PASSION'S PERILOUS CROSSROADS

Alexandre Rochforte was everything a woman could want in a husband, as gentle and understanding as he was superbly sensual, making Faith feel like a cherished wife, even as he taught her how to be a tantalizing woman.

Brad Alleyn was everything a woman craved in a lover, incredibly attractive, strong, daring, irresistibly reckless, breaking down every barrier in the way of his pleasure and Faith's desires.

Two different men, two different ways of love, and so few clues to know which would lead to happiness—and which to death. . . .

YESTERDAY'S TEARS

YESTERDAY'S TEARS

Susannah Leigh

NAL BOOKS ARE AVAILABLE AT QUANTITY DISCOUNTS WHEN USED TO PROMOTE PRODUCTS OR SERVICES. FOR INFORMATION PLEASE WRITE TO PREMIUM MARKETING DIVISION, THE NEW AMERICAN LIBRARY, INC., 1633 BROADWAY, NEW YORK, NEW YORK 10019.

SIGNET TRADEMARK REG. U.S. PAT. OFF. AND FOREIGN COUNTRIES
REGISTERED TRADEMARK—MARCA REGISTRADA
HECHO EN CHICAGO. U.S.A.

SIGNET, SIGNET CLASSICS, MENTOR, PLUME, MERIDIAN AND NAL BOOKS
are published by The New American Library, Inc.,
1633 Broadway, New York, New York 10019

First Printing, September, 1982

1 2 3 4 5 6 7 8 9

PRINTED IN THE UNITED STATES OF AMERICA

I

ECHOES OF MIDNIGHT

The room was a deep midnight blue, the air heavy and brooding in its own stillness. Only an echo of moonlight played across the rippled glass of tall French windows, open to the piazza. She stood just inside the threshold, a young woman, beautiful and lonely in the darkness. The sweet, familiar scent of flowers, cloying in the sultry night, lingered in her nostrils.

She hesitated a moment, uncertain, puzzled, trying to orient herself in the darkness. Then, slowly, she began to step forward. She thrust out her left hand, groping blindly with her fingers to feel her way. Her right hand, strangely heavy, dangled at her side as if it had been trapped in the rich folds of green silk that floated to the floor.

A sudden burst of gold bathed the room with light. The woman lifted her head, tilting her face upward, but she did not even cast a curious glance toward the solitary grease lamp in a corner of the room. She did not need to. She was sure of herself now, sure in a way she had never been before. Tension crackled through the air like static, but it did not frighten her, for she knew it emanated from her.

When at last she turned, she saw exactly what she had expected. Masculine features, potent and strong in the soft light. An iron will, too proud to unbend. She caught her breath at the savage perfection of it all. The boldness, the excitement of the challenge, the duel, for duel it was—and in the end the sweet triumph that would be hers.

Sensuality strained every muscle as she moved toward him. He was close now, so close his physical presence seemed to stifle her. He towered over her, a tall man, powerful, exuding virility with every breath. Blond hair, caught in the lamplight, burst into coppery flames; deep-set eyes blazed with blue fire; strong, hard lips opened, ready to scorn or to kiss.

What would he do, she wondered, if she reached out to him? Would he give himself to her, this man who had never known defeat, his body shuddering in surrender?

Or would the surrender be hers?

The idea thrilled her, more than anything that had gone before. One last victory for a masculine ego before the bitterness of defeat. She raised her hand, playing with him, tempting, provoking. Only as her fingers neared his face did she ease the other hand from the folds of her skirt.

She did not see the gun in his hand until it was too late. Her eyes, pale and catlike in the lamplight, widened into circles of astonishment, but she felt no fear. She knew he would not hurt her. Not this man. Not when he needed her so much.

"Chérie," she whispered, the word a low caress in her throat. Her hand hovered inches from the masculine roughness of his cheek. She opened her lips to repeat it one more time, *"Chérie,"* but the sound was lost in the deafening explosion that shattered the still night. Pain, sharp, excruciating pain, ripped through her chest.

She could only stare at him in dull amazement. How could he have done this to her? How could he? Where was the victory she had longed for so intensely? Where the sweetness of besting this strong man at last? Then the pain swelled in her breast, and she could feel nothing, think of nothing, but the need to escape from it, and she knew she was dying.

With a hoarse cry, Faith Eliot pulled herself upright in bed. The sheets twisted around her, catching her limbs in a straitjacket grip as she struggled to work them free. Sweat poured from her body, plastering fair curls against her forehead and saturating her nightdress, but she did not feel it. There was room in her consciousness only for the pain, wrenching, tearing, devouring her. Every drop of vitality seemed to ooze from her pores until the mattress beneath her was drenched with her own blood.

Her eyes, half blind in pain, turned upward, searching for blond hair, fiery in the lamplight, and cruel, cold lips. But there were no lips. No lamplight. Only the lacy purity of clean white curtains, caught in the faint breeze that blew through a half-open window. There was no exotic perfume floating on the sultry air. Only the somber gray of London fog, damp and impenetrable in an April dawn.

At last, the pain began to subside. Trembling, Faith pulled

herself to the edge of the bed, trying desperately to regain her composure. It took her a moment to realize that all the agony, all the terror she had just experienced was nothing but a dream. It took another moment to realize what the dream meant.

Fleur was dead.

II

BETWEEN YESTERDAY AND TOMORROW

One

"Fleur . . . Fleur. Où es tu? Viens à Maman, mon ange. Dépêche-toi."

Desirée Devereaux Eliot was a short, slight woman with thinning gray hair pulled back severely from washed-out features. Only when she called her daughter and her face took on a brief flicker of animation, could anyone guess she had once been a beautiful woman.

"Viens ici, chouette," she called out again in her native French. *"Tout de suite. Tante Anne est ici, et, elle a apporté un jolie cadeau pour son petit ange."*

Fleur materialized in the doorway, called to obedience by that magic word, *cadeau*. She did indeed look like a *petit ange*, a little angel. Honey golden curls bobbed fetchingly around rosy cheeks, and wide hazel eyes took on reflections of green from the mint-toned satin that trimmed her party frock.

"Un cadeau? Pour moi?" Her feet barely touched the floor as she danced into the room and dropped a graceful curtsy to the elderly woman who sat beside her mother. "A present for me, Great-Aunt Anne? How nice of you to remember my birthday. Do you know, I am nine today?"

"Indeed I do, child. Could I ever forget my little Fleur Anne?"

The emphasis was on the *Anne*, and Desirée did not fail to catch it. What a stroke of luck it had been, setting on a simple second name for her vivacious little daughter. Lady Anne Gordon had always been inordinately vain about the name she shared with her distant cousin, the great Queen Anne, predecessor to the Hanoverian upstarts who now sat on the throne of England. It was a vanity she clung to even more tenaciously after she married Andrew Devereaux, a

French Huguenot with nothing to set him apart from the masses but his great wealth.

And that vanity, Desirée reminded herself now, might one day be all that stood between a poor relation and starvation.

A second child peeked in the doorway that separated the salon from the long second-floor gallery. Her delicate features, virtually a copy of the little girl inside, marked her instantly as a sister. There was a sweet, wistful quality about her as she lingered on the threshold, waiting for someone to look up and notice her.

Ah, there you are, Faith, they would cry when they saw her. We've been looking everywhere for you. Come inside. There is a present for you too.

But no one looked up. All eyes were on Fleur as she squealed with excitement.

"Oh, Aunt Anne, it's lovely!"

The perfectly styled garment she pulled from its wrapping was an exquisite miniature of an adult ball gown. Emerald satin, cut in a coy imitation of womanly curves, was designed to cling to a tiny bodice, then fall to the floor in full folds over a silver lace petticoat. Echoes of the same silver laddered the breast in a graceful echelle. Faith watched enviously as her sister lifted the gown and, pressing it to her shoulders, began to spin round and round the room, following the beat of music she alone could hear.

"Isn't it perfect, *Maman?* Don't I look all grown up?"

"Prends soin, mon chou," Desirée protested, her face glowing with pride. "Take care. Don't hurt yourself."

"But don't I look grown up? Don't you think so? And don't I look pretty?"

"Comme un ange, my precious. *Comme un ange."*

She did truly look pretty, Faith had to admit as she followed the little whirling figure with her eyes. Fleur always looked pretty. Desirée had long ago insisted she wear nothing but green—"to bring out the color in your eyes," she had said—and it was a conceit that suited Fleur well. Faith did not really mind. It had not yet occurred to her that her own eyes were the same hazel tone. But she did sometimes wish she had a color of her own, too. A color that was just for her.

Lady Anne was enchanted. "A beautiful child. And so well behaved. I must give you credit, Desirée. It isn't easy raising a child alone."

Desirée stiffened at the reminder of her estrangement from the man who had fathered her two daughters. It was a thing that was not discussed in polite society, and Anne with her innate snobbishness knew it well. No matter how kind her voice might be, Desirée sensed a subtle rebuke in its depths.

"I do what I can."

"I'm sure you do." Lady Anne leaned forward, patting her hand with unconscious condescension. "I'm sure you do."

Faith followed the interplay from the doorway, but she was too young to understand it. All she could think of was her aunt's voluminous skirts, draped in bulky splendor across the divan, and she searched them anxiously with her eyes, wondering if somewhere in all that mass of fabric there might not be room for a second package.

It's *my* birthday, too, she longed to cry out. I am nine, too. But caution held her back. Could they have forgotten about her? she wondered, her mother and this old woman whose skin smelled like dead flowers. It hardly seemed possible. How could they remember Fleur's birthday and forget hers?

"Oh, Faith."

Fleur caught sight of her sister and, pausing in her dance, raced over to show off her present. She did not miss Faith's quivering lower lip, and she could not resist a childish bit of gloating.

"Don't you love my new dress?"

And don't you wish you had one just like it? her eyes seemed to add.

Faith stared back at her helplessly. She wanted to be angry with her sister. She wanted desperately to reach out and slap the smugness off her face, but she did not dare. Mama would be furious with her if she did.

"Faith! What on earth is the matter with you?"

Guiltily, the child turned to face her mother. Fleur danced away again, leaving her alone under that stern gaze. She had a terrible feeling for a moment that her mother had seen through to the blackness of her soul. Then she realized what was really wrong.

"I'm sorry, Mama." She raised a hand to brush back the wisps of hair that spilled onto her forehead, marring the studied perfection of carefully arranged tresses. The other hand brushed futilely at her skirt, as white as her sister's only an hour ago, now streaked with dirt. "Uncle Andrew told me Rags's new puppies were playing outside the stable, and I wanted to see them. I know I wasn't supposed to pick them up, but——"

"That's enough, Faith. We'll discuss it later. You haven't greeted your aunt yet."

"Of course, Mama. I'm sorry." Faith dropped a hasty curtsy. "It was good of you to come. . . ." . . . on my birthday, she started to add, but she bit her tongue. She was still not sure her aunt remembered.

Lady Anne scowled her disapproval. "I must say, Faith, I am not at all pleased to see you running around like a little hoyden, all dust and tatters. Still, it is your birthday. I suppose it would not be kind to slight you."

Faith felt as if a heavy weight had been lifted off her chest. Great-Aunt Anne had remembered her birthday, after all. She watched wide-eyed as her aunt reached down into the folds of her skirt. But when she saw the size of the package the old woman held out to her, her heart sank again.

She turned the small parcel over in her hands, unwrapping slowly. It was all she could do to control her disappointment when she saw the small, leather-bound volume inside.

"Pilgrim's Progress."

"A most edifying work, child. I want you to read it for an hour every morning and an hour again every night. If you do, I am sure you will find yourself intellectually and spiritually uplifted."

Faith struggled to swallow the big lump in her throat. She knew she needed to be uplifted, truly she did. It was just hard to want to be uplifted when there were pretty party dresses all around.

Lady Anne shook her head as she watched her. How could identical twins be so different?

"Quel dommage!" she said, turning to Desirée. *"L'une si belle, si charmante, et l'autre . . . sans espoir."* Then, French failing her, she added in a loud whisper, "Better not to encourage that one in frivolity, my dear. Teach her to cultivate her mind. That will be her only salvation—a well-cultivated mind."

Faith wanted to cry out in frustration. Did her aunt, with her few words of French, really think she could not understand? Or did she simply think children were too stupid to know when they had been insulted? She had only said what Faith had known all along, that Fleur was beautiful, and somehow, by some strange quirk of fate, she was not. But still it hurt.

"Where are your manners, Faith?" Desirée prompted. "Thank your aunt for the gift."

"Thank you, Great-Aunt Anne."

"Don't you want to kiss your aunt, Faith?"

Faith did not want to, but she knew what would happen if

she said no. Reluctantly, she stood on tiptoe, pressing her lips against the old woman's cheek. She concentrated with all her might on loose wrinkled skin, velvety beneath a coat of fuzz, and tried not to think about the smell of perfume, like roses left too long in the vase.

Desirée saw the relief on her daughter's face as she pulled away, and she knew the old woman had seen it, too. It frightened her, but her fear seemed like anger to the child.

"That will be all, Faith. Take your book and go to your room."

Faith looked back only once from the entrance. Fleur was watching her, her eyes dancing with mischief. As long as she could remember, Faith had always been able to read the expression in her sister's eyes. She knew exactly what they were saying now.

I am in here, Fleur was telling her. I am in here, and everyone adores me.

And you are out there.

You are out there.

Faith swung her legs over the edge of the bed, touching bare feet to the floor. The sheets, still damp with sweat, felt cold as she pushed them away.

It was always like that, she thought bitterly. Always. Fleur was on the inside, gazing out with knowing eyes at the sister who hovered on the fringes of her world. Faith had hated her that day. She had hated her with all the passion in a nine-year-old heart.

Yet it was the same Fleur who had come to her room that night, creeping into bed beside her and throwing her arms around her.

Faith could still remember every detail of that night. Fleur had brought her favorite doll, Caroline, with her, propping her up on the pillow between them. How she had envied her then! Caroline was a precious little beauty, so pretty and elegant it broke Faith's heart to look at her.

She had reached out a timid hand, barely daring to let it rest on Caroline's painted hair. Fleur was intensely proud of the doll, and from the moment Aunt Anne had given it to her, she had been fiercely possessive of it.

But this time Fleur did not rebuke her. Sitting up in the bed, she had stared down at her sister in the moonlight that drifted through the window. Then, impulsively, she thrust the doll in her arms.

"You can have her if you want."

"But she is yours. . . ."

"It doesn't matter. I am too old for dolls."

Mama had been horrified when she learned what Fleur had done, and so had Lady Anne, but the child was adamant. She had given the doll to her sister, she said, and that was all there was to it. Only Great-Uncle Andrew seemed to understand the inherent generosity in her act, and he bought her another doll, even grander than the first. Fleur thanked him sweetly, as she always did, then set the doll on a chair in the corner of her room and never looked at it again.

"Perhaps she *is* too old for dolls," Desirée had said.

But Faith knew different. Fleur had loved Caroline, with a love only a child could understand, and no other doll would ever take her place.

And now Fleur was dead.

The fog had grown heavier. Faith stepped over to the window and stared out. She could see nothing through the thick gray haze. A tree grew just outside the window, an ancient gnarled elm with branches so close she could almost reach out and touch them. Now she could not even see where it was.

Fleur was dead. The finality of the words were as cold as the dawn. Somewhere in the last few minutes, in violence and pain, her sister had died, and now she was alone.

"What a ninny you are, always mooning over that portrait."

Faith looked up to see her sister staring down at her from the stairway. Fleur was the picture of calculated coquetry. Already, at fourteen, her figure was well-developed, and she was not afraid to show it off to best advantage. Printed calico, touched with hundreds of pale green carnations, stretched tightly across breasts that promised to be unusually full, and a lemon-colored satin apron, trimmed with dainty Persian muslin, was designed to emphasize ripening curves. Faith was grateful now that Desirée had never insisted on dressing them as twins. Tall and gawky, she had felt self-conscious enough before she began to turn into a woman. At least she could keep her new maturity hidden beneath loose, childish frocks.

"I am not mooning over her. I just think she's pretty, that's all. She has such sad eyes."

"She has big brown eyes, just like a cow!"

Faith turned away. It was the summer of their mother's last illness, and young as they were, they both knew it. Lady Anne had been dead for three years, and Great-Uncle Andrew, at a loss to know what to do with two lively young girls in a house of death, had sent them to relatives in the country. Fleur had hated the place instantly, missing the gaiety and bustle of the city, but Faith did not mind it at all. She loved the woods and the fields, and even the stodgy old house with its narrow corridors and funny little attic windows and all the ancestors that looked down on them from heavy frames in every hallway.

"Well, I think she's pretty. And she doesn't look like a cow at all! What a dreadful thing to say. Look how lovely her hair is. I think dark hair is romantic, don't you? Even her name is romantic—Judith Bradford."

"Romantic? What a silly little dreamer you are. What difference does 'romantic' make? Now look at this portrait over here. This woman is beautiful. That's what really counts."

Neither girl paid the least attention to the portrait hanging between the two women. The men of the past did not interest them. Their daydreams were still centered on the elegant ladies who filled the roles they themselves longed to play.

"She *is* beautiful," Faith admitted. The woman's hair, thick and golden, was piled abundantly on her head in the fashion of a bygone era, and dainty features were rendered even more enticing by a skillful application of the cosmetician's art.

"Rosaline Devereaux." Fleur picked out the name as if she were reading it for the first time. "She was the first wife, you know, and that makes her so much more important. Besides, she belongs to *our* family."

"Well, that's true." Faith compared the two faces, skimming over the man between. "Isn't it amazing how different they are—and yet so much alike."

"Alike? How can you say that? They're not alike at all."

"They are too. They were married to the same man, weren't they? John Alleyn—James—whatever his name was. They both bore him just one son. And they both died when they tried to give birth to another."

"Oh, you *are* a silly dreamer." Fleur sat on the steps, tucking her skirt around her so the white lace on her petticoat would not get soiled. "It's all romantic to you, isn't it? Love and marriage—and childbearing? Well, let me tell you, it isn't so romantic to have your body pulled out of shape carrying a child. And it certainly isn't romantic to die in childbirth!"

An intensity beyond her years vibrated in her voice. Leaning forward, she caught her sister by the arm.

"Listen to me, Faith! I am going to have lovers. Lots of

them. But I am not going to be married. And I am not going to bear a child. Not ever!"

"Fleur!" Faith was shocked, not so much by her sister's challenge to nature as by the daring of her words. "You can't have . . . have . . . I mean, you can't do that."

"Can't I? That's the difference between us, sweet sister. You are a dreamer, and I am a doer. You'll sit around all your life, spinning romances in your head, and one day—if you're lucky—you'll catch some stuffy man and raise a passel of brats and watch life pass you by."

Her eyes glowed unnaturally as she dug her fingernails into her sister's wrist.

"But I'm not going to let life pass me by. While you are dreaming, I will be living. I am going to grab hold of life for all it's worth and cling to it and never—*never*—let it go!"

"Oh, Fleur. . . ."

Faith rested her head on the window frame. The wood felt cool against her flushed cheeks. The fog had grown so dense she could feel the moisture in her nostrils as she inhaled.

Poor Fleur. Poor pretty Fleur. So young . . . and so naive. She had not yet learned that life was a pawn in no man's game. That she could hold it, cling to it, grasp it against her heart, but she could not keep it from slipping away between her fingers.

And it had slipped away, Faith was certain of that. She knew it as surely as she knew that she herself was alive.

She did not for a moment doubt the reality of her dream. She had shared sensations with her twin before, the sort of things that made people uncomfortable when they found out about them. Like the time Fleur fell down the back stairs and broke her arm, and Faith had felt the same sharp stab of pain through her own body. Or the time her sister was lost in the woods, and she had been able to describe the place so exactly Uncle Andrew knew just where to look for her.

Of course, those were subtly different, she had to admit. Those were fleeting sensations, instincts, flashes of pictures that came and vanished again. They had never been so terrifying—or so complete. The act of dreaming had opened up feelings that were vivid beyond recall. Pain, ripping her body with wrenching power. Fear, paralyzing her limbs so she could not fight. Eternity, hurtling toward her until she felt death in her soul.

"Oh, Fleur, what have you done?"

What *had* her sister done? Where had she been tonight? What had happened to her?

Whatever it was, one thing was certain. Fleur had left no clues to her fate. Months ago, she had decided to go to the Colonies, wheedling and coaxing Uncle Andrew to let her sail for New York, but it was not that northern land Faith sensed in her dream. The sultry air, the moody darkness, the sweet scent of flowers—those were not New York. If anything, they were Havenhurst.

Havenhurst. . . .

Faith shut her eyes, trying to picture the place. It was so long ago—so very long. She was just a child when her mother took her from the Carolina plantation where she and her sister had been born. It did not even belong in the family anymore, for her father had lost it sometime in the year before he died. She had not expected to think of it again, nor wanted to.

The past had been dead to her. Only yesterday, it had seemed as if it had never existed. Now, suddenly, it was all coming back again, and she could not escape it. Somehow, in ways she could not begin to comprehend, it was all tied up with her sister's death.

"But I only have two arms," Fleur protested, glancing up through lowered lashes at the three young men who flocked around her. "Whatever am I to do?"

"I suppose you must grow another," one of them replied with mock seriousness. He was two years older than the others, and he did not intend to let them forget it. "You must give one arm to me, and it would be heartless to leave my brother or young Peter Ramsey alone. I would be absolutely devastated if they were disappointed."

"Fie, you don't fool me for a minute, James Gilbert. The only disappointment that would devastate you is your own."

James laughed easily. "I must admit you've caught me out, Miss Fleur. I *would* be devastated if you didn't let me escort you to the summerhouse. Ah, but I have it! Of course! You shall come with me, and Kendall and Peter can keep each other company. They shall dance attendance from a respectful distance behind."

Faith stood a little apart from the group, watching the three young men squabble over her sister. It was obvious that they had forgotten all about her. She could not truly blame them. Fleur had never looked more beautiful. Summer became her. Pale linen, sheer as silk, flared around her, emphasizing a waist cinched so tight it could be circled by a pair of strong hands, and a ruffled bodice, fashionably low-cut, pushed plump white breasts daringly out of a frame of artificial flowers.

"Why, James, whatever are you saying?" Fleur's tongue flicked across pink lips, a deliberate reminder of stolen kisses. "Do you think that's quite fair?"

"Not fair at all." Kendall Gilbert protested. "Come, Fleur you must choose. You cannot disappoint us both."

Faith watched as Fleur cocked her head prettily, studying them all as intently as if the world hinged on her decision. It was easy to see why they were taken with her. She had a way of making them feel they were so clever, so entrancing, that she could not take her eyes off them.

"Now let me see. James, of course—he is the oldest. And then. . . ."

Faith knew Fleur had already made her choice. Peter Ramsey was the handsomest and her sister had always favored him, but she was just playful enough not to let him know it.

"The two brothers then. James and Kendall. Peter, you follow with Faith."

Peter had the grace to blush as he turned and saw her standing at the edge of the grove.

"I'm sorry, Faith. I had forgotten you were coming with us."

Faith's own cheeks reddened as he took her arm. She wished she had the courage to brush him aside, telling him disdainfully she did not need his services, but she was afraid it would only make her look more foolish. She kept her eyes resolutely fastened on her slippers, peeking out from beneath the pink lawn of her skirt, but she could still feel him looking down at her, and she knew he was studying her figure, shrouded in layers of ruffles, and wondering why she did not look as tantalizing as her sister.

But when she finally glanced up, he was not looking at her at all. He was watching Fleur, and there was no mistaking the longing in his eyes. In that instant, Faith knew the truth. This boy beside her, so young and handsome, had shared more than kisses with her sister.

Faith had always known things like that about Fleur. She knew the very night her sister kept her vow and took her first lover. She had sensed the same masculine strength beside her in her own lonely bed; she had quivered with the same fear and excitement. But she had not known it was Peter, a companion of her own childhood.

"It's good to see you again, Faith," Peter ventured gamely, trying to dispel the awkwardness between them. "I haven't talked to you for a long time."

"No, I—I suppose. . . That is, I. . ." What was wrong with her? Peter was an old playmate. She ought to be able to chat as easily with him as if they were climbing trees in the woods or stealing carrots from the garden for the horses. The things he had done with Fleur shouldn't change anything. "No, I guess I've been busy."

Peter sensed her discomfort, and it seemed to make him uneasy, too. He did not try to make conversation again, and they walked the next few minutes in silence.

Halfway around the lake, Fleur whirled to face them. Shaking off her two admirers, she held out her hands.

"Faith! Come and walk with me."

Bewildered, Faith slipped her hand out of Peter's arm and hurried to her sister. She wondered if one of the men had done something, if he had committed some slight, real or imagined, to bring down Fleur's wrath. But one glance at the pair of them was enough to tell her she was wrong. They were as confused as she. Laughing, Fleur linked her arm through her sister's and drew her down the path, leaving her suitors to follow behind.

"You are my sister, Faith," she whispered conspiratorially. "My twin sister. I will have lovers—lots of them—but I only have one sister."

She paused, catching hold of Faith's hands as she looked deeply into her eyes.

"We are a part of each other. Don't ever forget that, Faith. You are me, and I am you—and nothing will ever keep us apart."

Faith ran her fingers down the window frame. Chipped paint caught at her skin, reminding her how rundown the house had become since her great-aunt's death. She had never understood before what it would mean to be alone.

Nothing will ever keep us apart.

How confident they had been then. And why not? Nothing had kept them apart before. Oh, they had quarreled, they had competed, they had laughed at each others dreams, but they had not for a moment doubted that they were inextricably tied to each other. She and Fleur, a single force, united against the world.

But now that union was broken, and she had become a separate entity, alone and vulnerable in a way she had never imagined.

The fog, so thick only seconds before, began to lift, easing away until vague forms drifted out of the mist. Faith watched, half hypnotized by the subtle play of shapes and shadows, as gray dissolved into illusive wisps of white. Slowly, she began to pick out the branches of the tree outside her window.

But it was not the tree that should have been there. Faith's heart caught in her throat as she stared at it. She knew she was being silly. There was nothing frightening about it, just a trick of nature, a deceptive haze that made even the familiar seem alien, but she could not stop herself from shivering.

It was not the old elm now. It was a massive live-oak, its broad branches, weary with thick gray moss, dipping to the earth. Faith could feel herself standing beneath it, feet sinking into the slime that oozed around her ankles, clutching at her, pulling her, drawing her into timeless depths. She gripped the window frame to keep from screaming out loud.

It was cold. She knew it was cold because foggy London dawns were always cold. But all she could feel was the heat. Steamy heat, humid and oppressive. Sweat drenched her nightdress and it was an effort to breathe.

In every tightly drawn breath, she sensed death. Death, as it had been there before. Remembered death, still fresh and painful, belonging not to the distant past but to the moment. Her own death, the final reality of her life.

Then the last breath caught in her throat, and it was all over. The earth had won at last, sucking her down, covering her face, choking her until her strength was gone. And it was dark. Dear God, it was dark. She could not see—and she could not breathe.

Gasping, Faith opened her eyes. The sensation was so real for a moment she could not believe she was alive. Only as she forced a cool gulp of air into bursting lungs did she realize that, once again, her pain was nothing but an illusion. She was alive and unhurt. But Fleur. . .

Turning back to the window, Faith tried to pick out the live-oak again, shadowy and mysterious beneath its mantle of moss. But it was no longer there. The fog, cold and arbitrary, had taken it away again, and the gray was as impenetrable as ever.

"Havenhurst?"

She barely whispered the word. She could remember nothing about the place of her birth. She could not have drawn a picture of it or described a single room, she did not know the man who lived there now, she did not even know if rice plantations in the Carolina Colonies had swamps with old, moss-draped live-oaks, but there was no doubt in her mind that she had returned there twice that day. A journey through space, or only a journey through memory, she did not know which, but she knew she had seen the past again, hidden somewhere behind the present.

And the present was the terrifying, tangible sense of her sister's dying.

Or was it tangible? Faith leaned back against the wall, shaken by her own conflicting visions. She had felt her sister's death, shared it with her, barely an hour ago in a dream. But she had felt the same thing again just now, every bit as compelling and urgent. She wondered if she dared to trust her own feelings.

Was it real? Had it all happened? The lamplight, the gun, the pain?

Or a brief, agonizing moment of suffocation in an unknown swamp?

A still wind, icy and biting, blew into the room. Shivering, Faith raised her hands to her neck, tightening the strings of her gown. She was surprised to feel her fingers come in contact with cold metal.

The locket! She had worn it so long, she had forgotten it was there. Twin lockets, hers with a tiny diamond, Fleur's with her own green emerald. They had clipped a lock of each other's hair and hidden it inside and sworn never to take the lockets off again.

Abruptly, Faith turned from the window. What on earth was she doing, thrashing her doubts over and over in her mind? Blond hair, catching her eye in the lamplight? Mud seeping into her slippers in the swamp? What did the details matter? The reality was still the same. Fleur was dead—and she had died at Havenhurst.

And only one person cared enough to do anything about it.

"I haven't forgotten, Fleur," she whispered. "We are sisters."

She would go to Havenhurst. She would pack her trunks and pretend she was as brave as Fleur and set out for a place that was only a name to her—the Colony of South Carolina.

And somewhere in the shadows of her own past, somewhere between yesterday and tomorrow, she would find out what had happened to her sister.

Fleur's death would not go unavenged.

Two

The light of oil lamps reflected on the window, catching the spray that coated the outside until it looked like frost in the night. Faith stared at it idly, imagining the scene that lay on the other side. The sea would be calm, a sleek, cold mystery, like a vast expanse of polished black marble. And above it, only an empty pit of darkness.

She was distracted by a sound behind her. Turning, she saw a young man standing alone, his hand resting on a railing at the side of the room to brace himself against the roll of the ship.

"Oh, it's you."

She turned away, determined not to look at him. She had known Rolfe Stephens, the son of her uncle's business partner, all her life. It was insulting to have him set over her as a watchdog now.

Rolfe ignored the snub. "Such warmth," he quipped lightly. "Such cheerfulness. Tell me, what have I done to deserve this enthusiastic welcome?"

Faith knew he was only trying to be pleasant, but his clumsy attempts at humor did nothing to ease an intolerable situation. Why, in heaven's name, had her uncle saddled her with this unwelcome escort, a man whose very presence could destroy everything she had vowed to accomplish? The frustration was so infuriating, she forgot to be tongue-tied.

"You look positively green, Mr. Stephens. Dare I presume you are not a good sailor?"

If he noticed her sudden formality, he chose not to acknowledge it. "I have made four crossings already, *Miss* Eliot. I expect I will survive this one. You would do better to look after yourself."

"Myself?" Faith could hardly believe her ears. Was the

man deliberately mocking her? The last traces of shyness vanished as her exasperation mounted. "We have been at sea five days, sir, and I have not felt so much as a twinge of squeamishness. I think we will see soon enough who bears up best under the rigors of a long voyage."

He did not answer, but shrugged and turned away. Faith did not know which irritated her most, the arrogance that prompted him to force himself on her again and again—or the galling indifference he showed now. She wished she could think of a tart, clever comment to put him in his place.

Against her will, she found herself studying his profile. Rolfe Stephens was far from unattractive. His hair, a rich chestnut color, was tied neatly at the nape of his neck with a plain black riband, and his eyes were a deep, velvety brown. He was not tall, but a lithe, slender figure lent the illusion of height, and the fashionable claret of his waistcoat, set off by a white cambric shirt, gave him an air that was both modish and casual. In truth, despite her trepidations, Faith had not been totally dismayed when her uncle told her she would make the long sea crossing in his company. But that, of course, was before she learned what an insufferable prig he could be.

The silence was beginning to get on her nerves. "I can imagine what a bore it must be for you, Mr. Stephens, making small talk with an empty-headed, frivolous female. But I find that no excuse for your rudeness."

"*My* rudeness?" His veneer of courtesy vanished as he turned to face her.

Faith could see that his patience was at an end, and for a moment, she was sorry she had gone so far. She hated herself for being so waspish. It would be so much easier if she could just tell him to leave her alone and be done with it. But that could ruin everything.

"What else would you call it, sir?" She tilted her head to the side, trying to imagine what Fleur would do to make the gesture coy and fetching. "When I try to make conversation, you find fault with whatever I say, or turn away in utter indifference. I am quite beyond myself to know what to do with you. If you are trying to drive me to tears, I fear you will succeed at any moment."

He studied her intently for a long time. At last he spoke. "You know, you are incredibly like your sister."

"My . . . sister?"

The words stunned Faith. It was true, for the first time in

her life, she had been consciously imitating Fleur. But she had not expected to succeed.

She caught a glimpse of her image in the glass. Surely Rolfe Stephens must see the same thing when he looked at her. Bland, ordinary features, colorless against a simple gray frock and chaste white lace. Dark blond hair, contrary and unruly. Lips a little too full, cheeks too ruddy from the sea air. Eyes a disappointing contradiction, golden in the glow of the lamp, grayed in the reflection of her dress.

"I am not like my sister at all."

"Not like her? What nonsense. You are identical twins."

"That's not true. That we're alike, I mean. Our style . . . our—our manner. . . ." Why, Fleur would have been flitting all over the room, laughing, teasing, posing in the lamplight until it caught the green of her dress and cast it up to her eyes. "Fleur is so . . . different."

"I used to think so," he admitted. "Fleur never walked if she could dance. She never talked, she teased and flirted. And she never let anyone's eyes stray from her, even for a moment. You were just the opposite, quiet and solemn. I expected something gentler from you. Something deeper. Obviously, that was naive."

"How bitter you sound, Mr. Stephens." The conversation was beginning to take an intriguing turn. Faith had never enjoyed this kind of bantering repartee with a man before. "Rather like a rejected suitor. Tell me, did my sister refuse you the sweetness of her kisses?"

"Your sister refused me nothing, Miss Eliot—as she refused no man who asked her."

"Rolfe!—Mr. Stephens." The game had gone too far now. This was her sister whose name he bandied about so unchivalrously. "I know what Fleur was—what she *is*. But you don't understand. Fleur was exquisitely beautiful. Not just on the outside—after all, I have the same features—but inside, too, with a kind of inner radiance that made her irresistible. I don't blame her for enjoying the fascination men felt for her. I envy her for it. I don't even blame her if she let that fascination go beyond a kiss—as she obviously did with you."

Rolfe saw her trembling indignation, and he regretted his roughness. Sitting beside her on the long bench, he took hold of her hand. Then, realizing his forwardness might be unwelcome, he dropped it awkwardly.

"No, Faith, I did not . . . do those things with her. I kissed her many times, but nothing else."

Faith felt a surge of relief. "Then you didn't mean what you said. All those terrible things. You really *were* a rejected suitor."

"Rejected? Hardly that." He rose abruptly and moved away from her. When he finally turned back, his face was set with determination. "I think we'd better get one thing straight. I don't like your sister. I never did, and I don't now. She is very pretty, just as you are when you want to be, and charming, but she is a sly, shallow creature who loves nothing more than playing selfish little games with other people's feelings."

"How can you say that?" Faith burned with shame for her sister. This man had put his arms around her, touched his lips to hers. "How can you be so unchivalrous? You took her kisses willingly enough."

He leaned down, his breath hot on her cheeks.

"I am a man, Faith. Do you understand that? Of course I responded to her beauty and sensuality. But that doesn't mean that I liked her—or myself for wanting her."

Faith pulled back from him. "That's not fair." Fleur *could* be shallow, even cruel sometimes, but there was another side to her, too. "You didn't know her like I did. No one could. When I find her, when I find out what——"

"Find her?"

His voice was too sharp. Faith looked down so he wouldn't see her confusion.

"I didn't mean *find* her." What a fool she was! She had already said too much. I mean, when I see her again in New York—when I find the friends she is staying with—well, then I'll prove you were wrong."

"What do you mean, *find* the friends your sister is staying with. Don't you know them?"

"Of course I know them." God in heaven, why was she being so careless? Above all, she had to keep him from guessing the truth. If he knew what she was really up to, he would ship her back to her uncle in a minute. "I mean, I know who they are. I know their names. It will be simple enough to locate them."

She wished he would stop staring at her. Jumping up, she flounced across the room. How could he say she was like her sister? She wasn't like Fleur at all. Fleur would never have been so stupid and clumsy. She would have known exactly how to get what she wanted from this handsome young man, no matter how he claimed to dislike her.

"It seems clear to me, Mr. Stephens, that you have no

more use for me than you did for my sister. I wonder that my uncle chose such an unseemly escort for me." She tried to look haughty as she headed for the door. It was not the perfectly timed exit Fleur would have pulled off so well, but it would have to do under the circumstances. "I am going out on deck. I am sure the air will be fresher there."

The wind rushed at her in a cold blast as she tugged the door open, then struggled to pull it shut behind her. She had not realized the gusts would be so strong. For a moment, she was tempted to turn back, but that was a luxury she dared not allow herself. Even if a storm was brewing, she would rather brave its furies than face the questions that waited inside.

The moonlight was deceptive. Even as it illuminated the water with brilliant clarity, it bathed the vessel in murky shadows. Faith gave a sharp cry of pain as her toe stubbed against a coil of rope lying on the rough boards of the deck. She reached down awkwardly, catching at it to keep from stumbling, then recoiled as she drew back her hand, smelling of grease and filth. Heavy canvas sails flapped on masts high above her, and the tangled rigging groaned heavily, like ghosts of men in pain.

She had never hated any place so much in her life. She hated the wind that mocked and threatened her. The salt that stung her skin and clung to the inside of her nostrils. Even the sea that seemed to stretch on forever.

And more than anything, she hated Rolfe Stephens for forcing her out in the cold.

How could Uncle Andrew have done this to her? A childish spate of tears embarrassed her, and she tried to pretend her eyes were watering from the wind. Why had he insisted on finding a nursemaid for her, as if she were too incompetent to do anything for herself? Only months before, he had let Fleur travel by herself.

But then that was Fleur—and Fleur always got what she wanted. She wheedled and flirted, cried and coaxed, and no one ever stood up to her.

"But why not *me?*" she cried out to the darkness. Only the wind responded, a shrill. lonely whistle through the sails. Why not her, indeed? Why, just this once, when it was so desperately important, couldn't her uncle have pampered her the way he had always pampered her sister?

Andrew Devereaux took a deep drag from the pipe clenched between his teeth, then exhaled slowly. Bless Walter

Raleigh for bringing the filthy weed back from the Colonies. There was nothing quite like it to relieve his tension.

"I daresay I'm a blasted idiot to let the little baggage out of my sight. Eh, Thomas?"

Thomas Stephens settled back in his chair. He looked remarkably like his son. His body was a little stockier, and his graying hair hidden beneath a powdered wig, but he had the same handsome features, the same air of quiet confidence. "Come now, Andrew, you don't seriously expect me to agree with you. If you did, you wouldn't have asked me."

"I daresay, I daresay. Well, dammit, man, disagree with me then! Tell me I'm an old fool for fussing so much."

"You *are* an old fool, Andrew. The girl is on my own ship, after all. Besides, I'm trusting my son with vital business affairs. Don't you think he can be trusted with a troublesome grandniece as well?"

"Oh, I trust Rolfe all right. The lad has a good head on his shoulders. It's the girl I'm not sure of."

"But you let the other go off without a qualm. I would have thought. . . ."

Thomas dropped the statement in mid-sentence. Everyone knew Andrew Devereaux had a blind spot when it came to Fleur. There was no point provoking a quarrel about it now.

"Ah, well," Andrew admitted, chuckling as he read his partner's thoughts. "The little minx always could do whatever she wanted with me. A giggle, a kiss on the cheek, a well-timed tear, and she has me eating out of her hand. But then, you see, I've never really worried about her. I know she's a brazen little hussy sometimes, and sly as the devil, but at least she can take care of herself."

"I wonder. Fleur is manipulative—and hard to resist, I admit—but is that really equal to taking care of herself? It always seemed to me Faith was the sensible one."

"Sensible? Quiet, yes—but sensible? I doubt it." Andrew leaned forward, pausing to capture the other man's attention. "Here's what really worries me, Thomas. She and Fleur were always close. Much too close."

"Close?" Thomas arched an eyebrow.

"I know, I know. They've had more than enough squabbles for an army of sisters. And more than their share of friction and jealousy. But they are twins, you know. Identical twins. The bond between them is so close it's uncanny."

"I wouldn't have thought so. If anything, Faith seemed relieved when Fleur left for New York."

"Don't you see, man? That's just what I mean. At first, she

was almost giddy, as if she had been released from a heavy burden. Then, all of a sudden, with absolutely no warning, she tells me she wants to join Fleur in the Colonies."

Thomas burst out laughing. He stretched his legs as he walked across the room, tugging casually at a bellcord on the far wall. "You can't have it both ways, Andrew. Either the girl is close to her sister, in which case it is natural to want to join her, or she isn't—in which case there isn't any uncanny bond between them. Besides, all this carrying on is after the fact. Don't you think it's time you offered me a glass of that excellent brandy of yours?"

"Of course, of course." Andrew nodded to the servant who had slipped soundlessly into the room. He did not try to speak again until he felt sharp edges of cut crystal in his hand. Then, lifting his glass, he said pointedly: "To my two girls, wherever they are."

Thomas took a sip of his drink. "You worry too much, Andrew. You're too old to start playing the protective father now. Your little birds have grown up, that's all. It's time they flew the nest."

Andrew drained his glass in a single gulp. "I hope you're right, Thomas. With God as my witness, I hope you're right."

Faith saw little of Rolfe Stephens in the long Atlantic crossing. Much to her surprise, her own prediction proved to be right. For all his "experience," Rolfe was nowhere near the sailor she was. After the first few days, he took to his cabin, surfacing only occasionally for a breath of fresh air.

"I thought you were accustomed to the sea, Mr. Stephens," she taunted one morning as he clung to the railing with taut hands. "Why, you look pale as a ghost."

Rolfe did not try to answer, but smiled wanly and made his way back across the deck. It occurred to Faith that he was being a remarkably good sport about the whole thing. She hoped he was not going to turn out to be nice after all. She did not want to be tempted to like him.

Without Rolfe watching over her every second, Faith had expected to find life on board pleasant and relaxing. Instead, it turned out to be amazingly dull. She got over her fear of the strangeness of the vessel, and even the savage gusts of wind that tore across the deck, but all the daring in the world could only tempt her to explore the ship. It could not help her find anything interesting on it.

She stood on deck one morning, barely noticing that the wind had ripped her hair out of its pins, and stared up at a hopeless jumble of ropes twisting into webs among the masts. From where she stood, it was impossible to distinguish one massive square of canvas from the next, much less figure out where each rope went or what its function was. It was as frustrating as it was bewildering. A great ship like that, once a powerful man-of-war, now part of an important merchant fleet, ought to have been fascinating. If only she had someone to teach her about it—or even someone to talk to—the monotony of her days would not be quite so unbearable. But there was no point hoping. Most of the time, she felt as if she were the only person on board.

After the first few nights, she had begun taking dinner alone in her cabin. Rolfe was too uncomfortable to eat with her, and while she was free to join the captain, she quickly learned he was a dour, uncommunicative man, and she could find no pleasure in his company. At the beginning, she had caught occasional glimpses of other passengers toward the stern of the vessel. They were shabby at best, nothing more than poor, pale figures who seemed to climb out of the hold with the cargo, but at least they gave a touch of humanity to the ship, and Faith had felt less alone with them there. But now even they were gone. Now the only signs of life were the slovenly, ill-bred sailors who scrambled up the masts to work on the sails or skittered like insects across the deck.

She turned her face into the wind, letting it whip her hair out behind her. At least there was one good thing about being alone. She didn't have to worry about what she looked like—or whether her behavior was seemly or proper. Laughing, she tossed back her head, loosening the last pins in long golden tresses.

It was a moment before she realized her solitude was an illusion. An uncomfortable feeling alerted her, the eerie sensation that someone was watching. Glancing around, she saw a short, dark man only a few feet away.

Her skin crawled as she watched him. He was a typical sailor, with leathery, pockmarked skin drawn tight over sunken cheeks, and filthy, matted hair. Only a handful of teeth showed in his mouth as his lips curled up in an unmistakable leer. Faith did not for a moment doubt what he was thinking. With a sinking feeling of horror, she realized they were alone on that part of the deck. If he took even a step, he could thrust out coarse hands to touch her, and there was no one there to help her. If she was going to protect herself, she had to do something, and she had to do it quickly.

"How dare you approach me, varlet?" She could not hope

to stand up to him physically. All she could do was bluff him down. "Don't you know who I am? I am under the protection of the owner of this vessel, and if you lay a hand on me, I'll have the captain throw you overboard."

It was a desperate gamble. She was not at all sure what would happen if the captain were forced to choose between an experienced seaman and a young woman who could be nothing but a nuisance, but she had to try. To her astonishment, it seemed to work. The man glowered at her, surly and brooding, but he backed away.

Faith's fear dissolved into excitement as she watched him disappear. She could not believe how beautifully she had handled the situation. For the first time in her life, she had been bold—bolder than she had ever dreamed. She had been faced with danger, and she had not trembled or cried, she had not called out for help, but she had stood up to it, all by herself. And she had won!

Her excitement carried her across the deck, toward the stern. She had rarely ventured so far from the uncomfortable little salon that had been set aside for her and Rolfe, but she did not care. Nothing could intimidate her now. She felt as if she could conquer the world.

She did not see the small group of men standing at the railing until she had nearly reached them, for it took all her concentration to pick her way through the tools and rigging that blocked the deck. When she caught sight of them, she paused, staring at them with rising curiosity. She could not for the life of her figure out what they were doing. They seemed to be clutching a bundle in their hands, a rough bag of some sort, made of canvas or coarse gray sheeting. They held it tightly, poised against the railing, as if they were about to toss it into the sea.

Faith stepped closer, craning her neck to see it better. As she did, the captain noticed her. His face darkened with fury.

"What the devil are you doing here? Get back, do you hear? Get back!"

Faith stopped abruptly. The force of the man's anger was so powerful it seemed to reach out and slap her in the face. "But what . . . what's wrong? What have I done?"

One of the men loosened his hold on the bag and grinned slowly. Faith recognized his expression instantly. She had seen it only a short time before on the face of another sailor, and it sickened her now. She did not know if she could find the strength to stand up to him, too.

Her fears were groundless. The captain, with a single

brusque gesture, shoved the man back, forcing him to grab hold of the filthy sack again. Then he scowled at Faith.

"This is no place for a woman. Get back to your cabin if you know what's good for you. Or does it give you a thrill to watch a burial at sea?"

"A burial?" Faith stumbled backward, inching toward the stairway that led down into the hold. She could not take her eyes off the sack, dangling clumsily over the rail. "But it's . . . it's so little."

"It was a lad," he replied grimly. "Five years old."

"Oh, dear God." Faith reached out to steady herself against the door jamb. She remembered seeing a few children, darting in and out among those anonymous figures the first few days at sea. Now she wished she had been friendlier, venturing close enough to talk to them. Perhaps she could have done something to help. "But where are his parents? And couldn't you wrap him in something more decent than a filthy rag?"

"The sharks won't know the difference."

The captain raised his hand to his men. The little body seemed to hang for a second in the air, then slipped noiselessly out of sight. The splash that followed was so faint and far away it hardly seemed real.

Almost as an afterthought, the captain turned back to Faith. "As for the parents, they're below deck where they belong."

"Below deck?" Faith couldn't believe what she was hearing. How could anyone be so unfeeling? She turned toward the stairway, gasping at the stench of filth and decay that rose from beneath. "You let them stay down there? All the time? With the children?" She forgot her own squeamishness as the full force of it hit her. "How can you allow that, sir? They need fresh air every day, even if they're too ill or uncomfortable to realize it. They should be forced on deck if need be. No wonder that poor little boy died."

The captain glared at her furiously. "You'd do well not to interfere in things you don't understand. Those people are nothing but slime. God knows what diseases they are carrying, perhaps even the pox. I'd be a damned fool to let them on deck where they could contaminate my men—or you."

"To *let* them on deck?" Faith's stomach turned as she realized what he was saying. "You mean you keep them locked up in the hold? Who do you think you are, playing God like that? Choosing who will live and who will die—all because of what *might* happen?"

Faith did not know where all the rage came from—even Fleur had never been so fiery—but she did not try to question it. It had started somewhere on the other side of the deck when she faced down a nameless sailor, and she was not going to let go of it now. The welfare, even the lives, of too many people depended on it.

"I've put up with a great deal on this ship—dirt, discomfort, even insolence. But I tell you, sir, I'll not put up with this. Those people are going to come up on deck, and they are going to come right now. And if you won't get them, I will!"

The captain raised his hand as if to strike her, but Faith held her ground. Her defiance seemed to work. He hesitated briefly; then, his face still black with rage, he dropped his arm to his side. Only when she saw that his eyes were focused beyond her did Faith realize some outside force had affected the balance of their confrontation. Turning, she saw Rolfe Stephens hurrying toward them.

"What on earth is wrong, Faith? I could hear you all the way across the ship."

"Oh, Rolfe!" Faith threw herself into his arms, completely forgetting she had vowed to have nothing to do with him. "It was terrible. They just threw him overboard. In a filthy sack. And he was only a baby."

Rolfe looked confused. Then, realizing what she was saying, he wrapped comforting arms around her. "There, there, Faith. It's all right. It *is* terrible, I know, but it can't be helped. The long voyage is hard on everyone, especially the children."

"It's *not* all right!" she cried, pulling away from him. "Those people are shut up all the time, without even a breath of air. If they stay below deck, they'll die before we reach port."

"Don't be ridiculous, Faith. Of course they're not shut up. They're free to come out whenever they want. That's one of my father's strictest orders."

"But they are shut up, Rolfe. You don't know what it's like. You're hardly ever on deck." It suddenly occurred to her that the other passengers had disappeared about the time Rolfe began staying in his cabin. She pointed an accusing finger at the captain. "He admits he keeps them locked up. Because they're slime, he says."

Rolfe faced the captain resolutely.

"Is this true?"

The man's eyes were shifty, darting this way and that.

"What do you care if it is? You know what those people are. Nothing but indentured servants, off to serve terms in the Colonies. It's no skin off my nose—or yours—if some of them don't make it."

"By God, sir, I'll hear no more of this. My father doesn't run a slaver. Those people are human beings, not animals, and I won't have you treating them that way."

The captain, cunning in his anger, did not attempt to reply, but turned instead toward Faith. His face was black with hatred. Rolfe drew her close to him, resting a protective hand on her waist.

"Don't be frightened, Faith. I'll take care of everything. Why don't you go to your cabin and rest?"

Faith caught her breath as she felt the pressure of his hand, so light, yet strong and masculine. She had never been so intensely aware of a man's touch before. Slowly, she looked up.

His eyes were as tender as his touch—and as masculine. There was nothing of the guarded appraisal she had seen in their depths before. Nothing of the faintly veiled disapproval. It was as if he were seeing her for the first time, and it was obvious he liked what he saw.

Faith could not resist glancing over her shoulder as she walked away to see if he was still watching her. A tremor of excitement coursed through her veins when she saw that he was. She did not mistake the look on his face. It was an expression she had seen often enough in the past. But always before, it had been directed at Fleur.

Rolfe roused himself enough that evening to join her for dinner and, although he barely touched his food, he at least managed to keep up an interesting conversation, telling her about the ships his father owned and the businesses he ran, and the growing part in that vast commercial empire that he himself was beginning to play. Faith was fascinated, but she listened with only half an ear. She could not take her eyes off this handsome young man across the table from her, just as she could not for an instant forget that his eyes, too, had never left her face.

It was flattering, the way he looked at her, it was exciting, it was tantalizing beyond her wildest dreams—but it was frightening, too. The new emotions, the new feelings in her body, were so confusing she could not sort them out. It was almost a relief when he pushed back his chair and said it was time to retire.

Wrapping a shawl around her shoulders, Faith wandered

out on deck, hoping the cold air would clear her troubled thoughts. The wind was faint, the sea as calm as the day they set sail. The metal railing felt like ice as she rested her fingers against it.

She stared into the night, and she could see him again, looking back at her, telling her with dark, melting eyes that he adored her. She could feel the touch of his hand once again on her waist, gentle, strong, vibrating with unknown temptations. If he were to step behind her now, slipping the shawl from her shoulders until only the thin silk of her dress stood between his fingers and her quivering flesh, she would lean into his arms, lifting her lips to enjoy the excitement of her first kiss in his embrace.

She had never envied her sister so much. If Fleur were here, she would not be standing alone at the rail, confused and intimidated by the yearnings of her body. Fleur would tilt back her head and laugh at caution—and propriety. She would slip through the passages of the ship into the arms of the man she wanted. And in the darkness of a narrow bed, she would give herself up to the moaning of the wind and the rhythm of the sea in a passion that held neither doubt nor fear. At that moment, Faith longed desperately to be like her sister. It would be so good to stop struggling at last and abandon herself to her own desires.

But not with Rolfe. Oh, dear heaven, not with Rolfe. She could not let herself get involved with this man. There was too much at stake. If he was overprotective now, simply on his father's bidding, what would he be like when he learned to care for her?

Someday, all too soon, the ship would dock in the harbor at New York, and she would have to find a way to get rid of him. It would only make things harder for her—and for him—if they grew too close now.

She leaned against the railing, trying to work it all out in her mind. Was she being a fool, chasing after straws in the wind? A room she had never seen, a swamp she didn't even recognize—could she ever hope to find these things? And if she could, what then? Fleur had been so much cleverer than she, so much more resourceful, and she had not been able to save herself. Was she only racing headlong toward the same dark fate?

Faith's doubts continued to plague her on the last days of the voyage, but she did not let herself dwell on them. She could not. If she did, she knew she would never find the courage to go on. Instead, she forced herself to concentrate on how she was going to elude Rolfe once they docked in New York.

It proved far easier than she dared to hope. The instant she hit on a plan, she knew it was perfect. There was no way it could fail.

She waited until the morning they were due to land. Then, tying the laces of her corset so tight she could barely breathe, she sat down at her dressing table and began to arrange her hair in the latest fashion. When she had finished, she donned her most becoming dress, a sheer, softly feminine lawn, and stood back from the mirror to survey the effect.

She was bewitching, and for the first time, she knew it. The gold pattern in her dress brought out the highlights of her hair, and ruffled petticoats, full over wide hoops, accented the slimness of her waist and the ripe curves of her breast. A gauzy fichu, snowy white with delicate webs of silver, floated down from her shoulders, barely disguising the low neckline that dipped temptingly beneath daring cleavage.

She did not need a second glance at her mirror to reconfirm her loveliness. Rolfe's eyes, when she opened the door to him, told her all she needed to know. No man had ever looked more adoringly at Fleur.

Her heart ached as she looked at him. He was so handsome, this young man she had once despised. So tender. She could not forget that he was the first man who had made her feel beautiful. The first man whose touch told her she was a woman. With him, she had shared that magic moment when her youthful body awakened to passion, and she hated herself for the way she was about to repay him.

"I am sorry, Rolfe."

He looked puzzled as he followed her into the room. "Sorry for what?"

She held out her hands. "I'm afraid we got off to a bad start. Can you ever forgive me for the way I treated you?"

"Oh, that." He laughed easily. "I knew you were just miffed because your uncle wouldn't let you travel alone, the way your sister did. Believe me, Faith, I would forgive you much more than that."

I hope so, she thought, but she did not speak the words aloud. She wished he would not look at her so solemnly. It made her feel even guiltier.

"You have always been so kind . . . so understanding." She stepped as close as she dared, letting her fingers run along the edge of his jacket. "I wonder . . . dare I ask one more thing of you?"

"Anything, Faith. You know I would give you anything within my power."

"I know I'm being silly, honestly I do, but I dread going to that terrible, rough city unprepared. I'm sure I shall faint in that awful dock area if I have to stand there with those coarse sailors staring at me while we try to find a hired cab. Do you suppose you could take my trunks in and engage a room for me? Then you could come back in a proper carriage."

Rolfe gazed at her tenderly. "Find a room for you? I won't hear of it, Faith. You'll stay with my cousins. I'll go and arrange things now."

"Oh, Rolfe. . . ." Faith didn't know if she felt more guilty or relieved. She could not believe he had made it so easy for her. "You are so good to me."

"Any man would be good to you. Don't you know that?"

He was standing so close to her, Faith could feel the heat of his body. She was intensely conscious of her breasts, warm flesh beneath a lacy veil, barely an inch from the rough black wool of his coat. She had to smile as she remembered how embarrassed she had once been by her own budding voluptuousness. She had not known then how exciting it could be to feel like a woman.

She did not know how it happened. One minute they were barely touching, the next she was in his arms, lifting her face to his. His kiss was sweeter than she had ever imagined, soft and tender, demanding as he forced her lips apart, gentle as his tongue teased hers. She could feel his hardness, strong and muscular, as he crushed her against him, sliding his hands down to urge her hips toward his. Frightened, she drew her body back, but still she could not tear her lips away. She felt as if she were drowning in the passion of his kiss.

It was Rolfe who finally ended the moment. Easing his lips from hers, he traced a line of tender kisses down her cheek, sinking at last to her neck.

"Oh Faith, Faith. You don't know how beautiful you are."

"Rolfe . . . please." Trembling, she pushed him away. She was sick with shame at what she had done.

Misunderstanding, he pulled back, his face stricken. "My dear, forgive me. I don't know what got into me. I had no right to treat you like that."

"No, no, that's not it." How could she explain? How could she tell him she had delighted as much in the force of his assault as he had in the softness of her acquiescence? "It's just that I can't . . . I can't. . . ."

"My God, Faith, I know you can't," he broke in, horrified. Suddenly, he was painfully aware of the bed only inches away. "Damn it, I am a cad—and twice the cad for cursing in front of you. I have only respect for you, and admiration. Believe me, I never intended. . . ."

Or hadn't he? he asked himself wryly. Who did he think he was kidding? It was he who had drawn her against his chest, he whose lips sank hungrily on hers. The bed seemed to fill his whole range of vision now, mocking him for his protests.

He took a step backward. "I'd better see to your trunks."

"Rolfe. . . ."

He turned in the doorway. His eyes were filled with hope. It hurt her not to be able to say the things she knew he longed to hear.

"Thank you," she whispered. "Thank you for everything."

She watched the door swing slowly shut, then listened to his footsteps echo down the hallway. At last they vanished, and he was gone.

She dared waste no time. Pulling a small hand valise out of the closet where she had secreted it, she set it by the door. It contained little—a nightdress, a change of lingerie, a few toilet articles—but she dared not steal away with more. Picking it up, she opened the door and glanced down the passageway to make sure no one was in sight. She had bribed one sailor to get the assistance she needed. She could not afford to let anyone else see her.

Her feet faltered on the threshold. It was so absolute, this thing she was about to do. So irrevocable. Another minute, another step—and there would be no turning back.

Am I being a fool? she asked herself for the thousandth time since her long journey began. Am I throwing my life away, just like my sister? And for the thousandth time, she had to give herself the same answer. It did not matter. It simply did not matter. No matter how frightened she was, no matter how desperately she longed to throw herself into Rolfe's arms and forget everything else, she had to go on. Fleur was her sister. She could not let her die unavenged.

The passageway was dark as she stepped into it. Dark and empty. Silence was her only companion as she slipped down its length, hurrying toward the rendezvous she had already arranged.

Rolfe leaned forward in the carriage, sticking his head out the window. The noise of the street muffled his voice as he called out to the coachman.

"Can't you get that nag to move any faster? We'll never get there at this rate."

It was intolerable to think of Faith waiting even another minute in a cramped, stale-smelling cabin. Almost as intolerable as it was having to wait another minute to be with her. The whole thing was crazy. Only a few weeks ago, there had been no thought in his head of love or attachments, no plans for the kind of long-range commitment he knew his family expected of him. Now, suddenly, he had found a woman, a beautiful, enchanting young woman, and the world had turned upside down.

Impatiently, he settled back in his seat, staring out at the passing scene. He had visited the Colonies twice before, and both times he had been fascinated by the brashness that contrasted so strikingly with his own cautious refinement. Now, for the first time, he saw the place through Faith's eyes, and he was glad she had had the sense to remain behind until he could arrange everything for her. New York was not a city to be subjected to unawares.

There was an overall crudeness about everything that could not fail to appall her. The streets, narrow dirt lanes in the best of times, were slick with the spring rains, and horses' hooves spattered an indiscriminate coating of muddy yellow-brown on carriage doors and low brick walls, on the rags of passing beggers and the smooth woolen breeches of fastidious gentlemen. Piles of dung sank into the oozing mud, matching the filth of the street until only their fetid stench gave them away.

The surroundings grew rougher as they approached the docks. Farther inland, nearer the wall that separated the city from the Indian-infested frontier beyond, tall narrow town-houses huddled together, quaint and colorful with an Old World charm, but here there was nothing but offices and warehouses, drab gray blocks with a saloon on every corner. The sounds were a raucous symphony: horses whinnying shrilly, impatient with the ropes that tethered them in semi-circles at the edge of the road; rough male voices, boisterous in disagreement and in song; the barking of a dog, fierce in his disapproval of the groaning wheels of a passing carriage; the cries of a drunken sailor as he called out bawdy greetings to a friend.

Ordinarily, Rolfe would have been intrigued by the men who hurried down the street or huddled in groups in the doorways. They were all kinds and all colors. A clerk in somber black, his nose pinched in distaste, stepping gingerly over heaps of dung—he could have been nothing but an Englishman, lonely and homesick in his self-imposed exile. A dark-skinned frontiersman, all buckskin and cambric, brass buttons and glassy beads, covered by a threadbare blanket and capped with a jaunty tricorne—some half-breed trader, no doubt, as down on his luck in the city as he had been in the raw countryside. A black Spanish sailor, dark skin glistening, bright red shirt stained with sweat and dirt, a golden loop swinging in his ear—what tales of daring and adventure would he have been able to spin, what sagas of piracy on the open seas, if only they had a common language and the courage to speak to each other.

But he had no time to think of such things now. There was room in his thoughts for one image and one only. The lovely young woman he longed to hold in his arms.

Faith. Sweet, gentle Faith. He could not believe how soft she felt in his embrace. How tenderly she trembled with yearning and innocence. Not like the other. . . .

Damn it, why did he have to think of that now? It was Faith he loved, Faith he wanted—not Fleur. He had wanted never to think of Fleur again.

And yet he could not forget her. Perhaps, in a way, he never would. She had been too sultry—too exciting. And he had been too new to love. His body had been ready to explode when she opened her lips to him, wriggling her hips against his with a suggestiveness that could not be misinterpreted.

He had never understood why he had denied himself the joy she offered. He knew well enough, despite his harsh words to Faith on the ship, that Fleur was not the little slut he tried to pretend she was. She had loved to experiment, testing the kisses of every boy or man who wandered within arm's reach, but anything more than that had always been reserved for the handsomest—the most dashing—of her suitors. He should have been flattered. Instead, he had been frightened and run away.

He had hated himself for it then. He had called himself a prude for thinking it cheap or demeaning to be involved in the kind of casual encounter that demanded no commitment on either side. He had been filled with self-loathing for rejecting the same excitement he would have accepted eagerly from a common prostitute. Now, at last, he understood what he should have realized all along.

Even then, even in adolescence, it was Faith he wanted. Faith, a boisterous tomboy one minute, solemn and timid the next. Faith, with the huge, limpid eyes that spoke a thousand words, even when her lips were silent. Instinctively, he had known that one day he would want this beautiful girl with all the passion and hunger in his soul.

And any dalliance with the sister would only have defiled his love for her.

He did not wait for the coach to come to a stop at the docks, but thrust the door open while it was still moving and leaped out. A pair of sailors, struggling with a heavy carton on the gangplank, called out an angry curse as he pushed them hastily aside.

He was disappointed when he knocked at her cabin and received no answer, but he was not unduly alarmed. He paused only long enough to shove the door open, making sure the room was empty, before he hurried toward the salon. He had not begun to worry yet. After all, it was not reasonable to expect her to wait in the stuffy cabin.

It was only when he reached the salon and found it empty that the truth began to dawn on him. Still, he could not believe it. He was angry at first, then puzzled, then angry again. It was a long time before he could bring himself to admit what she had done to him.

"Damn!" He pounded his fist against the door jamb, concentrating on the surge of pain that raced up his forearm, as if it had the power to take his mind off another, deeper pain. What an idiot he had been, believing in that little vixen.

What was it he had said to her that night? *You know, you are incredibly like your sister.*

And she was, goddammit, she was! Oh, their styles were different, their ways of working with men. Fleur had excited him with brazen lips and hips that writhed against his, Faith had trapped him with a frightened, innocent kiss—but in the end it was the same. They had both used their sexuality to manipulate him, and they had both known exactly what they were doing! The only difference was that the first had failed. The second had succeeded devastatingly well.

He did not jostle the deckhands this time as he returned slowly down the gangplank. He barely even saw them. He had learned a bitter lesson that day, and it was one he was determined never to forget. It would be a long, cold day in hell before he trusted a beautiful woman again.

He did not turn his head as he reached the dock and headed toward the waiting carriage. The small, ill-fitted packet anchored in the harbor meant nothing to him. He could not know it waited only a favorable wind to carry its load of trading goods to Charles Town. Even if he had, he would not have associated it with Faith. He had no reason to believe she had even heard of South Carolina.

Three

Thick yellow dust stained the hem of Faith's skirt as she stood at the edge of the crude dirt road and stared around her in dismay. The small southern town—though, in truth, the word *town* hardly seemed an apt description for such a primitive place—was barely a score of wooden buildings, each a little more dilapidated and ill-kept than the last. It had not occurred to her that the strip of cultivated land separating the ocean from the wild, unexplored interior of the continent would be so narrow, or that it would leave her feeling so vulnerable. Why, this place was nothing but a frontier town—and a rough one at that!

"Hardly what you imagined, I daresay," a voice beside her broke into her thoughts. "Where are all the quaint little shops? you are asking yourself. The thatched roofs and white picket fences? Primroses and buttercups, providing gay splashes of pink and yellow across tidy green lawns?"

Faith glanced at the speaker with distaste. She had not liked Eleazar Carstairs when she first met him in Charles Town, and his flippancy now did nothing to amend her opinion. Still, she knew it would be foolish to antagonize him. Carstairs, the owner of a nearby plantation, had just returned from a year in England, and he had been invaluable in helping her get this far. She was not at all sure she could go even the last few miles to Havenhurst without him.

"Now you're making fun of me, Mr. Carstairs," she replied, as politely as she could manage. "I may be naive, but even so, I didn't hope to find an English country village in the middle of the Colonial landscape. I must admit, though, I hadn't expected anything quite so—so unrefined."

Carstairs laughed. He was a slender, middle-aged man, impeccably dressed, with a ruffled cambric shirt, still crisp, even in the midday heat, and a broad-brimmed black hat tilted at a rakish angle on his head. Dark eyes, too small for his face, shifted almost continuously, pausing only on occasion to linger with unnecessary obviousness on the bare skin of Faith's arms and bosom.

"Permit me to speculate, Miss Eliot, that you will find much in the Colonies that is—as you so charmingly put it—unrefined."

"I'm sure I will," Faith snapped. His words made her uncomfortable, reminding her once again how poorly she had prepared herself for this impetuous journey. "Tell me, is Havenhurst like this, too? I remember nothing about it, of course—I was just a child when we left—but somehow I can't picture it as a tumbledown wooden shanty, with leaks in the roof and rotting boards on the veranda."

"Good Lord, neither can I! What a vivid imagination you have. Surely you don't think we planters are anything like the poor squatters in town."

"Well, no, of course not, but. . . ."

Faith looked around doubtfully. The worst of the noon heat was over, and one by one, men had begun to straggle onto the road. They moved slowly, with the lethargy common to inhabitants of subtropic climes. A black-skinned man, coarse tow-linen pants rolled halfway to his knees, dragged bare feet through the dusty road, then disappeared into one of the huts. A pair of even blacker lads, twelve or thirteen years old, struggled silently with a large crock, hauling it between them as they left a gouged-out trail in the earth. In the center of the road, a short, stocky man, a shock of thinning yellow hair spilling onto his forehead, adjusted a sack of grain on shoulders no longer young enough to bear the weight, and waited patiently for the boys to make their way around him. The color of their skin marked the blacks as slaves, the white man as a farmer, but nothing in their manner or their dress set them apart from each other.

Carstairs ignored her skepticism.

"My own home, Cypress Hill, is a showcase, elegant enough to put many a palace in Europe to shame—and so, in its day, was Havenhurst. Adam Eliot spared no expense building it for his bride, and the lovely Desirée, much to her credit, knew how to spend his money well. Nothing was too good for her. The finest furnishings, the richest brocades, the most delicate crystals—everything was imported from France to suit her exquisite taste."

Faith felt as if she were listening to a description of two

strangers. The Adam Eliot whose very name had been banned as long as she could remember had never seemed in her imagination either generous or extravagant. As for Desirée, earthly pleasures must have been repugnant to a young girl still haunted by nightmares of the Huguenot persecution in France which had claimed the lives of her parents and crippled her young brother, Olivier. If she spent her new husband's money to adorn Havenhurst, the plantation she herself had bought with her family fortune, she could only have done it to please him.

"Did you know my mother?" Faith asked curiously. She did not like Carstairs, but she wanted to know more about Havenhurst, and he was one man who could tell her.

"Regrettably, no. It is a pleasure I would have enjoyed enormously. They say she was a great beauty—like her daughter."

"But my father?" Faith pressed, deliberately ignoring the insinuation in his tone. "You did know my father, didn't you?"

"Oh, yes, I knew your father very well."

"Well enough to know why he lost Havenhurst?"

It was a blunt question, but Faith had the feeling tact would be lost on a man like Carstairs. If she was right, if Fleur's death was somehow connected with Havenhurst, she could not afford to be subtle.

"My dear child," Carstairs sputtered, taken aback by her directness. "I couldn't begin to tell you. Adam didn't confide in me. That's hardly the kind of thing a man chats about with his acquaintances."

"But there must have been speculation at the time."

"Speculation? Oh, my yes, I should say so. There was gossip galore, and for months, too. But that's just it, don't you see? It was *only* speculation. No one had the vaguest notion beforehand that Adam was managing his plantation poorly. It was a complete shock to us when he sold out to pay his debts—though not, I must admit, an unwelcome one."

"Why not?"

"Let us be frank, Miss Eliot. Your father was not—how shall I put it?—the most popular man in the Colony. When he died, a short time later, there were more than a few dry eyes in the neighborhood."

The man's coldness touched an unexpected chord in Faith, stirring a tentative feeling of empathy for a man who had never truly been a father to her. For the first time, she dared to wonder consciously what Adam Eliot had been like. It seemed to her that anyone at odds with a person like Eleazar Carstairs could not be totally without redeeming qualities.

"And what of the new owner?" she asked, changing the subject adroitly. "Mr. Alleyn? What is he like?"

Jeremy Alleyn was only a name to her. He had never been anything more. Faith had been just fifteen that summer when she crouched outside a half-open door and listened to her aunt and uncle discuss the disgraceful loss of Havenhurst in shocked, hushed tones. She had been curious about it then, had longed to ask for more information, but even as a child she had understood that the subject of Adam Eliot was forbidden to her.

"You mean you don't know Alleyn?" Carstairs took no pains to hide his surprise. "Not at all? You came all the way across the ocean without talking it over with the owner of Havenhurst—or asking what kind of welcome you could expect?"

"Of course not," Faith lied. She had already admitted her foolhardiness to herself. She was not about to admit it again to a man she didn't even like. "Mr. Alleyn is a distant relative. His mother, Rosaline Devereaux, is a second cousin to my mother. I merely meant, what kind of a man is he? It's hard to tell from letters and hearsay."

"You mean, will you like him?" Carstairs asked, studying her with a look Faith could only interpret as sardonic amusement. "Oh, yes, I think you will. I don't like him, of course, nor do any of the other planters, but the man does seem to hold an inexplicable attraction for women. If you are typical—and you certainly seem to be—I doubt you'll hold out long against his charms."

Faith clamped her mouth shut, forcing back an angry retort. Carstairs didn't think much of her, and perhaps she hadn't given him reason to, but he was wrong. Jeremy Alleyn, whatever his charms, was definitely not going to appeal to her. Fleur would have adored him—she always thrived on the kind of man who held an "inexplicable attraction" for women—but to Faith he only seemed intimidating, even frightening. There was no danger whatsoever she would be tempted to like him.

She did not try to speak again, but followed obediently as Eleazar Carstairs guided her toward the blacksmith's shop at the far end of the street. For the moment, she had had quite as much as she could take of Havenhurst and all its mysteries. She already had enough qualms about her self-imposed mission, qualms that had heightened day by day as she approached her destination. She did not need Carstairs, with his questions and insinuations, to add to them now. The smartest thing she could do was concentrate on immediate problems, not the least of which was finding some way to cover the last few miles between town and Jeremy Alleyn's plantation.

Walking was not easy. The street was less a street than a series of hoof prints and wagon ruts, molded in once-soft mud, then solidified with the coming of the dry season until nothing remained but sharp ridges and deep holes. Faith negotiated the path gingerly. Head down, toes testing each foothold, she moved as best she could, struggling to keep from twisting her ankle or throwing herself off balance. She was so engrossed, she barely noticed when a rough sleeve brushed her arm.

Looking up, she was startled to see a young black man no more than a few inches away from her. She stopped, forgetting her precarious footing, as she stared at him in frank fascination. She had been both frightened and intrigued the first time she had seen these strange, dark creatures on the docks in New York, but never before had she been so close she could reach out and touch one with her hand. She shivered with anticipation as she studied the youth, searching for visible traces of the jungle savage who once had killed wild beasts with bare hands or torn missionaries and slave traders apart with sharpened teeth. She was more disappointed than relieved when she detected none of the exotic violence she had imagined. The young man was certainly a disagreeable specimen, ragged and unwashed, with the unpleasant smell of sweat rising above the stench of dung-strewn streets, but there was nothing either wild or threatening in his mien. If anything, he seemed dull, almost timid, as he backed away with a mumbled apology.

Carstairs' fingers dug into Faith's arm as he steered her away. "Filthy, insolent beasts!" he cursed soundly. "We should put a curb on importing any more of them before we're overrun with the swine."

Faith did not try to reply. She had heard that the Colonials were bringing in more and more blacks every year to expand their slave force, but she was wise enough not to pursue the subject. She had no interest in the politics of South Carolina, and she would not be here long enough to develop one. She had no desire to stay in this dreadful place a minute longer than she had to.

The blacksmith's shop was a sweltering furnace. Faith tried to follow Carstairs inside, but fell back, gasping, as gusts of hot air swept into her face. Eyes burning from smoke, she stood in the doorway and stared in at what seemed to be a blazing inferno. Sparks sizzled through the air, a fireworks show in miniature, accompanied by the rhythmic clang of metal against metal. A massive man, his muscular body half naked, was barely visible in the semidarkness. Swarthy skin, reddened in the reflection of the flames, was so distorted in color that Faith could not tell if he was black or white. Carstairs did not seem to be sure either, for he stood tentatively to the side, as if it disgusted him to get too close.

When Carstairs at last emerged from the shop, he told Faith what she had expected to hear, that there was not a horse for sale or rent anywhere in town. She did not know whether to cry in frustration or sigh with relief. She had never been much of a horsewoman, and the idea of riding with a full set of petticoats and nothing but dress slippers on her feet hardly appealed to her. Besides, she was not at all sure she wanted to be alone on deserted roads with a man like Eleazar Carstairs. But now, without a horse—and no such thing as a hired carriage anywhere in the countryside—she had no idea how she was going to get to Havenhurst.

The problem was postponed, for Carstairs had caught sight of a plump, white-wigged man riding toward them from the far end of the street. Removing his hat, he waved it back and forth in broad gestures, trying to catch the man's attention.

"Hey, Sam Hardin, you old scoundrel! What are you doing out in all this heat?"

Hardin did not accelerate his pace, but rode toward them slowly, letting his horse pick its way through ruts and debris on the street. "Carstairs?" he called out skeptically. "Carstairs, is that you?"

"Who else?"

Carstairs donned his hat again, tipping it back on his head. Stepping up to the older man, he caught the horse's reins deftly in his hand, pulling it to a stop.

Hardin scowled down at him. "You certainly tarried long enough in England. Mundane tittle-tattle had it you would never deign to grace us with your presence again. More's the pity. I had begun to surmise the tale had veracity on its side."

"More's the pity I was gone?" Carstairs quipped good-naturedly. "Or more's the pity I came back? Come on, Samuel, 'fess up. You're only burned because I had the good sense to go away at the right time."

"Indubitably, dear Eleazar, indubitably," the man admitted with an affected sigh. "A most calamitous year in the Carolinas, I must agree. Most deplorable. I tell you, 1739 will go down throughout eternity as a year of infamy."

"A year of infamy?" Faith was surprised to hear her own voice. A minute ago she had thought she was totally disinterested in the Colonies. Now, a chance conversation had piqued her curiosity. "I'm afraid I know very little about South Carolina, sir. What happened last year that made it so infamous?"

Hardin looked down, open-mouthed, at the slender figure he had not noticed before. He leaned forward, squinting to make out her features. When he pulled himself upright again, he seemed vaguely dissatisfied, as if he still had not seen her clearly. He did not try to speak, but left it to Carstairs to answer Faith's question.

"The black rebellion. I'm surprised you didn't hear about it in England. They rose up at a place called Stono River, not far from here. There were only twenty of them in the beginning, led by the slave Jemmy, but before it ended, they had turned into a mad, howling mob of more than a hundred. They were trying to get to St. Augustine. The Spanish rile them up, you know. They promise them freedom if they can get to Florida—anything to stir up trouble in the English Colonies. I wonder if the dumb bastards even know how barbarously the Spaniards treat their own slaves."

"Did they make it?"

Faith found the story strangely touching. The poor savages, how frightened they must have been, captives in a strange land. She hoped, if they got that far, the Spanish had kept their promise.

"I suppose it all sounds romantic to you," Carstairs told her contemptuously. "Well, try this on for a pretty tale, why don't you? They broke into Hutchinson's store, ostensibly to steal small arms and powder. But by the time they had finished, the heads of the storekeeper and two other men were sitting on the steps in front."

Faith gasped in horror. The "poor savages" no longer seemed quite so sad and helpless.

"You mean they—they killed them?"

"Decapitation usually results in death," Carstairs replied grimly. "Next, they went to the house of a man named Godfrey, where they went through an orgy of plunder and burning. And, yes, they killed Godfrey—and his son and daughter. Need I say more? By the time they were caught, more than twenty whites were dead."

"But they *were* caught?"

"Hanged, shot and gibbeted alive," Carstairs agreed cheerfully. "The ones that didn't escape, that is."

"The ones that didn't escape?"

Faith looked around anxiously, horrified at the thoughts that were beginning to whirl through her head. No one was on the street now, but she could not forget the sight of two scrawny black lads, wrestling manfully with a heavy crock, or the unexpected feel of coarse fabric against her arm a few seconds later. And yet they had seemed so harmless, all of them. So diffident.

"Are these people dangerous then?"

"Are they dangerous?" Hardin burst into the conversation with a roar. "Of course they are dangerous, you frivolous little trollop."

Faith pulled herself up tall with indignation. She did not know whom Hardin had mistaken her for—perhaps the very fact of being with Eleazar Carstairs was enough to justify the slur in his mind—but she did not care. No man was going to treat her like that, especially not a man like Samuel Hardin. His manner was as pompous as his speech, but his shirttail had slipped out of his breeches, exposing an inch of soft pink belly, and the acrid odor of sweat was no more appealing on him than it had been on the black slave in the street.

"I am not a trollop, Mr. Hardin, nor am I frivolous. I merely asked a civil question, and I expected a civil answer."

"Bravo!" Carstairs punctuated the word with a burst of laughter as he clapped her familiarly on the back. "A woman of spirit! I like that. Hold onto that quality, my dear. It will serve you in good stead at Havenhurst. Alleyn likes his women feisty and fiery."

Faith refrained from retorting that she was not Jeremy Alleyn's woman and she didn't give a fig what he liked or didn't like. Moving away from the men, she sauntered partway down the road, trying to pretend she had found something so fascinating in the front yard of one of the huts she could not tear her eyes away. In reality, she saw only one small, scraggly chicken, and that—poor thing—was in no danger of being made into anything heartier than soup, for there wasn't an ounce of meat on its bones.

Snatches of conversation carried to her ears. She could not understand everything they were saying, but she knew the men were still discussing the rebellion. From what she could hear, each seemed as much at cross purposes with himself as with the other. Hardin's "At least the scurrilous knaves can't go out after dark anymore without a paper signed by their master," brought a sharp rebuttal: "What the devil does that accomplish when men like . . ." Faith strained to hear the name. What was it? Alleyn? ". . . give the wretches a paper whenever they want it?" Decisions were made and unmade in minutes. "A quota on importation," the two agreed. Then, "A ban on importation." And in the end, "Oh, hell, why don't we just ship the savages back to Africa where they belong?"

How naive they sounded, Faith thought, listening to the two men babble self-importantly as if they thought they were making logical points. Even she knew that the economy of the Colonies, particularly the southern ones, depended on a heavy agricultural output from the large farms and plantations. Who did they think would harvest all that rice and tobacco if they shipped the savages back to Africa? How would men like Eleazar Carstairs and Samuel Hardin get rich then?

At last the conversation ended, and Carstairs ambled over to where Faith was standing. She was uncomfortably aware, as she had been before, of dark eyes scrutinizing her form, but this time the man seemed bolder than before, more sure of himself. She had the feeling that he had decided she was at his mercy and could do nothing about it.

"I've been thinking about your problem," he drawled, leaning with deceptive carelessness against a tethering post at the side of the road. He made not the slightest pretense of raising his eyes above her bosom. "There is only one reasonable way to get you to Havenhurst. I shall put you behind me on my horse."

Faith's dismay must have shown on her face, for the man began to smile, not at all pleasantly, she thought.

"Unless, of course," he added sarcastically, "you would prefer a dugout canoe."

Faith did not have the vaguest notion what a canoe was, though his tone warned her she would not find it attractive, but she did not truly care. It seemed to her the choice was a simple one.

"I think the canoe would be more comfortable."

She expected Carstairs to bristle with indignation at the insult, but she quickly learned she had underestimated the man. He only laughed as he took her arm, leading her toward the riverbank. He was still laughing, minutes later, when they arrived. It took Faith only a second to figure out why.

A dugout canoe was not a real boat at all, but a cypress log, with the center hollowed out. Faith eyed it with distinct suspicion. Jagged splinters ruptured the sides, and a half inch of muddy water sloshed in the bottom, making her doubt it could stay afloat for more than a few minutes at best. Such a conveyance might look serviceable to native Indians, or even to less discriminating white settlers, discouraged by the lack of roads and transportation, but to Faith, it seemed an idiotic way to risk one's life.

She cast a last dubious glance at Eleazar Carstairs. All it took was one look at the self-satisfied smirk on his face to make up her mind. She could not possibly consider riding through dense woods and lonely fields behind this man, not when she knew he could feel her breasts pressed into his back, her arms around his waist. Gamely, she stepped into the canoe, trying not to look alarmed as it rolled precariously.

Carstairs reached out a hand to steady her, but Faith noticed he took care not to get the long, rounded toes of his riding boots wet in the process. He made no attempt to help, but stood on the sandy shore, grinning as he watched the elderly black boatman wade into the water. The canoe scraped harshly against the riverbed, then slid out into the current.

"Watch out for Old Sharper," Carstairs called as the boatman climbed aboard. Faith could not tell whether he was laughing or not. "These black gaffers may look feeble and arthritic, but they're wily as the devil."

Faith regarded the old slave apprehensively. Surely even Carstairs would not let her go off with the man if he could not be trusted. His face looked benign enough, with thin lips sunken into toothless gums, and eyes that were dark and empty. He did not seem to have noticed Carstairs' words, and Faith wondered if he was deaf or perhaps too dim-witted to understand.

"I'll take my chances," she called back.

There was no mistaking Carstairs' laughter this time. The sound was brittle and metallic.

"Just don't let him steer you near the swamps. That's where the black bastards who escaped the rebellion are hiding out."

Faith shuddered. What an awful man, she thought, turning to block him out of her sight. He knew very well there were no swamps at Havenhurst—not if it was truly the civilized place he had described—but he couldn't resist one last chance to frighten her. If he was any example of the men in this new land, he and that obnoxious Sam Hardin both, she wasn't going to be the least bit sorry when it was time to leave.

It took only an hour to reach Havenhurst, but the afternoon heat made the last leg of Faith's journey seem longer than it was. Perspiration dripped from her hair and forehead, trickling down her neck until the silvery fichu she had tucked into her bosom was drenched. Huge black horseflies tormented her mercilessly, buzzing in her ears every minute of the time, stinging when she tried in vain to brush them from her arms and face. Even the water smelled hot and steamy, as if it were not a free-flowing river, but a stagnant, fetid pond.

The banks that drifted slowly by on either side were a far cry from anything Faith had imagined. In her daydreams, Havenhurst was a lush tropical paradise. Extravagant vegetation sparkled in the sunlight like translucent emeralds, highlighted with fiery bursts of scarlet and gold, and sweet floral perfumes wafted on warm breezes across waters mystic and green. But reality was a brutal disappointment. Try as she would, Faith could detect nothing languid in the scene around her, nothing moody or sultry. This land was a wilderness, raw and frank, and no one looking at it could forget that for a moment.

The earth was only half tamed. New sprouts peeked out of flooded rice fields, with sturdy banks of soil cutting them into even squares, like an enormous patchwork quilt of brown and green and gold, but the shores held more than rice alone. Tall cypresses stood at the river's edge, thrusting long, twisted limbs like so many tangled roots into the water, and ancient live-oaks, somber and mysterious in their drapes of gray moss, dozed in the shadows, oblivious to the intrusion of man in their midst.

Even the hillsides, easing gently upward from the edge of the fields, did not truly belong to civilization. Orchards, ripening with plums and apples, peaches and figs, nectrons and mulberries, dotted the slopes, and the golden-beige of grain alternated with row upon row of familiar and exotic vegetables, but nowhere did cultivated land have more than a tenuous hold on its space. Dark blue-green pine forests threatened on every side; copses of poplar and black gum were overgrown with wild grapes; and pea vines, tall as a horse, spilled across plowed boundaries to flaunt their disdain for man.

Faith turned back to glance at the boatman. She was beginning to be curious about this land they were passing through.

"Have we come to Mr. Alleyn's plantation yet?" she asked, none too hopefully. The man looked as placid and dull as before, and she doubted he could understand her question.

Much to her surprise, the dark, wrinkled face lit up instantly.

"Yes'm," he drawled softly, the strange word sounding to Faith's ears like a contraction of "yes" and "madam," though she couldn't be sure. "Sho' be Mist' Alleyn land. Ain't nothin' here but what it be Mist' Alleyn. Far as yo' eye kin see and farther."

Far as your eye can see—and farther. The words tore at Faith's heart as she studied the shores and slopes again. Once all the land in sight and beyond had belonged to Desirée Devereaux and her brother, Olivier. Faith blinked back the tears that stung her eyes at the thought of such cruel injustice. Her mother had suffered so much in the long, agonizing flight from France. The New World should have been a beginning for her, not an ending. Even after Olivier died, the plantation they had bought together should have provided security for Desirée. Hers should never have been the humiliation of ending her days as a poor relation in someone else's house, always conscious that the price of every piece of bread she put into her daughters' mouths was her own pride and independence.

The boat rounded one last bend in the river, and the slave's voice rang out.

"Havenhurst," he told her excitedly. "Yo' see that house, one up on the hill? That be Havenhurst."

Havenhurst. Faith squinted into the sunlight, trying to see the place better. At first, it seemed almost an illusion, airy and sparkling, like a perfect diamond magically set in the yellow-gold of tall, waving grasses. Then, slowly, her eyes adjusted to the glare, and the contours of the house where she had been born began to take shape for her.

Eleazar Carstairs had not lied—Havenhurst was nothing like the miserable hovels in town—but he had been wrong to compare it to a palace in Europe. Nothing about it was even vaguely reminiscent of the stodgy stone bulwarks and gaudy rococo facades that typified the castles of the Continent. There was an elegant, understated grace in its open simplicity and clean, fluid lines that lent it a style all its own. Slender columns supported a gently sloping roof, and the starkness of pure white was relieved by a colorful accent of wisteria, entwining the railing of the piazza that circled the house.

Faith was surprised to feel how fast her heart was beating as the boatman steered the small canoe toward the sturdy landing that served the plantation. She had known she would be frightened when she reached Havenhurst, but she had not realized how helpless and alone fear would make her feel. What if she was wrong? she asked herself now, acutely conscious that it was too late to turn around and go back. What if she had just concocted the whole thing out of one fantastic nightmare? What if Fleur had not perished in the steamy wilderness of South Carolina after all? What if she had never even been here?

The boat slid into the shore, stopping with a disconcerting jolt. Faith sat absolutely still, not even hearing the puzzled tone in the boatman's voice as he told her again, and one more time again, that they had arrived. At last she rose, catching hold of the handle of her satchel. Her palms were so slick with sweat she could barely hang onto it.

She had already set foot on the sandy shore when she looked up and saw a man riding toward her from the fields. This time, when she felt her heartbeat quicken, she knew it was not from fear alone.

He made an awesome picture. Leaning forward, he merged into the white mane of the horse, heightening an illusion of unleashed power, until the strength of his body seemed to flow into that smooth, effortless gallop. Sun-streaked hair whipped back from his face. His shirt, half open to the waist, clung to his chest, then flared out behind him like a defiant banner. Everything about him was electric and untamed, like a pale savage, riding bareback across a wild, windswept plain.

Clouds of dust swirled around the stallion's hooves as the man reined him in abruptly, a few feet from Faith. He did not hurry to dismount, but eased his muscular body with a fluid, catlike grace to the ground. Flaxen hair emphasized the darkness of bronzed skin, and strong features seemed even stronger in the glare that reflected off the sand. Deep-set blue eyes vibrated with the intensity of midnight.

He was the man in her dream.

Faith stood absolutely still, fighting the wave of dizziness that swept over her as she tried to piece together what was happening. Out of the corner of her eyes, she could see the small dugout canoe, slipping closer and closer to the bend in the river, until it was nearly out of earshot, and she was painfully aware that she was alone with a man who was almost certainly a killer. She had the sudden mad urge to rush at him in fury, accusing him of the violence that had found a painful mirror in her dream, but she knew she did not dare. This was his land, his territory, and anyone who came in answer to her cries would not be there to help her.

It was a minute before she realized he was as shocked by the sight of her as she had been by him. His eyes narrowed until they were barely slits in tanned skin, and his lips parted silently, as if he wanted to speak but could not find the words. Slowly, Faith began to understand what was going on in his mind. If she was right—and she was sure she was—this man had to think he was looking not at her, but at her identical twin.

And he had to think he was seeing a ghost.

Faith set her bag carefully on the earth, then took a slow, deliberate step forward. If only she could keep up the illusion, if only she could trick him into believing for just another minute she was really Fleur, perhaps he would make some kind of slip. She was going to need a lot more proof than a dream if she wanted to go to the authorities.

"Hello, Jeremy," she said softly.

The reaction was dramatic. His facial muscles tightened briefly, then eased with an unexpected suddenness. Faith was dismayed to see deep, crinkly lines form in the flesh around his eyes. His voice, when he spoke, was rough and masculine, softened only slightly by a slow, ironic drawl.

"Miss Faith Eliot, I believe."

Faith bit her lip to keep from crying out in frustration. She could not believe the man had seen through her ruse so quickly. Whatever advantage surprise had given her was rapidly slipping away. Raising her chin with a bravado she did not feel, she looked him square in the eyes.

"Where is my sister?"

If she hoped to catch him off guard, she was disappointed. He merely threw back his head and laughed.

"By God, you're the spitting image of your father. Adam Eliot was not a man to mince words either."

Now it was Faith who was caught off guard. She was not used to being reminded of her father, much less compared to him. The idea made her uncomfortable.

"You haven't answered my question," she said, anxious to get the conversation back on course. It occurred to her that a small lie might be in order, especially if it was a lie he could not prove. "I know Fleur was here, Jeremy. She wrote me a long letter and told me all about it."

"Did she now?" He seemed disconcertingly unimpressed. "And you, I suppose, couldn't resist coming to see for yourself. But tell me, aren't you supposed to be playing this scene with a little more style? Shouldn't I be hearing, 'Cousin Jeremy, how thoughtful of you to receive me so unexpectedly'? Or better yet, 'Jeremy, I've heard so many lovely things about you'?"

Faith was beginning to feel at a distinct disadvantage. The man obviously had a maddening ability to make people feel two inches high, though it was a talent that seemed strangely out of place now. He was right, of course, she had been rude—but it seemed to her he was overreacting.

"I didn't come here for social niceties. I came to find my sister. It was perfectly natural to ask for her first."

"Without so much as a 'How do you do?' or a 'Pleased to meet you'? No, I don't think so." His body was relaxed as he ran one hand lightly along the horse's neck, but his eyes were wary. "Besides, you're a little behind the times. My brother Jeremy—my half brother—shot himself in a hunting accident four years ago. Or perhaps one of his faithful retainers did the job for him, I don't know. At any rate, Havenhurst belongs to me now. I am Bradford Alleyn."

"Bradford . . . Alleyn?"

Faith stared at him in dismay. Everything was beginning to fall into place now. What a fool she must have looked, stepping up to him, as plain as you please, with a simpering, "Hello, *Jeremy*." No wonder he had known she wasn't Fleur—and no wonder he was so unconcerned about Fleur's letter. If Faith had really heard from her sister, she would know all about the new master of Havenhurst.

He saw the color rise to her cheeks, and much to her surprise, he relented.

"In truth, your sister was here, Faith, but she left quite a while ago, and rather abruptly at that. Frankly, I'm surprised to find you so concerned. From what I've seen of the young lady, I'd say she was used to coming and going as she pleased, without so much as a by-your-leave from anyone."

Faith hesitated. For the first time since she had seen this rugged man, she was unsure. Bradford Alleyn might not be her idea of a gentleman, but he didn't exactly fit her preconception of a murderer either. If he had a guilty conscience about Fleur, surely he would be more evasive, more conciliatory.

"Fleur *can* be inconsiderate. . . ."

It would be just like her sister to depart as impulsively as she had come, not even bothering with a thank you or a goodbye to her host. Faith could picture her, slipping away in early morning mists, relishing the adventure of making her way into town. And if she had found herself in a deserted swamp at dawn. . . .

If only it weren't for her dream. If only every detail had not been so undeniably clear.

But it had been clear. There was no doubt about it, she thought, letting her eyes linger frankly on Bradford Alleyn's features. Blue eyes, set so deep they seemed to sink into hollows above high cheekbones. A strong nose, almost aquiline in its sharpness. A square jaw, jutting outward, proclaiming a stubbornness that could not be moved. Full, sensual lips.

The memory was so real, Faith could almost feel it happening again. It was all there for her now. A darkened room, touched only by the light of a solitary grease lamp. A tall, fair-haired man, rough, arrogant, brash, but so compelling she could not draw herself away. In that moment, Faith became her sister again, every nerve in her body charged with searing excitement. If she raised her hand, she wondered, as she had raised it that night, would he let her reach out, running sensitive fingertips across his cheek? Or would he raise his own hand one last time, pointing a small, deadly pistol at her breast?

"Do I fascinate you?"

Faith gasped at the words that called her back to reality. Too late, she realized, she had been staring openly at this man, and he had not failed to see it. She blushed to think what must be crossing his mind.

"I don't know what you mean, sir."

"Oh, come now." He spoke teasingly, but there was no mistaking the bold challenge in his tone. "You haven't been able to tear your eyes from my face. Dare I presume you find me so seductive you cannot resist me?"

"Mr. Alleyn!"

Her blushes only encouraged him. White teeth flashed against sun-darkened skin as he laughed. "You protest, madam? Can you be telling me those intriguing yellow-green eyes were not glued rapturously on my face?"

"Certainly not. At least not—not. . . ." Faith stumbled over the words. How could she explain to him? That was not *her* sensuality he glimpsed just now, but Fleur's. "I assure you, sir, I do not find you appealing in any way. You are not the kind of man I could ever be attracted to. I was just curious because—because I've seen you before."

The instant the words were out, Faith realized what she had done. How could she have been so stupid? she berated herself furiously. And she had hoped *he* would make a slip!

To her relief, he did not seem to catch her mistake. "Ah, yes, the portrait."

"The portrait?"

"Of my father, Jonathan Alleyn. Fleur said she had seen it in one of the old Devereaux family homes."

Slowly, Faith began to remember. Two beautiful women, the fair Rosaline Devereaux, the darkly sad Judith Bradford. And hanging between them, a man whose features she had barely even noticed. It took a minute for her to call them back now. When she did, she was numb with astonishment.

"Why, it could be a portrait of you. The resemblance is uncanny."

"So I've been told. I don't see it myself."

There was a sharp edge to his voice, but Faith did not hear it. She was too caught up in the maelstrom of her own thoughts.

The dream. Why had she trusted the dream? She had never been sure of it, not really, not from the beginning. It was too different from the telepathic experiences she had shared with Fleur before. What if it was not real at all? What if her sister had only sent her a fleeting montage of sensations—pain, bewilderment, the scent of magnolias on a humid night wind—and her subconscious mind, lulled by sleep, had translated those very sensations into visible forms? The man? But the man was only a portrait she barely remembered. And the room? Perhaps it was a room she had known before.

"Is there a study here?" she asked abruptly.

He seemed amused by the question. "Of course there's a study. Plantations are businesses, too, with records to keep and financial affairs to be transacted. As a matter of fact, the study I use is the same one your father had when you were a little girl. I doubt if it's changed much since then, except to add a layer or two of dust. Perhaps you'd like to see it before you leave."

So there it was, Faith thought dully. Only this morning, her mission had seemed so clear. Find a man, if he existed—find a room, if it was real. But now she had found the man, and if she was not very much mistaken, she had found the room, too. Only she was no nearer the truth than before.

"Yes, I would like to see it. But I am not leaving. I am staying until—until my sister returns."

"The devil you are!"

Faith took an unconscious step backward, stunned by the blatant opposition she had not expected. It was almost as if this man had decided not to like her the instant he saw her, and nothing was going to change his mind.

"Why, where is your hospitality, Mr. Alleyn?" she quipped,

trying to make light of the whole thing. "Is that any way to receive a cousin?"

"Don't 'mister' me. My name is Brad, and that is what I expect to be called. As for my being your cousin, that's ridiculous. Jeremy was your cousin, not me. Don't think I feel bound to honor my half brother's obligations."

"But surely a few day's hospitality——"

"A few days—or a few weeks?" Brad slipped the horse's reins over a low post beside the dock, then took a step forward, studying Faith with an intensity that was as insulting as it was flattering. "You're a very beautiful woman, Faith Eliot—any man with eyes in his head can see that—but I'll be blasted if I'm going to disrupt my life by letting a female in my house again. I'm not going to dress for a boring evening of chitchat in the parlor. I'm not going to watch my language because little ladylike ears tend to blush pink at the first foul word, and I'm certainly not going to listen to a lot of ridiculous gossip at the dinner table when I would rather read a good book and improve my mind."

If she hadn't been so nervous, Faith would have burst out laughing. Obviously, Brad Alleyn was a confirmed bachelor. She was beginning to see the lure Havenhurst had held for Fleur.

"Then I give you my promise," she retorted, as acidly as she dared, "that I will not get in the way of your dinner-table reading."

Reaching down, she grasped her valise firmly in her hand. If she gave Brad Alleyn enough time, he was going to find a dozen excuses not to have her there, and she had come too far to let herself be turned away now. Swinging the satchel at her side, she began to march resolutely toward the house.

It took him only an instant to catch up with her. Faith tensed in anticipation, knowing only too well that this was a man capable of throwing her over his shoulder and carrying her, kicking and screaming, back to the dock. To her relief, he only leaned forward, taking the bag wordlessly from her hand.

He did not attempt to speak until they reached the base of the stairway that led up to the house. Even then, he took his time. Dropping the bag on the ground, he glanced down at it with a look that was obviously intended to be sarcastic.

"Is this all? No trunks and crates piled up on the dock? No boxes of parasols and pomanders? No frilly feather bonnets?"

"Feather bonnets are out of style this season. But don't worry, I won't disgrace you in front of your neighbors. I intend to purchase whatever I need for my short stay from one of the local seamstresses."

Brad glowered, his face darkening, and Faith braced herself, waiting for him to throw up a whole new set of obstacles. Instead, he surprised her with a sudden burst of laughter.

"Dammit, I should know better than to argue with a daughter of Adam Eliot. Very well, stay if you must. You'll regret it—*I'll* regret it—but stay."

Faith was too stunned to reply. Had this strong, stubborn man let her win so easily? Suppressing a small, self-congratulatory smile, she began to move up the steps, leaving her bag behind for him to carry. She had gotten what she wanted, for the time being at least. She would be a fool to risk it all by being too smug now.

She had nearly reached the top when she became aware of a figure standing beside the railing looking down at her. Turning, she found herself face to face with the most astounding creature she had ever seen. Coal black skin, blacker than the darkest face she had seen in town, was molded into an almost perfect square, set atop a bulky body, accented by stout arms and a massive bosom, sinking with its own weight over the waistband of a vivid scarlet apron. Thick lips jutted out in a deliberate pout over a jaw that would have done credit to a bulldog.

"Well, Beneba." Brad's voice sounded in Faith's ear as he moved up the steps beside her. "Don't just stand there. Air out one of those musty rooms on the second floor. Miss Faith Eliot is going to stay with us for a while."

The woman's eyes narrowed into thin slits of white at the sound of Faith's name, but she did not move. Sucking in her lips, she set her jaw even more tenaciously than before.

"Doan' yo' got the sense yo' was born with, Mist' Brad? Yo' lets that woman in this house, yo' ain't got nothin' but grief, and yo' knows it."

Faith stared at her in amazement. She knew nothing about these strange black slaves, she had never had any dealings with them before, but she could not believe this was the way they were supposed to behave. Casting an anxious glance toward Brad, she half expected to see his volatile temper reach the boiling point. To her surprise, he seemed to take the woman's insolence in stride.

"Air out the room, Beneba."

Beneath the amusement in his voice was a firmness that could not be mistaken. The woman he had called Beneba hesitated, contemplating, or so it seemed to Faith, a tempting assortment of objections, before turning away at last. Her back, as she headed toward the door, was as expressive as her face; the set of her shoulders no less square, no less stubborn, than the set of her jaw had been.

Faith glanced helplessly at Brad. Was there no one here to offer her even a superficial word of welcome? She had known the task she had set for herself would be a difficult one. She had expected doubt, she had expected danger, she had even expected fear, but never had it occurred to her that everyone at Havenhurst, from the master right down to the lowliest of his slaves, would set up a united front to shut her out. For the first time since she had left England, she was tempted to turn around and go back.

A glimmer in Brad's eye warned her he had seen what she was thinking, and she knew he would not hesitate to use it against her. The surge of indignation that welled up in her was enough to steady her resolve. She might give in to her own fear, she might even betray her sister's memory—but there was no way she was going to let a man like Brad Alleyn laugh at her again. She tilted her chin upward, determined to look saucy and carefree as she stepped through a shadowed doorway into the house.

A pair of myrtle candles, sturdy and reassuring in their polished brass holders, cast a clear light over unfamiliar furnishings. Faith lay in the middle of a high four-poster bed and pulled clean holland sheeting all the way up to her chin. The room Beneba had led her to was plain, but comfortable. A solid mahogany bureau, fitted with glass doors, stood against one wall, and opposite it, beneath the windows, a long table held a looking glass on a small stand and a simple ceramic pitcher and basin. A colorful Marseilles quilt, neatly folded on a wainscot chair, eclipsed the delicate white of lace curtains hanging limply in the breezeless window. Only a thick layer of dust in one corner, carelessly overlooked in too hasty a cleaning, testified to the loneliness of a room that had not been used for years.

The silence was heavy and oppressive. At first, Faith had been grateful to learn that no one else occupied the second floor of the house; now she felt unexpectedly isolated and vulnerable. She half wished she had not taken the cowardly way out, pleading fatigue so she could avoid Brad Alleyn for the evening. It had been naive to think she could put this strange, enigmatic man out of her thoughts so easily.

It seemed to her she had never met anyone so complex—or so exasperating. He could be the model of courtesy when he wanted, humorous, almost friendly, but his was a fickle friendliness, dissolving without warning into a brittle, mocking sarcasm. It almost seemed to Faith, looking back on that afternoon, that he had deliberately set out to dominate her with his will, disarming her one minute, cutting her into ribbons the next. She could not help remembering the magnetic power he had had over her, if only for an instant, when memory had drawn her back into another world. Of course that was only a dream—and the dream was more Fleur's than her own—but still the power had been there.

Brad Alleyn was a dangerous man. Only a fool would let herself forget that, even for a moment. He was a man who knew how to manipulate people, to use them for his own ends, and no woman would ever be safe with him. If even Fleur, who knew so much more about men, had not been able to outmaneuver him, what hope did her less worldly sister have?

It was late when Faith finally fell into a fitful sleep. Even then, she could find no rest. Disturbing images swirled through the haze of half-consciousness, twisting and teasing as if they were daring her to reach out and catch them in her hands. Fleur—she could have sworn she saw Fleur, a little girl again, tears streaming down her cheeks, the white of her skirt smudged with dirt—but Fleur had never ruined a dainty frock in her life. And Desirée? Was that really Desirée, dressed in widow's black before she was a widow, picking out the same monotonous tune with one finger over and over again on the white keys of a white virginal? And Brad Alleyn. . . .

What was Brad doing in her dream? Confused, Faith tried to pull herself out of her troubled sleep. This was the past that was enveloping her now, and Brad had no part in her past. He was an intruder there, just as she was an intruder in his house. Then, slowly, his features began to change, distorting subtly, moving out of focus, until he was Brad no longer.

A new man faced her now, a man she could feel but not see, recognize but not acknowledge, and somewhere in the depths of her soul, Faith sensed a tangible threat to all the stability that was left in her world. Who are you? she wanted to cry out. Who are you—and what do you mean to me?

A low sound, more a sob than a cry, cut through the stillness, awakening Faith with a start. She lay motionless, waiting, listening, until at last she realized the sound had come from her. Slowly, she opened her eyes.

The candle had burned down, but it had not gone out, and the room was still bathed in a pure light. The burning wax sputtered, a harsh, sibilant crackle, unnaturally loud in the silence. Pulling herself up, Faith leaned over the candle, blowing gently as she dared the darkness to frighten her again. The fragrant scent of myrtle faded with the flame until only the musty reminders of years of disuse remained.

Four

The dining room was ablaze with light when Faith came downstairs the next evening. She paused in the doorway, clutching a leather-bound volume in nervous fingers as she stared at a display of opulence that would not have shamed the finest baronial manor in England. Candles gleamed in crystal and marble candelabra, highlighting an elaborately set table and casting rich streaks of gold across dark paneled walls. Snowy damask made a perfect backdrop for delicate imported china, so translucent it seemed to glow from within, and the brittle luster of silver, polished to a high sheen, added dramatic accents to the scene.

Brad was already seated when she arrived. He rose politely, but made no other effort to greet her. For all his protests, Faith noticed he had taken the time to dress for dinner. In spite of herself, she could not help admiring the way superbly tailored clothes emphasized the masculine lines of his tall, powerful body. A Van Dyke brown jacket, so modish it might have come from the pages of a fashion magazine, set off tanned skin to perfection, accenting blue eyes and dark blond hair, tied with stylish simplicity at the nape of his neck. Strong muscles stretched taut fabric across broad shoulders, a subtle reminder that elegance could be a mask for rugged virility—and the same man who seemed a perfect gentleman planter might also be a cold-blooded killer.

Brad scowled irritably when he saw the look on her face. "Confound it, woman, if you must be tardy, don't stand there gawking. Surely you've seen a table set for dinner before. Or did you think we Colonials were such a crude lot we ate with our hands from wooden trenchers?"

Faith felt the heat rise to her cheeks. He was right—she *had* been thinking that—but only an ill-mannered boor would call attention to her naiveté.

"I'm sorry I'm late. The clock in the library seems to be stuck on six o'clock, and I had no idea what time it was. It won't happen again, I assure you."

She slipped quietly into her place, grateful that she had had the good sense to select a book from the library shelves and bring it with her. Naiveté and tardiness were sins enough for one evening. She didn't want to be accused of interfering with his reading, too. She laid the volume beside her plate.

Brad did not miss the gesture. Reaching forward, he tilted the book up, letting candlelight play on gold letters on the spine: *Poor Richard, An Almanack—1737.*

"Ben Franklin?" His voice had a quizzical, amused tone. "An interesting choice for a dinner companion, I must admit."

Faith could not tell whether he was laughing at her or not. She had never heard of this Mr. Franklin, and she had no idea if he was suitable reading for a young lady, but she was determined not to let Brad bully her.

"You did say you were a man who prefers his book at the table, or did I hear you wrong?"

He leaned back, half dropping heavy lids over his eyes. "And you, I suppose, are the kind of female who delights in throwing a man's words back in his face. Well, I daresay it serves me right for taking you in in the first place."

Dry humor underscored the gruffness in his voice, giving Faith the uncanny feeling that he actually enjoyed her impudence. She began to catch a glimmer of the excitement Fleur always felt when she sparred with a strong man.

"Don't tell me you forgot your own book?"

He did not rise to the bait. Ignoring the challenge, he lifted his hand, beckoning toward the doorway.

The man who stepped into view, moving stealthily on soft-soled slippers, was impeccably garbed in the stark black and white of the servant class, with neatly pressed broadcloth framing a clean muslin shirt, and immaculate white gloves slipping discreetly beneath dark cuffs. The black skin of his face was so smooth it seemed almost ageless, and gray-white hair grew in fuzzy tufts out of his head, making him look like some prankster had perched a ball of cotton on his shoulders and forgotten to take it away again.

Brad pointed his finger—rather more obviously than necessary, Faith thought—at the book beside her. "You may take that away, Cuffee. I don't think Miss Eliot will be needing it."

His overbearing manner was enough to make Faith stiffen with indignation, but she did not protest. She sensed she had won the first round with this man. It would be foolish to press her luck. Besides, if she wanted to find out anything about her sister, she was going to have to learn to get along with him.

Dinner was as elaborate as the table that had been prepared to receive it. Massive platters, heaped with succulent joints and golden-brown fowl, had been set beside steaming tureens of soup and fresh vegetables on a sturdy sideboard. Waste must certainly be one of the watchwords of the southern Colonies, Faith thought, as she watched Cuffee carry dish after dish to the table, for the food that had been set in front of two diners was enough to serve a small army. The variety seemed infinite: ham, sweet with a crisp red glaze; roast beef, dark and crusty on the outside, just the way she liked it, strangely pink when she cut into it; wild turkey, pungent and gamey in contrast to the more familiar taste of chicken; fresh bream, caught that afternoon in their own stream. Even the vegetables were exotic: sweet yellow corn, dressed with herbs she had never tasted before; cucumbers, sliced as thin as parchment; turnips from the garden, and peas, carrots and Indian beans; and an odd orange-colored casserole made from boiling a root with the unlikely name of yam.

Long before the meal was over, Faith was glad she had not been too stubborn to give up her book. For all his earlier rudeness, Brad turned out to be a gracious host, regaling her with tales of a Havenhurst that had long since vanished, and Faith found herself hanging on every word. Brad had been only seventeen—"A callow youth with barely enough tail-feathers to fly," he told her with a grin—when he came to the Colonies to join his half brother, already engaged in an unsuccessful attempt to build his own plantation along the riverbank. It was there that he met Adam Eliot.

"Jeremy was a lazy son of a bitch," he said, laughing away the harshness of his words. "Adam knew I would never learn anything from him, so he took me under his wing, He was a hard taskmaster—dammit, was he demanding!—but when he finished with me, I knew how to run a plantation."

"What was Havenhurst like then?" Faith was surprised at her own curiosity. She had spent so many years trying to forget her father, it was hard to admit she wanted to hear about him now. "In the early days, I mean. When the plantation was still being developed."

"I don't know as I'd call those 'the early days.' By the time I arrived, your mother had already left, taking you and your sister with her, and Havenhurst was very much as you see it now. Most of the marshes had been cleared and drained, and channels and sluices were built to control the flooding. Rice fields lined the river, potatoes and potherbs grew in the gardens, and the hillsides had been tamed, with orchards blossoming in the spring and Indian corn reaching toward the sun in the summer."

"And the house? Was the house here then?"

"Of course. The house was Desirée's doing, built to her specifications and filled with all the extravagant furnishings and decorations she ordered from Europe. Lord, how it overwhelmed me the first time I saw it. I remember wandering from room to room, looking at the gilt and the velvet and the cut glass, and thinking to myself, 'By George, this must have cost Adam a pretty penny!' "

Faith wrinkled her brow thoughtfully. Eleazar Carstairs had said the same thing, and she had been disinclined to believe him.

"Why does everyone keep talking about how much the house cost my father? I thought Havenhurst belonged to my mother."

"The land, yes, but that was all. The money Desirée and her brother smuggled out of France was pitifully little compared to the enormous wealth the family had once possessed. When Adam married your mother, gaining title to her half of the land, Havenhurst was nothing but a swamp. The house, the outbuildings, the equipment, the army of slaves needed to run the place—all that was purchased with Adam's personal fortune."

Faith dropped her eyes, confused. As long as she could remember, she had thought of her father as an opportunist, a man who had had no qualms about marrying a woman for her money, then cheating her out of it. It was hard to accept the idea that her parents' relationship had once been a truly symbiotic one. Together, they had forged a plantation out of the wilderness; without each other, they had both died penniless.

Brad did not intrude on her thoughts, but used the silence to study her carefully. It disturbed him vaguely to see nothing of the bold, aggressive young woman who had pushed her way into his house yesterday. Where was all the brashness that had irritated and intrigued him? The perky insouciance that surrounded her like a protective shield? When she finally looked up, he could see that she was troubled.

"Brad, how—how did my father die?"

Brad picked up a crystal decanter, pouring a steady stream of Madeira into his glass. The girl had a way of cutting right through to the heart of things. He wasn't sure he liked that.

"In all honesty, I don't know. I was away in England when it happened. Adam insisted on sending me to school, and Jeremy for once in his life didn't bluster on about how spoiled I was, but let him get away with it. Do you suppose they detected a few rough edges that needed smoothing out? At any rate, I was there when Jeremy wrote and told me Adam had drowned."

"Drowned?" Faith was surprised, although she knew she shouldn't be. "I don't remember my father, of course, but somehow I . . . well, I always pictured him as a powerful man. You know, tall and athletic."

"And a strong swimmer?" Brad did not like the turn the conversation was taking, but he didn't know what he could do about it. "Adam *was* a strong swimmer, Faith. But he was with someone—a friend—when it happened. He was the kind of man who would risk a current to save a friend."

Faith curled her fingers around her glass, staring contemplatively into the amber liquid. Could this be her father he was describing? Could this brave, generous man be the same Adam Eliot who had never sent a single letter to his daughters in all the painful years of growing up?

Brad watched her closely, intrigued by the careless way she turned away from him. If all this was new to her, if she really hadn't heard it before, why wasn't she pelting him with questions? Where did my father drown? What was he doing? Who was with him? Who was the "friend" you spoke of?

What the devil was she up to anyhow? he asked himself, eyeing her suspiciously. It was hard to imagine anything devious about this lovely girl sitting across from him, long lashes brushing her cheeks as she gazed into the reflection of candlelight in wine. But then Fleur had looked like that, too. As sweet and pretty as an angel.

"It's amazing how like your sister you are. If I had the two of you here, side by side, I wonder if I would be able to tell you apart."

"Do you?" Faith had the feeling he was making fun of her. "I think men could always tell the difference between Fleur and me, even when we were little girls. Besides, can you honestly picture my sister sitting here, as calm as you please, in a faded dress with a little patch on her sleeve, like some poor country cousin?"

Brad leaned back in his chair, drumming his fingers against the tabletop. So there was rivalry between the two sisters, was there? He wondered why Faith had really come to Havenhurst. Not to be with her twin, that was for sure. She was up to something, and he was damned if he was going to let her get away with it.

They finished the rest of the meal in silence, lost in their own thoughts. The sound of rich Java coffee being poured into china cups seemed unnaturally loud in the stillness as Cuffee slipped unobtrusively around the table, clearing away the last traces of melon and wild strawberries. At last it was time to scrape back their chairs and rise from the table.

Brad escorted Faith to the door, then stood politely to the side. A teasing whiff of perfume floated up from her hair as she passed, tantalizing his nostrils, reminding him excruciatingly of Fleur and all the captivating loveliness he had thought he would never see again. He had the sudden, insane urge to invite this girl to sit beside him on the piazza and laugh with him, flirting, pretending the nights were never long and lonely.

Damn! he cursed himself furiously. This girl was Faith, not Fleur. She was nothing like her sister—and if she were, he would have nothing to do with her!

"I hope you enjoy Poor Richard," he said curtly, retrieving the book from the sideboard where Cuffee had put it. "I think you will find him most diverting."

Faith stood alone in the doorway after he had gone, listening to his footsteps die away in the darkness. Really, the man was impossible! she thought, confused and indignant all at the same time. He had played the perfect gentleman with her, courteous, charming, even attentive—and then he turned around and dismissed her like a common servant!

She was still thinking about him minutes later when she settled in a comfortable chair in the library and leafed halfheartedly through her book. It was getting harder and harder to tuck Brad Alleyn into a neat pigeonhole in her mind. An aristocratic planter, leading a life of culture and good taste? That image hardly suited him. A rough Colonial upstart, hard-drinking and fast-living? But that wasn't Brad either. An ambitious climber then? A moody recluse? A half-tamed brute, used to getting his own way? A savage killer?

Brad Alleyn as a killer. The idea was oddly intriguing.

Faith could just see him, all decked out in the armor and plumes of another era, riding boldly into battle. Or standing tall and silent in the cold gray dawn of a deserted plain, a pistol raised in his hand, as his second called out the paces. Even brawling crudely in a waterfront bar, smashing his fist into the face of a drunken bully who had insulted him.

But turning his gun against an unarmed woman and ruthlessly pulling the trigger? Would he really do something like that?

And why? That was the question. Even if she could imagine him gunning down her sister in cold blood, why would he want to? Fleur had been an outrageous flirt, of course, playing with the heart of every man she met, but Brad was obviously a match for any scheming woman. Love was the one passion Faith was sure he would never kill for.

Giving up at last, Faith flipped the book shut. Mr. Franklin might be every bit as diverting as Brad claimed, but she was in no mood for diversion this evening. Putting the book back on the shelf, she scowled at the hands of the clock, still stubbornly set on six o'clock. She had no idea what time it really was—no doubt much too early to go upstairs to her room—but anything was better than sitting in the library brooding.

The hallway outside was dim and shadowy, illuminated only by a pair of slender tapers set in matching brass holders on a long mahogany side table. Faith chose one of them at random and, picking it up, began to head for the steps. She had almost reached them when her eye fell on a tightly closed door, half hidden in the darkness at the rear of the hall. Eager to put off the moment she had to go upstairs, Faith decided to see what lay behind it. There had to be a reason why only one door in the entire hallway had not been left open.

An odor of dust and dead roses drifted out of the room the instant Faith turned the handle, sweeping her up in a haunting sense of familiarity. She lingered briefly on the threshold, confused by sensations she had not expected, then stepped slowly inside, raising the candle high in her hand. Nothing was immediately recognizable, no furnishings or objets d'art brought back the past with a swift rush of remembrance, but she knew beyond the slightest doubt that this was a place she had been before.

Only the dust was real; the roses had been an illusion. No flowers livened the color of the room now, nor had they for years. Rotting draperies, once a deep, rich hue, had faded to dusky pink, touched with streaks of gray, and the timeworn carpet that sprawled across the center of a dark wood floor was so dulled by age its pattern was barely discernible. In front of the windows, a white virginal, dainty and pristine in the midst of decay, looked like a ghost of itself, as if somehow it knew that the sweet sonatas and lilting airs of yesterday were no longer even memories.

Faith went over to the instrument, wondering what there was about the promise of music that evoked such strong feelings when nothing else at Havenhurst had seemed familiar. Its shiny white surface darkened to ivory in the light as she set the candle down and lifted the cover. Laying her fingers lightly on the keys, she began to pick out a simple melody. The sound that rose to her ears was sweet and pure of tone.

"Yo' lookin' fo' somethin'? Or yo' jes' pokin' yo' nose where it doan' belong?"

The voice seemed to leap out of the darkness. Looking up with a start, Faith caught sight of a bulky form hovering on the edge of the faint circle of candlelight. It took her a moment to pick out the features of the woman who had shown her to her room the day before. A dark chocolate-colored apron and drab brown dress blended into the deep tones of her skin until it almost looked as if she had been molded out of the night. The strange, twisted talisman that dangled from a cord around her neck gleamed white in the darkness, giving Faith the eerie sense of a primitive jungle snake, carved from a long, sharpened fang.

"The—the door was ajar." Faith hated herself for the lie, but she could not help it. "I saw the virginal and I——"

"Doan' yo' fool wit' me, chile." The woman's jaw clamped down with practiced tenacity. "Yo' can't pull the wool over ole Beneba's eyes. Ain't nobody opened that door since—since longer'n I kin remember, and that's a fact."

Faith pulled herself together with an effort. She could set her jaw just as forcefully as Beneba's if she made up her mind to it. She wasn't going to let a servant intimidate her like that.

"I saw the virginal, and I was curious. Tell me about it. Was it my mother's?"

The woman's reaction was so unexpected, Faith did not know what to make of it. Her lower lip pouted out in characteristic obstinacy, but her eyes betrayed her, widening superstitiously until the whites seemed to glow in the darkness.

"Now how's I s'posed to know that? Lawdy, I ain't been

here but long after yo' mama was gone. I doan' know nothing 'bout her, yo' hear? Or that virginal."

For an instant Faith was tempted to press her, but she sensed it would only bring out the old woman's stubbornness. Picking up the candle, she headed toward the door, pausing only long enough to look her straight in the eye.

"See that this room is aired out, Beneba. I intend to play that instrument—and often. The house is much too gloomy. It needs to be filled with music."

She turned to look back over her shoulder when she reached the stairs. Beneba was still standing in front of the door, testing it to make sure the latch had caught. She did not even glance at Faith as she ambled down the hall, disappearing through one of the open doors.

Faith could only shake her head as she began to move slowly up the stairway. What was there about Beneba that made her so hostile? she wondered. Was it only because Faith was white that the woman hated her so much—or was it because she was the daughter of Adam Eliot? Faith paused on a narrow landing, then continued up the last few steps to the second floor. Or was Beneba suspicious of her because of Fleur? Had something happened while her sister. . . .

Faith's ankle twisted painfully beneath her, breaking abruptly into her thoughts. With a sharp glance downward, she saw to her horror that one of the steps had broken. Clutching at the railing, she tried desperately to keep her balance, but it held only a fraction of a second before giving way with a snapping sound. The candle flew from her hand, plunging the stairway into darkness as Faith hurtled helplessly into space.

A sharp pain shot through her knee as she slammed into the landing. Gasping for breath, she crouched awkwardly on the floor, then pulled herself up cautiously, running her hands down her leg to make sure she had no broken bones. By the time she finally managed to stand, a soft golden glow had begun to envelop the hall. Turning, Faith saw a woman standing at the base of the stairs, a candle flickering in her hand.

Beneba. It made Faith shiver to look at her. It was almost as if she had been there all the time, lurking in one of the shadowy doorways, waiting for something to happen.

"The—the step broke. It came apart under my foot."

Beneba studied her coolly, then glanced down at the jagged edges of a broken board. "Them's old steps, that's fo' sho'. Shouldn't nobody be on 'em. Them rooms up there's been empty mebbe fifteen year now."

"But the railing!" Faith was furious. How could the old woman be so calm? Didn't she know Faith could have been killed? "The railing broke in the same place—and at the same time!"

Beneba's expression did not change. Stooping with an audible sigh, she picked up Faith's candle where it had fallen.

"Why yo' makin' such a fuss, chile? Yo' ain't hurt t'all, far as I kin see. Couldn't nobody be hurt, not with that landin' right there. Why, they ain't but six, seven steps in all."

She held the wick of Faith's candle calmly against her own flame, coaxing it into a blaze of yellow before extending it toward the girl. Faith reached out to grasp it, but her hands were trembling so badly she could barely hang on to it. She had the uncomfortable feeling that Beneba was chuckling under her breath as she turned and waddled back into the darkness, her broad hips jiggling from side to side with a rhythm of their own.

Faith was still shaking when she reached her room and pulled the door shut behind her, leaning against it to steady herself. What had really happened out there? she asked herself again and again. Had the step really been rotten, just as Beneba claimed? Had the railing been so badly cracked it was ready to give at the first pressure? Or had someone helped them along?

She drew a cool linen nightdress over her head and slipped into bed, but it was a long time before she fell asleep. Threats—tangible threats, not the vague fantasies that had frightened her before—seemed more real now than she had ever dreamed. Every shift in light as a cloud passed over the face of the moon looked like the shifting rays of a lantern, peeking in through the window. And every natural groan of the old house seemed an unnatural footfall right outside her door. It was well past midnight before she finally dozed off.

When she opened her eyes in the morning, bright rays of sunlight were already streaming through the open window. Sitting up sleepily, she focused her eyes on familiar objects, warm and richly colored in the cheerful light, and for the first time, she dared to smile at her own fears. Last night, when the hall had been drenched in black shadows and sounds were distorted by darkness, the world had seemed grim and sinister. This morning, she wondered if she wasn't letting her imagination run away with her.

Throwing a wrapper over her nightgown, she stepped into the hallway, determined to have another look at the place where she fell. The stairs had already been repaired, but shiny new boards told her where the break had been, and Faith had to admit Beneba was right. No more than half a dozen steps led from that spot to the landing. No matter how clumsily she had fallen, she could not possibly have done more than twist her ankle or perhaps sprain her wrist. If somebody had wanted to hurt her—really hurt her—they would have found a better place for it.

She was beginning to feel a little foolish as she sat down at her dressing table and took the pins out of thick honey-golden curls. The long, rhythmic strokes of the brush through her hair were wonderfully relaxing, easing away tension, and she almost felt like herself again when she heard a sudden, sharp rapping sound. Dropping the brush with a clatter, she jumped up, then caught herself with a smile. And she had thought she wasn't nervous anymore! She drew the wrapper tightly around her body and walked over to the door, pulling it open.

A strikingly lovely young woman, no more than a year or so older than Faith, stood on the other side of the threshold, a length of bright red fabric draped carelessly over her arm. Lustrous black hair had been pulled into a knot at the nape of her neck, and her skin, a smooth, creamy brown, was much fairer than that of any of the other blacks on the plantation. Her coloring marked her as a slave, but nothing in either her bearing or her manner confirmed that status. She carried herself with a tall, regal grace, as if she had been born to be mistress of the manor, not one of its handmaidens. Beauty was a quality she wore the way someone else might wear an old cloak, comfortable and accepted, a thing she hardly thought of anymore.

"Please—" Faith stepped aside to let her pass. "—please come in." She had not realized until that moment how long it had been since she had someone her own age to talk with. If only she could make friends with this girl, perhaps everything at Havenhurst would not seem quite so dark and frightening anymore.

If the girl noticed the warmth of Faith's smile, she did not acknowledge it. Indeed, she barely seemed to notice Faith at all. Her eyes fixed straight ahead, she walked over to the bed, laying the fabric neatly across its unmade surface. Faith followed her, curious to see what it was. The instant she got a look at it, everything else vanished from her mind.

"Why, it's a dress!" It was not elegant, but it was charming, fashioned in a gay floral print with full sleeves and a frilly, feminine skirt. "But where on earth——"

"One of the younger girls, Fibby, stayed up all night making it for you." The girl spoke in low, cultivated tones, but her voice was so expressionless, it was almost a monotone. "Mr. Alleyn thought you might need it."

"Brad?" Faith picked up the dress, running smooth cotton between her fingers. Brad Alleyn was getting more and more complex all the time. Last night, when he dismissed her so abruptly, Faith had been certain he put her out of his mind. Yet obviously he had spared at least a minute to think of her again. "How pretty it is. I never expected him to do anything like this."

"The dress should fit. Fibby is next to useless most of the time, but when she takes up a needle, there is magic in her fingers. Besides, she made dresses for your sister so she already knows your size."

Faith looked up, her attention drawn by the emptiness in the girl's voice. "I don't think I've seen you before. What's your name?"

"They call me Estee. You haven't seen me around the house because I prefer to work in the garden. Mr. Alleyn has assigned me to be your personal maid."

"My personal maid?" Faith tried not to laugh, but she couldn't help herself. No wonder the girl was so aloof. Why, who on earth wanted to be a lady's maid when the "lady" only had one dress to her name, and that faded and patched. Even a servant had her pride. "I've never had a maid in my life, Estee. I'm not sure I know what to do with one. Couldn't we just be friends?"

The girl's eyes dilated, flashing with emotion for the first time since she had entered the room. "It doesn't matter whether you want a maid or not—any more than it matters whether I want to be one. Mr. Alleyn has given the order. That's all there is to it."

Faith stared at her in amazement. Estee had seemed so lovely, so approachable, when she appeared on the threshold. It was hard to believe she was as hostile as the other blacks. Perhaps it was her own fault, Faith thought guiltily. Perhaps she had insulted the girl when she burst into laughter a moment ago.

"Estee—that's an interesting name," she said casually, trying to make peace as best she could. "Is that your real name, or is it a nickname?"

"My mother named me Esther."

"Esther?" Faith laughed brightly as she tossed the dress back on the bed. "That's one of my favorite names. It's from the Bible, did you know that? From now on, I shall call you Esther."

"No!"

The vehemence in the girl's voice was so stunning Faith could not think of a thing to say. She stood in silence, waiting until the black fire in her eyes died away and she was ready to speak again.

"Esther was the name of a queen. It is not suitable for a slave."

"Well, I never!" Faith could hardly believe her ears. Even in this rough new land, surely servants were expected to behave with at least a modicum of propriety. "I don't know the customs here, Estee, but I'll tell you one thing—if a servant at home ever spoke so tartly to her mistress, she'd be dismissed on the spot."

She regretted the words instantly, but it was too late to call them back. The hard, closed look on Estee's features warned her that whatever chance she had had of making friends with this girl was gone now.

"I am not a servant," Estee replied quietly. "I am a slave. I think you will be happier here when you learn the difference. You can have me beaten if you like, you can sell me onto a sugar plantation on the Islands, you can even kill me—but you can never dismiss me!"

What a strange girl, Faith thought, watching her turn and head toward the door. Beautiful, but decidedly strange. It was almost as if she had made up her mind to hate Faith before she even set foot in the room, and nothing was going to shake her from her resolve.

One thing was becoming increasingly clear about these black slaves, Faith decided, mulling the problem over later in her mind. Whether from stubbornness or willful pride, she could not tell which, they had erected a wall around themselves, a wall so high and sturdy no white person would ever climb it. The thought made her feel unexpectedly vulnerable. For the first time it occurred to her that fear and danger were not the only enemies she faced at Havenhurst. There was another, subtler enemy, one that might prove far more insidious in the end. That enemy was loneliness.

Faith had more than enough time to contemplate her loneliness in the days that followed. It was not that Brad was unkind. Quite the contrary, he turned out to be surprisingly generous with his money—he sent to town for bolts of fabric so Fibby could fashion a new wardrobe for her, and even gave her carte blanche to order anything else she wanted—but he was no more generous with his time than he had been at first, giving her only an hour or two each day at dinner, nothing more. As for neighbors, Faith soon discovered, they might as well not have existed. Summer was hardly a pleasant season in the south, with insects swarming over stagnant rice ponds and unhealthful vapors rising out of the marshes, and virtually everyone who could afford it fled to the mountains or the seashore, leaving his property in the hands of an overseer or driver.

Only one of the neighboring planters came to call, an Englishman named Lord Warren, and in truth, he was hardly a planter at all for he had come to the Colonies only temporarily to secure a nearby plantation, Oakwood, as the inheritance of his infant nephew. Brad was obviously fond of the man, perhaps because he had known him in England, but to Faith he seemed nothing more than a loutish rake. If this was what their neighbors were going to be like, she would just as soon they stayed at the seashore!

"By Jove, Alleyn, you do have all the luck!" he had said, smacking his lips with undisguised vulgarity when he saw Faith. "Where did you find such a toothsome morsel?"

Faith glared at him in open fury. She didn't know which she minded most, having this odious man leer at her—or being reduced to such a ridiculous cliché!

"I hope you are not implying that Mr. Alleyn has not been a gentleman, sir. Or that he has treated me as anything but a lady."

To her consternation, both men burst out laughing. "How the wench defends you, lad," Lord Warren cried with a bawdy wink at his friend. "Ah, my dear, when will you sweet young things learn that a handsome face is no match for maturity and experience? Find yourself an older man—he'll adore you so much more."

And he meant it, too, Faith thought later, appalled at the very idea. It was not that Lord Warren was unattractive—he still had a trim physique, and he wore his clothes elegantly, even in the heat—but after all, he was old enough to be her father! What was there about these Colonial men, from Eleazar Carstairs who undressed her with his eyes to Brad Alleyn who hardly even bothered to look at her, that made them so cavalier with a woman's feelings?

She was sitting on a stump near the side of the house, halfway down the hill that sloped toward the river. The sun was beginning to set, and afternoon shadows lengthened across perfectly manicured green lawns. A few yards away, a thick azalea hedge rose above the red-brown earth of a garden path. On the other side, a low iron railing served as the last defense against tangled shrubs and vines of an encroaching wilderness.

Really, the situation was hopelessly frustrating, she told herself with a frown. She had been at Havenhurst a week now, and she was no closer to learning her sister's fate than she had been the day she arrived. Brad had a maddening way of communicating absolutely nothing when he wanted to, changing the subject adroitly whenever she asked about Fleur, and the servants were even worse.

"Yo' sister, Miz' Faith?" Cuffee had said, shaking his head vaguely, as if he could not make out what she was trying to say. "Cain't say as I rightly recall her. Th' older a man gits, the more his mind up and goes on him."

Cuffee was not the only one whose mind seemed to "up and go" when Fleur's name came up. Even the little seamstress, Fibby, a chatterbox with barely a brain in her head, got the same vacant look in her eyes whenever Faith dared to mention her sister. What was it with these touchy blacks? Faith wondered. Had Fleur, always careless and self-centered, done something to offend them—or had they been warned to keep their mouths shut?

Well, there was no point worrying about it now, she thought, rising from the stump and brushing a damp wisp of hair back from her forehead. She looked cooler than she felt in a summery white saque, fashioned from a length of sheer handkerchief linen. A slim, loose skirt clung seductively to her long legs, and the bodice dipped so low in front she was almost embarrassed to be seen in it. Fibby might not be willing to talk about her sister, Faith mused with a smile, but she had not forgotten how to cut gowns to Fleur's taste.

Just above her, on the hillside, Faith caught sight of Brad chatting with a pair of black fieldhands. Something in the manner of the three men—the casual way Brad pushed a broad-brimmed straw hat back on his head as he laughed, the nonchalance of the two workmen leaning lazily against their hoes—made her vaguely uneasy. Surely such loose camaraderie between master and slave was unfitting, even unwise. Could Brad have forgotten that Stono River was barely a year in the past?

Brad stayed with the men for a few minutes, then left them with an easy wave and cut across the lawn. On impulse, Faith decided to join him. He might not welcome her company, but he could hardly refuse to walk with her as far as the house.

To her surprise, he greeted her with an easy grin. Faith would have been encouraged by his friendliness if she had not been aware of bold eyes running up and down her figure.

"No more poor country cousin?" he teased. "I'm glad to see our worthless little Fibby is finally earning her keep."

Faith averted her eyes, embarrassed by his gaze. Why hadn't she had the good sense to have Fibby fashion a modesty bit to tuck into her bosom?

"I was just admiring the landscaping," she said, eager to change the subject. "Everything is so beautifully cared for—well, until you get to that railing over there. What did you do, just give up on the gardens when you reached the other side of the path?"

Brad followed her gaze, laughing good-naturedly at the dense vines that twisted through the low iron fence. "That's the old cemetery. It's been overgrown so long, I hardly notice it any more."

"That's a cemetery? So near the house?"

"Actually, it was meant to be the family plot, but your mother left the Colony, taking you and your sister with her, and Adam's body was never found. So only your Uncle Olivier is buried there."

"My mother's brother?"

Faith spotted a gate in the fence and went over to it. Her Uncle Olivier had always seemed a sad, romantic figure to her—the handsome young hero cut down in his prime—and she did not want to pass his grave without at least pausing for a moment. Brad caught up with her in a few long strides. Bending over the rusty gate, he gripped the latch in strong hands and forced it open.

"It looks like the jungle's taken over, doesn't it? Adam seemed to like it that way, and I never saw any reason to change it."

Faith took a tentative step through the gate, then stopped as she felt her skirt tangle in the undergrowth. The place did indeed look like a jungle. Nature had reclaimed the land with a vengeance, choking it in a thick mantle of green, dotted here and there with the cascading color of wild trailing roses. In the center, a single gray stone, overly ornate with the baroque curlicues of a bygone era, looked oddly out of place, like a self-conscious monument to the vanity of man in the savage beauty of a desolate Eden.

"He was only fifteen when they fled from France," she said

softly, uttering the words as much for her own benefit as for his. "My mother was barely seventeen. They must have suffered terribly, both of them."

"So I gather. Lord knows, Fleur prattled on about it often enough, hinting at violence and dark secrets until she got so melodramatic I wouldn't listen to her anymore."

Faith had to smile. How like her sister that sounded! Only Fleur could embellish tragedy until it seemed like glamor.

"I hope you didn't take her too seriously. Of course, Mama did talk to her more—she was much closer to Fleur than she was to me—but I suspect most of her stories were just what you called them—prattle. Fleur had a vivid imagination and she loved to use it."

Not that there wasn't a core of truth to the tales, Faith reminded herself with a shudder. Huguenots had been persecuted by the Catholic majority in France for over a century, and with the repeal of the Edict of Nantes in 1685, they had lost their last hope of official protection. By the time Claude and Marie-Thérèse Devereaux finally converted their vast land holdings to gold and jewels and loaded their seven children onto a crude farm wagon, the plight of French Protestants had become desperate. The journey was as painful as it was long, and when at last Claude whipped an exhausted horse the last few miles to the coast, only two of his children still huddled together in the back of the wagon.

Arrival at the docks brought no change in the bad luck that had plagued them. Word of the wealthy refugees spread quickly, and one of the local barons, a man renowned for his Christian zeal, was only too happy to relieve the heretic and his wife of an ill-deserved fortune—and a comely daughter. If he had known the couple's fifteen-year-old son was carrying a share of the family gold, he would gladly have thrown him in the dungeon, too.

Faith had never been able to sort fact from fantasy in her sister's account of the night that followed. Now she supposed she never would. Had her grandparents really been tortured for a few sacks of gold, or had they simply succumbed to exhaustion and hunger? Had her mother been so brutally used that the rest of her life was scarred by the memory? And had Olivier, barely more than a child, cowered in the darkness outside, listening to his sister's screams, vowing to rescue her, no matter what the cost?

Only the outcome was certain. Whatever the reason, Claude and Marie-Thérèse did not survive the night. And Olivier, when he was finally reunited with his sister, had been so savagely beaten his broken legs would never be straight again.

"What did it get him?"

Faith whispered the words, too soft to be audible, but Brad seemed to sense her mood, for he laid his hand on her arm and urged her gently toward the gate. She did not resist, but followed obediently, turning only at the last moment for one final glance over her shoulder.

What *did* it get him? All the courage? The will to fight? An elaborate tombstone on an alien hillside could be no more comforting than a wooden cross beside a country road at home. How much easier it would have been for him—yes, and for Desirée, too—if they had been laid to rest beside their younger brothers and sisters early in that agonizing journey.

They did not try to speak again, but walked the rest of the way in silence. The first shadows of twilight accented the softness of Faith's features, lending her a look of childlike innocence, and Brad found himself watching her with more than the casual interest he had intended. Her beauty was a magnet, drawing his eyes even against his will, reminding him in ways that made him distinctly uncomfortable of how long it had been since he held a woman in his arms.

They had just started up the steps to the piazza when Faith stumbled, catching her toe painfully on the edge of a rough plank. Without thinking, Brad reached out, grasping her arm tightly, forgetting until he felt warm flesh beneath his fingers how much he had wanted to touch her an instant before. Faith raised her eyes tentatively, disturbingly aware of masculine strength in the hand that gripped her arm. Slowly, she pulled back.

"I'm not usually this clumsy," she said breathlessly, anxious to dispel the awkwardness that had risen between them. "I guess my knee is still stiff from the last time I fell. At least then I had the broken step for an excuse."

Brad's expression changed subtly as he looked down at her. "What broken step?"

Faith was so grateful for the diversion, she did not even notice the sharpness in his voice. "The one on the main staircase. You know, the step near the top. It scared me half to death when it gave out underneath me. Then when the railing broke, too, I was sure I was going to be killed."

"Why didn't you tell me this before?"

"I—I thought you already knew. When I went out in the

morning and saw that the step had been fixed, I just assumed. . . ."

Her voice trailed off, lost in a flood of unwanted memories. How frightened she had been that night, standing just inside the door to her room, leaning her cheek against smooth, hard wood. And how desperately she had longed for a stout bolt to shut herself away from the dangers outside.

"Then you think——"

"I think I've been a damn sight too careless," he broke in, a little too quickly to be convincing. "I've been so busy working in the fields, I haven't paid any attention to the house. The first thing tomorrow, I intend to go over it inch by inch to make sure nothing else is unsafe. This isn't going to happen again, Faith—I promise you that!"

Faith barely moved as she watched him. So instinct had served her right after all. Someone *had* been trying to hurt her that night, clumsily perhaps, ineffectually, but deliberately! And if he had tried once, what was to keep him from trying again? Suddenly she felt very lonely—and very far from home.

Brad did not miss the glint of moisture on her lashes. He lifted his hand, ready to lay it on her arm again, then thought better of it. Leaning forward, he looked thoughtfully into her eyes. His voice, when he spoke, was gentle but firm.

"Why don't you go home, Faith?"

Faith was caught off guard by the question she had not expected. She hated herself for the tears that welled up in her eyes. The last thing in the world she wanted was to leave her emotions raw and exposed in front of this man.

"You know I can't do that! I came here to see my sister. I'm not going to leave until she comes back."

"But Fleur isn't coming back. Surely you know that by now. Look around you, Faith. Where are the dazzling balls that would have delighted her? The elegant soirees? The flocks of handsome young men at her beck and call? Don't you see, my dear? There's nothing for your sister here—or for you."

It was the kindness in his voice that hurt the most. All the frustration, all the despair Faith had been bottling up seemed to burst inside her, and she could hold it back no longer. A single tear betrayed her, running warm and wet down her cheek, followed by another and yet another.

Brad could only stand by and watch her helplessly, touched as he always was by the fragile softness of a woman in pain. He was acutely aware of the hard calluses on his hand as he raised it to her cheek, gently brushing the tears away.

"Damn!"

Why was he always so adroit with the women who amused him, and so clumsy with the ones he cared about? More than anything, he wanted to take this beautiful girl in his arms and cradle her, caress her, kiss away her tears. He felt her tremble beneath his fingers, a light, provocative quivering she could not control, and he knew she sensed the yearning that flooded through his soul.

Faith held her breath, afraid to move or speak, as he leaned over her. She had never been so intensely aware of anything in her life as she was now of the rough feel of male fingers against her smooth skin. The sensation was so sudden, so unexpected, she did not know how to deal with it. Even Rolfe, when he had drawn her into his embrace, intoxicating her with the fire of his kiss, had not stirred the same primitive longings this man awakened now with no more than the touch of his hand.

He looked down at her with glowing eyes. His voice was tender as he cupped her chin in his hand, tilting her face toward his.

"By God, you are a winsome little witch."

He held her an instant longer, then, dropping his hand, turned and walked down the steps. Faith felt the solitude intensely as twilight closed in around her, cutting her off from the distant fields. The cry of a boatman, invisible in the enveloping darkness, drifted up from the river, then the world sank into silence again.

What was she doing? Faith asked herself, frightened now that he was no longer there to confuse her with the compelling magnetism that drove the last traces of reason from her mind. How could she be attracted to this complex, dangerous man? This man who almost certainly had killed her sister?

If she was right—if he had really pointed a gun at Fleur's breast and pulled the trigger—then the day of reckoning would come all too soon. She had vowed to avenge her sister's death, and she would keep her vow—even if vengeance had to come from her own hand. God help her on that day if she had let herself fall in love with the man she had to kill.

Five

Brad Alleyn was a tall man, but he looked even taller in the saddle as he rode down the oak-lined drive toward the river. Broad shoulders strained the tan rawhide of a plainly cut jacket, and black trousers blended into the flank of the powerful stallion beneath him. Golden streaks in his hair looked as if they had caught on fire in the blazing rays of a hot morning sun.

Faith sat on the railing of the veranda, watching him vanish into the blinding light that shimmered off the river. She had been more than a little surprised a few seconds earlier when she caught sight of a tall, sunlit silhouette cutting through the stableyard and realized who it had to be. She could have sworn she had overheard Cuffee telling Beneba that his master planned to spend the entire morning in his study, working on the books.

Well, no matter, she thought, rising and brushing the wrinkles out of sheer white linen. She had not been looking forward to dodging Brad all morning, and after what had happened the day before, she had no intention of letting herself run into him. Besides, she had wanted to have a look at his study since the day she arrived, and she would never have a better chance than this. If he was heading toward town, he couldn't possibly be back for hours.

The piazza was still bathed in late morning shadows as she walked slowly toward the west wing, where Brad's study opened directly onto the wide wooden walkway. Tall French doors were ajar, giving a glimpse of the darkened room inside. Faith paused when she reached them, surprised to feel how fast her heart was beating. She knew she was being foolish—even if she recognized the room, it would prove nothing—but the memory of her dream was still vivid enough to make her hand tremble as she laid it against warm glass panes and pushed slowly inward.

The room inside had a rugged, masculine feel to it. Dark wood set off sparse, functional furnishings, and books had been crammed to overflowing in tall bookcases that lined the walls. The only concession to comfort, if indeed it could be called that, was a sagging, threadbare couch, set behind a low table at the side of the room. Just to the left of the door stood a plain mahogany desk, so sturdy and compact it looked as though it would be more at home in a sea captain's cabin than the study of a great plantation. Only a man's hand could have scattered papers so haphazardly across the surface, setting a clumsy grease lamp on top as a careless afterthought to hold them in place.

Faith did not try to move for a moment, but stayed where she was, waiting for instinct or memory to close in on her. It was a moment before she realized it was not going to happen. In all the times she had imagined this moment—in all the times she had asked herself how she would feel when she finally saw the room where her sister might have died—one thing had not occurred to her. That she could see it and not feel anything at all.

It *could* have been the room in her dream, she thought helplessly. That could be the same desk—certainly it looked the same—but the desk she had seen only once before was barely a blur in her memory. And that could be the lamp—but it was a common, ordinary lamp, no more than a saucer-shaped iron container with a wick floating in it. There must have been thousands just like it all over the Colonies.

Sighing with frustration, she shut the door behind her and stepped inside. If the room couldn't tell her anything about Fleur's death, at least it could give her some badly needed information about the man who might be her murderer.

Clues were everywhere, but they were not the clues Faith had expected. A rack of pipes, built into one of the low bookcases, filled the room with the pungent, masculine scent of tobacco, and old gazettes, frayed and yellowing at the edges, cluttered the area in front of the windows, giving the room a casual, relaxed feeling. Well-worn slippers had been kicked under a corner of the couch, and nearby, on the table, lay a slender volume, its pages carelessly marked with a torn piece of paper. Faith smiled as she picked it up and noted the title: *The Sonnets of William Shakespeare.* Who would ever have picked Brad as a man with poetry in his soul?

On a counter behind the desk, Faith spotted a stack of old

ledgers, so battered and dusty they looked as if they had been there for years. She lifted the cover of the one on top, half hoping it would be able to tell her about the days when Adam Eliot still owned Havenhurst.

She was quickly disappointed. If the ledgers had any secrets to divulge, they were not in a form she could decode. Row upon row of dry figures rose to her eyes, telling her nothing beyond the fact that the plantation was meticulously run. She studied the numbers curiously, wondering if the writing was her father's. Somehow she had imagined his hand would be bold and undisciplined—big black scrawls splashing across the pages. These were neat, prim ciphers, all carefully tucked one under the other in their own straight——

"What the devil are you doing here?"

Faith jumped nervously. Whirling around, she saw Brad standing in an inner doorway leading to the dressing room beyond. He had changed into a simple pair of gray breeches, and his white shirt was open at the neck. The scowl on his face was anything but welcoming.

"I—I thought you had gone."

"Obviously. Do you always take advantage of my absence to snoop through my things?"

"I wasn't snooping. That is, I . . . Well, I wanted to see your study. You told me I could, you know. The day I arrived."

"I did think you'd have the courtesy to wait for an invitation. Or was that too much to expect?"

Faith met his eyes with a bravado she did not feel. If she was going to avenge Fleur's death, she would have to be as bold as Fleur. Lowering her lashes, she let them tremble lightly against her cheeks, just as her sister would have done. It was a dangerous gambit, especially after what had happened yesterday, but it was a chance she had to take.

"I know why you're so angry with me. You're afraid I'll discover your secrets."

The ploy worked better than she had hoped. The color drained from Brad's face, almost as if he took her seriously, and she had a sudden heady sensation of power over this man. With a sweet half-smile, she stepped over to the table and picked up the book, flipping it open to the page that had been marked. Her voice was low and seductive as she began to read.

"Shall I compare thee to a summer's day?
Thou art more lovely and more temperate:

Rough winds do shake the darling buds of May,
And summer's lease hath all too short a date."

Still smiling, she closed the book. "I never realized such tender sentiments dwelled beneath that gruff exterior."

The little minx, he thought, captivated in spite of himself. What a beauty she was, with that gamin smile, as innocent as it was knowing. She must have studied the volume carefully before he came in, or else she knew the sonnets well enough to pick out the most romantic phrase on sight.

"Well, you have caught me out—I admit it. I should have hidden the volume, I swear, had I known my retreat was so vulnerable. I could never bear to look unmanly in your eyes."

His easy humor caught Faith unawares, breaking through her cautious reserve. She could not help being intrigued by a man who not only read poetry, but was sure enough of his masculinity to admit it out loud. She decided to press him a little, now that he seemed to have given up some of his anger.

"I didn't mean to snoop, really I didn't. I was just curious because you told me this used to be my father's study. I thought it might bring back old memories, though honestly, the place is so messy I can't make heads nor tails out of it. Why, I've never seen so many out-of-date newspapers in my life—and just look at that pile of old ledgers! Someone may have run a dustrag over the top every now and then, but I doubt if anyone's opened them for years."

Brad laughed good-naturedly. "I don't suppose they have. Those were Adam's books. When Jeremy took over, he had his own system, such as it was, and he never bothered with them. By the time Havenhurst came to me, they were already out of date."

"Then they *were* my father's. Was that his handwriting?"

Brad shook his head. "Adam may have made a note or two in them, but the books were kept by a slave named Friday, a shrewd old man who had persuaded his previous owner to have him educated so he could read the Holy Scripture. As a matter of fact, he died a few days after Adam. If he hadn't, Jeremy might have kept him on and saved me a hell of a mess when I took over."

Faith turned away, confused by emotions she could not understand. Her eye fell on the desk beside the door, and she tried to imagine that a man was sitting there, absorbed in his work, glancing up only occasionally to bark out orders to a slave working on ledgers across the room. She could not make the picture come to life. Troubled, she turned back to Brad.

"What was my father like?"

Brad was fascinated by her eyes, open and curious, yet strangely timid, as if she was afraid of the answers he would give her. He had to force himself to remember that this soft, appealing woman was in reality a calculating vixen who would stop at nothing to get what she wanted.

"Adam is hard to describe," he said slowly. "He was a big man—bigger than life. I don't mean just physically, but in the impression he created. He could stand in the middle of a roomful of strangers and command attention. He seemed to tower over everyone else, a tall, muscular figure, with fair hair streaked almost white from years of working in the sun."

"A little like you, then?"

"Good God, no!" Brad burst out, startled by the comparison. "I'm not at all like Adam, at least no more than superficially. He was about my height, maybe an inch or so taller, and his hair was the same color, but that's where the resemblance ended. He was much broader shouldered, and he had strong, almost classical features." He leaned forward, unable to resist the urge to tease her. "And he had those same devastating yellow-green eyes."

Faith dropped her gaze, suddenly frightened by the new intimacy in his tone. She could not forget the way he made her feel yesterday, when she was certain he was going to draw her into his arms.

"I—I didn't mean that. I meant, what kind of person was he? What kind of man?"

Brad watched her closely, trying to figure out what she was after. She knew how to work her way under his skin, that was for sure, with her wistful looks and sudden bouts of shyness. He cursed himself soundly for his weakness. The last thing in the world he wanted was to get involved with pretty Miss Faith Eliot.

"Don't you remember your father at all?"

"How could I? I was only six when we left."

In spite of himself, Brad felt caution give way to sympathy. Maybe he was being too hard on the girl after all. Maybe he was making too many comparisons to her sister.

"Adam was not an easy man to know, Faith. He kept to himself much of the time. Whatever passions or pains were in his heart, he didn't share them, even with—" He paused, breaking the rhythm of his speech for a split second. "—even with those who were closest to him. But underneath that veneer of aloofness, I always sensed a great capacity for love—especially for you."

"For me?" Faith could remember only the long, empty years with no communication from her father. "I find that hard to believe."

"Adam rarely talked about the past—it was a closed book to him, like those dusty ledgers on the counter—but sometimes on a rainy evening, after a glass or two of whiskey, he'd stretch his legs out in front of the fire and stare into the flames. Then I knew he was thinking about you."

"You mean he missed us? My sister and me—and my mother?"

"I didn't say your sister, Faith—or your mother. You. I think Adam used to feel guilty because you were always his pet. He called you his 'little diamond' after that locket you still wear around your neck. Do you know, you refused to take it off, even for a bath?"

Faith shook her head, bewildered. Try as she would, she could not recognize the child he was describing as herself. Was that really her, that giggling, happy little girl who climbed into her Papa's lap, secure in the warmth of a love that was constant and all-encompassing? But surely love wasn't a thing you forgot.

Brad sensed the need she could not put into words. His hand was light as he rested it on her arm. "Your father was a good man, Faith."

Faith pulled back abruptly. Stepping over to the window, she drew the curtain aside, letting bright rays of sunlight flood into the room. She was not sure which upset her most, the touch of his hand on her arm, gentle and provocative, reminding her of emotions she did not want to admit—or the lies he told her about her father.

"If my father was a good man, then why——"

She caught herself just in time. She had started to say: Then why did mother get a vacant look in her eyes, as if dark shutters had been drawn across them, every time his name was mentioned? The thought was too personal to be shared.

"Then why did he lose Havenhurst?"

Brad stood beside her, turning her toward him, taking her hands in his. "I told you, Faith, I was away at the time. I suppose I'll never know for sure. I heard later that he was too ambitious, that he overextended himself and the creditors closed in, but that never sounded like Adam to me. I sometimes wonder——"

He broke off, irritated with himself for having said so much. The past was over and done now. What good would it do to rake up all the pain again?

"It's all right, Faith," he murmured. Unable to resist her poignant sweetness any longer, he drew her slowly, comfortingly into his arms. "It doesn't matter anymore, my dear. Don't you understand? Whatever happened, whatever your father did, it can't hurt you anymore."

The touch of his lips on her hair was soft and undemanding, a soothing invitation to sink into the haven of his embrace. Faith fought the feeling as long as she could, remembering the impulsive fascination that had nearly swept her into his arms once before, but the temptation of tenderness was too much for her. She had been lonely and frightened too long to deny herself the solace of his closeness now.

She yielded with a sigh, resting her head against the rough strength of his shoulder. His lips grew bolder, tracing a course of kisses down her forehead, her cheeks, the soft curve of her neck. Faith knew she should not allow such liberties—she knew only too well what he would think if she did—but she could not find it in her heart to resist. Just one kiss, she promised herself. Just one sweet, lingering kiss they could both savor and then she would pull away from him.

She slipped her hands around his neck, coiling her fingers into coarse silken strands of hair as she urged his head downward. Brad held back for an instant, as if he sensed he was taking advantage of her vulnerability, then surrendered, devouring her with the ravenous excitement of a kiss that knew neither gentleness nor innocence. There was an urgency in the moment, a sudden tormented longing that awakened dormant passions, and Faith felt her body respond instinctively, arching tautly, brazenly against the lean, hard muscles that assaulted her.

Horrified, she realized what she was doing. Forcing her hands against his chest, she pushed him roughly away. What on earth was she thinking of? she asked herself with a rush of dismay. She had only wanted to flirt with this man, to tease and tantalize him. How could she have let things get so out of hand?

She took a cautious step backward. His face was grim, his eyes dark and clouded, and she knew she had angered him. Trying desperately to look bright and sophisticated, she raised her brows into a pair of amused question marks. This was not a man she could afford to offend.

"Are you always so . . . so forceful?"

The hardness in his eyes relaxed. He saw the game she was playing—the shyness, the wanton aggressiveness, the sudden primness, all alternating at a dizzying pace—and it excited him.

"Always."

He gripped her wrist tightly in his hand. Had he really thought he would be able to hold out against her, this ravishing, seductive creature who could pull him back and forth like a puppet on a string? The hard, throbbing pain that had already begun to swell his groin warned him she was about to defeat every cautious instinct he possessed.

Faith felt the tension in his grip, and she knew it would only be an instant before he drew her toward him again. Terrified, she wracked her brain, trying to think of something—anything—to distract him.

"Were you this bold with my sister, too?" she blurted out. "Is that why she left so abruptly?"

The words were no sooner out of her mouth than she realized how appallingly appropriate they were. A man like Brad Alleyn would have been a challenge to Fleur—and Fleur had never resisted a challenge in her life! It gave Faith a heavy feeling in the pit of her stomach to imagine her sister in the embrace of the man whose arms had just held her.

Brad did not give her time to pursue the thought. "What the devil does your sister have to do with this?"

"I just wondered . . . I mean, you never want to talk about her. Don't you like her?"

"Do *you* like her, Faith?"

Faith narrowed her eyes in surprise. What kind of man answered a question with a question? "Of course I loved her. She was my sister."

"I didn't ask if you loved her—I asked if you liked her. There is a difference, you know."

Faith hesitated, aware of a need to analyze feelings she had never questioned before. *Had* she liked her sister? Heaven knows, Fleur was never the easiest person in the world to get along with. She had been spoiled, she had been self-centered, she had to have her own way, no matter what. But she had been warm, too, and loving—and fun. Above all, Fleur had been fun.

"Yes, I liked my sister very much. But what a strange thing to ask. Aren't siblings supposed to like each other? You had a brother. Didn't you like him?"

Brad's face was a noncommittal mask. "No, I didn't like

my brother," he said coldly. "I suppose I loved him—there are ties of blood that go beyond reason or comprehension—but I never pretended, even to myself, that I liked him."

Suddenly, he was tired of the games she was playing. They had amused him before, stirring his blood to the boiling point, but now he was weary of them. Tightening his hold on her wrist, he drew her toward him.

"You didn't come here to talk about my brother—or your sister."

He knew damn well what she had come for, and he was just the man to give it to her! Without another word, he clasped her in the forceful vise of his arms, pressing her body urgently, demandingly against his. All he wanted now was to thrust her down on the couch and tear that absurdly innocent white dress off her flesh.

Terrified, Faith tried to pull back, but he was too strong for her. His body, hard and taut, vibrated with compulsive intensity, calling out to an answering hunger that would not be denied. Faith summoned all her strength to fight him. She couldn't give in to him, she told herself frantically—she couldn't! Not this man who might be her sister's killer! Raising her foot, she jabbed a pointed toe again and again into his shin, determined to kick and scratch as long as she had to. She might not be able to stop him, but at least she could make him earn his savage victory.

He stiffened at the sudden fury of her resistance, but he did not loosen his hold. Damn the bitch, she was playing her stupid games again, forcing him into the violence that would prove his masculine virility. Well, if that was what it took to excite her, it was all right with him. It wasn't what he wanted, but it would do. He tangled his hand in her hair, pulling her head back until her parted lips turned upward.

His mouth was a fiery challenge, a quenchless, volcanic force that sucked her strength away. Feverishly, Faith struggled to pull back, but even as she did, she felt the unbridled urges of her own flesh overcome her. The brutal, rousing power of his passion drew her like a magnet, kindling sparks of awakening desire into open flames. She wedged her arms against his chest, trying one last time to hold him off, but her hands betrayed her, clutching instead at his shirt, clawing, clinging, thrilling to the sensuality of his assault.

He did not relent, but pushed her slowly, surely down onto the couch, pausing only long enough to tear open the front of his breeches. He was trembling almost as much as she, although he did not feel it. He knew only that he wanted this woman—*needed* this woman—with a hunger he had never known before.

Faith felt the hard edge of the couch dig into her back as he pushed her down, and she closed her eyes, terrified and excited by sensations she could no longer control. This man was going to hurt her, he was going to use her—he was going to shame her horribly—but he was going to teach her at last what it was to be a woman!

She lay on the couch, quivering, weak with surrender, all her fears melting into the wave of longing that swept over her, as she waited for the force of his body to press her deeper and deeper into the cushions. When nothing happened, she opened her eyes cautiously. She was surprised to see him standing immobile, a few inches away, his hands still resting on the waistband of his breeches. He was looking, not down at her as she had expected, but toward the half-open window. It was a moment before Faith's ears picked up the sound of hoofbeats outside, faint at first, then louder as they approached the house.

Brad's voice was dry, his expression almost amused as he looked down at her. "It seems Cousin Alexandre has his usual good timing."

Faith huddled in a corner of the couch, barely daring to return his gaze. The brittle sarcasm in his eyes, the total lack of concern, made her sick with shame and confusion. In a moment of madness, she had tossed her innocence to the winds, offering up maidenly virtue like a pagan sacrifice, and all he could do was stand in the doorway, casually fastening the front of his trousers, as if she were a cheap little tramp who did this sort of thing every day.

He saw her tears, and they irritated him. Wasn't that just like a woman? he thought angrily. What a blasted fool he had been to think she was less devious than her sister! She had teased him from the second he entered the room, she had thrown herself into his arms, she had clung to him as if her life depended on his passion—and now she just sat there, misty eyed and silent, trying to make him feel guilty for something he hadn't even started!

"Don't be in a hurry to leave," he said harshly, pausing in the doorway. "We have unfinished business to take care of, you and I."

Faith buried her head in her hands, shaking with horror and self-disgust as she listened to the door close quietly behind him. What was wrong with her? How could she have let this happen? Was she so wanton, so steeped in sin, that any man with a handsome face and virile body could have her for the asking?

Damn him! she thought furiously, directing the force of her anger outward. All right, she had been foolish, she had played with fire when she flirted with him—but surely he saw what she was going. He was a sophisticated man of the world and she barely more than a teenager. How could he take advantage of her innocence like that?

It was a long time before she lifted her head, letting her hands drop helplessly into her lap. She strained her ears, listening for the sound of voices outside, but she could hear nothing. She dreaded going out there, dreaded the mocking eyes that would follow her as she slunk around the corner and headed for the front door, but she knew she had no choice. Brad would come back soon, and when he did, she couldn't let him find her there, looking for all the world as though she were waiting for him. And she couldn't risk trying to make her way through his dressing room into an inner corridor either, she reminded herself grimly. Not when she might find herself trapped by a locked door at any second.

The midday sun was high in the sky, drenching the earth in a burst of white heat when she finally stepped outside. Brad was standing in the yard a few feet from the base of the steps, his back turned toward the piazza, as he conversed with a tall, slender man beside him. Faith was tempted to slip past them, trying to sneak into the house unseen, but she knew only too well how she would feel if they turned around and caught her. No, stealth was not the best course now, she decided firmly. If she was going to salvage what was left of her pride, she had to hold her head high and walk straight toward them.

She paused briefly at the top of the stairway, studying the stranger. He was about the same height as Brad, but beyond that, there was nothing to mark them as cousins. Where Brad was athletic and muscular, this man had the lean, lithe body of a dancer, accented by the flowing lines of a stylish midnight-blue riding jacket. His features, in profile, were so perfectly formed they looked as if they had been chiseled by a master sculptor out of alabaster. His hair, blond, but much paler than Brad's, shone like silver in the light.

She had just taken the first tentative step when the stranger, sensing her presence, turned toward her. Faith gripped the railing, steadying herself as she watched him. He looked even more striking now than he had in profile, his face dominated by high cheekbones and wide, sensual lips.

Soft blue-gray eyes lit up with undisguised admiration at the sight of her.

Faith stood where she was, mesmerized by the unexpected force of his gaze. Was this attractive, aristocratic man really looking at her? She had seen that expression often enough in men's eyes—but only when they had been looking at Fleur. The feeling made her so giddy she forgot everything else.

It was like floating in a dream, she thought, catching her skirt in her hands and gliding gracefully down the steps. Like a fairy tale dream come true. The dashing young prince meets the beautiful commoner and falls hopelessly, desperately in love at first sight. It could not have been more romantic—or more exciting.

"Hello," she said breathlessly. "I am Faith Eliot."

The dream was shattered with her words. Faith watched his expression change, doubt and disbelief merging into an unmistakable air of disappointment. It did not take a mind reader to know what had happened.

How could she have been such a fool? she berated herself bitterly. Only seconds before, she had asked herself if this man was really looking at her. She should have known he was not. He may have been staring in her direction, but he had not seen Faith Eliot at all. He had seen only her twin sister—Fleur!

Harsh laughter in her ears did nothing to ease Faith's discomfort. Nor did the distinctly unpleasant smile that twisted Brad's handsome features.

"May I present Alexandre Juilliard?" he said smoothly. "My cousin and none-too-motivated overseer. Or perhaps I should say Jeremy's cousin, to be more precise. It seems Alex has taken quite a fancy to you, my dear."

Faith's cheeks burned with embarrassment. If she could have dug a hole and climbed in after it, she would have. Brad no more thought his half brother's cousin had taken a fancy to her than he thought his favorite white stallion could jump over the stable. It had amused him to see her puff up like a peacock, preening with vanity at the illusion of being admired. Now he was looking forward to watching her squirm.

Well, she wasn't going to let him get away with it! Faith thought with a sudden flash of rebellion. She had already been humiliated enough for one day. Brad Alleyn was not going to laugh at her again—not if she could help it!

Taking a deep breath, she cocked her head prettily to the side, ignoring Brad as she concentrated on the suave stranger he had introduced as his overseer. So Cousin Alexandre wanted Fleur, did he? All right, she would give him Fleur!

"Why, Alexandre, I'm really quite put out with you." She pushed her lower lip out in a little-girl pout. "You haven't greeted me yet. I was told that men in the Colonies were handsome. I had hoped they would be gentlemen as well."

Alexandre's reaction was everything she had wanted. Even Fleur couldn't have handled the situation more perfectly.

"*Milles pardons, chère mademoiselle.*" His voice, soft and seductive, was lightly accented with his native French. "A thousand pardons, I beg you. Had I known I would encounter such loveliness at Havenhurst, I would not have been struck speechless with surprise."

Faith could not help being amused by the outrageous flattery of his words. Alexandre played the game well—and it was clear that he enjoyed it. Now that he had recovered, his eyes once again glowed with delight. Only this time Faith was sure he was looking at her.

"I hope I didn't startle you. I look exactly like Fleur, you know. Men can never tell us apart. I suspect, sir, that my sister was quite enchanted with your charm. I hope you will turn my head as well."

She allowed herself a subtle glance to the side, searching for Brad out of the corner of her eye. She could not resist a secret smile when she saw him. He was glowering—positively glowering!—with the darkest, angriest expression she had ever seen.

Why, he's jealous, she thought, biting her lip to keep from laughing out loud. Of all the arrogance! He had been rude, he had been crass, he had tried to force himself on her in the most vulgar way possible—and now he was furious because she dared to flirt with someone else!

Linking her arm through Alexandre's, she guided him toward the house, smiling a sweet, intimate smile she knew Brad would not miss. It suddenly occurred to her that Alexandre Juilliard might well be a man worth cultivating. He had obviously known her sister as well as Brad had—and he was the kind of man who would be much more likely to let go of his secrets. Besides, he was handsome, he was charming—and he knew exactly how to flatter her! She would not in the least mind spending every minute of her time with him.

And if she just happened to teach Brad a thing or two in the bargain, that was all right too!

"Are you really Jeremy's cousin?" she asked, batting her

eyes so obviously it was hard to believe he couldn't see what she was doing. "So am I, you know. Does that make us cousins, too?"

"We are related, yes, on your mother's side. But I am afraid, pretty *mademoiselle*, that the relationship is a very distant one."

"Ah, but that's good." Faith made her voice deep and throaty, the way Fleur always did when she wanted to tease a man. "We wouldn't want the relationship to be *too* close."

She gave his arm an extra squeeze, just in case Brad was still watching. Perhaps, after all, she thought, suppressing the urge to turn and give him one last triumphant glance, it was going to be fun playacting the part of her sister.

Six

"What a contradictory little creature you are, *chérie*." Alexandre leaned nonchalantly against the virginal, gazing down at Faith with a look that was only half teasing. "First you tell me you will be devastated if I don't come and listen to you play—then you say the music makes you moody and you're not fit to be with! Are you trying to drive me to despair?"

Faith only laughed. Alexandre was so transparent—and so easy to manipulate. He must have been putty in the hands of a woman like her sister.

"To despair, Alexandre?" She ran her hands lightly up and down the keys, accenting the playfulness of her words. "You don't expect me to believe that, do you? A handsome, sophisticated man like you? Why, you must have known dozens of beautiful women."

It was almost too easy. Alexandre leaned even closer, letting his hand rest inches from hers on the keyboard, waiting for the invitation he knew would not come.

"None so beautiful as you, *ma belle coquette*—and none so fiendishly provocative."

Faith was still smiling to herself the next morning as she sat alone in the library, *Poor Richard's Almanack* open but unread on her lap. Fleur had certainly been right about men. Tease them, she had told Faith once, provoke them, play with them, but don't ever let them see into your heart—not if you want to hold their interest. What a silly goose she had been, not listening to her sister years ago. It was much more fun flirting with a man than turning crimson and stammering every time he came into the room.

A sound in the doorway attracted her attention. Looking up, she saw Brad frowning at her.

"Well, don't you look smug?" he grumbled irritably. "Rather like the cat that just swallowed a nice fat canary."

Faith only sweetened her smile. Brad had made a point of ignoring her ever since that afternoon she rebuffed him, but his feigned indifference did not fool her for a minute. It was amazing how little it took to get a rugged, virile man to act like a spoiled adolescent.

"I don't think cats swallow canaries—I think they just chew them into little bits. And why shouldn't I be cheerful? Things have been much pleasanter around here the last week or so, don't you agree?"

"Ah, yes, since dear Alex deigned to forsake the gaming tables and salons of Charles Town to take up his duties again." His slow, sarcastic drawl made him sound maddeningly unruffled, not at all the way Faith had hoped. "It does add to the savor of the game, doesn't it? Having two men to play off against each other."

Faith not quite so sure of herself now, but she was determined not to let him see it. She closed the book, keeping her finger in it to hold her place.

"Why, Mr. Alleyn, I do believe you're jealous."

"Jealous?" If anything, he looked amused. "Of whom, pray tell? Of a worthless overseer who's too incompetent to earn his keep? Or are you laboring under the delusion that I am so besotted with you I can't bear it when you look at another man? Hardly, my dear. I've seen quite enough of the way you and your twin sister operate to be immune to your charms."

Faith was not sure who had been insulted most—she or Alexandre. "You're very free with your criticism, sir. Tell me, why do you keep Alexandre on if he is so—how did you put it?—'worthless'?"

"Pity perhaps?" He raised a brow, tossing the question back at her. "Or more likely an uncharacteristic twinge of guilt. Alex was Jeremy's special pet, as docile as the horses he kept in the stable, or the dogs in the yard. Jeremy was grooming him to take over Havenhurst, and no doubt he would have, had I not been inconsiderate enough to come back. Poor Alex, you can't really blame him for hating me. I'm all that stands between him and a life of fast horses and fancy frock coats—and an overseer of his own to do all the work for him."

His callousness stunned Faith. "How can you talk like that? So—so coldly? You drive Alexandre constantly, you work him like a slave from sunup to sundown, then you make fun of him behind his back. You don't have an ounce of warmth in your heart. Or feeling!"

"Don't I?" Unperturbed, he glanced down at the book in her lap. "Still working on Ben Franklin? It doesn't look like you've gotten very far. Don't they teach young ladies of quality to read nowadays?"

A dozen biting retorts rose to Faith's lips, but she was too late for he had already disappeared through the doorway. What an exasperating man he was, goading her on while he stayed cool as a cucumber himself! Obviously, she had been right about him—he *was* jealous. Well, maybe not jealous exactly. That was the wrong word. Thwarted was more like it. His prodigious ego couldn't stand the idea that one woman in the world could actually say no to him.

Still irritated, Faith looked up at the clock, reading the same time she had read since the day she arrived. Six o'clock. Always six o'clock, whether it was noon or midnight or halfway through the morning, like now. What was wrong with this place anyhow, with clocks that didn't work and musical instruments shut up in dusty rooms—and people who never spoke to each other except to be unkind? With a sudden burst of energy, Faith forced herself to jump up, tossing the book into the chair behind her. It was going to be another hot day, with humidity rising like steam out of the flooded fields, and if she stayed inside, mopping the sweat off her forehead and thinking about how aggravating Brad was, she would make herself miserable.

The air was much fresher outside. Verdant branches swept in a wide arch over the garden path, shading the earth beneath, and the pungent scent of greenery tempered the pervasive stench of nearby rice paddies. The barest hint of a breeze floated up from the river.

Faith paused beside the narrow iron gate that opened into the small family graveyard. She could not forget Brad's words the day she had first seen the place. *Adam seemed to like it that way,* he had told her. *I never saw any reason to change it.*

But why? she asked herself now. Why would a man deliberately neglect his own brother-in-law's grave? Had her father hated her Uncle Olivier for some reason—or had he hated the idea of death itself? Was it an abomination to him? An affront to be challenged at all costs?

A bright trill of laughter, light and elusively feminine, broke into her thoughts. Forgetting the graveyard, Faith turned toward the house, but a tall azalea hedge blocked her view and she could see nothing. Who on earth could be there? she asked herself, puzzled. Not a neighbor, she was sure of that, for the neighbors never ventured to call. And which of the slave girls—even Estee—would be impertinent enough to gambol on the front lawn?

The hedge resisted stubbornly as Faith thrust her hands into its branches, trying awkwardly to part them, but she persisted until she had managed to make a small opening. Pressing her face against the leaves, she peered through to the other side. At first she could see nothing, for the sun, glaring off the white of the house, nearly blinded her. Then, slowly, a pair of figures, hazy in the shade of an old maple tree, began to materialize.

They made a handsome couple. The girl, a vision of softness in an old-fashioned rose-colored gown, floated through the air on the seat of a crude rope swing, dangling from one of the branches. Behind her, garbed in a deeper version of the same rich hue, a laughing young swain caught the swing as it came back, holding her teasingly against his body for a split second before setting her free again.

Faith stared at them curiously. Something about the young pair, something in their faces, their mannerisms, was so familiar she had the feeling she had seen them before. For a long time, she could not figure out what it was. When she did, she gasped with surprise.

"Why, they must be my cousins!"

She was so startled, she almost shouted the words. The pretty, fragile features of the girl on the swing were almost a carbon copy of her own mother's. She could be nothing but a Devereaux! Yes, and the young man, too, with the blue-black hair and milky skin that made him look more like the girl's brother than an ardent lover.

Pulling up her skirts, Faith abandoned all propriety as she raced like a hoyden down the path, heading for the end of the long hedge. How strange it seemed to think that she had cousins she had never heard of—and how strange that Brad had never mentioned them! She fairly flew around the corner, starting across the wide yard, then stopped abruptly.

The lush, well-kept expanse of green was totally empty!

Bewildered, Faith turned around slowly, scanning the area with her eyes. A young black man, powerfully built, with hands jammed deep into his pockets, whistled carelessly as he sauntered along the edge of the woods. Two small children, half naked and crusted with dirt, tore across the yard, then skidded to a stop when they saw Faith and veered off toward the river. A lone boatman, barely a black silhouette against the silvery current, poled his raft lazily along the shore. No one else was in sight.

But where could they have gone? Faith asked herself, confused. The hedge was too thick to penetrate, and no doors opened onto the yard from that side of the house. Besides, why would the young couple want to leave? They seemed to be having so much fun on the swing.

It was almost as if they had heard her coming, she thought uncomfortably. Almost as if they had deliberately run away from her.

But why? It didn't make any sense. Why should she have cousins that no one had told her about? And why would they be afraid to meet her?

A layer of dust hovered like a low-lying mist over the parched earth in back of the house. Estee held her apron out in front of her with one hand, using the other to rub away the beads of perspiration that trickled down her forehead. From the unpainted wooden steps that led into the main dwelling to the cookhouses and outbuildings across the yard, everything was the same monotonous shade of ocher. Black-skinned toddlers playing in the dirt, an old yellow dog sprawled against the fence, a pile of Indian corn waiting to be husked—all seemed to have been dyed in the same indiscriminate vat. Even the chickens, squabbling querulously as they pecked at the grains of corn Estee scattered on the ground, were so coated with dust it was hard to imagine their feathers had ever been white.

"Cluck, cluck, cluck," she mimicked irritably, dipping her hand one more time into the outstretched apron. "A bunch of gossipy old women, that's all you are, with nothing better to do than chatter and feed your stomachs. Don't you know you're going in the cooking pot with all the others, you stupid old hens?"

There was nothing dumber than a chicken, that was for sure. Not a fence in sight, not a thing to hold them in the yard but their own laziness, and still they hung around. Maybe they'd have a rougher time of it in the wild, maybe they'd have to scratch a little harder for their food, but at least they wouldn't end up as Sunday dinner for some overfed white man!

"All right now, shoo!" she called out sharply, tossing away the rest of the grain with a quick shake of her apron. "I've had enough of you, you hear me? Just get along now! Shoo!"

She lifted a bare foot, jabbing at the nearest hens until they scurried off in a shrill chorus of protests. How she hated it when Beneba made her feed the chickens! She would rather work in the flower gardens any day, or even one of the vegetable patches. Digging with her hands in fertile earth, planting seeds and watching them grow—that was work even a slave could take pride in!

A loud wail rose up in the yard behind her, drawing Estee back. One of the children, Little Tom, Cud Joe's youngest boy, was huddled in the meager shade of a storage shed, tears streaking his dark cheeks. The other children had already begun to gather in an uneven semicircle around him. Estee frowned as she caught sight of Cato, a youth of twelve, standing at the side with his faithful shadow, ten-year-old Sammee, a few paces behind him.

"What's going on? I thought I sent you two to dig potatoes in the garden. What are you doing here?"

Sammee hung his head, unable to look up at her, but Cato was not afraid of a tongue-lashing, especially from a woman.

"Aw, Estee, we was jes' playin'."

"And a fine game it must have been, too! Little Tom is beside himself. What did you do to him?"

Cato grinned. "Shucks, we was jes' funnin'. I was Black Amos, the driver up to Cypress Hill, and Little Tom here—well, he was a bad nigger, and he had t'be whupped."

And with a real switch, no doubt, Estee thought grimly, glancing around in vain for the weapon. Cato was too shrewd to leave the evidence in plain sight. No wonder the boy had been shrieking his head off. It turned her stomach to think of Black Amos, or any other slave for that matter, serving as overseer for a master as sadistic as Eleazar Carstairs. How could children make something like that into a game?

"You get out of my sight, the lot of you," she told them brusquely, flapping her apron at them just as she had with the chickens a moment before. "Get out from underfoot. Shoo, shoo, shoo!"

She could not shake a feeling of annoyance as she circled around the house, following the path that led between the garden and the old abandoned graveyard. It seemed to her that nothing had gone right lately. Not since *she* arrived, that white bitch with her insipid smile and her oh-so-sweet manners. The men were already fighting over her—God knows, there was enough bad blood between them as it was—and even Beneba was always on edge now. Cantankerous as the old woman was, she had always been family to Estee, especially since her mother died six years ago. It made her feel lonely to be at odds with her all the time.

A footfall sounded on the earth behind her, but Estee heard it too late to react. Strong arms grabbed her roughly, knocking the breath out of her as they whirled her around. Flashing teeth, bold against dark skin, mocked her upraised eyes.

"You!" Estee pulled back tensely. "What are you doing here? Are you mad?"

"Mad with love, *querida*." The man's voice, deep and melodic, was heavily accented with Spanish. "I could not live another day without seeing you."

"Now I know you're mad, Prince. This is no——"

"Don't call me that!" Black eyes flashed with sudden fury, a stunning contrast to the infectious richness of his laughter. Catching her arms in his hands, he gripped them so tightly she had to bite her lip to keep from crying out. "How often must I tell you? Prince is the name of a slave. I am called Rodrigo—and I always will be!"

"Rodrigo indeed!" Estee shook her arms free. Even after he was no longer touching her, she could still feel the bruising pressure of his fingers against her flesh. "You are no more Rodrigo than Prince. You were so young when the Spanish enslaved you, you can't even remember your African name."

"At least the Spaniards give a man a chance to earn his freedom. Show me an Englishman who will let go of a slave! I was a free man when my ship pulled into the harbor at Charles Town. Do you hear me? Free!"

Estee shook her head sadly. It was an old story, one that had grown all too familiar with the telling. How many strong, reckless slaves had served on Spanish galleons, mingling with whites in a world where strength and recklessness counted for everything? Soon there had been nothing to distinguish one pirate from another, and the price of freedom was a casque of stolen gold. But in the end, freedom proved elusive. A venture into foreign waters, a gambit too rash, too arrogant, and suddenly the privateering days were over. The captured whites were hanged on a gibbet in the public square, and the blacks were branded as slaves.

"Oh, my dear," she said softly. "My Rodrigo, if you will. What does it matter what you were? You are not free now, neither you nor I. You cannot come here in broad daylight."

He broke the mood with a quick smile, as compelling as it was unexpected. That was one of the things she loved most about him, the sudden, breathtaking changes from laughter to fury, then back again.

"You are too cautious, you worry too much. Where is your courage? Your daring?"

"One of us has to be cautious, Rodrigo. If your master finds you here——"

"*Diablo* take my master." He spit the words out, retreating into rage again. "I was born free, I earned my freedom once—I will be free again! He thinks he has us trapped with his whips and chains. He thinks he can sit in his house on the hill with walls around him like a fortress and feel safe, but he is a fool. We almost had him last year at Stono River. Next time——"

"Stop it!" Estee cried out, her voice trembling with fear. "You know I hate it when you talk like that." Where would all that misplaced bravado get him? Strong black men had tried his way at Stono River, and every last one of them was dead. Only fools like Rodrigo believed some of them were still hiding in the swamps, waiting to come out one dark night and form them all into a band of bold *conquistadores.*

"But why do you hate it?" he asked, deliberately provoking. His fingers were gentle as he ran them along her arm, lingering on the bruises he himself had caused. "Why do you want to protect the white man? Ah, but I forget—you are light-skinned yourself. Perhaps there is some white blood flowing through those proud African——"

"No! Don't say that! Don't ever say that!"

The words were a torrent of sound, bursting from her lips. Rodrigo roared with laughter as he drew her into his arms. His lovely Estee. So proud and so predictable. He always knew how to touch her secret fears.

"*Mi amada,* don't you know I am teasing you?"

"No, you are not teasing," she said quietly. "You are not teasing at all. But you are wrong. I was born in the Islands. Many there have fairer skin."

"*¿Que importa, querida?* What does it matter? You know your creamy golden skin drives me mad with desire. What do I care where it comes from?"

The closeness of his body was a bold challenge, tempting her to lay her head against strong shoulders. Cautiously, she forced herself to step backward. Somehow, she had to fight the contagious madness that threatened to engulf them both.

"We mustn't, Rodrigo. Not now, not here."

"Tonight, then. You know where."

"I tell you, no! It is too dangerous, especially with the

white woman here. She snoops everywhere, opening doors, peeking in drawers, prowling all over the grounds. If she sees——"

"Tonight," he repeated, his voice slow and sure. "You cannot resist me, you know you cannot. You've never been able to resist me—not since that first time in the woods."

Estee eyed him uncertainly. Against her will, her body was beginning to remember. She had been so young that day. So vulnerable.

"You took me by force. You know you did."

"And you had nothing to do with it?" His face was solemn, but his voice rang with laughter. "You didn't walk along the fence, swinging your hips so I couldn't ignore you? You didn't pause to look at me, telling me with your eyes that you wanted me as much as I wanted you?"

"Of course not! How can you say such a thing?" She *had* found excuses to wander through the fields at the edge of the plantation, knowing he would be certain to see her, but that was only because she had been flattered by his attention. How could she know he would react so violently?

"You didn't enjoy it? Not at all?"

She couldn't meet his gaze. He was beginning to catch her out, and she was not at all sure she liked it.

"You were so rough. . . ."

He bent over her, touching his lips to her hair, daring her to look up at him. "Then why did you stay for more?"

Why indeed? Even now, she was not sure. Perhaps because, after all the roughness and the passion, there had been a moment of tenderness that took her breath away. Or because, beneath the strength and brute animal force, she had sensed a vulnerability that called out to softer, feminine instincts. Or simply because, somewhere in her own body, she had found a need that matched the need in his.

"You know I love you, Rodrigo. I would die for you."

"Tonight then."

It was not a question. Boldness was a part of his life, as it always had been, and it would be a part of hers if she was going to love him. Lowering his head without once looking to see if anyone was in sight, he kissed her full on the mouth. Then, shoving his hands in his pockets, he strolled away, heading for the woods that drifted down the hillside almost to the rice fields below.

Estee stood alone, watching him grow smaller and smaller in the distance. She did not know if she wanted to laugh or cry. Had there ever been another man quite as impulsive as this lover of hers? Quite as foolhardy? He would be the death of them both one of these days.

Only when he had slipped into the trees did Estee at last turn away. Hurrying to the end of the hedge, she rounded the corner and began to walk briskly toward the front door. She did not even see a slender figure clad in buttercup yellow until she had nearly stumbled over her. The instant she recognized Faith, her body went rigid with apprehension. How long had the girl been there? How much had she seen?

Faith was so engrossed in her own thoughts, she did not see the tension on Estee's features. "Did you see them?" she asked breathlessly. "That young couple just now?"

Them? Estee's throat was so dry she could hardly swallow. *That young couple?* Faith had seen them, then. She had seen Estee and Rodrigo reach out and touch each other, perhaps she had even seen them kiss. But had she recognized them? Would she be standing here discussing it so calmly if she had?

Estee decided to bluff it out. "Are you sure you didn't imagine it? I didn't see anyone. Maybe the sun was in your eyes."

"No, no, I'm sure of it. They were here just a minute ago. A beautiful girl with jet black hair and fair skin, and a young man. . . ."

"Oh, white folks." Estee shrugged exaggeratedly, trying not to let Faith see her relief. "I can't keep track of the comings and goings of white folks."

"But you must have seen them. They were right over there. On the swing."

"The swing?" Estee squinted narrowly, studying Faith with dark, troubled eyes. This girl, with her pretty manners and strange ways, made her more than a little uncomfortable. "There *was* a swing there, but that was years ago. I remember once, when I was a little girl, not long after your mother left, Adam caught me on it. 'Don't go near there again,' he shouted. I'd never seen him so angry. 'No one is ever to go near that swing. Do you understand?' Hah! I was bold as brass in those days, and I guess he knew it. When I came back in the morning, there was nothing left but a stump."

Faith felt a chill seep into the hot swampy air as she listened. Slowly, she turned back to the spot where she had seen the young couple. Estee was right. Nothing was there but a worn gray stump.

"What's the matter, white girl?" Tension had sharpened Estee's tongue until she could no longer control it. "Are you seeing things? Why don't you go inside and lie down and let us darkies wait on you so you don't strain yourself?"

Faith was more astonished than angry. Estee had always had a chip on her shoulder, about the size of a small house, but she had never been quite this rude. There was not even a veneer of courtesy left in her voice.

"You've hated me from the beginning, haven't you?" she said softly. "But why? You had never laid eyes on me before."

"Hadn't I?" Estee was surprised at how calm she felt. She was being foolhardy, but she didn't care anymore. Rodrigo was right. She couldn't spend her whole life being afraid. "I was just six years old when my mother and old Beneba brought me here from the Islands—only Beneba wasn't so old then. She was a handsome, fiery woman, and fun to be with. You were still here with your mother and twin sister."

"You came here with Beneba? Before we left?" But Beneba hadn't come to Havenhurst until after Desirée was gone, or so she said at least. Had she lied? Or was it Estee who was lying now?

Estee hardly noticed the interruption. "You were younger than I, you and your sister, maybe five, maybe four, and I wasn't allowed anywhere near you, but I remember you well. Your mother always dressed you in frilly white frocks with gay little sashes, and your hair was all done up in golden ringlets that bounced up and down when you ran. You trampled the flowers when you chased each other through the gardens, but no one ever scolded you, and you shrieked as you slid down the banisters in the hall. My playground was the dirt yard out in back—when I was allowed to play, that is. Most of the time I was scrubbing pots and pans in the cookhouse or digging up potatoes for your dinner."

"Oh, Estee. . . ." Faith had never felt more helpless. How could she fight a hatred that had been simmering for fifteen years? "Fleur and I were little girls then. We couldn't help the way things were."

"So you just wash your hands of it, and that makes everything all right, is that it? You don't know the first thing about me. You don't know who I am, how I feel inside—and you don't care. What would you say if I told you my mother was the daughter of a king?"

Faith tried not to let the doubt show in her face. "Well, I—I'm sure if you say so. . . ."

"Not a petty tribal chieftain, the way you're thinking." Estee tilted her chin upward, reinforcing the heritage she claimed. "But a real king, a ruler of men so wealthy they could have bought and sold your father a dozen times over. You were *raised* as a princess, but I was *meant* to be one. And I would have been if the white man hadn't come to Africa with his greed and his gold! Would you like to know what happened to my mother? She was dragged out of her home like a jungle animal and loaded into the hold of a ship—not by slave traders, mind you, but by her own people, seduced by a shipload of china and polished brass pans. And a dozen silk umbrellas!"

Faith heard the pain in Estee's voice, and it touched a responsive chord in her heart. Hadn't her own childhood been haunted by the shadows of a mother's pain?

"Exploitation isn't a matter of black and white, Estee. My mother may not have been the daughter of a king, but she was the granddaughter of a duke, and she, too, was used brutally by her people."

"Oh, yes, my heart bleeds for her," Estee replied scornfully. "Poor abused little white woman. She didn't come to this land of her own free choice—she was carried here in chains! And it's only a rumor that she ended up as mistress of a great plantation with every indulgence her heart could desire."

"Estee!" Faith was appalled. It was one thing to build up fantasies of royalty to foster a sense of pride, but this girl was wallowing in a sea of her own venom. "Surely you don't begrudge her that one period of happiness. She paid a high enough price for it."

"She never paid for anything in her life! She had a husband to give her everything she wanted—a man to call her sweet, honeyed endearments from dawn to sunset." All the anger poured out now, complete and undisguised. How proud Rodrigo would be if he could see her. There was no fear left in her. "Do you know what he called *my* mother? He called her Katherine!" She spit out the word, as if it were a bitter poison she could not keep in her mouth. "Katherine! It wasn't her name, but he didn't care. Katherine was easier to remember than one of those funny-sounding African names. She wasn't a person to him, an individual with a soul and a heart of her own. She was just someone to be used——"

She broke off, checking herself with visible effort. Her eyes were cold as she stared at Faith.

"Don't force me to say things you don't want to hear, white girl."

Slowly, coolly, she turned, and without another word,

walked away. Faith could only stand and look after her in amazement. What on earth had prompted such a display of fire? Of unleashed boldness? All she had done was ask an innocent question about the young couple on the swing.

The couple on the swing. . . .

Faith was stunned to realize she had completely forgotten about them. Looking back slowly, she searched the empty landscape for the tall shade maple she knew she would not find. The weathered gray stump that met her eyes seemed small and lonely in a wide expanse of green.

Perhaps Estee had been right, she admitted reluctantly. Perhaps the sun *had* been in her eyes. And yet. . . .

Yet it must have been real once. The tree, the swing, perhaps even the young couple. She must have seen them as a child, watching as they laughed and frolicked with each other.

Could that be what had happened just now? Sunlight shimmering in her eyes, a moment of distorted images—and the memories that had been buried deep in her subconscious leaped to life again.

But memories of what? Was that lovely, gentle girl her mother? The same Desirée who had never been known to laugh? And the young man who gazed down at her with the look of an ardent swain—could that have been Olivier, the doting younger brother? Not a helpless cripple at all, as Faith had imagined, but a lean, trim youth, barely favoring one badly mended leg over the other? The idea made her lightheaded, almost dizzy, and she sank down on the old, worn stump to turn it over and over in her mind.

She was still there an hour later when Alexandre strolled around the corner of the house, pausing to take in the sweetness of a vision he had not expected. How like a little girl she looked, an innocent elfin figure with her elbows propped up on her knees and her chin cupped in her hands. But hers was an innocence seasoned with the sensual excitement of a woman's full, ripe body. His heart beat faster as he slipped up behind her, bending to whisper in her ear.

"So solemn, *jolie* Faith. Where are you now. A million miles away?"

She rewarded him with a quick smile, as guileless as it was softly feminine. He felt his body begin to respond. What an enchanting illusion she created, like a delicate child-woman hesitating just on the threshold of her own seductiveness. It was an image that never failed to captivate him.

"You caught me daydreaming, Alexandre. I was thinking of the past."

He leaned closer, dropping on one knee to the earth beside her. "The past, *chérie*? What can the past matter to one as young as you?"

"Do you believe . . . ?" Faith faltered, half afraid he would laugh at her. "I mean, do you think that people can—well, can see things that aren't really there? Visions perhaps. Or illusions—I don't know what to call them."

To her surprise, he seemed to take the question seriously. There was a depth to Alexandre that always surprised her, a kind of mysticism hidden beneath the surface gaiety of his laughter.

"How earnest you are, *enfant*," he teased gently. "Haven't you learned yet there are many things on earth we cannot explain—or understand? Do you know, you look exactly like Fleur right now? All misty-eyed and lost in dreams."

Fleur? The sound of her sister's name on Alexandre's lips was strangely disconcerting. Since the day she arrived, Faith had spent all her time trying to coax people to open up about Fleur. Now for the first time, she was conscious of a need to turn away from her.

"What is wrong with all these slaves?" she asked abruptly, anxious to change the subject. "These black people? Why do they hate us so much?"

"Hate us?" Alexandre looked amused. "Are you sure you aren't exaggerating?"

"I don't think so. I try to be friendly, really I do, but no matter what I say, I can't seem to get through to them. Beneba lurks in the hallway, watching everything I do as if she's afraid I'm going to steal the silver, and as for Estee—well, Estee can't even bring herself to be civil."

Alexandre pinched his lips together, trying to keep from laughing. "What a little girl you are, *chérie*. Always eager—always enthusiastic. You want everything *tout de suite*—just like a child. You have to remember, these people don't feel things the way we do. They don't want what we want."

"What do they want, then? Why are they so hateful all the time?"

Alexandre set his face in patient lines, like a schoolmaster who had already explained the same thing a hundred times and would explain it a hundred times again. "They miss the jungles, Faith. They miss their beastly savage ways and their huts built right on the dirt. You can dress them in clean clothes and whitewash the walls of their cabins, but all your pretty reforms will never even scratch the surface. If you spent half your life trying to elevate them, it wouldn't do a whit of good because they don't want your ways. They simply don't *want* them. If we had any decency—or common sense—we'd pack them back to Africa where they belong."

"Back to Africa?" Faith remembered how dubious she had felt when she heard the same words on Eleazar Carstair's lips. "I don't think I understand, Alexandre. Wouldn't that be foolish? The whole economy of the southern Colonies is based on plantations. If you eliminate the blacks, who will work the fields?"

"Only here a few weeks and already *la belle dame* is an expert on the economy." Alexandre shook his head in mock dismay. "Black men aren't the only ones who can work, Faith—though it may seem that way at times. In the north, most of the labor force is made up of indentured servants—men and women transported from Europe for specified periods of time."

"But the needs of the South are different. It takes hundreds of slaves to run a plantation. You could spend a fortune on indentured servants and you'd only have them ten years, maybe even five——"

"And if we bought black men, we could keep them for life. That does sound more practical, doesn't it? But remember, Faith, those five or ten years we're talking about are healthy, productive years. You don't have to continue to maintain indentured servants when they're too old—or too sick—to work. You don't have to feed and house and clothe a passel of men and women who'll never turn a penny's profit for you again. Add to that the tremendous cost of trying to keep order among savages—and the terrible toll in human life and property when we fail—and it doesn't seem like such a bargain anymore."

Faith was silent for a moment. "That never occurred to me," she said at last in a contemplative voice. It was obvious there was more to running a plantation than she had thought.

"That's just the trouble," Alexandre said wearily. "It hasn't occurred to anyone that our whole society isn't feasible. It simply doesn't work. And if we don't do something about it now, before we are too set in our ways to change, it's going to destroy us all."

Faith studied him curiously, fascinated by the passion in his voice. She couldn't help remembering how cavalierly Brad had dismissed him only a short time before.

"You really love Havenhurst, don't you?" she said slowly.

"Tell me, did you think—when you were here with Jeremy, I mean—that one day this would all be yours?"

He rose and stepped away from her, gazing down at the silvery ribbon of water that wound into the distance. When he turned back, there was a hardness in his eyes.

"I expected it, yes. Jeremy had no children. I was like a son to him—or perhaps only an extension of his own ambition, I don't know. He should have left a will, I suppose, but who thought little brother Brad would give up all the advantages of England to come back here."

"And now you're only here at his sufferance." Angry tears stung Faith's eyes at the thought of Brad's cruel disdain toward the man whose place he had taken. She longed to say more, but the pain that flickered across Alexandre's features warned her to stop. Fleur would never have made a man look like that—and Fleur knew how to hold onto her men!

"Why Alexandre, whatever are you thinking of?" she chided coyly, pushing her lower lip out in a perfect imitation of Fleur whenever she wanted to catch a man's attention. "How can you let me prattle on about all these tiresome, serious things. If I don't bore you soon, I will most certainly bore myself."

It worked perfectly. Alexandre laughed as he came toward her, teasing her eyes with his own. What an enchanting creature she was, all sensuality and mischief. He wondered if she had injected a serious note into the conversation just to make the flirtation that followed more dazzling by contrast. He wouldn't put it beyond her. It was the sort of thing Fleur would have done, and Faith was very much like her twin.

"*Petite sorcière,*" he said softly, making no effort to hide the longing in his tone. "My own little sorceress. Where did you get those bewitching yellow eyes? I could have sworn Fleur's eyes were green."

"They were, silly." Faith loved the way he could tease her out of her solemnity. There was an effervescence about this man, an almost reckless humor, that intrigued her. "That's because Fleur always wore green—and I am wearing yellow."

"Ah, you disappoint me, *ma chère*. All this time I thought the color was in your eyes. Now you tell me it is your dress."

"The color *is* in my eyes. All the colors are there. The dress only brings them out."

"And if you wore blue?"

"Then my eyes would be blue," she lied. "And don't you dare say, 'What if you wore pink?' "

"Black then?" he pressed. "If you wore black, would your eyes flash with dark fire like a Spanish seductress?"

Faith could hold out no longer. Laughing, she reached out her hands, not even thinking how forward the gesture would look to him.

"I will never wear black. It is much too depressing."

He held her hands lightly, then clasped them tighter, drawing her slowly toward him. The laughter was gone between them now, the teasing merriment that had held them in its tender bond only a second before. All that was left was a sudden, intense awareness of each other.

He's going to kiss me, Faith thought, surprised and frightened by the conflicting emotions the realization called up in her. She could remember only the brutish violence of Brad Alleyn's mouth, hard and demanding on hers, and it tormented her to think of that same mindless, bestial passion tarnishing her feelings for Alexandre. Yet she knew that once it began—once it caught her body in its grip—no power on earth could hold it back.

Alexandre saw her confusion, and it touched him in a way he had not expected. He wanted her more than ever now, he knew he must have her no matter what the cost, but instinct warned him he would be a fool to push her too far, too fast. Backing away, he raised her hands slowly, pressing them to his lips.

Faith felt his mouth, warm and moist against fingers that trembled with longings she could not understand. The sensations that swept over her now were different from the urgent hunger she had felt in Brad's arms, much purer, sweeter, yet they swelled her body with the same primitive stirrings, reminding her once again it was too late to retreat into the safety of naive adolescence.

"Sir, you are too bold," she protested, pulling her hands back, though not quite as quickly as she had intended. "I fear you will think me very brazen for letting you take such liberties."

He did not try to stop her as she turned and began to walk toward the house, but contented himself to follow a few paces behind her. She seemed to him the perfect woman, her golden hair wrapped like a shining halo around her head, the soft yellow muslin of her dress emphasizing every tantalizing curve of a body made for love. He adored the way she toyed with him, luring him on, then flitted away, leaving him, charmed and bewildered, to scurry after her as best he could.

A woman like that would be well worth the time it took to pursue her.

Faith paused halfway across the lawn to smile at him. It surprised her to realize she had completely forgotten Fleur in the last few minutes. She had looked at Alexandre, and it had not occurred to her that he had once been deeply attracted to her sister—and she had thought of Brad and not said to herself, "This is the man who may have caused my sister's death." They were just two men to her, two exciting, very diverse men who had awakened new and compelling passions in her heart.

But which was the man she truly wanted? she wondered, covering her confusion by turning away again. She was intensely conscious of Alexandre's eyes following her as she moved slowly up the steps to the wide piazza. Which man offered her only the easy gratifications her sister had always sought—Brad, with the raw lust that made no claims on her heart . . . or Alexandre, with the unquestioning admiration that posed no threat to her vanity? And which offered that strange, unfathomable, awesome enticement that she had always thought of as LOVE with four great big capital letters in every fantasy she had ever known?

And how was she ever going to find the wisdom to tell the difference?

Seven

Brad made an imposing figure as he rode down the drive, a tall man, erect on a strong, spirited stallion. Faith stood alone in an upstairs window, watching him round one last curve and disappear from sight. To an artist's eye, she thought idly, the picture would be a perfect study in black and tan: blond hair against a faded buckskin jacket, black gloves, black boots, and the glossy jet of a black mane whipping in the wind.

Turning slowly from the window, languid in the heat that spilled through rippled glass, Faith barely noticed another tall, powerfully built man standing in the yard just below. It was a moment before she realized who it was. When she did, she spun around for a closer look. There could be no doubt about it—the man in the yard was Brad Alleyn!

The thought was distinctly unnerving. She could not forget another morning, not so long ago, when she had seen a blond man on a black stallion ride down the drive. And only minutes later, she had encountered Brad in his study!

But if the man wasn't Brad, then who——

The thought broke off even before it could take form in her mind. The answer, if only she'd had the sense to see it, had been obvious all the time.

"Papa?"

It was more a cry than a question. It came from her own lips, but the sound was another, smaller voice. A voice she could barely remember.

"Papa, Papa!"

A little whirlwind of gingham and white petticoats flew down the path, feet barely touching the ground. The tall man reined in his horse, smiling as the child skidded to a stop beside him, clutching at his leg to keep from falling.

"There's Papa's little jewel," he called out, pulling her up so she could stand on his boot in the stirrup. "There's Papa's little diamond. And in such a hurry, too."

The child raised her arms, begging to be set in the saddle in front of him. "Did you bring me a present, Papa? Did you?"

"What makes you think I brought something for you, you greedy little thing?"

"Because you always do when you go away."

The man laughed loudly, clasping her in strong, tight arms. Touching his heels to the stallion's flank, he turned toward the stable. "When we get inside, precious," he promised. "When we get inside." The child did not coax again, but snuggled in his embrace. Papa was home, and he smelled of leather and tobacco and whiskers, and everything was comfortable and familiar again.

Faith turned away from the window, fighting the flood of confusion that swept over her as she sat gingerly on the edge of the bed and stared at the far wall. The tall man she had just pictured was not the Adam Eliot she expected to remember—surely this warm, generous, loving father could not be the same man who had turned his back on his family a few months later—yet the image was so intense, it was hard to believe it was not real. First the young couple on the swing, now a tall, laughing man on horseback—*was* the glare of the sun playing tricks on her eyes? Or had the past at last begun to come to life?

Faith was determined to get at the truth, that very night if possible. Brad looked surprised when she accosted him, demanding to know about Adam's horse, but he wrinkled his brow thoughtfully, making an effort to remember.

"Adam did have a black stallion—a magnificent animal. I had forgotten about him, or perhaps I put him out of my mind. Jeremy had him shot after your father died. The horse would never let anyone but Adam touch him. My brother was not a man to tolerate a beast who scorned him."

Shot! The thought made Faith sick, even after so many years. The stallion *was* magnificent, a beautiful, fiery mount, his darkness an exciting contrast to the tall, blond man who rode him.

The tall, blond man. . . .

The words sank slowly into Faith's consciousness. Adam Eliot had been tall and blond, too, so like Brad Alleyn it was impossible to tell them apart from a distance. Could it have been her father and not Brad she had sensed in her dream? A shadowy presence, tall and featureless, so ill-defined in her mind she had to grasp at a portrait to flesh him out?

But that was ridiculous! Faith was furious at herself for her foolishness. How could her father have caused Fleur's death? He had been dead himself for five years.

Still, dreams *were* funny things. All played out in murky symbols, dark and difficult to understand. It did make a perverse kind of sense, now that she thought about it. The portrait, a symbol for the man she did not want to remember—the man, a symbol for the past she did not know. Was that what Fleur's last fleeting message meant? "Look to the past, sweet sister. You will find clues to my fate in the past."

But where in the past? And what if she was misinterpreting the dream? Everything was so confusing, Faith thought helplessly—and it was growing more confusing with each passing day. The Havenhurst of her childhood was finally returning to memory, but it was a Havenhurst that was totally alien to her, as far removed from the preconceived notions she had when she first set foot on the sandy shore as her own comfortable England was from this brash Colonial frontier.

The Desirée she remembered when she stepped into the music room was not the pale, black-clad, tight-lipped woman she had always known, but a laughing, flirtatious girl, her porcelain delicacy exquisitely enhanced by a soft rose gown. Faith could almost hear music and laughter floating into the hall again, tempting Adam to pause in the doorway, smiling at his wife before he slipped away again. Olivier, slender and darkly handsome, lingered longer, leaning over the virginal to tease his sister when she hit a sour note, provoking gales of infectious giggles from merry pink lips. And all the while, Fleur sat at their feet, so enrapt Faith could not coax her away, even when she wanted to run out and romp in the fields.

Nor was the Adam who cleared away the last of the swamps along the riverbank the stern, uncompromising father she had expected, but rather the kind, laughing man who once leaned down to pull a little girl up into the saddle. How strong he looked to her then, a bronzed giant, raising a heavy ax above his head to sink it with resounding force into the flesh of an ancient cypress. Faith stood at the edge of the field, watching patiently, knowing any minute he would look up and see her. "What are you waiting for, little diamond?" he would call out. "Come and help your father." And she would run up to him, trembling with excitement as he placed a small hatchet in her hands. Together, they would lift it over her head, pretending it was a massive ax, just like his, and in that moment, she, too, would be a giant.

Even she and Fleur were not the same two girls who grew to young womanhood in the prim, stately halls of an English manor. It felt strange to pick up a candle and follow the dark, narrow stairway that led to an attic room with two child-sized beds, still gaily covered with bright red quilts. Setting the candle on a small table, Faith sat on one of the beds, surprised to find how low it was. It seemed to her her feet should dangle over the edge, barely touching when she pointed her toes toward the floor. Leaning back, she shut her eyes, letting the past close in on her again.

"That's my sash!" a baby voice shrieked out. Was that her? Faith wondered—or was it Fleur? They sounded so alike she couldn't tell the difference.

"No, it's mine! It goes with my white dress."

"You don't have a white dress!" Petulant anger rang out in childish tones. Such indignation! Faith thought with a smile. How seriously children took everything. "You got your white dress dirty, and now it's spoiled."

"Well, I have the sash anyway. Give it to me—it's mine!"

"No, it's mine!"

Faith laughed out loud as she opened her eyes. Had they ever been that young, she and Fleur? That typical? Why, they were no different from children all over the world. Fleur had not been too prissy to sit all day on the floor, and Faith had not been afraid to talk back to anyone, even her twin sister. They were as alike as two little buttons then, and she could not even begin to guess which speaker was which and whose sash belonged to what dress.

Where had all the years come from? she wondered. When had they stopped being "they," and become Fleur and Faith, two separate, distinct people with personalities all their own? When had laughter gone out of the house, and music? And love? When had the past ceased and the present begun?

"I don't think I remember things the way everyone else does," she said to Alexandre as they strolled through the garden, enjoying the first cool hints of approaching autumn. "Nothing comes back to me in dribs and drabs—you know, a piece of furniture that seems vaguely familiar, or a pretty trinket that brings back hazy memories. With me, it's all or nothing."

Alexandre drew her into the shade of a tall live-oak and leaned against the rough bark as he studied her intently. They were holding hands, as they often did now, freely, without self-consciousness.

"I doubt if you do anything the way everyone else does, *chérie*." He was fascinated by her lashes, curly and surprisingly dark as they quivered against pink-white skin. Any second now she would look up, giving him just a glimpse of melting hazel eyes. "You are enchanting, but of course you know that."

"How can I know it? You haven't told me for at least an hour. A girl does need reassuring, you know."

Alexandre laughed, delighted with the coquetry that was so polished it almost seemed natural. That was exactly what Fleur would have said—and she would have uttered it with the same coy tilt of the head!

"Ah, *mon coeur*, you don't need me for that. I only wish you did. You have your mirror, and I know exactly what it says to you when you tilt your head, *comme ça*, and practice fluttering your lashes against your cheek."

Faith turned away, hiding a quick blush. She *had* been studying herself in the mirror, just the way her sister always did, but she had the feeling Fleur would have never let anyone catch her at it.

"You mustn't make fun of me Alexandre. You know I would never do anything so—so calculating."

"But of course you would! You wouldn't be Faith if you didn't—and I wouldn't adore you so much."

He took hold of her hands, pulling her toward him. Faith's body tingled with the nearness of this man, so strong yet so tender, and her heart began to beat rapidly. This was not the Alexandre she had come to take for granted. The eyes that gazed down at her were filled with gentle admiration, as they always had been, but now their depths glowed with a new hunger. His lips parted expectantly, as if to suck her into his mouth with the same savage force Brad had poured into his kisses.

"You mustn't stand so close," she whispered throatily. The fabric of his shirt was coarse against her fingers as she pushed him back.

"Why not, *chérie*?"

"Because—because I don't like it."

"Because you don't like it? Or because you like it too much?"

Faith *did* like it, she had to admit. She liked the gentleness, the passion, even the fear this man aroused in her. But somehow, for some reason she did not understand, she could not let herself give in to it. Bitterly, she cursed her own prudery. Fleur would never have been afraid. Fleur would have thrown herself into Alexandre's arms, abandoning her inhibitions in the rapture of his kiss before flitting away to savor the sweetness of the moment in solitude.

"I told you, I don't like it." She stamped her foot childishly to emphasize her words. "I don't like it *at all!*"

Alexandre only laughed. The excitement, the longing, that made her hands quiver as she pushed him away tempted him to draw her back again. What would she do, he wondered, if he crushed her against his chest, bruising her flesh with eager hands, tearing the clothes off her voluptuous body? Would she pull away from him in shock and horror—or would she sink into his arms, sighing for the passion they both knew she wanted? He decided not to take the chance. She would be his soon enough. He could afford to bide his time.

"What a devil you are, *coquette,*" he said lightly. "Your eyes invite me and your hands push me away. When will you stop tormenting me?"

Faith was relieved by the teasing tone in his voice, but the memory of that afternoon did not leave her, even in the long hours of the night that followed. How could she be so like her sister, she asked herself again and again—and yet so different? She had learned Fleur's games almost frighteningly well, yet she had learned them only by half. And a newly maturing body, lonely in a wide bed meant for two, warned her she had chosen the least satisfying half.

Perhaps, she consoled herself, things would be different soon. Perhaps, when she put the pieces of the past together and discovered who she had been, she would at last be able to figure out who she was now—and what she wanted out of life.

Yet, two days later, as she stood on a windswept hillside staring down at three simple stone gravemarkers set flat in rustling grasses, the secrets of the past no longer seemed quite so tantalizing. The spot was cool and green, shaded by a copse of tall pines, and wild flowers dotted the slopes that opened onto a breathtaking panorama of the river, but Faith found no beauty in the setting.

How strange the truth seemed. Like a series of veils, some pretty and softly colored, others somber and black, all layered one on top of the other. You pulled one of them away, and you thought you saw what lay beneath. But then you looked closer and saw that that was only a veil, too—and under it was another and yet another. Until you reached out a hand that no longer expected to find anything and pulled aside that one final veil, and at last the truth lay naked and exposed to your eyes.

The markers spoke for themselves:

ADAM JOSEPH ELIOT
Born January 29, 1726 - Died April 12, 1726

AARON ELIOT
Born September 29, 1727 - Died December 24, 1730

JACOB ELIOT
Born July 17, 1729 - Died July 17, 1729

Faith sank to her knees, reaching out a tentative hand to brush dried wisps of grass off the stones, as if somehow she could change the inscriptions by making them more readable. She wondered why it bothered her so much. The tall man who had ridden spirited stallions through the wilderness and hewn down trees with strong arms seemed to her both impulsive and virile, not at all the sort to settle for a lonely, monkish existence. That he had taken another woman after his wife left was only natural.

Faith sat back on her heels, tucking her skirt around her legs, and tried to imagine what she was like, this woman who had borne her father three illegitimate sons. A spinster neighbor, she decided at first—a slender, sad-eyed creature, sneaking out on moonless nights to meet the lover she could never hope to wed. Or a brazen hussy, a wonderfully wanton, henna-haired creature, living openly in her father's house and thumbing her nose at all those scandalized neighbors. Faith liked that picture best of all. Though most likely, she had to admit, she had been that typical stereotype, the faithful housekeeper, content to tidy her master's rooms by day and ruffle his bed by night, and never, *never* beg a crumb for reward.

No, hardly a housekeeper. Faith smiled a little at the thought. In England perhaps—but not in the Colonies. Here the only housekeepers were sultry women with sloe eyes and dusky skin, and . . .

. . . and they were the property of the men who bought them.

Slowly, Faith stood up, drawing her breath in a long, low hiss between clenched teeth. She knew now she had finally lifted that last veil. All she could see was the remembered image of Estee's eyes, black and blazing with hatred.

He called her Katherine. That was not her name, but he didn't care. She was just someone to be used.

Oh, dear heaven, no wonder the girl hated her! Every time she looked at Faith, she must have seen reflections of a brutal man who held women in no higher regard than livestock and furnishings. A man who did not understand—or care—that the tears of a ruined woman could scar her daughter's life. Who buried his bastard sons, not in the black cemetery with their mother's people—and oh, God forbid, not in the Eliot family graveyard!—but high on some isolated hillside where no one would see them.

Suddenly, Faith could stand the place no longer. Hiking her skirts to her knees, she began to race down the hill, not even caring that she exposed a pair of shapely calves to the view of anyone who happened by. No wonder they *all* hated her! Beneba, with her surly stares; Cuffee, polite and indifferent; even chatty little Fibby, who grew taciturn and uncomfortable whenever Faith brought up the past—every one of them must have known her father's shame.

Brambles caught at her ankles, drawing blood where they scratched, but Faith did not even notice. All she wanted was to feel hot air blow in her face as she ran, to let the wind tear carefully styled hair out of its pins, streaming it out in back of her—to leave the past and all its pain behind.

She was almost down the hill when she felt her feet skid on a layer of sand, hidden beneath the grass. Her ankle twisted suddenly, threatening to give out beneath her, and she struggled to hold her balance. Gasping for breath, she stopped where she was, releasing her skirt to float airily down to her ankles.

Well, she had only herself to blame, she thought ruefully. Thick tresses felt hot on her neck, and she reached up to tuck wayward curls untidily back in their pins. She had deliberately flirted with the past for weeks, she had wooed and coaxed and courted. Now, like a shy young lover, it had slipped out of its hiding place, and like it or not, she was going to have to meet it face to face.

Brad sat in silence at the crest of the hill, leaning forward in the saddle as he gazed down the slopes toward the silver-green river below. His jaw tensed when he caught sight of Faith, tracing her way through parched, waving grasses, her skirts caught up in her hands like a teenage tomboy. Blast it! he thought irritably. He had told the woman she could stay at Havenhurst. He hadn't given her the run of the place.

Slowly, his eyes drifted up the rise of the hill, following in reverse the pell-mell course she had just run. They stopped when they reached a shady ledge, just at the edge of a cluster of pine. So she had found her father's secret, had she? He wondered what she made of it.

He saw her stumble, and he thrust out his hand, then caught himself with a harsh laugh. Below him, oblivious to his concern, Faith let her skirts fall around her legs, shaking them out with a careless wiggle of her hips. The little minx, Brad thought with grudging admiration. If she had known he was watching, she couldn't have made the gesture more provocative—or more appealing.

The horse stirred uneasily beneath him. Brad reached forward, laying a steadying hand on his neck. They were new to each other, he and this stallion, a magnificent Arabian gray, so pale it looked pure white. They had yet to try each other's strength and weaknesses. He gripped the reins firmly in his fingers, giving a slow, even pull to remind them both who was master.

The sight of Faith on the hillside brought back memories he had no desire to recall. The softness of full breasts pressing against his chest, the sweet scent of perfume, silken strands of hair teasing his cheek. . . . Damn her, she had trembled in his arms, she had fought and flirted, kicked and kissed with an abandon that set his blood on fire—and then she had simply stepped outside, as cool as you please, and linked her arm through Alexandre's, squeezing the same supple body against his!

The wind picked up, swirling Faith's skirt away from her ankles, teasing Brad with glimpses of lacy petticoats and soft white skin. He was uncomfortably aware of the hard leather of his saddle, pressing into his groin, and he hated himself for the physical sensations he could not control. The girl was a cheap little baggage—a bitch without a trace of conscience—but by God, she was beautiful, and he wanted her more than ever.

"Yo' think mebbe they is sum'pin down there for yo', eh?"

Brad started guiltily, like a small boy caught in a forbidden prank. Glancing down, he saw dark, disapproving eyes glaring back at him.

"What the hell are you doing up here?" he snapped. "Don't you have better sense than to climb a hill in this heat?"

Beneba's ample bosom heaved as she planted a stout walking stick firmly on the ground, shifting her weight forward. "I bin climbin' hills since afore yo' was born, Mist' Brad, an' I ain't about t' stop now. 'Sides, where's a body t' find nice red cocoa pods, 'ceptin' here? Or a silk fig or two?"

Brad tightened his lips, trying to keep from smiling. Silk figs and cocoa pods weren't native to the hills along the river, and they both knew it.

"And a little eye of newt and tail of frog, no doubt," he replied dryly. Beneba had a going concern on "the street," the section behind the main house where the huts and hovels of the slaves were located, and she was forever gathering cockroaches and land turtles to boil into tea, or stirring anise and nutmeg mace into an aprodisiac for some lovesick young swain. "Save that mumbo-jumbo for the gullible simpletons who believe it."

"An' yo' doan' believe?" Beneba tugged at a filthy leather thong around her neck, pulling out a long serpentine amulet carved from bone in the image of the snake god, Damballa. "They's plenty folks doan' believe—leastaways they *think* they doan' believe. But jes' yo' wait 'til the white man doctor, he doan' do 'em no good—or the white man priest—then they come a'runnin' to ol' Beneba. Then they begs—wi' tears in they eyes, they begs—'Beneba, gimme th' magic o' ol' Africa.' "

"Africa, hell!" Brad stared at the amulet, all yellow and stained, like a decaying tooth, and thought how he hated the thing. To him, it symbolized all that was primitive and repressive about the black culture. "You don't know the first thing about Africa. You've never even been there."

"I was born in the Islands, Mist' Brad. They is still a lot o' Africa in the Islands."

There was more truth in that than Brad cared to admit. The Island blacks, with their lilting speech and strange, haunting music, stirred deep chords of superstition in even the most practical of men. Dropping the subject, he turned toward the hillside again. He was surprised to find Faith still there, standing immobile, just a few yards from the narrow footpath that wound the rest of the way down the hill. She looked compellingly fragile, like a little girl with a woman's body, and he felt himself harden again with the longing he could not resist.

A harsh sound, somewhere between a grunt and a laugh, jolted him back to reality. He composed his face quickly, determined to hide his feelings.

"You think I'm tempted by that? Hell! I've done some fool things in my time, but I know trouble when I see it."

"Yo' ain't tempted, eh?" The sound turned into a deep

throaty chuckle. Beneba lowered her eyes pointedly, letting Brad know it was not his face that gave him away. "Jes' 'cause a woman's old, doan' mean she cain't tell a man when she sees one."

"Confound it, Beneba!" Brad liked the old slave's earthy frankness, but he was damned if he was going to let her see she was the one woman in the world with the power to make him blush. "I'm the master of this plantation. If you can't behave with humility, at least show me a little respect!"

Beneba narrowed her eyes until they were shadowy slits in a dark face. She had known this man since he was a boy, barely out of short pants. She wasn't about to take any sass from him now.

"Yo' know what's wrong wi' yo', Mist' Brad? Yo' been alone too long. Why yo' doan' go down to the street an' fine yo'self a nice black girl? Ain't no shame in that."

Brad leaned back in the saddle, stretching out muscles that had been cramped too long. He had had a black woman once, a full-bodied, big-boned woman who folded him into her arms and shut out the rest of the world, and he had wallowed for hours in the sensual pleasures of her bed. But when it was over and he lay beside her, silent and withdrawn, he had been bitterly conscious of the fact that she had had no choice in the matter. She could love him or she could hate him, she could revel in the things he did to her body or she could be repulsed by them—but she could never say no.

"That's not for me, Beneba."

Beneba had heard that quiet finality in his voice before, and she did not try to argue. Instead, she let her eyes scan the hillside, lingering on Faith, still motionless beside the path. Her dark face puckered with a worried frown.

"Yo' know where she's been, doan' yo'?"

Brad nodded calmly. There was no point denying the obvious. "She was bound to find out sooner or later."

"She doan' belong here, that one. She doan' belong here t'all. Yo' knows it, Mist' Brad, well as I does."

Brad turned cool, assessing eyes on her face. "You wouldn't be thinking of doing something about it, would you, Beneba?"

The only acknowledgment was a slight tensing of her jaw. "She doan' worry yo' none, Mist' Brad?" she grumbled. "She gonna dig up all th' ol' graves, yo' knows she is—an' she gonna lay all them ol' corpses out in the sun. An' that doan' worry yo' t'all?"

Brad looked off in the distance, following the river out to

sea. He understood the old woman's concern. Faith's curiosity ought to worry him, it ought to worry the hell out of him, but it seemed so natural, so inevitable, he couldn't work up the will to fight it.

"It's her father, Beneba. Her heritage. She has a right to know."

He touched his heels to the horse's flank, eager to get away from the old woman and all the dire predictions he did not want to hear. The wind whipped his shirt away from his body, cooling hot sweat and giving him the feeling he was wild and free. The past was the past. If it was all going to come up again, it was, and if it wasn't, it wasn't. That was all there was to it. He could have gotten rid of Faith the day she arrived—blast it, he *should* have gotten rid of her!—but there wasn't a damn thing he could do about it now.

He was nearly to the bottom of the hill before he realized where he was going. He reined in his horse, stopping for a moment as he stared at the footpath, barely a quarter of a mile ahead of him; then, with an impulsive laugh, he spurred the stallion on again.

Hell, he had made a fool of himself over women in the past—and he'd make a fool of himself over enough in the future. One more or less wouldn't make any difference.

The path leveled off when it reached the foot of the hill, angling sharply to the right to join the wide, fenced lane that led to the house. Faith shuffled idly through the dirt, so lost in thought she barely noticed a long shadow stretching across the road. Looking up, she saw Brad perched on top of the fence, the heels of his boots hooked over the rail beneath him. The stallion, tethered to a post beside him, pawed impatiently at the earth, kicking up clouds of yellow dust.

For an instant, Faith was tempted to turn and walk away, pretending she hadn't seen him. But she knew Brad well enough to realize he would never let her get away with anything like that. Besides, even if she could ignore him, there was no way she could ignore those three little graves.

She paused a few feet away. Dropping her eyes, she sucked in her breath, making her waist look as tiny as possible. It was a perfect Fleur pose, and one that never failed to get results.

"Why, Mr. Alleyn, how lazy you are. I thought you spent all your time toiling in the fields, and here I catch you daydreaming."

He eyed her warily, wondering why he was doing this to

himself. It was going to be that morning in the study all over again. She would tease him, play with him, promise him everything—and ten minutes later she'd pull the same thing on Alex!

"You really enjoy your little games, don't you? Tell me, do you dally with me to annoy Alex? Or do you flirt with that poor wretch to drive me mad with desire?"

Faith opened her mouth in indignation, but not a sound came out. Really, the arrogance of the man was incredible! As if she would have anything to do with him if she could avoid it! No matter how much she wanted to know about the graves she had just found, it wasn't worth the aggravation she would have to put up with from him. Turning on her heel, she raised her chin as high as she could and began to march down the road.

Brad choked back the laughter he knew would do him no good. Damn the vixen! She was even prettier when she was angry. He raised his voice to call after her.

"I see you were up on the hill."

The words had exactly the effect he desired. Her face was pale as she turned around.

"I found three graves," she said slowly. "Three little boys with my father's name."

Brad nodded knowingly. "Your brothers."

"My . . . brothers?"

Faith choked on the words. How could anyone possibly find kinship between legitimate offspring and such ugly bastardy? She was sick with shame for a man who found his pleasures groveling in the filthy hovels of the street, forcing his body on helpless women who had no way to protect themselves. It seemed to her it was time to bring the whole disgusting business out in the open.

"They were black, weren't they?"

Brad studied her coldly, misinterpreting the disgust he heard in her voice. "They were your father's sons, Faith."

"But their mother? She was black."

He fixed her with a noncommittal stare. Where had it come from, all that prejudice? Not from Adam, that was for sure.

"Yes, she was black."

Faith closed her eyes, swaying dizzily as the final reality of her father's disgrace swept over her. Three bastards—and the first born less than a year after Desirée had fled to England. How long had it been going on before?"

"At least I know now why my mother left my father."

"Do you?" Brad's voice was cold. "I never did."

He wondered why he wanted her so much, this spoiled bitch who looked like she wanted to throw up because her father's mistress was black. But want her he did, and he was determined to have her.

He pushed off the fence, moving toward her. His hands were light as he laid them on her arm, careful not to frighten her. His voice was kinder than he had intended.

"Let the past lie, Faith. It will only bring you pain."

Faith sensed tenderness in his tone. She held back for a moment, still cautious, still afraid of this man who had such power to hurt her, but in the end, the pain was too much and she surrendered, letting her head sink onto his shoulder. Even a man like Brad had to know how devastated she was by the discovery she had just made—even he would not deny her the solace she needed so desperately.

The sweetness of his embrace was more intense than she had expected, and she quivered in his arms, barely noticing as his hands slipped downward, caressing, enticing, urging her hips tighter against his. It seemed so natural, the feel of his lips on hers, the invasion of his tongue into her mouth, that at first she did not realize what he was doing. When she did, she pushed him away with a rush of horror.

She was shaking as she stood and faced him. The bastard! What kind of man would treat a woman like that? He knew she needed comfort—and all he did was take advantage of her!

"You—you son of a bitch!"

Brad roared with laughter. This was the way he liked her, open and honest, with all the pretense stripped away. What a savage fury she would bring to some lucky man's bed! It galled him to think it might be Alex's.

"By God, you'd make a magnificent harlot!"

Faith recoiled, too stunned by his words to think of a retort. She had always sensed an anger in his passion, a kind of leashed violence that simmered beneath the surface, but never, *never* had she thought he would insult her so grossly!

He watched her confusion, and it afforded him a certain satisfaction. Why was it that a slut never wanted to be called by that name?

"Oh, not a creature of the streets," he assured her. "Not some wretched whore who can barely keep body and soul together. An expensive courtesan, that's what you should be. All decked out in diamonds and brocades. Some poor devil of a prince would sell his kingdom for you."

And it wouldn't be a bad bargain, either. Fire and ice, all for the price of one. Grabbing her wrist, he pulled her roughly toward him.

"Come, Faith, stop pretending. You know you want this as much as I do."

Faith felt a sickening sense of longing swell through her body as he drew her nearer, and she realized her mouth was hungry for the pressure of his again. God help her, all those hours of soul-searching, all the sweet tenderness she had shared with Alexandre, and still she could not fight the baser urges of her own nature!

"Oh, no," she whispered despairingly. "Oh, please. . . ."

Brad caught the scent of her fear, and it diminished his pleasure. Damn the little bitch! Who was she to pull her tears on him?

"What now, my fine lady? Sweet innocence again? Do you take me for a fool? You kissed me like a little tramp, you writhed your body against mine like a tramp, and neither you nor I will ever believe you are anything else! I could have you right now if I wanted—right here in the dirt—and you wouldn't do a thing to stop me!"

His body trembled with controlled anger as he watched the tears slip out of her eyes and run down her cheeks. Hell, he had been right about her all along. She wanted to tease a man, she wanted to work him into a frenzy to feed her ego, but she didn't want to give him a damn thing!

"But I don't want you, so you can relax!"

He thrust her angrily away. Faith stumbled awkwardly, clutching at the fence to keep from falling. He tossed the reins over the horse's head and mounted with a flowing movement to the saddle. His eyes were blue ice as he stared down at her.

"Did I say you should be a harlot, my dear? It seems I was mistaken. At least a harlot is honest about what she is."

Faith burned with fury all the way back to the house. She was still seething an hour later as she sat alone in her room, her chin cupped in her hands, staring at her reflection in the candlelit mirror. The man was a brute, an animal, an arrogant stallion who thought every mare in the field was his! How dare he call her a harlot? She, who had kissed only one man before him? How dare he treat her like a common tart?

Still. . . .

Faith held her breath, appalled by the nagging doubts that were beginning to creep into her mind. Still, there *was* a little of the common tart in her. She could see it in the image that faced her in the dark glass.

Her eyes seemed to have been magnified by the mirror. Huge, wide, frightened orbs of shimmering golden-brown. Faith stared at them, fascinated and awed by the new realities that leaped out of their depths.

There was more of her sister in her than she cared to admit. Her body, like Fleur's, had changed with maturity, awakened by the rough touch of a man she did not even like. And once awakened, new longings would never be stilled again. The passion she craved was going to be hers—and there was nothing she could do to stop it.

Only the choice of passion was hers. She could drift along as she had been, letting the yearnings she denied lead her straight into the arms of a man who only wanted to use her, a man who inspired nothing but fear in her—a man who might well be a merciless killer!

Or she could take her fate into her own hands and give herself freely, joyfully, to a man who adored her.

She was surprised how steady her hand was as she slipped the sheer nightdress over her head. Gauzy linen felt cool against flesh that was flushed with anticipation. Taking a blue silk wrapper from a peg by the door, she tied it over the gown and turned to give herself one last look in the mirror.

Funny, she thought, studying her reflection with a detached air. She had always thought it was so easy to tell her and Fleur apart. Now she was not sure.

The doorway stood open, letting perfumed night breezes drift in from the piazza. Faith hesitated on the threshold, staring in at a room so sparsely decorated it seemed more like an office or study than a sleeping chamber. The impression was heightened by the furnishings: a small, compactly built writing desk to the left of the door, a pair of bookcases on the far wall, a low narrow couch just in front of the dark draperies that covered the window. On the couch, half reclining, his long legs stretched out in front of him, Alexandre leaned over a sheaf of papers, scowling as he shuffled them back and forth in his hands. His pale hair, caught in the fiery rays of a single grease lamp, shone almost as golden as Brad's.

Faith did not move as she stood in the doorway, acutely conscious of the presence of a man who did not even know she was there. The cry of an owl, a lonely wail in the distance, broke the silence, then died away, leaving the night emptier than ever. For an instant, she was tempted to turn and run away, slipping into the darkness, but she knew she could not give in to her doubts. It had been hard enough coming here. She could not go back now.

She took a slow step into the room, pausing before she dared to move again. It seemed forever before Alexandre looked up and saw her.

His face lit up instantly, mirroring the delight he made no effort to conceal. How exquisite she looked, his adorable Faith, with her long hair hanging down her back and deep blue moonlight framing her golden beauty. He was glad now he had not tried to push her. He had been right to trust her to come to him.

He rose and went toward her, his outstretched hands coaxing her forward. "I knew you would come tonight, *chérie*."

Faith pulled back, confused by the open, confident sensuality in his tone. A dozen excuses rose to her lips—I couldn't sleep, I was just passing by, I saw your light and thought I would stop for a chat—but she knew she could never make them convincing, even to herself.

"What am I doing?" she whispered miserably. "What must you think of me?"

He smiled indulgently, enchanted with this last show of maidenly modesty, just as she was about to give herself to him. "I think only that you are beautiful, *mon ange*—and that I want you very much." He laid light hands on her shoulders, caressing the silk of her wrapper, then slipped them inside the forbidden edge of her neckline, his fingers tingling with the warmth of her skin.

Horrified, Faith realized he was about to open the wrapper and ease it off her body. This was what she wanted, she told herself frantically—this was what she had come for—but now that the moment was here, she felt a sudden need to back away and look at what she was doing.

"Alexandre, please. . . ."

Alexandre's face hardened. There was a strange look in his eyes, almost as if he had expected her words.

"Please what, *chérie*? Please rip this fragile gown off my body? Please show me what a big, strong man you are?"

"No!" Faith drew back, stunned by the harshness of his words. "Oh, dear heaven, no!"

Was this Alexandre? This cold, coarse man whose features were so contorted with lust they barely seemed familiar? He should have been gazing at her with lovesick eyes, courting her tenderly, telling her every minute how much he adored her. She wondered if it was too late to change her mind, too late to tie the wrapper tighter around her waist and turn and leave. Did a woman have the right to come into a man's room in the middle of the night, arousing all his basest passions, and then just walk out the door? And would he let her if she tried?

The confusion written plainly on her face was enough to make Alexandre relent. "Shhhh, *petite,*" he whispered hoarsely. "Do not struggle so. You know I love it when you play your games with me, but the time for games is past."

This time Faith did not resist as his hands slid down the neck of her robe, parting it slowly, pushing it along her shoulders until there was nothing to hold it on her body any more. She had made a bargain, with this man as well as herself, and she would have to keep it.

Alexandre caught his breath in sheer excitement as he watched the silken robe slip away. Never in his life had he seen anything more alluring. Filmy, translucent white hugged rounded hips and full breasts, taking on subtle hints of pink, darkening provocatively into round circles where hard nipples jutted out at him. His body ached with longing, and he was tempted to take her as she was, pressing her down against the floor, not even bothering to rip off her gown as he entered her.

The naked hunger in his eyes fascinated Faith almost as much as it terrified her. These were not Alexandre's eyes any more—they were Brad Alleyn's eyes, dark blue and blazing with passion that offered nothing in return. Too late, she realized what she should have known all along. No matter how she tried, no matter how cool and sophisticated she pretended to be, she would never be her sister. She needed the security of love as much as the excitement. She needed all the words and promises that Fleur would have scorned.

"I am sorry. I am so desperately sorry. I cannot do this."

His eyes turned cold as he glared down at her. "You cannot—or you will not?"

Faith drew her hands upward, crossing her arms protectively over her breast. She knew she deserved all the bitter anger he was hurling at her.

"Try to understand, Alexandre. I—I. . . ." Why was it so hard to find words? Why couldn't she just blurt out the truth and have done with it. "You see, I'm . . . well, I—I've never done this before."

His face twisted into a puzzled expression, as if he was not sure he had heard her right. Then something seemed to snap inside him, and he threw back his head and laughed. It was a brittle, staccato sound.

Faith could only stare at him, trying to figure out what was going on in his mind. Then, slowly, she realized. He did not believe her. He simply did not believe! And God help her, she had only herself to blame. She had tried so hard to pretend she was Fleur, she had ended up convincing him.

She opened her mouth to plead with him again, then stopped even before she could form the words. There was nothing she could say to this man, no way she could convince him how sorry she was. Slowly, she inched toward the open doorway.

He reached it before her, thrusting out a long arm to block her way. With a sudden, swift movement, he raised his hand, bringing it down with a resounding crack on the side of her face.

"*Vache!*"

Faith reeled from the blow, crying out as she felt her back jam into the doorframe. Dear God, what had she done? Alexandre was a good man—a gentle man! Had she tormented him that cruelly? Had her selfish games driven him to such desperate extremes?

Her misery only angered him more. Gripping a corner of the desk, he squeezed it until his knuckles were white, as if he had to work himself into a frenzy to deal with her.

"Do you want me to hit you again? Is that it? Do you want me to throw you on the bed and force myself on you like a filthy animal? That's the way you like it, isn't it? That's the only thing that excites you."

"Oh, no—no!"

"No?" His voice was so rasping, Faith could hardly recognize it. "Are you lying to me—or yourself?"

Faith had the terrible, sickening feeling he was looking straight through to the depths of her soul. That *was* what she had wanted, that very afternoon when Brad grabbed her and pulled her toward him. She had wanted the force that would take away her right to decide—her need to admit her own responsibility. But she didn't want it now. Not with Alexandre.

"No, I am not lying. Not to myself, and especially not to you. I do want this passion that has risen between us—I want it desperately—but not like this. Not without love. Without commitments."

She did not wait to hear his answer, if indeed he had any answer. Spinning around, she raced through the door and out onto the piazza. All she wanted now was darkness, welcome, enveloping darkness, wiping away the ugly images of pain and betrayal in the eyes of a man who had once adored her. The night air was cold on her skin, the boards rough beneath bare feet as she fled along the side of the house and down the steps into the yard.

Eight

Faith flew down the rough path, barely feeling the ruts and stones that cut into her soles. She did not know where she was going—she did not know if instinct guided her or random chance—and she did not care. All she wanted was to put as much distance as she could between herself and the nightmare she had left behind.

Slender wisps of clouds, stretched into ribbons by the rising wind, floated across the moon, plunging the path into the eerie half light of undulating shadows. The darkness was almost a relief, even though it made each step a treacherous gamble. At least it offered an illusion of invisibility—a comfortable, deceptive feeling that the same black veil that hid her blushes could hide her shame as well.

At least a harlot keeps her promises.

Dear heaven, why did she keep hearing Brad's words? Why was it *his* scornful face that seemed emblazoned in the darkness around her? It was not Brad she had hurt so deeply, it was not Brad whose tender passions she had used until she twisted them all around, bringing out violence in a man intended by nature only to be gentle—and it certainly was not Brad she was running from now.

But, oh, God help her, it *was* Brad who had found the words to call her what she was.

Faith choked on the thought, gasping painfully as she stopped in the center of the path and tried to catch her breath. Tears dimmed her eyes, and she could no longer make out even vague hints of light in the open fields that surrounded her.

What a fool she had been to play at being Fleur. She had perfected the part all too well. She flirted with Alexandre, looking up at him through lowered lashes, but when he looked back, he saw only her sister. She went to him in the dark of night, slipping into his room with nothing but a thin silk wrapper covering her lacy nightgown—and he reached out and drew Fleur into his arms!

The minute she let him see Faith, the minute she gave him a glimpse of the soft, innocent, guileless girl who needed at least the illusion of love, he had turned away in anger and disgust.

Faith began to walk down the road again, moving slowly now, carefully, sliding her feet along the ground to feel the obstacles she could not see. The moon played games with her, coming out from under the clouds for a brilliant, blue-white instant, then pitching the world into darkness so thick she could almost reach out and touch it. Something about the path seemed hauntingly familiar, giving her the uncanny feeling she could walk all the way to the end and still come back, without once losing her way.

Fleur. It had always been "Fleur this," and "Fleur that," all those long years of growing up. Never, "Where is Faith?" "What does Faith want?" Now it was Fleur all over again.

No, not Fleur *again,* she reminded herself bitterly. In some dreadful, inevitable way, it had been Fleur all along. Oh, she had known a few moments of happiness with Alexandre, and she had been naive enough to think they were hers, but she had been wrong. Even those were Fleur's.

Slowly, almost imperceptibly, the quality of the air around her began to change, growing sultrier, more stifling, with each step she took. Faith paused, trying to pick out something in the pervasive darkness that would tell her where she was. A musty, stagnant odor, heavy with the scent of water, rushed into her nostrils, and she realized that somehow, without knowing it, she had wandered down toward the river.

A glimmering patch of gold shivered on the ground in front of her. Faith inched forward, curious to see what it was. To her surprise, she found not the optical illusion she had expected, but clear rays of warm light, reflecting off moist yellow dirt. Glancing up, she saw that the moon was free of its web of clouds. Only the branches of a thick grove of trees kept it from flooding the earth with color.

But there were no groves on the riverbank, she thought, suddenly apprehensive, though she couldn't tell why. At least she didn't think there were. Surely Brad had told her all the trees along the shore had been cleared away years ago—or had she just assumed it because somehow the thought made her more comfortable? A tight feeling contracted her chest as she forced her feet to the side of the road, groping toward dark, indefinable forms that were only vaguely visible. Even before her fingers came in contact with the tree trunk, she knew what they would feel—the slickness of moss on bark that had never been touched by the sun. And she knew the tree was a live-oak.

A live-oak . . . Faith could almost see it again, dark gray against the murky gray of a London fog. Branches dripping with long streamers of moss, hanging heavily to the earth; mud oozing around her ankles, threatening to suck her into warm, moist depths. And any minute now, the first pale light of dawn would quiver through the trees, and she would know her sister's fate had been sealed.

No wonder her feet had been so eager to bring her to this spot—this was the swamp she had seen the morning Fleur died! And no wonder the patch seemed so familiar. Her hand was trembling as she drew it back from the tree, curling her fingers around the diamond locket at her neck. Whatever had happened to her sister, this place had something to do with it. If she ever hoped to find the truth, she could not run away from it now.

The ground turned to soft slime, seeping up between her toes, as Faith left the path and began to twist a circuitous course between the trees. She had no idea where she was, or even what direction she was going, but she was not alarmed. Instinct had brought her this far. Surely it would carry her the rest of the way as well.

Long, clinging fingers of gray moss brushed against her cheeks, stretching out slimy tendrils to coil in an unwanted embrace around her neck. Faith jumped back, slipping through the mud in her eagerness to get away from them. Rubbing her cheek with her hand, she tried not to think of all the vile insects and vermin that must be nesting there. It was enough to hear faint splashes in the mud around her, low, slithering, sinister sounds, and know she was not alone in the swamp.

Faith had always hated snakes, even when she lived in London. Only it was easier to hate them there, she thought, forcing a rueful smile to her lips. There, she had known she was safe in the city, and every snake in England was off somewhere in the woods or countryside. Here, every time her foot slid into a pool of slush, she cringed with revulsion, waiting for some adder or water moccasin to crawl across her toes or twine its way up her leg. Irritated with herself, she brushed the thought aside. She could not afford weakness now, she reminded herself sternly. She could not think of snakes or vermin swarming through gray moss, or even the dangers that lay ahead of her in the darkness. All she could think of was Fleur and the vow she had made to avenge her death.

An owl screeched somewhere in the distance, and Faith paused, listening to its eerie wail. How different it had sounded only a short time before, when she had stood in the doorway of Alexandre's room and looked in at him where he sat with his head bent over his papers. If only she hadn't been so foolish then—if only she told him how desperately she needed tenderness and love—perhaps she would be lying in his embrace now. She stood and listened for a long time, but the owl did not cry out again, and the night was heavy with silence.

Even the stillness was deceptive, teeming with unseen life as if somewhere beneath the dark surface of muddy waters, faint rustles and subtle movements could be heard if only the ear was sharp enough to pick them up. The wind began to rise again, gently, for Faith could not feel its cooling touch, but with a low moan through the trees, like the cry of a woman in pain.

Faith shivered as the sound faded away, wondering if it had really been as poignant as it seemed, or if she had imagined it all. But as it came again, a little louder this time, a little sharper, she knew imagination had nothing to do with it. That was no wailing of the wind. And it was no animal howling either!

Rigid with apprehension, Faith turned around slowly, trying to pierce the darkness with her eyes, but she could see nothing save the faint outline of nearby trees. Someone was in trouble, she was sure of that now, and she was almost certain it was a woman. But who could she be? And how could Faith hope to find her in the darkness?

And what would be waiting for her if she did?

What if Eleazar Carstairs had been right after all? The thought sent cold tremors up and down her spine. What if the slaves who escaped the Stono River uprising really were hiding out in the swamps? She had dismissed the whole idea as a sadistic joke the first time she heard it; now she was not so certain. If they were somewhere nearby, if they were quarreling among themselves tonight, if one of them was beating his woman. . . .

If, if, *if!* Angrily, Faith brushed all speculation aside. What did a thousand if's count against a single cry of pain? She could feel the wind now, sharp and biting through the thin fabric of her nightgown, but she knew she was not shivering from the cold. Somewhere out there, a woman needed help. Free woman or slave, it did not matter—if Faith turned away now, she would never be able to live with herself again.

She did not try to move for a minute, but stood absolutely still, waiting for the cry to reach her ears again, hoping against hope that when it did, she would be able to figure out where it was coming from. At first she had no luck. Then, slowly, she began to pinpoint the direction. Turning to the right, she managed to pick out a dark blot against the sky, marking the spot where a low hill sloped up from the river.

The woods grew less and less dense as she climbed, the ground more solid under her feet with each step, and Faith realized with a deep breath of relief that she had left the stale swamp air behind her in the lowlands. The moon was up to its old tricks again, giving no more than brief, tantalizing glimpses of the scenery around her, but at least the land was relatively clear, and there were few trees to block out the light. Faith paused a few yards from the crest of the hill, letting the wind whip her long white skirt out in front of her. The sensation of coldness was a welcome caress against skin hot with the sweat of exertion and fear.

By the time she reached the top, the clouds had at last begun to thin, and a hazy light settled over the shallow hollow that greeted her. Faith stopped, marveling at the silhouettes of deep-blue-green trees against the sky, and thought how good it was to be able to see everything again. It was a moment before she realized that the light that illuminated the landscape for her also made a tall, white-garbed figure frighteningly visible to anyone lurking in the shadows below. Reacting belatedly, she ran for the nearest tree, pressing her body against it as if somehow its slender trunk could shield her from watching eyes. Catching her breath, she waited, listening for the telltale sounds that would tell her she had been seen. When she heard nothing, she knew her luck had held. If anyone was there, they had not spotted her—at least not yet!

The bark felt surprisingly dry in her hand, a welcome contrast to the moss that draped the live-oaks below. Faith let her head sink gratefully against its smooth surface as she scanned the hollow, waiting for her eyes to adjust to the dim light. A sudden movement, just where the drop of the slope began to rise again, caught her attention, and she turned toward it, squinting to make out figures she could barely see.

There were two of them, a man and a woman, crouching

against the earth. No, not crouching—sprawling across a patch of grass so deep and green it looked black in the moonlight. To her horror, Faith saw that they were engaged in a fierce struggle, writhing and twisting on the ground, and the woman seemed to be getting the worst of it! The man lay on top of her, a huge, muscular savage, his clothes so black it was impossible to tell where fabric left off and glistening skin began. Beneath him the girl looked slight and fragile, a helpless victim, squirming to free herself from the terrible vise of his brutality.

Frantic with fear, Faith searched the ground for a weapon—the fallen branch of a tree, a stone lying loose on the soil, anything she could use to protect herself!—but she could find nothing. Not that it mattered, she reminded herself harshly. The man was too powerful, too menacing, to face, even with a stout stick in her hand.

One last cloud passed over the face of the moon, blotting out the light for a brief second. As it withdrew, the world was bathed in a new white clarity, almost as bright as day. For the first time, everything was sharp and distinct to Faith's eyes. What she saw made her gasp with shock.

The man was not clothed in black, as she had assumed—the blackness was his flesh, naked from head to foot. And the girl was not fighting to tear herself from his clutches, scratching and clawing for her freedom. She was lying willingly beneath him, her long limbs entwined around his torso. The cry that escaped her lips could no longer be mistaken for a cry of pain!

Faith stared at the two of them, mesmerized by the feverish rhythm of their movement. The man's body was a powerful machine, heaving up and down, thrusting again and again into pliant flesh beneath. The girl's legs caught him in a wrenching grip, holding him close, then setting him free to plunge even deeper into her body. Faith could feel the pain of every thrust in her own flesh—she could sense the same primitive madness that was driving them both to peaks of frenzy. Unconsciously, her lips parted, letting out a soft cry.

The couple heard it instantly. The man paused, his muscles tensing, his head rising slowly to search the slopes. The woman eased herself from beneath him, clutching patterned blue gingham against bare breasts in an instinctive shield. After a moment, she, too, raised her head, shaking long, dark hair away from strongly molded features.

Estee! A rush of anger welled up in Faith as she recognized her. One of their own household servants! How could the girl have done this to her? Faith had been so worried, so frightened, when she heard the cries. She had been ready to risk her own life to help. And now she found it was only Estee out on the prowl, no better than a cat in heat! It was like a slap in the face—a personal act of betrayal!

The male had spotted her now. He stood up, slowly at first, then with a speed that seemed out of place in so big a man. Faith stared at him, fascinated and horrified both as she realized that nothing—absolutely nothing!—covered his nakedness. It was a second before shock receded enough for her to understand what was going through his head.

The white girl had seen them! That was what he was thinking—that was what he had to be thinking! The white girl had seen them, and now she was a threat to them both. Slave justice was swift and brutal. For them, the punishment for fornication might well be as savage as the punishment for murder—if they were caught!

Terrified, Faith began to race down the hill, trying desperately to reach the woods at the bottom. Pain scraped through her knee as she stumbled, sliding along the sandy soil, but she forced herself up, limping on at the same breakneck speed. The hill had seemed so short when she climbed it; now it was interminable. Oh, God, if only the trees were not so far away! If only she could reach the dense undergrowth before the man caught up with her!

"No. Rodrigo—no!"

Faith heard the cry, a long, anguished plea somewhere behind her, but she did not stop, or even pause to look over her shoulders. She knew Estee was calling out to the man—she knew she was begging him to stop—but she did not know if he would listen, and she dared not take the chance.

She reached the trees at last, but instead of the security she longed for, she found only renewed fear. The earth made a hideous, squishing sound every time she slapped her feet against it, spattering mud on the hem of her gown, and she was sure the man must hear her, no matter where he was. But there was nothing she could do about it, no way she could slow down enough to slip silently through the trees. Even now, he might be right behind her!

Heaven help her, what had she done to herself? Why had she been such a prude? That could have been her—that *should* have been her—entwined in Brad's embrace on a sunswept hillside instead of running in terror through the night. Those should have been Brad's muscles, strong and hard, pressing against——

Brad? Even in her frantic flight, Faith realized how absurd she was being. What was she thinking? Fear must have dulled her brain. Brad was not the one she longed for. Not Brad at all. Alexandre. If only she were safe in Alexandre's arms right now.

She did not feel the pain that shot through her ankle, it all happened too suddenly. She was conscious only of the swift, terrifying sensation of flying forward through empty space. She thrust out her hands to break her fall, but it was no use. Her fingers slid through the mud, and her head snapped to one side, cracking against a rock embedded in the earth. A blinding flash of pain raced through her body; then she felt nothing.

"Faith!"

The voice seemed to swirl through the darkness around her, sharp and demanding, yet strangely elusive. Faith tried to focus on it, but she could not force her mind to concentrate. Her sister. It sounded like her sister. But Fleur wasn't here—she couldn't be.

"Faith—Faith!"

There it was again, the same voice, too persistent to ignore. Groggily, Faith opened her eyes, trying not to feel the awful throbbing that beat against her temples. At first, she could see nothing. Then the faint outline of a tall feminine form began to emerge from a blur of nausea and pain.

"Estee . . . ?"

The black girl leaned forward, dark eyes brimming with concern.

"Oh, Faith—Miss Faith! Thank heaven you're all right."

"But what . . . ?" Faith barely mouthed the words, trying to figure out what the girl was doing there. Slowly, hazy images began to come back. Tall grasses, deep green in the moonlight. Black skin, glistening as if it had been rubbed with oil. Long, lean limbs twisted into a lover's knot.

"Oh, my God, that was you! There in the hollow."

"We didn't mean any harm, Miss Faith. I swear we didn't!" Estee knelt in the mud, slipping anxious hands under Faith's head, trying to urge her up. "We had no idea you were there. We would never do anything to hurt you!"

With an effort, Faith forced herself to a sitting position. Her head hurt worse than ever, and waves of nausea flooded her body.

"Oh, Estee, how could you? In the open fields—like an animal!"

Estee pulled back, retreating into herself again. Moonlight filtered through the trees, lingering on features so rigid and expressionless they might have been carved from ebony.

"Where would you have us go, white girl? We are not like you. We do not have grand houses with rooms of our own to cavort in."

Faith watched the last traces of warmth fade from Estee's eyes, and she hated herself for her childish outburst. That had been jealousy talking, not reason. Reason would have reminded her it was wrong to envy another woman the courage she herself lacked.

"I am not judging you, Estee." After what had happened that day, how could she judge anyone? "But if you care enough about this man to . . . well, to do *that* with him, why don't you marry him?"

Estee stood, rising with a single fluid motion. She held her head high as she looked down at the young woman in the dirt at her feet.

"You think I do not want to marry him? You think he does not want to marry me? We love each other, my Rodrigo and I. We would give our souls to live together as man and wife!"

Faith rose more slowly, feeling through the mud with bare toes to find a foothold. What on earth had she said to make Estee so angry? "But I don't understand. Really I don't. If you want to marry——"

"No, you *don't* understand!" Estee's nostrils flared with contempt. "And you never will. You aren't a slave—I am! 'Go live in a little room in the back of the house, Estee,' they tell me, and I go live in a little room in the back of the house. 'You are going to eat hog jowl and beans while we have venison and syllabub and cider from Virginia in the main house,' and I eat hog jowl and beans! 'Go and work in the gardens, Estee.' 'Go be a lady's maid.' Like it or not, I do what I'm told—and when the time comes, I'll marry whom I'm told. If I marry at all!"

With a quick, defiant gesture, she tossed her hair in the wind, and turned and began to follow the path again, leaving Faith to catch up as best she could. Night sounds seemed unnaturally loud in the uncomfortable silence between them. Twigs snapped beneath their feet with the force of firecrackers; a frog croaked somewhere nearby, startling them as it splashed into a rice pond; an owl hooted its haunting call in the distance.

The sky was clear as they emerged from the swampland,

the moon so bright Faith could see every blade of grass on the banks that divided the rice fields into tidy squares. Surreptitiously, she stole a glance at Estee's profile. How beautiful she seemed—and how unyielding. Had *she* looked like that, too? she wondered. The tragic, ill-fated Katherine.

"Estee. . . ."

The soft hesitation in her voice was more compelling than a command. Estee stopped, fixing cautious eyes on her face.

"What do you want?"

"I went for a walk on the hillside this afternoon. There were three graves there."

Estee nodded coolly. Her expression did not change. "I wondered when you would find them."

Faith hesitated, half sorry now that she had spoken. But she had to finish what she had begun.

"Those children, those three little boys . . . were they born to your mother?"

"Why do you ask? You know they were."

"And the father?"

Estee did not answer; she did not need to. Adam Eliot's name was on those markers, his shame branded indelibly in cold stone. Faith was sick with revulsion as she looked at Estee, seeing in her the same exotic beauty that had proved her mother's downfall. *I am not a servant,* Estee had told her once. *I am a slave.* Faith was beginning to understand at last what that meant.

"Is that why. . . ." She faltered on words too ugly to utter aloud. She didn't give a fig about Brad—he could be as much of a beast as he wanted!—but she would weep if Estee's fate were to be her mother's. "Is that why Brad won't let you marry your lover? Because you are too beautiful to give away?"

To her surprise, Estee only shrugged, as if the whole thing did not matter. She looked tired, even bored, as she headed for the house.

"I do not know if Mr. Alleyn would let me marry Rodrigo or not. I never asked him."

"You never asked?" Faith hurried forward, grabbing Estee's arm and whirling her around. "Well, I never! Honestly, Estee, what a ninny you are. I know Brad is a hard master, but he's not cruel. Surely he'll let you marry your young man if you ask him."

"You still don't understand, do you? I do not ask Mr. Alleyn because it is not for him to say yes or no. Rodrigo—no, not Rodrigo, Prince! His name is Prince, no matter how we both pretend—*Prince* does not belong to him."

"To whom, then?"

"Eleazar Carstairs."

The wind picked up, biting through the thin fabric of Faith's nightgown. She shivered in the unexpected cold. Eleazar Carstairs. She still had a vivid picture of him in her mind. A small man, nattily dressed, fond of a one-sided joke. He did not strike her as the kind who would be generous with his slaves. This time it was she who turned away, leaving Estee to follow her across the wide lawn.

"Perhaps we can work something out," she mused thoughtfully. After all, slaves were shuttled from plantation to plantation all the time. Sometimes it seemed inhumane, with father separated from son and friend from friend, but maybe this time, the system could be used to advantage. "Your Prince seems strong and healthy. I'm sure Brad would be willing to buy him."

Estee's only reaction was a sharp, mirthless laugh.

"Haven't you figured out yet that Eleazar Carstairs hates my master? He and everyone else in this God-forsaken place. As far as he's concerned, Brad Alleyn is 'a damn sight too easy on his niggers!'—and that's a sin around here. Carstairs would cut off his arm before he would sell him a strong black man. And so would everyone else!"

"But there must be a way. If I were to ask Brad——"

"No!" Estee's voice cracked with emotion. Her hand trembled as she stretched it out to Faith. "You must not tell—promise you will not tell! If my master knew I had a lover, he would forbid me to see him again. If he had to, he would lock me in my hut to keep me from him."

Faith wavered, unsure of herself. She had the terrible feeling Estee was right. If Brad didn't buy the girl's lover, how else could he protect her from Carstair's spiteful wrath?

"You mustn't tell!" Despair had driven away the last traces of pride. She was ready to plead now—to grovel and beg if she had to. "You must promise not to tell. Promise! I will die if I cannot see my man again."

Her hand still quivered in the air, but she did not try to press it closer. Slowly, Faith reached up and clasped it in her own.

"Oh, Estee, I don't know. . . ."

But she *did* know, she told herself objectively. She had known all along, only she was too frightened to admit it. Estee might be foolish, she might have made the wrong choice—but it was her choice to make. It was her future, her life, she was gambling.

"All right," she whispered. "I won't tell."

It had been a good bargain and a bad one both, Faith decided later as she nestled into soft pillows, relishing the feel of clean sheets against freshly bathed skin. Long hair, brushed until it shone, cascaded over bare shoulders, covering her breasts and belly. Good, because the warmth of a hand in hers at last was like nourishment after a long famine of loneliness. Bad, because it left the burden of someone else's life on her own slender shoulders.

Her eyes slipped down to the blue wrapper, neatly folded at the foot of the bed. It had been there when she returned, mute witness to the fact that Alexandre had come and gone—and not bothered to leave a word for her! Just a casual gesture, the return of a robe she had left carelessly in his room, but it was eloquent enough to tell her everything she needed to know. For Alexandre, what had happened that night had been trivial and unimportant. A thing too insignificant even for anger.

The whole evening had been a farce of misunderstanding, Faith thought, wishing she had the objectivity to laugh at it. It was certainly funny enough. What a picture she must have made, standing in the swamp in nothing but a sheer nightdress, trying to pretend she was some sort of latter-day Cassandra. Every call of the owl was an omen, every brush of gray moss against her cheek a prophesy of doom. All that mystical power—and what had it gotten her? A nasty crack on the head!

She had felt so grown up, so daring, when she slipped into Alexandre's room—and all she had done was prove what a child she was! She had made a fool of herself, a complete, utter fool, and in the bargain, she ruined all her chances with the one man she truly wanted.

And the worst of it was, she was going to have to face him every day of her stay at Havenhurst!

Well, there was nothing for it, she thought, grimacing at the idea. She was going to have to make her peace with Alexandre, and that was that. They could not spend all their time tiptoeing around the house, trying to avoid each other and turning crimson with embarrassment every time they failed. Tomorrow she would bare her soul to him—humiliating as the whole idea sounded!—and it would all be out in the open at last.

Yes, tomorrow, she promised herself sleepily, wrapping her

arms around the pillow and pressing it against her cheek. Tomorrow she would tell Alexandre everything. She could not make him care for her again—it was too late for that—but at least she could make him understand.

Tomorrow, Faith thought as she sat on a hard wooden bench in the library and tried not to listen to the sound of footsteps in the hall outside, was one thing when it was really tomorrow, and quite another when it became today! Just the thought that it might be Alexandre out there—that she might have to utter the careful little speech she had rehearsed over and over in front of her mirror—was enough to make her heart flutter with pure terror.

She strained her ears, but she could not hear the footsteps any longer, and she knew someone was standing in the doorway, just a few feet away from where she sat. It took all her courage to raise her eyes. Her face grew ashen when she saw the man she both longed for and dreaded.

All the pretty speeches vanished from her mind. "Oh, Alexandre, I—I don't know what to say to you."

He strode into the room, then stopped abruptly, his face as red as hers was pale.

"Faith, don't. Please don't say anything."

"But I want to. I *have* to."

"No, *ma chère*. If anyone is going to say the words, it must be me. I was a beast last night—a scoundrel! I have no right to ask you to forgive me, but——"

"Forgive *you?*" Faith was stunned. This was not at all the way she had expected things to go. "Oh, Alexandre——"

"No, let me go on. I didn't sleep at all, thinking about this, wondering what I was going to say to you. I tried to find you last night—I tried to tell you how badly I felt—but you weren't in your room."

The wrapper! He hadn't just tossed it on her bed, then left without another thought. It was only an excuse. He wanted to see her—he wanted to be with her!

"I couldn't sleep either. I went for a walk."

"Oh, my sweet Faith—if only you knew what you looked like, standing in the doorway of my room with the moonlight behind you. And that absurd negligee, so thin every contour of your breasts——" He broke off, pounding his fist angrily against the wall. When he turned back to her, his face was tense. "Blast it, Faith, I know it's no excuse, but can you imagine what I thought when I saw you there?"

Faith flushed guiltily. Of course she could imagine! He thought exactly what she had intended him to think.

"Alexandre, I'm so sorry. . . ."

"Don't be sorry, *chérie*. The fault is mine, not yours. I saw a flirtatious smile, and I read things into it that were not there. I saw lashes quivering on pink cheeks, and I forgot how tempting it is for a pretty young girl to try her wiles on a man."

"You make me ashamed of myself. You are so understanding, and I——"

"Ashamed? Of what? Of being young and lovely? Of making me want you so much I couldn't control myself?"

Faith listened in a daze. She had been so frightened of this encounter, so sure he was going to look at her with ice in his eyes—just the way Brad would have—and tell her what a bitch she was. Instead, he leaned over her, taking her hands tenderly in his.

"I still want you, Faith—more than ever. Only now I'm wise enough to know I will never conquer your body without first surrendering my own heart."

Faith tried to respond, but she could think of nothing to say. She felt a light tremor in the masculine hands that held hers, but she could not for the life of her understand what it meant.

Alexandre smiled at her confusion. "Why so silent, *chérie?* I have never seen you at a loss for words before. Don't you know I am asking you to be my wife?"

"Your . . . wife?"

The room seemed to spin around. Faith caught her breath, trying to get her head straight. Wife? Had he said wife? But no one ever said that to her. Fleur, yes—men were always flinging their hearts at Fleur's feet—but not her.

"Aren't you going to give me an answer? Ah, but perhaps my proposal was not good enough. I suppose you want me down on my knees on the floor."

"On your knees?" Faith was intoxicated with excitement. This was every dream she had ever dreamed. This beautiful, sophisticated, gentle man actually wanted her! "Of course on your knees! I never consider proposals from men who are not on their knees."

He laughed, delighted with the childlike exuberance he had not expected. Still holding her hands, he sank down on one knee.

"No, no, not *one* knee!" Faith took back her hands, folding them primly in her lap. "Two! I demand two knees."

Still laughing, he complied, dropping the other knee to the floor. The corners of Faith's lips turned up as she watched him. How awkward he looked, how touchingly clumsy, kneeling on the carpet in front of her.

"I must warn you, my love. If you persist in this insane folly, I fully intend to say yes."

"Ah, Faith. . . ." All the laughter was gone now. Only tender devotion shone in his eyes. "My sweet, darling Faith, I cannot give you one-half the riches I want for you, and I am not one-tenth the man you deserve. But if love counts for anything, you have all of my heart, now and forever. Will you do me the honor of becoming my wife?"

"Oh, yes!" Even the words were perfect. It was just the way she had imagined it, the first time she saw him. The fairy tale prince and the princess lived happily ever after. "Yes, Alexandre—yes, yes, yes!"

She had dared, and she had won! She had finally stopped imitating Fleur and let him see that she was really Faith. And miracle of miracles! it turned out to be Faith he wanted all the time.

"Come, sweet love," she teased, extending coaxing hands to him. "Don't you feel silly there on the floor? Come to my arms where you belong."

Nine

Fleur should have been there.

Faith stood at the top of the stairway, listening to the sound of music floating up from the grand salon, and thought how much sweeter this day would have been if she could have shared it with her sister. Sighing, she stepped over to the narrow window at the end of the hall and stared down into the empty gardens below. This was the moment she had waited for all her life—the day that had filled her fantasies for years—but it was not the same without Fleur.

Fleur should have been right there beside her. No, hardly *beside* her, she thought with a smile. Not for Fleur the role of the prim bridesmaid, waiting patiently in a quiet hallway while all the guests were giggling and gossiping downstairs. Fleur had to see everything—she had to be a part of it all! She would have been halfway down the steps by now, leaning precariously over the balustrade to check out each new arrival.

"There's Eleazar Carstairs' wife," she would have called up. "Oh, do come and look, Faith! She's just like we imagined. Thin and pale—and she might as well be a widow already in frumpy black. And Frances Hardin! Good Lord, purple satin? And she's fatter than Samuel!"

"Shhh!" Faith would have whispered, trying very hard not to laugh. Laughter always encouraged Fleur. "They'll hear you."

"What does it matter if they do? Those old biddies are so puffed up with their own importance, they'll all think I'm talking about someone else!"

And they would have, too, Faith thought, letting herself laugh at the idea. She could almost see Fleur's green eyes sparkling with mischief as she tossed out one outrageous insult after another, managing to make them all funny. And somewhere between a deft verbal autopsy on the minister's spinster sister and a devastatingly droll sketch of poor Lord Warren, Faith would completely forget she had ever been nervous.

Fleur would have waited until then to tease her—and she would have picked her moment perfectly. Looking very solemn, she would have walked up the stairs, shaking her head as she paused to study her sister.

"Didn't I always say you'd settle down with some stodgy man and raise a passel of brats?"

She would have been joking—Fleur was always joking—but Faith would rise to the bait.

"Alexandre is not stodgy. He's not stodgy at all!"

"Of course he is! He's the stodgiest man I ever saw—and not a bit good-looking! I don't in the least envy you a wedding night in his arms."

How she would have laughed then. But her laughter would have lasted only a minute. Turning suddenly very serious, she would have reached out and caught her sister's hand.

"Be happy, Faith—oh, please be happy! I do love you very much, dear little sister. I want nothing in the world but joy for you."

Faith turned away from the window, conscious of tears on her lashes, dimming the empty hallway until it was barely a blur of light. The music was hushed now, even the last flurry of excited whispers had died away, and she knew it was time to move slowly toward the head of the stairs, leaving yesterday and all its longings behind.

No bride could have looked lovelier. A deceptively simple sacque, tailored from a length of white kincob brocade, was so elegant it might have been imported all the way from Europe, not fashioned in a few days to suit an impatient bridegroom who could wait no longer to claim his prize. Softness and purity were emphasized by the deep point-lace ruffles that trimmed the sleeves and formed a charming cap for golden curls. Delicate pink rosebuds, meticulously embroidered along the hem of a sheer silk petticoat, picked up the subtle flush in Faith's cheeks; the color was repeated one last time in a tiny nosegay pinned to her bosom. She wore only one jewel—the diamond at her throat.

She had nearly reached the bottom of the stairs when she looked up and saw the one man she had not expected standing in the doorway of the salon. He made a compelling figure—she had to admit that, even now—but then he had always been compelling, right from the beginning when she stepped out of the dugout canoe and saw him riding like a savage down from the hills. She gripped the banister tightly in one hand, clinging to it to keep her balance.

She had not seen Brad for several days, not since the morning after Alexandre proposed, but she would never forget a single detail of that painful encounter. Even now it made her blush to think of it.

He had looked especially attractive that day, too, as he glanced in the doorway of the music room. Tight russet britches emphasized slender hips and strong masculine thighs, and a clean white work shirt, open at the neck, showed glimpses of dark blond hair beneath.

"What are all these rumors I've been hearing?" he asked dryly. "Surely you aren't serious about committing holy matrimony with old Alex?"

Faith let her fingers rest idly on the keyboard. She had enjoyed the moment, then, without a touch of apprehension. It was wonderfully satisfying to see the look of annoyance in his eye.

"And why not, pray tell? Who better to share my life with than Alexandre?"

"Who better? Anyone, my dear. Choose another man—a dozen, if you will—but leave Alex alone. He'll never be right for you."

"Why, Bradford Alleyn, do I detect a hint of green in your eyes? Don't tell me you're jealous?"

"Call it what you want. But for God's sake, use a little common sense, Faith. It's easy to put on a white dress and say the right words in front of a minister. It's a damn sight harder to spend the rest of your life regretting it."

Faith was fascinated with the turn the conversation was taking. She had expected opposition, but not like this! This wasn't the way a man talked when he had just gotten a mild boot in the ego. This was the way he talked when he loved a woman and wanted her for himself!

It occurred to her that it might be amusing to make him admit it out loud.

"A dozen men? But what on earth would I do with a dozen, pray tell? One is quite enough."

"Then make sure he's the right one."

"And who might that be? You?"

He leaned against the doorframe, his eyes a little too candid for comfort.

"You could do worse, you know. You want me—and I want you. We'd be fools to deny it, either of us."

Faith could hardly believe how easy it was. Just a few well-chosen words and she'd have this man eating out of her hands. Not that she wanted him, of course—she wouldn't have him if he were the last man on earth!—but after the misery he'd put her through, she had a right to make him squirm.

"Dare I trust my ears, sir? What have I done to encourage such boldness? When have I ever given you cause to believe I would abandon Alexandre and marry you?"

"*Marry?*" Up went an eyebrow, with just enough of a question to be distinctly disconcerting. "Did I say anything about marriage?"

"Well, I—I just assumed. . . ."

White teeth flashed against sun-bronzed skin. "Never assume, my dear. You can get yourself in a lot of trouble that way. I am not a marrying man—and I never will be."

Oh, sweet heaven! Even days later, Faith's stomach still turned somersaults at the thought of it. Why—oh, *why*—hadn't she had the sense to pick up what was left of her dignity and walk out of the room? Why had she had to open her mouth again?

"But—but you said you wanted me."

He had roared with laughter. An ugly, humiliating sound that went right through her.

"And so I do, my pet. I want you passionately! In my *bed*—where you belong."

A wave of faintness swept over Faith as she drew her hand back from the railing and forced herself down the last few steps. At least Brad's vulgarity had accomplished one thing. If she had had any last lingering doubts about whether she was marrying the right man, they were gone now.

She raised her chin defiantly when she reached him, waiting for the sarcasm that did not come. Instead, his smile was generous, his arm almost inviting as he held it out to her.

"How very beautiful you look. Your father would have been proud of his little diamond today."

His words caught Faith off guard. She hesitated, confused by the tears that came to her eyes for the second time that day. First Fleur—now her father. It had never occurred to her a bride could feel so lonely.

For once, feminine tears evoked no scorn in Brad. He waited patiently, then when she did not move, took her hand and slipped it through his arm.

"As Adam's friend, let me stand in for him today."

Only a few impressions of the next half hour stood out in Faith's mind. The comforting strength of Brad's arm as he led her down the long aisle toward a makeshift altar at the end of the grand salon. The funny feeling when she looked up and saw dozens of faces all around her—no, not dozens, hundreds surely!—and realized that every one of them belonged to a stranger. The bored, nasal tones of the minister, a Huguenot imported especially from one of the French settlements on the Santee to recite the words she had memorized years ago. The way Alexandre's hand shook when he tried to slip the ring on her finger and she had to reach up and help him.

Then, suddenly, everyone was crowding around her, congratulating her and telling her how pretty she looked, and Faith realized with a burst of excitement that it was all over. It had actually happened! That wonderful, magical moment that girls whispered about and dreamed of—and always secretly feared would never come for them. No longer was she plain little Faith Eliot, unwanted by any man. Now she was *Mrs.* Alexandre Juilliard, a married lady, with a whole new place in the world.

The festivities began almost the instant the ceremony ended. Long rows of chairs were whisked away by dark-skinned men in clean white gloves, and tables laden with crystal and silver appeared under the windows, transforming the sweet serenity of a flower-decked chapel into a glittering banquet hall. Faith watched with wide eyes, fascinated by the activity. Did these bizarre Colonials always outdo themselves when they got together, she wondered, or was all this extravagance only Brad's way of letting her know he had a conscience after all? Not that it mattered, she thought, smiling to herself. This was quite the liveliest gala she had ever been to, and she was going to enjoy it to the hilt!

So much food had been heaped on the tables, the long boards literally bent under the weight of it. Huge spiced hams, dotted with cloves and peppercorns, and all crusty with a white wine glaze on top, dominated the buffet, but they had more than ample competition: pale slices of cold roast veal in savory meat jelly; pheasant from the woods, succulent in a smooth claret sauce, accented by shallots, mace, and pepper; oyster-and-sweetbread pie, baked in a thick crust and topped with heavy cream; mutton with cucumbers fried in lemon juice; a salmi of wild duck, dressed in bacon and sweet herbs;

whole platters of spiced cantaloupe, cherries steeped in brandy, and heavenly little wafers of paper-thin lemon.

Faith took at least a bite of everything, heaping her plate until she couldn't stuff another morsel on it. She had been too nervous to eat before, and she had not realized until now how hungry she was. The whalebone stays of her corset dug painfully into her ribs, but she popped one last piece of tipsy cake into her mouth anyway, greedily licking her fingers. The Colonials might be crude, but she had to give them one thing at least—they set an uncommonly splendid table.

Champagne corks popped amidst loud bursts of laughter, and the band struck up a lilting tune, perfect for the rollicking round of dancing that would follow. The music sounded strange to Faith's ears, with far too many violins and basses, and not a single flute, but it was rousing and fun, and she could not help enjoying it.

Twilight had already fallen, and the polished hardwood floor sparkled with reflections of a thousand tiny candle flames. Faith took a glass of champagne from one of the overladen trays and lifted it to her lips, letting the bubbles tickle her nose.

"Here, here! A toast! A toast!"

The cry was too loud to ignore. Faith couldn't help laughing when she caught sight of old Samuel Hardin, balancing on tiptoe on the seat of a straight-backed chair. The lower buttons of his waitcoat had come undone, and his wig was so crooked, one pudgy ear stuck out, but he looked as stiff and pompous as the day she had met him. A half-empty glass was raised in his hand.

"I avail myself of this auspicious opportunity to propose a libation. Unite with me, friends, in proffering to this resplendent couple our most lugubrious blessings."

An expectant titter ran through the crowd. Sober, Samuel Hardin was preposterous enough; drunk he was like a caricature of himself. With cries of "Here, Sam!" and "You show 'em, Sam!" they egged him on.

He was only too ready to oblige.

"Felicity, dear children," he called out, his voice quivering with enthusiasm. "Felicity, complacency, prosperity! May you find the Elysium you seek, the temporal garden of Eden, the golden Arcadia——"

"Enough, Samuel!" a raucous voice chimed in. "Spare our ears and let us wet our whistles!"

Hardin's round cheeks reddened with disappointment.

Robbed of his verbosity, he hardly seemed to know what to say.

"Well, then, here's to . . . here's to the gride and broom!"

Faith laughed with the others. Could this be the same Sam Hardin she had despised so much yesterday? Now that he was no longer calling her a frivolous little trollop, she almost found him endearing. Turning, she saw Lord Warren at her side.

"I wonder if I'm supposed to be the gride—whatever that is. Or, heaven forbid, the broom!"

"Ah, not a poor stick of a broom surely. Not with those voluptuous curves."

Faith was surprised to hear herself giggle. She wondered if it was the champagne, or just her own high spirits, but even Lord Warren couldn't upset her today. What a phony he was! Trying so hard to look like a lecher, when all the time he was nothing but a kindly, rather clumsy man who only wanted to be friendly.

The orchestra began to play again, and Faith whirled from partner to partner, leaving her new husband to take the hands of men she had never met before, then floating back to him with a carefree abandon that took her breath away. Fleur had always loved to dance; at last she understood why. The music wove a spell of magic around her, the rhythm caught her body in its subtle enchantment—and nothing in the world was quite as exciting as seeing a handsome young stranger gaze down at her with adoration in his eyes.

Only when she found herself face-to-face with Brad did she feel a sudden rush of trepidation. She wished she could think of an excuse to stop dancing—how much easier it would be if only she could bat helpless lashes at him and tell him how very, *very* tired she was and how *desperately* she longed to sit this one out—but how could she refuse the man whose money had paid for the music? Besides, this was her party, her night, and she was not going to be cheated out of a second of it!

"Well, who are you this time?" she quipped, careful not to let the steps of the dance bring them too close together. "Are you that thoughtful man who met me at the foot of the stairs a few hours ago? Or are you the arrogant scoundrel who delights in making fun of me?"

He laughed easily, spinning her into the center of the room. "Why are we always sparring, Faith? Is there some reckless streak in me that can't resist taunting pretty young things—or are you just devilish enough to goad me into it every time?"

Faith stopped right in the middle of the floor. If this was the way things were going to go, she wasn't sure she wanted to finish the dance.

"Well, I seem to have my answer. A whole evening of thoughtfulness from you—that would have been too much to expect, wouldn't it?"

His lips turned up in a wry grin. "I guess I deserve that." Laying a light hand on her waist, he led her away from the other dancers, toward a quiet corner next to the windows. "I promised myself I wasn't going to be flippant, but you see how I keep my word—at least to myself! There's something in my nature that abhors the need to apologize, and I am trying very hard to say I'm sorry to you. I know you won't believe me, but I never meant things to turn out like this between us."

"You're right—I don't believe you. You made it very clear, right from the start, that you didn't like me."

"Oh, no, I didn't. He tried not to laugh, but he didn't quite succeed. "I told you I didn't want you at Havenhurst, and I still don't—but I never said I didn't like you. You're a beautiful, exciting, desirable woman, and I have *always* liked you. Much too much for my own good!"

Faith could not tell whether he was teasing or not. She only knew his words made her uncomfortable.

"Sir, I cannot allow——"

"Shhh!" He raised his hand, as if to lay it on her lips, then drew it back again. "Not another well-earned barb, I beg you. What I am trying to say, and saying it badly, is that you are very dear to me—both for yourself and because you are Adam's daughter—and all I have ever wanted is your happiness."

The words were so unexpected, Faith could think of nothing to say. She stood in silence, watching him slip into the throng of dancers, and wondered if she could possibly have heard him right. Had this cool, sarcastic, self-possessed man actually admitted to a tender emotion? And could he really have meant it?

He sounded sincere, she could not deny that. His voice fairly rang with honesty and conviction. But then he had sounded sincere before, and that hadn't stopped him from being perfectly beastly five minutes later. She could not help wondering if he had sounded sincere to Fleur, too—just before he raised his gun and pointed it at her breast!

The air was stifling in the crowded room, even with the windows open, and Faith felt as if she could not breathe. Smiling a sweet apology at the young men who were already bickering playfully over her next dance, she made her way through a narrow side door to the cool, deserted gardens that lay beyond. She needed a few minutes to herself. A few minutes to clear her head of champagne and the giddy whirl of dancing—and above all, the need to analyze her feelings for a man she would never understand.

The music sounded faint and far away, like a carnival off somewhere in the distance, and Faith paused beside a japonica tree to listen to it. The melody was sweet and haunting, but underneath it, she sensed another sound, a jarring, almost discordant beat that seemed to come from somewhere behind the house. Her curiosity aroused, she decided to follow it and see what it was.

She stopped in amazement the instant she reached the large dirt yard that stretched all the way to the outbuildings in the rear. Brad had told her the slaves would have their own celebration tonight—they always did, he said, when there was a party in the big house—but it never occurred to her it would be like this. Brightly colored lanterns had been strung on cords between the trees, giving the whole area a festive air, and a half-dozen bonfires flooded the earth with red-golden light. Plump roasted chickens rested on rough-plank tables beside huge iron pots filled with beans, and a whole roast ox—or what was left of it, at least—still turned on a spit over a firepit in the center.

Beside one of the smaller fires, so close to the flickering flames their dark skin looked almost red, a small band of musicians beat out the exotic rhythm that had drawn Faith toward them in the first place. She stepped forward now, eager to get a better look at the instruments that could produce such strange sounds. The drums were not drums at all, she saw at once, but hollowed-out logs with skins drawn tightly across their heads, though they were capable of producing a pure, clear sound, at once eerie and exciting. An odd, three-stringed instrument, rather like a clumsy mandolin, looked more whimsical than practical, for the comical figure that had been crudely carved at the end of its long neck added nothing to its primitive sound. A pair of gourds, filled with pebbles or seeds—Faith was not sure which—completed the unlikely ensemble.

A few of the blacks had already gathered around the musicians. Now, more and more of them began to leave the food tables, squatting and sitting in a wide circle as they clapped their hands in time to the music. A tall, angular girl leaped up, enticed into the center of the circle by a rhythm she could not resist. Her eyes transfixed, her feet planted firmly on the ground, she began to sway to the rhythm, first with her head, then her upper torso, then at last a slow, sensual swinging of her hips. It was only a minute before another black figure joined her and then another, and soon the circle was filled with dancers.

Faith stood on the sidelines, intrigued by the complex beat that stirred these people into motion. No, not *the* beat, she corrected herself, listening more closely. There were at least two beats, or three—perhaps even four—all mingling together with a subtlety that made the orchestra inside sound naive and childlike. Her toe tapped the ground, and she hated herself for the inhibitions that would not let her tie her skirts halfway up to her waist and run into the circle with the others.

One of the musicians glanced up and, catching sight of her, let his fingers drop from the strings of his instrument. The drummers stopped their beat a second later, and soon the gourds, too, were still. Faith was uncomfortably aware of dozens of pairs of dark eyes, all fastened on her face.

She backed self-consciously out of the firelight. Too late, she realized she had no business being there. She was as unwelcome at these slave festivities as black visitors would have been in the big house with all her stuffy, status-conscious guests.

She had just opened her lips to murmur an awkward apology when a young woman detached herself from the group sitting on the ground and began to hurry toward her. Faith barely had time to recognize Estee before black arms caught her up in an impulsive embrace.

"We saw it all!" she told Faith breathlessly. "We peeked in the window the minute the ceremony started, and we didn't leave till the end. You looked absolutely beautiful—but, oh, so pale! Don't tell me you were frightened?"

Faith caught the teasing in her tone, and her heart broke for the girl. She knew what it cost Estee to rejoice in the happiness that could never be hers.

"White girls are always pale, Estee. Don't you know that?"

The laughter that followed dissolved whatever awkwardness was left, and soon everyone was flocking around her, admiring her gown, oohing and ahing over expensive brocade, even reaching out with shy fingers to touch the delicate point lace in her cap. How friendly they all seemed now. Sweet little Fibby, bubbling over with excitement; quiet, dignified Cuffee, taking a minute off from his duties in the house; Estee, proud for the first time to claim a white woman as a friend—even dour, disapproving Beneba seemed to have forgotten that Faith was an outsider, and one of the wrong race at that.

"Sho' do look purty, honey!" she enthused, her big, square face filled with a grin that went from ear to ear. "I ain't never seen a purtier bride—an' that's a fac'. Not in all my days!"

Faith still glowed with excitement as she crossed the lawn and slipped back through the doorway into the ballroom. For the first time since she had arrived at Havenhurst—no, for the first time in her life!—she felt like she belonged.

What a wonderful thing a wedding was, she told herself, delighted with the idea of it all. How she wished she could have one every day of her life! Weddings did the most amazing things to people, filling them with thoughts of love and kindness, reminding them of all the promises they made to each other when they, too, were young and believed in romance.

Alexandre looked up quizzically when she came through the door, and Faith knew he had missed her. How handsome he looked, this new husband of hers. How exciting. She did not try to go to him where he stood chatting with friends, but caught his eye across the room, flashing him a slow, secret smile.

"Soon, my love," she whispered silently, forming her lips around the words. "Soon!"

Soon the guests would leave, and the champagne glasses would be cleared away; soon the candles would all be blown out, one by one—and she would be his wife at last.

Brad braced his feet awkwardly on the ground, digging his heels into the soil to steady himself. Dammit, he was drunk! He hated it when he was drunk. He hated anything that made him lose control of his body.

A heavy, rough-hewn door stood squarely in front of him, blocking his way. He stared at it impatiently, trying to figure out what the devil it was doing there. He couldn't imagine why the blasted thing was closed—but then he couldn't think of a reason why it should be open either. He thought about knocking on it, but even in his drunkenness, he knew he couldn't do that. This was his door, after all. Every door in the place was his! A man didn't knock on his own door. Raising one foot, he banged it against the crude wood, ramming it inward with a single strong blow.

Inside, the room was dim and smoky. Embers glowed in the great open fireplace that stretched along one wall, but their hazy red light was barely enough to pick up the outlines of a few flimsy pieces of furniture: a narrow bed, its faded mattress stuffed with gray moss; a rickety wooden table, set with a tin plate and a tin cup; a single straight-backed chair in front of the fire, and a pair of three-legged stools across the room. The walls were rough logs, clumsily chinked with cracking mud and clay; the floors, rough planks, littered with firewood and shavings.

A woman with dark golden skin crouched in front of the fire. She did not move at once, but rose slowly to her feet. Brad knew she must be surprised to see him, but she was careful to let nothing show in her face.

"I had not thought you would come tonight." Her voice was soft and unusually cultivated for a slave. "There is much music in the big house still. Much laughter."

Brad took a step inside, then stopped, thrusting his hand against the wall to keep the room from reeling.

"Watch out for me tonight, Eva. You see before you a man totally, unashamedly drunk."

Eva grinned. Crooked teeth gave her face a puckish, bawdy look.

"But not *too* drunk, eh?'"

Brad sank down on the side of the bed. Thank God for women who knew how to be open and free. The smartest thing he'd ever done was take Beneba's advice and stop denying his own strong needs. Who the hell cared about Faith anyway? The little bitch! Prancing around in that ridiculous white dress. As if anyone actually believed she was a virgin bride.

"Beautiful little Evita. Come to me."

Eva was neither beautiful nor little, but it pleased him to tease her, and they both knew he meant it affectionately. She was a big, solid woman, a warm, comforting presence, as sheltering as the earth from which she had been molded, and he always drew strength from her. He laid his hands on her hips, pulling her toward him.

She twisted away with a sly laugh. Dropping to her knees, she wrapped her hands around his boot. It was a minute before he realized what she was doing.

"No, dammit!" He jerked his leg back, trying to free himself. "I won't have you groveling at my feet like a—like a. . . ."

Like a what? he thought bitterly. Surrendering, he lay back on the bed, letting her do what she wanted. Like a slave? Hell, she *was* a slave. All the anger in the world wasn't going to change that.

Eva tugged patiently at his boots, her face impassive as she pulled them off one by one, lining them up at the foot of the bed. Her breath was warm against his cheek when she leaned over him, unfastening his shirt and easing it off his body.

Brad lay on his back and looked up at her, fascinated by the unexpected grace he saw in her movement.

"Why do you put up with me, Evita? Why don't you tell me to go to hell and send me packing?"

She smiled uncertainly. How strangely he talked sometimes. Not at all like the other white men she had know.

"How can I send you away? You are my master."

"Confound it, woman, I'm not an animal! I won't force you—you know that! You can send me away any time you want."

"No, I cannot—but it does not matter. You are a strong man. You know how to please a woman."

"Don't you ever get angry? Don't you hate the men who use your body?" He lifted his hand, running it lightly down her cheek. "Don't you ever hate me?"

Eva looked puzzled. She liked this man who had just begun coming to her, but she did not understand him.

"Why should I? You are good to me. You have given me a cabin of my own, and——"

"But what about tomorrow? Dammit, Eva, what about next year—the year after that? Have you thought about it at all? Have you asked yourself who'll take care of you when I get bored and cast you off?"

She shook her head slowly. "Tomorrow is tomorrow—I cannot change it. Why would you have me worry about it?"

"Blast that serenity of yours!" He caught hold of her wrist, jerking her angrily toward him. "I want you to yell at me! Don't you understand that? I want you to fight and rail. I want—I want. . . ."

"What do you want, master?" He was hurting her, but she did not try to pull away.

Brad knew she was staring down at him, but he could not bring himself to look back at her. How could he tell her that the one thing he wanted was the one thing she could never give? Long, fragrant strands of gold spilling across his pillow, teasing his face, his shoulders, his chest. Pale, smooth skin touching his naked body when he woke in the morning; slender arms reaching out to draw him——

"Oh, hell, Eva, I just want to forget."

She did not miss the pain in his voice, nor did she fail to understand it. She had seen the way he looked at the white girl. She knew the loneliness that was his tonight.

"Then I will help you forget."

Her fingers slid slowly down his body, resting at last between his thighs, caressing him, tempting, exulting when she felt him grow hard in her grasp.

He let her hold him for a minute, then he caught her hand, taking it briefly in his. A peasant's hand, he thought as he looked down at it. Big-knuckled, calloused, honest in its toil. Why couldn't that be enough for him? Why couldn't he take love where he found it and let it go at that? If only he were more like Adam. . . .

But Adam had had Katherine—and that was the difference.

Brad put his arms around Eva, drawing her down on the bed beside him, and he knew that between himself and this woman there would never be anything like love. Need, yes; passion, of course—but love? For her, it would only be a hut of her own, a new dress every now and then, better food than she had had before. And for him——

"Make me forget, Eva."

He pressed her closer, urging her body under his. Make me forget that her hair is on *his* pillow now. Make me forget that those pale, slender arms are twined around his body. Make me forget you are only a slave and don't care for me any more than I care for you.

But across the yard, in the big house, Faith was not lying in Alexandre's arms. Not yet. She was sitting alone on the edge of a double bed and thinking how silent the house seemed now that the last guest was gone and even the servants had finished their chores, shutting the front door behind them as they disappeared into the darkness.

A slight noise, more a rustle than a footstep, broke the stillness. Faith reacted with a start. Looking up, she saw her new husband standing in the doorway, waiting, she supposed, for an invitation to enter. He wore a deep blue dressing gown, so soft and velvety it seemed to catch the candlelight and hold it inside. The color was mirrored in eyes that glowed with the dark excitement of the midnight sky.

Faith tried to smile, but she did not quite succeed.

"What a handsome bridegroom comes to me."

The tremor in her voice gave her away. Was every bride this nervous on her wedding night? she wondered. Yet it seemed foolish. The worst was over now, the doubts, the questions—the need to decide. All that was left was the one thing she had longed for since she had first laid eyes on this dashing stranger.

Alexandre did not move, but stood and watched her, entranced by the seductive sweetness of her innocence. How fragile she looked, his *belle enchanteresse,* with her lips trembling and her long hair floating down to her shoulders. He hungered to take her in his arms and make her his—truly his—as she had never been before.

"And what a beautiful bride awaits."

Faith managed a smile at last. Darling, gentle Alexandre. Why had she been so afraid? Didn't she know he would always find the right thing to say?

"Come, dear heart," she urged, holding out her arms. "Come, sit beside me and tell me one more time how much you love me."

He laughed as he came to her. "So I will, *chérie*—and often. But not now. Now I have other things in mind."

His arms were strong as they enfolded her, drawing her slowly, confidently, toward his body. His mouth was hard and forceful, warning her the moment had come to forget the sweet security of flirtation and give herself up to more tempestuous raptures. Faith quivered in his embrace, confused by the conflicting passions that tore her apart. She did not know which frightened her most, the yearning in her body to surrender or the need in her heart to draw back and shield herself from the turbulence of love's demands. She knew only that Alexandre's hands were too bold as they sought her breasts, squeezing, fondling, slipping inside sheer lace to linger against warm flesh.

"Alexandre, please. . . ."

Oh, dear heaven, why was she so frightened? It was not the physical act she dreaded, for she knew that would bring nothing but pleasure. Nor was it the pain—she could always endure the pain. But the closeness—the sense of joining with this man, of being one with him—wouldn't that strip away all her defenses, leaving her vulnerable and unprotected?

". . . please, my love, be gentle with me."

He stiffened, drawing away, and Faith realized she had displeased him. She longed to make things right again, she longed to pick up his hand and press it back against her breast, but she was afraid to touch him, so she stayed where she was, waiting for the coldness to fade from his eyes. At last, the moment passed, and he reached out, teasing her chin with his fingers.

"Did you think I was going to thrust you back on the bed and rip off your gown? Never mind, I suppose it can't be helped. I did threaten that once, didn't I?"

"Oh, no, my darling!" Faith was horrified at her clumsiness. How could she have been so dense? So tactless? "I didn't mean that, truly I didn't. What happened that night was as much my fault as yours. You know it was."

"You have forgiven me, then?"

"Oh, Alexandre, a hundred times—a thousand times!"

"Then let me show you how gently I can love you." His eyes were filled with ardor as he leaned toward her; his mouth soft this time as it rested on hers, tantalizing her with all the tender yearning of her dreams; his tongue so light she almost thought she imagined the feel of it flicking across her lips. "Here, *chérie,* let me help you take off that pretty gown. I want to cover your body with kisses."

"But Alexandre, shouldn't you. . . ." Faith hesitated, hating herself for the prudishness she could not control. This man was her husband, her lawfully bound mate—he would have every right to be furious if she tried to squirm out of his embrace again. "The light—shouldn't you blow out the light?"

He looked amused. "But you always liked the——" He caught himself, laughing. "I mean, I always thought you would like the light. You're the kind of woman who should revel in her beauty—and the effect it has on a man."

Faith could not meet his gaze. She had the feeling he was trying to tell her this was the kind of woman he wanted. Bold and uninhibited.

"And so I shall, my love, I promise you. Only not tonight. Just for now—just for the first time—won't you allow me the privacy of darkness?"

He did not reply, but bent over the candle, cupping his hand around it as he blew it out. Moonlight flooded the room with cool, clear rays, almost as bright as the luminous gold glow of the flame. Faith's hand was shaking as she raised it to the drawstring that gathered lacy ruffles around her neck, but she dared not ask Alexandre to draw the curtains. She had displeased her husband more than once that night; she could not chance it again.

Alexandre stared at her, fascinated by the last lingering

hesitance that held her hand on the string a brief moment, then let it go with a swift, sweeping movement. The gown floated to the ground, a bit of gossamer caught on the night air. Now her beauty belonged to him.

She had been right to play it her way, he admitted admiringly. The moonlight was more flattering than a candle could ever have been. Blue-black shadows caressed pale skin, slimming a slender waist into nothingness, accenting full, high breasts, darkening the soft down that nestled between her thighs until it looked like jet—deep, mysterious, inviting. At last she was his, this beautiful, maddening, exciting woman. All his. No other man had ever had her, and none ever would. Never again would he lie awake at night and wonder where she was.

He forgot her plea for tenderness as he pulled her toward him, crushing her in a vise so strong she could not pull away. Faith felt urgency in the fingers that dug into her back, bruising soft flesh with savage fury, and in the lips that sank to her neck, burying their longing in perfumed tresses, parting until she could feel teeth against her skin. Any minute now, any second, he would demand his ultimate right as a husband, and no matter how frightened she was—no matter how far from ready—she dared not deny him.

This was not the way she had imagined it, she thought, as she felt him push her roughly down on the bed. This was not what she dreamed of that morning in the library when he asked her to become his bride. She wanted love from this man, affection, a gentle courtship that would lull away her fears. She wanted him to stir those same emotions Brad had once touched—only without the ugly bestiality of lust without love.

The pain when he entered her was almost a relief, erasing everything else from her mind. It was worse than she had expected, but Faith did not care. If only she could focus on it, if only she could hold on to every shred of its throbbing force, perhaps then she could forget the humiliating things that were happening to her body. How could Fleur have loved this so much? she thought with disgust. It was awful, it was degrading—there was nothing romantic about it at all!

Then, just when she was sure she could bear it no longer, the pain began to subside, and in its place, to her surprise, Faith felt a warm, welcome glow, so sweet and satisfying she could not bring herself to resist it. She did not recognize the feeling—she had no idea where it had come from or why—but there was an excitement in it beyond anything she had ever known, and her whole body began to tingle with a new, unexpected anticipation.

She had barely begun to discover how good it felt to move in rhythm with him, letting the male strength of his passion swell the sensations in her body, when he stopped suddenly, collapsing with a low, hoarse grunt on her breast. Faith felt strangely bereft as he rolled out of her arms, lying on his back on his own side of the bed.

Was this all there was to it? she asked herself, bewildered by the emotions that had been roused, then suspended so abruptly. It was not nearly as dreadful as she had feared, that was for sure—but then it wasn't exactly fulfilling either! It hardly seemed worth all the fuss and carrying on.

She wondered if Alexandre would be understanding if she moved closer to him, telling him she needed the comfort of his arms around her—or if he would simply pull away with that same cold, displeased look on his face. She wished she knew what was expected of her now. She had spent so much time worrying about how she was supposed to behave *before* he made love to her—and what she was supposed to do *when* she was in his arms—it hadn't occurred to her she might need to know about afterward, too.

It was a long time before she dared look at him. Even then, she moved cautiously, raising herself on one elbow to gaze down at him.

He was even handsomer in repose. His face, almost classically perfect, took on the lines of a young Greek god in the cold light of the moon. Skin as pale as alabaster showed off the symmetry of a wide brow and sharply chiseled cheekbones, and full lips, parted a fraction of an inch, hinted at sensitivity and strength. Open eyes shone like two orbs of silver-blue glass.

Faith felt herself shiver as she watched him. She knew so little about men—she certainly did not know what they were supposed to look like when they finished making love to a woman—but she couldn't believe it was right for a bridegroom to lie on the far side of the bed, staring up at the ceiling with empty eyes.

She worked up enough courage to lay her hand on his arm.

"I am sorry, my love," she whispered. "I fear I disappointed you."

He jumped when she touched him, almost as if he had forgotten she was there. It took a moment for his eyes to focus on her, but when they did, they were soft and loving.

"Disappoint me? But, *mon coeur,* you could never do that. No, it was *I* who disappointed you."

"Oh, no, Alexandre—honestly! I wasn't disappointed. You were so—so. . . ."

He laughed at her efforts to reassure him. "Has no one ever told you, *fillette,* that a woman is always disappointed when her lover first possesses her? That first time, all the rough passion—that's a man's selfish way of satisfying himself. But the second time. . . ."

He was still laughing, gently, temptingly, as he drew her into his arms. She held back for an instant, studying him questioningly, but the warmth in his eyes reassured her. Did you think it was all over? they seemed to be saying to her. Did you think I wanted only my own pleasure, with nothing for you?

Faith could resist him no more. She wanted to believe the things his eyes seemed to promise—she *needed* to believe them—and she let herself go at last. With a sigh of longing, she sank into his embrace, all her inhibitions, all her fears finally gone. No longer were his hands intruders as they toyed with her body, caressing her breasts, her hips, her thighs, pausing to rest on the soft, moist hair that curled between her legs; no longer was that hard, pulsating proof of his masculinity a threat when, gentle enticements over, he slipped it slowly, demandingly into her body. Her arms tightened possessively around him, her hips pressed upward with a will of their own, as she waited breathlessly for this man she loved to initiate her into the tender mysteries her body longed to learn. This time he did not fail her.

Afterward, she snuggled close in his arms, feeling the miracle of his body, hot and damp with sweat against hers. How could he lie there so calmly? she wondered. Her own body seemed to be simmering with excitement, as if hundreds of tiny fires smoldered somewhere deep inside her flesh.

"Ah, my sweet love," she murmured contentedly. "How right you were. That was for me—*all* for me."

"And for me, too," he reminded her gently. But his voice was sleepy, and Faith sensed that he uttered the words only because he knew how much she wanted to hear them. She laughed lightly as she nestled closer, nipping his ear playfully before letting him go. It did not matter now that he wanted to slide over to the other side of the bed, retreating once again into the private shell of his own body. Nothing would ever matter again. She had belonged to him for one blissful, unbelievable moment—and she would belong to him forever. She laid her hand over his.

"I love you so very much, my darling."

She felt a gentle pressure on her fingers, so light and careless she knew he was almost asleep.

"And I love you, Fleur."

Fleur. . . .

Faith drew back slowly, looking at his face in the faint moonlight that muted his features. He looked so placid in sleep. So unaware.

Fleur . . . I love you, Fleur.

Too late, a dozen things came back to her. A hundred little hints that should have told her the truth if only she'd had the sense to see them.

You always liked the light, he had said to her. Not, *I thought you would like the light,* the way he tried to make her believe—but *You liked the light.* Only that was Fleur, of course. It was Fleur who loved undressing in front of a candle flame. It was Fleur who loved having a man ravish every inch of her body with eyes hungry with desire.

And that night she had gone to his room. *This is the way you like it, isn't it? This is what excites you.* That was why he was so rough with her. Not because he thought she would enjoy it—but because he knew Fleur would!

Heaven help her, what a fool she had been. What a stupid, naive little fool! She had been so eager to catch a handsome man—she had wanted so desperately to be a "married lady" with all the lovely status that title implied—she hadn't stopped to ask herself if Alexandre was marrying her because he loved her or because she reminded him of the woman he could never have.

Brad had been right. Even if Fleur were still alive, she would never have come back to Havenhurst. There *was* nothing for her here, none of the lively excitement she craved, and Alexandre was too intelligent not to have figured that out. He knew he had lost Fleur—and there was nothing he could do but take the sister who looked like her and try and content himself with that.

Faith slipped out of bed, moving carefully so she would not wake Alexandre, though he was sleeping so soundly there was little danger of that. She put on the same blue wrapper she had worn the night she thought she had won his heart forever and stepped over to the window.

Outside, the world was quiet and serene. The sky was a deep, mystical blue, the earth so black in shadow she could not penetrate it with her eyes. Only the river broke the darkness, shining and silver as it wound peacefully through invisible shores.

So Fleur was still with her. Even in death, she could not leave her sister behind. She thought she had outgrown old insecurities—she had been so sure she could stand on her own at last—but now she knew that would never be true. Now she was married to a man who would think of her sister every time he took her in his arms, and she would live in Fleur's shadow for the rest of her life.

A single tear ran down her cheek as she turned to look at her husband one more time. Impatiently, she reached up and brushed it away.

"Well, we're a fine pair, aren't we?" she said softly, daring to laugh a little at herself. "Here I am, afraid to live with my sister's memory—and you're afraid to live without it! I wonder what we're going to make of this marriage, you and I."

III

ANOTHER APRIL

One

April. Golden jessamine tumbled over the rice-field banks, mingling with blackberry blossoms and wisteria, and here and there, purple and white irises bobbed their jaunty bonnets in the breeze. Faith held a sprig of jessamine against her nose, picking out the scent of flowers from the pungent sap that stained her fingers, and tried to remember what it had smelled like that April morning in London when the fog was so heavy she could feel it in her nostrils.

April. How they had loved to play on the rice banks, she and Fleur, twining gaily colored blossoms into long chains and arguing over whose was the prettiest. They stained their hands then, too, and Desirée exclaimed with despair when she saw smears of green on their skirts where impatient little fingers had rubbed away the sticky sap.

Faith let go of the jessamine, tossing it idly into the wide central channel that divided the fields amost exactly in half. She watched for a moment as it drifted down the dark waters toward the river, then began to follow it, lifting her skirts when she came to one of the wobbly footbridges that spanned the canals. The fields had been drained for spring planting, and only an occasional pool of standing water still oozed dark red-brown in the drying soil.

April. Was it really only a year since her sister died? Faith could hardly remember the determined young girl who had set out that day from London, certain that somehow, despite her fears, she would find a way to avenge her sister's death. The whole world seemed to have turned upside down since then, yet in a strange way nothing had changed at all. She had come halfway around the world to find the plantation where she had been born, she had dared to face the past and all its memories—but nowhere in that dizzying maze of yesterday had she found even the slightest clue to her sister's fate. And she had surrendered her innocence to a handsome stranger, slipping from adolescence to womanhood in his embrace, but even after half a year of marriage, the man she called husband was as much a stranger as he had been on the eve of their wedding.

A stocky man, square and broad-shouldered, stood waist deep in the water at the end of the channel. Faith paused to study him. He was not as young as he seemed at first. Flecks of white grayed his hair, and deep lines cut into the skin around his eyes, but there was a slow, steady strength in his movements as he bent over the sturdy sluice that separated the channel from the river. Mud coated his pitch-black skin, muting it to a neutral reddish tan.

To Faith, the sluice seemed a fascinating device, ingeniously contrived, yet remarkably simple. Thick heart pine and cypress planks had been driven into the earth to form a foundation for a pair of gates, one adjacent to the river, the other farther inland. The river gate closed automatically with the pressure of the high tide, opening again as the tide ebbed; the inner gate worked exactly in reverse. By raising one gate and leaving the other in place, the entire area could be flooded or drained at will.

Perspiration drenched the man's body as he tugged at a rotting board, freeing it at last and flinging it onto the bank. Even with the breeze, the air was hot, a reminder of steamy summer months to come. Faith turned away, looking up toward the hills, cool patches of spring green against a crisp blue sky.

It had not been such a bad bargain, she had to admit, this marriage to a man who did not love her. Alexandre was a charming, witty companion, ever attentive, ever ready to please, and she could find no fault in the way he treated her, especially in front of others. It was exciting to walk into a festive party at one of the neighboring plantations on his arm and know that every young woman there envied her (and every older one secretly wished she could catch a handsome prize like that for her own unmarried daughter). If he looked at her strangely sometimes when they were alone, as if he were as unsure of her as she was of him, at least he was kind enough not to put his doubts into words. And if he came to her room only infrequently—and then as much from duty as desire—could she really complain when he was a gentle, considerate lover who rarely failed to satisfy the burgeoning passions of her body?

"What a pretty picture! I'll have to commission an artist to paint it. I think we'll call it *Shepherdess Who Has Lost Her Flock.*"

Faith looked up to see Brad Alleyn mounted on his favorite stallion a few yards away. Since her marriage to Alexandre, Brad had been unfailingly courteous, even aloof, but there were times, like today, when shadows deepened his eyes nearly to black, emphasizing a rugged, primitive masculinity, that she could not help remembering what had once passed between them.

"Don't be so patronizing. *Shepherdess Who Lost Her Flock*, indeed! You make me sound like a pathetic waif."

"You do look like a waif, I swear. You have a little smudge—right there on the tip of your nose. And your skirt! It looks as if you've been rolling in the grass."

Faith glanced down. It was true—buttercup-yellow ruffles, cleanly edged only an hour before in white holland tape, were now daubed with green.

"Oh, wouldn't Mama have been furious!" she said, giggling in spite of herself. "I can just hear her now. 'Little girls must learn to take care of their frocks!' Obviously, the lesson didn't take."

Brad grinned, "Good! I made you laugh. You were much too pensive, staring off into the hills like that."

"I was just thinking——" Faith caught herself just in time. She could hardly say, I was thinking it's been a year since Fleur died. Not when she didn't want this man to realize how much she knew. "I was just thinking that—that it's April."

He raised a quizzical brow. "Very astute of you."

"I mean, its just a year since I sailed from England. You have no idea how strange it felt to stand at the rail of that ship and wave goodbye to my uncle and his business partner, knowing I might never see them again."

"What do they think of your decision to stay here? Your family and friends. Do they approve?"

"Of course." Faith answered a little too quickly. She had made her peace with her uncle, writing to tell him of her marriage, but she knew she had disappointed him, just as she knew he must be desperately worried about Fleur by this time. "They are delighted for me. I have a thoughtful, considerate husband—who just happens to be the handsomest man I ever saw in my life! What more could any woman want?"

"I wouldn't presume to guess. It has occurred to me, though, that the qualities a young woman sees in a man before she marries him might not be the same ones she sees afterward."

"You may be right," Faith admitted with a smile. "You know, it's easy to say to yourself, When I marry this beautiful, perfect stranger, the world is going to turn into a dazzling paradise and we'll live happily ever after. Only it doesn't seem to happen that way. It's hard work, taking a stranger and making him into a friend, someone you really know, intimately and completely. Has there been any woman in the history of the world, I wonder, who has never looked at the man on the other side of the breakfast table and said to herself—Who on earth is this person?"

"Any woman, Faith? Or you?"

Faith turned toward the river, trying to look casual and unconcerned. The question had hit much too close to home to suit her. She was surprised to see that the black man had almost finished his task, whittling down a new length of board until it fit snugly into the sluice. Sweat was running down his body, washing away the mud and grime.

"Doesn't it bother your conscience to work your slaves so hard? That man looks like he's ready to drop from exhaustion."

Brad took the rebuke calmly. "I don't ask anything of my slaves I'm not willing to do myself."

"Well, maybe *you*," Faith conceded. Brad was out before the sun every morning and rarely returned home until long after dusk. She had seen him toiling in the channel himself, his skin so bronzed, his clothes so caked with dirt, that only the flaxen streaks in his hair set him apart from his slaves. "But I doubt if Samuel Hardin can *walk* in this heat, let alone work. As for Eleazar Carstairs—well, I can't picture him with dirt under his fingernails."

"I don't have to answer for Carstairs, thank God."

"Don't you?" Faith's eyes narrowed as she looked at him. "That's a little glib, isn't it? It seems to me that any man who supports the system has to answer for its evils. Alexandre says our whole civilization is flawed—slavery is the weakness that's going to destroy us in the end. He says the smartest thing we can do is take all the slaves and ship them back to Africa."

"Alexandre is a fool!" Brad paused, letting a wry smile twist his features. She knew how to get under his skin all right, accusing him of overworking his slaves and calling him glib when he denied it. "But I forget, the man is your husband. Perhaps you have a sentimental attachment to him."

Faith glared at him angrily. Did he always raise one eyebrow when he wanted to be sarcastic, she wondered, or did he only do it with her?

"Sentiment has nothing to do with it. I happen to think my husband is right, that's all. Alexandre says we can manage perfectly well with indentured servants, and I agree with him. We're just asking for another Stono River if we keep these people here. Besides, it's inhumane."

"What would you consider humane? To pack slaves into the stinking hold of a ship—'tight pack' and 'loose pack' as the slavers say—and see how many of them survive the journey? And even if we get them to Africa, what happens then? Most of these people have never even seen the place. They were born here, or perhaps on the Islands. They don't speak the native languages, they don't know the customs, they don't even dress the same. What kind of welcome do you think they'd find there?"

"But they hunger for Africa, Brad—you know they do. Take Estee, for instance. Do you know, she makes up all sorts of stories about her grandfather? She pretends he was a chief—or a king, or something like that—just to give herself a sense of belonging. Of being someone."

Brad shook his head as he looked down at her. Sometimes it amazed him, the way a woman's mind could work.

"What makes you think she made them up?"

"You mean . . . but I . . . well, I just assumed. . . ."

"Didn't I warn you never to assume anything?" Up went that brow again, just the way Faith hated. She had the awful feeling he remembered exactly when he had said those words before—and just what the circumstances were. "As a matter of fact, Estee's grandfather *was* a king. But don't fill your head with any romantic notions about that. He had gotten on the wrong side of a boundary dispute with another king—not an uncommon thing in that part of the world—and he and Katherine were already slaves when——

"Ah, but you don't want all the gory details, do you? Suffice it to say Katherine was a black slave in a black land with black masters, and if I'm ever 'noble' enough to send Estee back, doubtless she'll end up as a slave, too."

"Doubtless?" Faith's eyes flashed with undisguised fury. How could the man be so insensitive? "Doubtless, you say? By God, sir, you are smug! Is that your justification for perpetuating this abomination? Because Estee *might* be a slave in Africa. Well, she *is* a slave here!"

To her discomfort, he threw back his head and laughed. It was maddening, the way he never took her seriously, even when she was talking sense.

"Damn, what a spitfire! You're Adam's daughter, all right, through and through. You sound just like your father."

"My—father?"

"Adam hated slavery with that same fierce passion. He would have wiped it off the face of the earth if it were in his power."

Faith let her gaze sweep across the open fields. The sun had climbed higher and the heat was already uncomfortable, but blacks seemed to be everywhere, poking at tenacious green weeds with crude wooden hoes, leveling the earth out after themselves.

"Pardon me if I find that a little hard to believe."

"The man who owns the plantation can't hate the institution that shores it up, is that it?" Brad caught himself with a harsh laugh. "Sorry. I didn't mean to sound so defensive. Besides, I know what you mean. It doesn't ring true, even to me. Knowing Adam's convictions, I expected him to leave a will with specific instructions for the manumission of his slaves. It surprised me when he didn't."

"You mean because he had a black mistress?"

"Good Lord, woman, you do love to oversimplify things. No, not because of his mistress. Because he thought slavery was an abhorrent, malignant, evil thing. Like your Alexandre—whom he would have despised, by the way—he considered slavery the weak thread that would pull apart the fabric of our entire society."

Faith's back stiffened at the slur. Was that what this was all about? The whole tirade? Just another way of getting in a dig at Alexandre?

"I think you're making it all up. The man you're describing doesn't sound like my father at all."

"Now who's being smug?" Brad asked dryly. "You seem to know a great deal about your father, for a girl who only remembers one thing—that he rode a black stallion."

Faith set her jaw determinedly. He was right, of course—she *was* being smug—but she'd die before she'd give him the satisfaction of admitting it.

"I don't need to remember my father to know he hid his bastards' graves on an isolated hillside where no one would see them."

Brad eyed her coolly. "Where would you have put them?"

"Oh, not in the family burial ground, don't worry. We wouldn't want people to talk, would we?"

"And you think Adam was afraid of a little idle gossip. Hell, Faith, your father knew how the other planters felt about him. He didn't give a damn! Sometimes I think he goaded them on."

He paused, surprised at the anger in his tone. The girl had every right to delve into the past, even if that meant questioning her father's motives. Adam himself wouldn't have wanted it any other way.

"I was there, Faith, the day one of the little boys died, a few hours after he was born. Katherine was too ill to move, or even open her eyes. It was Adam who sat on a chair beside her bed, rocking the child back and forth, cradling him in his arms, comforting him as long as there was a breath left in his body. It was Adam who laid him in the pine box he made with his own hands. Adam who took up the shovel to bury him."

Faith tried not to see the picture he was painting for her. It was strangely disturbing to remember how loving those same arms had once felt around her.

"But not in the family cemetery," she reminded him softly.

"Not next to your mother's kin—no. Not in the shadow of the house he built for her. High on a windswept hillside, where the wild flowers grow free and the air is fresh, even in the summer."

Faith wished he would stop adding new dimensions to everything. She had just gotten used to the idea that the tall, strong man who could be so gentle with a little girl was the same shameful libertine who drove her mother away in tears. Now Brad was asking her to see him in yet another light.

Brad tried not to smile as he watched her bite her lower lip, determined to keep it from trembling.

"Don't be so quick to judge your father, Faith. You come here with your head filled with preconceived notions, and you try so hard to make everything fit in with them, you can't see the truth anymore. You want to know what your father was really like? Look at this land, this soil he took from the wilderness and shaped with his own sweat. The rice fields cleared from the swamps, that was Adam Eliot—not the fashionable house filled with crystal and geegaws from all over the world. The cornfields forged out of pine forests—not the gardens and bridal paths and the street in back where the slaves live."

He stopped to laugh at himself. How the devil did he expect her to know about the land if no one took the time to show it to her? Impulsively, he held out his hand.

"Come on. I'm just on my way to the barn to begin claying the rice. Do you even know what that is? No? Well, then, climb up in front of me and let me introduce you to your heritage."

Faith hesitated. The offer was tempting. No one ever wanted to show a woman anything but the parlor and the gardens—or maybe a peek at the slaves working in the cookhouse out in back—as if the poor feminine brain was too weak and giddy to take in all the complex details of the male world. But to give her hand to a man who had once threatened to throw her down in the dirt and have his way with her! That was more than common sense would allow.

Brad laughed easily. "But maybe you're like our neighbors at Cypress Hill—afraid of getting your fingernails dirty."

That was too much for Faith. "I'm not afraid of soiling my hands and you know it! I wasn't raised like a little princess with servants to look after me every minute of the time. Don't you dare say I was!"

The gambit worked perfectly. Before she knew it, Faith was sitting in front of him, uncomfortably conscious of the hard strength of his chest against her back. His shirtsleeves were rolled up to the elbow, his forearms tanned and thick with masculine hair as they circled her body to grip the reins. Faith could not help remembering how safe and secure she had felt when she was a little girl and her father drew her up to the saddle and held her just like that.

Only this man was no Adam Eliot. There was no security in the rugged arms that held her in a casual embrace. Faith wished she could forget, even for a moment, that he was a man and she a woman—and he had already taught her how exciting a forbidden kiss could be. If only Alexandre had come to her last night, she thought desperately. If only she had not lain awake for hours, tossing and turning, longing for the feel of his body next to hers, perhaps then she would not be so aware of the physical presence of this man behind her.

It seemed forever, but they reached the barn at last, and Faith slid down gratefully, not even waiting for Brad to help her. She had been so absorbed in her own conflicting emotions she barely noticed the area as they rode up. Now she saw to her surprise that the normally lazy barnyard had turned into a bustling hive of activity.

Everyone on the plantation seemed to be there. An elderly

fieldhand, his calloused fingers running up and down the sides of coarse tow-linen trousers, stood beside an open barn door, chatting with one of the house servants, a white-shirted young man who might have been a carbon copy of Cuffee, had his features been softer and his hair streaked with gray. Cuffee himself was across the crowded yard, laughing and joking with a group of brawny, bare-chested young men as freely as if house and field got together every day of the week. A toothless old woman crouched in the meager shade of a small sapling, spitting coarsely in the dirt as she called out raucous greetings to everyone who passed. Beneba, resplendent in a vivid red-and-white checked apron, stopped to give her a cuff on the shoulder, then hurried off, rounding up a score of noisy, naked urchins and shooing them out from underfoot.

The girls and young women were especially colorful. Most of them had tied their hair back with gay cotton kerchiefs, and their dresses, faded and patched though they were, seemed like bright spring bouquets, with red gingham next to solid blue, and soft gold prints alternating with bold stripes of rose and peach and green. Bare feet tapped and shuffled on the ground, tracing out little circles in the dust.

Perhaps, Faith admitted reluctantly, Brad was right after all. She *did* have her head filled with a lot of silly notions. Who was she to denounce slavery so bitterly? If these people were really as put upon as she claimed, why weren't they all standing around looking miserable?

Even Estee had turned out for the claying. Faith was surprised to see her next to the barn with several of the younger girls. Raising her arm, she waved it wildly to attract her attention. The slave girl's face was alight with uncharacteristic excitement as she left her friends and hurried toward her.

"So you've come to watch us work, eh, white girl?"

Faith caught the laughter in her tone. It had been a good choice after all, keeping Estee's secret. Nothing dire had happened, and she had won a friend.

"Watch indeed! I suppose you think I'm afraid of hard work, too."

"We wouldn't want to get those pretty white toes dirty."

Faith tossed her head defiantly. First Brad with her fingernails, now Estee carrying on about her toes!

"My fingers and toes will wash off quite nicely, thank you! I'll tell you what, my friend. We'll work side by side, you and I—and let's see who gets tired first!"

Brad was standing in the center of the yard, deep in conversation with a pair of men, a middle-aged laborer Faith had seen several times before and a tall, slender lad with bright eyes and a lightning-quick smile. When he broke away from them, he spared a minute to come over and explain things to Faith. Planting was one of the busiest times on a rice plantation, he told her—and one of the most demanding. Every step had to be meticulously prepared and executed, and even then, there was no guarantee something wouldn't go wrong and the entire crop be destroyed. Coating each grain of seed rice with a layer of clay—claying the rice, as it was called—seemed simple enough, but it was vitally important. After the rice was sowed and the fields flooded with water to protect the seed from the birds, it was the clay that would enable the grain to adhere to the earth, keeping it from floating to the surface.

The process began in a special loft, high above the floor of the barn, where the seed rice had been stored for the winter. Faith followed Brad inside, then hesitated when she came to the foot of a ladder so narrow and rickety it looked as if it would never support her weight. Holding her breath, she forced her feet upward, trying to pretend she didn't notice how badly the thing swayed every time she took a step. She would have loved to turn back, but she could just hear Brad laughing at her if she did!

The loft was not much sturdier, with wide chinks in the flooring and knotholes where light showed through, but compared to the flimsy ladder, it felt like a rock under her feet. Faith moved as far from the edge as she could and looked around curiously. The place was larger than she had expected, nearly half the length of the barn, with more than enough room for a dozen young men who had gathered there, led by the bright-eyed youth she had seen talking to Brad in the yard. Everyone seemed to be in motion, bending to scoop up the rice, measuring it out in heaping bushels, carrying it over to the side and dumping it into a spout that shot it down to the ground below. Dust hovered in the air like a white mist, stinging Faith's eyes and coating the inside of her mouth and nostrils.

Faith was so engrossed in all the activity—and so intrigued by the rousing good spirits that made light of backbreaking labor—she did not even hear the discordant sound of musicians tuning their instruments somewhere outside. Only when one of the fiddlers broke into a spontaneous, off-key melody did she finally notice. Puzzled, she glanced at Brad.

"Some of the planters take claying very seriously," he explained. "But most of us find that things go just as smoothly if we dare to have a little fun."

A *little* fun, Faith decided as she stood in the yard and stared at the flurry of movement around her, was definitely an understatement. Excitement and laughter filled the air. A broad layer of rice had been spread on the ground, and the girls were already gravitating toward it, giggling boisterously with one another, breaking out in an occasional lighthearted jig. Old men chuckled to themselves as they strolled in from the street, their bodies bouncing up and down in time to music that had not even begun yet; the old women, catching their impatience, squatted in a circle around the musicians, egging them on with the restless clapping of their hands.

A brigade of older children began to run back and forth between the barn and the seed rice. Dipping wooden piggins into barrels that had been filled with clay and water, they sloshed the slimy mixture on the ground with shrieks of laughter, getting at least as much on themselves as on the rice. The girls leaned forward, pulling their skirts between their legs and looping them over the front of their waistbands, until every pretty dress had turned into a rough, comical pantaloon. The rice disappeared under a mantle of shiny gray, the fiddlers took up their bows at last, and the girls leaped forward, each vying with the other to see who could be the first to set her toes to the clay-soaked grains.

Faith watched in fascination. It had never occurred to her that anything as monotonous as agricultural labor could actually seem like a festive celebration. Yet festive the occasion was, with the girls singing and joking as they danced over the rice, grinding it beneath their feet until each grain was thoroughly coated with clay. When they had finished one section, the young men would move in, shoveling the rice into a pyramid where it would soak until morning. Then, with jests and songs of their own, they spread out a fresh layer, and the whole thing began all over again.

Estee danced as merrily as the rest, pausing only briefly when she caught sight of Faith hesitating on the sidelines. Her handsome features broadened into a grin, and she flashed an impatient wink.

Well, white girl, her bold eyes seemed to say—I thought we were going to work side by side!

Faith cast one last rueful glance at her dress, then pulled it up and looped it at her waist, the way she had seen the others do. There was no point worrying about it now—not when she had already made up her mind. Kicking off her slippers, she ran out impulsively to join the others.

The music was brisk and sprightly, a lively combination of unfamiliar tunes and old half-forgotten airs, and Faith soon felt the vibrant rhythm begin to take hold of her body. A dark, pretty girl thrust out a sweaty hand and Faith caught at it eagerly, extending the other to Estee. It seemed to her she had never known anything so exhilarating. The jokes were outrageous, but they were fun, the laughter flowed free and easy, and the clayed rice was slippery beneath her soles, tempting her feet to move faster and faster every second.

Faith had never felt so free in her life. She didn't know if it was the stimulation of the music or simply the fact that she had dared to pull her skirts up over her legs like a rebellious tomboy, but she felt as if she were a whole different person. What a fool she had been to turn up her nose at slavery. These people might share their simple quarters with a dozen others while she slept between clean linen sheets in the big house, they might toil and suffer and chafe beneath their chains, but at least they kept their spirit. They knew how to enjoy a laugh and a gibe better than most of the white folks she knew. And they weren't afraid of a fiddle that was out of tune!

By the end of the first hour, Faith was ready to admit a slave's lot was not quite as rollicking as it seemed at first. It was hard to believe anything as much fun as dancing could be so tiring. By the end of the day, every muscle in her back and legs had begun to ache, and every little grain of rice seemed a sharp pebble digging into the soft skin of her feet. Thank heavens Brad had had the good sense to bring out the fiddlers, she thought gratefully. Without their music, she didn't think she could have gone on.

It was a relief when twilight fell at last, and the musicians finally put down their instruments. The girls wandered off slowly, in pairs and small groups, still laughing and humming little snatches of songs, and Faith was left alone at the edge of the yard. Wearily, she sank down on the ground, not even bothering to loosen her skirt and tuck it around her legs. She barely even had the strength for a weak smile and a goodbye wave to Estee.

A few minutes later, Brad came over, squatting on his heels beside her. Faith glanced up reluctantly. If he had called her a waif before, what must he think of her now?

"Don't you dare laugh at me, Brad Alleyn! I've never been so tired in my life, and I don't care what I look like!"

But he laughed anyway, a low, easy sound that had no mockery in it. Faith was uncomfortably aware that he was looking at her more intensely than he had for months—and that her body was beginning to respond to the flattery in his gaze.

His voice was soft as he leaned closer. "Shall I tell you what you're thinking?"

Faith was thankful for the darkness that hid her blush. If he tried to tell her she was thinking about the way his shirt stretched across strong shoulders, or how appealingly boyish his hair looked when it tumbled down on his brow, she would deny it.

"Do you really think you can read my mind?"

"Good God, no! Only a fool would claim to read a woman's mind. But I can tell you what's in a corner of it."

"Oh?"

"You were thinking, just a minute ago, that it's not so bad to be a slave after all. That perhaps those nasty little comments of yours a while back were a bit premature."

"Well, in a way. . . ." Faith was startled by his words. That *was* what she had been thinking, but how could he know? "Of course, I wouldn't want to be a slave myself. It would be perfectly awful having someone tell me where I could live or whom to choose for a friend—or even whom to marry. But it isn't as bad as I thought. I mean, they really do have fun, don't they? And the work is hard, but it's not all that awful."

Brad's whole face contorted with laughter as he rose and looked down at her.

"Let's see if you can say the same thing tomorrow. Come out to the fields at dawn—if you can get your pretty head off the pillow that early—and we'll see if you're Adam Eliot's daughter after all, or just a pale imitation of your mother."

Faith stared at him helplessly. Every time they seemed to be getting along, he had to go and do something to spoil it.

"What's wrong with my mother?"

"Let's just say I can't imagine that spoiled little lady laboring with the darkies in the field. Or lifting a dustmop with the laziest housemaid for that matter."

Faith's lips tightened into a pout. "Now who's being smug? You seem to know a great deal about my mother—for a man who never even met her!"

The words did not work as well for her as they had for him. Her best insults seemed to slide off his back like water off a duck's feathers.

"*Touché,* my sweet. Tomorrow at dawn then—and we'll see what a daughter of Desirée Devereaux is made of."

Dawn cast an eerie gray light over a land that was only half awake. Estee laid her hand on the barn door, feeling the rough texture of unpainted oak against her palm, and stared up at a single streak of blood red threading across the horizon. They had already taken so many chances, she and Rodrigo. It was insane to be here now.

Come to me in the barn, querida, he had urged the night before, taking advantage of the confusion that followed the claying to slip over to Havenhurst for a few minutes. *Come at dawn when the workers are in the fields, and my master and his wife are still in bed.*

Come to Eleazar Carstairs' barn! And she like a fool had agreed!

She dared stand there no longer, a dark silhouette against the lightening sky. Rusty hinges creaked a loud protest as she pulled the door open, then drew it shut behind her, slipping into the dim interior. Outside, the air had been fresh, and a chill morning dew cut through the thin calico of her dress. Inside, it was hot and stifling, with the musty odor of mud and dung mixed with rotting hay.

"Hssst, *querida!* Up here."

Estee jumped nervously, then caught herself with an angry jolt. Looking up, she saw Rodrigo grinning down at her from the hay loft.

"Fool!" she hissed, as furious with him for startling her as for making so much noise. "Keep on shouting like that and you'll wake the dead, to say nothing of the living."

He laughed heartily, a full, booming sound that bounced off the empty walls.

You know what you are? *Una coneja pequeña*—a timid little doe rabbit. Always afraid of everything."

Estee gave him a sharp look as she started up the ladder. "If I were afraid, would I be here?"

Rodrigo tried to look stern as he glowered back at her. "What is it with you, *mujer?* Fire in the eyes and a tongue as tart as vinegar! Why can't you be sweet and docile like other women—and never talk back to me?"

"Because I'd bore you to death, that's why. You wouldn't put up with sweetness for five minutes, and you know it!"

He could hold back the laughter no longer. She could see right through him, this proud, hot-headed woman of his, and he loved it! Reaching down, he gripped her arms in hands so massive they made her look fragile. It took him only a second to drag her up the last few rungs of the ladder.

Estee struggled for a moment, holding on to the last vestiges of sanity, then gave up, sinking into the compelling power of his embrace. This was her man, imperfect and irritating as he was, and she would give up anything, risk anything, to be with him.

He held her briefly, teasing her with his arms; then released her suddenly, tossing her into the air as lightly as if she were a little girl. Estee thrilled to the swift changes in his mood, the passion and the playful exuberance that followed so easily on each other's heels. A surge of exhilaration raced through her body as he whirled her over his head, whipping her skirts out behind her. Crude, ill-fitting boots clomped heavily against the rough floorboards.

"Put me down, you idiot!" she protested, trying not to laugh. "They'll hear you a mile away. Put me down this instant!"

"Put you down? That's what you want?"

She missed the teasing in his eyes. "You heard me. I told you to put me down!"

"Anything you say!"

He flipped her neatly over his head, hurling her into a pile of hay on the other side of the loft. Estee's shrill cry of surprise dissolved into giggles as she felt musty, crackling straw envelop her body, half burying her. Horrified, she clapped her hand over her mouth. And she had told him not to make so much noise!

He did not give her a chance to think what she was doing, but dropped down beside her, pulling her back with him until her body was stretched out on top of his. His fingers were like iron as they twisted through her hair, forcing her head slowly, irresistibly down. Her lips parted, hungry to receive the scourging presence of his tongue, bold, exciting—the way she had taught him to kiss her. The way he knew she loved.

The smell of hay was damp in her nostrils, a stale accent to the odor of their sweat. Funny, she thought, how much she associated smells with this man. Grassy knolls, green and pungent in the spring; the aroma of mud and decaying ferns, carried on the wind from the swamps; jessamine on the rice banks, as sweet as orange blossoms. If it all ended tomorrow—if she could never see this man again—how would she ever bear to walk through the fields and woods again?

The power in his hands was potent, fiery, as he ran them up and down her body, making her flesh tingle with the roughness of his touch. Subtlety was no part of this man's nature. His fingers should not have hesitated as they searched the contours of her breast—his fist should have grabbed her dress and torn it away with one quick, violent wrench. But they both knew she could not go home with telltale rips and rents in her garb, and so a part of their pleasure in each other was diminished.

He sensed the pain in her surrender, and he recognized it for what it was, the despair of a woman trapped in a love that would not let her go until it had destroyed her. It excited him to feel her twist and writhe on top of him, wriggling her limbs to help him free her of her garments. His hands slid lower, curling around her buttocks, forcing her skirt down until she lay naked in arms that longed to crush her.

He was about to take her at last, when he felt her tense suddenly, drawing slowly upward. The movement angered him, stirring latent passions he could neither acknowledge nor understand. Sometimes she was magnificent, his beautiful Estee—earthy and free with her love. Other times, she turned all fussy and female on him, fretting over things no man could comprehend.

He held her at arm's length. Her skin, a light creamy brown, was so pale she almost looked white.

"Did you hear that?" she asked sharply. "That creaking noise? Like someone opening the door?"

In spite of himself, he picked up her tension. "I didn't hear anything," he said defensively. "You must have imagined it."

But he listened anyway, straining his ears into the darkness. All he could hear was a soft rustling, like a rat scurrying across the floor. Then there was only silence.

Estee knew she had angered him, but she could not think of a way to put things right. She longed to touch his face with her hand, caressing him gently, tenderly. But tenderness was a thing he could not accept.

"One of these days I'll be right," she said softly. "One of these days I'll hear a sound, and when we look up, there'll be someone there, standing over us. Then it will all be over."

"If we are stupid enough to stay around and wait for that to happen—yes!"

She knew what was coming, but she did not try to stop him. It was important for him to say the words. Important to have a sense of power over his own destiny.

"And if we don't stay here, love—where would you have us go? To the swamps with those mythical heroes of yours?"

He drew her down again, letting his lips rest soothingly on her hair. She knew he did it for her, and she loved him for it.

"Why not to the swamps, mythical or no? If we stay here—if we keep on as we have been—it will all be over anyway. At least in the swamps, we would have a taste of freedom."

Only a few months ago, his words would have terrified her. Now she had grown used to them—or perhaps it was only that she had finally come to admit he was right.

"We will be killed, Rodrigo. You know that."

"Perhaps. But is that so terrible? Is it worse to die than to live in chains?"

Estee studied his face in the shadows. His were strong features, eyes large and wide-set, a broad, noble brow, nostrils full and flaring. This was a man meant by nature to be a hunter or chieftain—a man meant to stand tall among men. Not a man to grovel on the ground, begging for crusts of bread, crawling through the night like a thief to claim his woman. The chains he railed at were robbing him slowly of his manhood.

"I love you, Rodrigo. If you go to the swamps, I will follow."

"And if I put a gun in your hand?"

She faltered. This was not a challenge she could face. She was ready to die for this man, but killing for him was quite another matter. But she sensed this was not a time to defy him.

"Wherever you go, I go, too. Whatever you ask, I will give you. I am your woman, and I belong to you."

The hay scratched her skin as she burrowed her arms into it, twining them around him. Her fingers were as impatient as his, clawing at the coarse trousers that stood between his naked flesh and her desire. There was no modesty left in her, no fear—no sense of the tomorrow that might never come. Her hips hovered above his, tantalizing him for a brief instant, then lunged down, meeting the potent upward thrust that tore into her body with a savage passion. There was only this man and this moment, and nothing existed beyond the boundary of his embrace.

Faith stooped down, ignoring the dull pain in her arm as she reached out for at least the thousandth time that morning, sprinkling a few grains of rice into a carefully drilled hole, then brushing the dirt back over it again. Shifting the heavy canvas bag on her shoulder, she inched forward, groping for the next hole with her hand. It had seemed so easy two hours ago. Just follow the men with the team of oxen and the rice drill, and pop a few seeds into every hole—what could be simpler? It hadn't occurred to her that the endless repetition might take its toll: bend and sow the seed, rise and walk a few steps, bend and tug at one of the countless weeds that evaded the hoes, rise and try to walk again.

Brad paused on a nearby bank to watch her. He wondered if she realized what a delightfully droll figure she made, dragging an oversized rice bag along the ground behind her, her jaw set in a stubborn square like a little girl determined to prove she could do anything the grown-ups could.

"Well, what do you think?" he called out. "Does a slave's work still seem like fun?"

Faith threw him a sharp glance. His boots were covered with mud, but a clean gray shirt, open to the waist, fluttered in the breeze, and a broad-brimmed straw hat cooled his brow.

"Oh, just—just go to hell!"

Brad grinned broadly. Blast it, she was a willful little thing! So tired she could barely stand and still she had the fire to curse him out like a fishwife. He hoped Alexandre appreciated all that spirit.

"Peace, you vixen! I didn't come to quarrel. Surely you see undisguised admiration in my eyes. How can I fail to be captivated by a woman who looks beautiful in a full coat of spring mud?"

In spite of herself, Faith giggled. He was being positively dreadful, but she couldn't work up the energy to get mad at him. Besides, it was fun engaging in outrageous banter with a man again, even if she couldn't believe a word of what he said.

"If only I could get my husband to say something like that."

Brad did not miss the wistful edge in her voice. So, Alex had managed to touch that deep core of passion after all. He didn't know why the idea surprised him. Whatever else the bastard lacked, he obviously had a way with feisty women. Even Fleur, that calculating little minx, had been attached to him—though he had never seemed to neglect her the way he was neglecting his wife.

Brad crouched down, fixing his eyes steadily on Faith. It seemed to him she looked even more like a little girl than before.

"Do you want some advice? Or perhaps I should say, would you take some advice, even if you don't want it?"

Faith fidgeted under his gaze. She had already given away more of herself than she intended. The last thing she wanted was to encourage another intimacy.

"I'm sure I don't know what you mean. What kind of advice could you have for me?"

Brad took in the picture of this woman before him, vulnerable and appealing, and he cursed himself for a fool. If she didn't find what she wanted in her marriage, sooner or later she was going to look for it somewhere else.

"I can give you a man's point of view. Sometimes that helps. It may have occurred to you that we're a bunch of ornery, self-centered sons-of-bitches—and you're not far from right. If you want to hold our attention, you're going to have to put out the right bait. Now a hot-tempered hussy up to her ankles in mud and swearing like a man might make *my* blood boil—but I can't imagine old Alex sidling up to someone like that, can you?"

Faith looked down, uncomfortably aware of the dirt caked on her skirt. Unsightly blisters were already beginning to form on her hands. It didn't exactly endear Brad to her to realize he was right.

"I'll thank you to keep your advice to yourself. My relationship with my husband is no concern of yours!"

Brad pinched the brim of his hat, pulling it low over his eyes. It *was* none of his concern, but how could he ignore that sad look? Besides, he had never gone after another man's wife in his life. He wasn't about to start now.

"You did cheat the man, my dear. You lured him to the altar with fluttering lashes and a flirtatious little simper, and the poor fool thought he was headed for heaven. Imagine his shock when he woke up one morning and found himself married to a woman with a will of iron and a frightening predilection to question everything in sight."

Faith stared at her shoes, fascinated by the way mud oozed around the pointed toes when she shoved them into the earth. He was right, she *had* cheated Alexandre. But if she lived up to her promises—if she gave him the silly imitation of Fleur he wanted—she would be cheating herself.

A sudden commotion erupted in the distance, breaking into their conversation. Faith glanced up quickly, half curious, half eager to snatch at anything that might prove a distraction. At first, she had no sense of trepidation. Slaves in the nearby fields, hoes and rice sacks in hand, had begun to drift slowly inland, but nothing in their ambling gait gave notice of concern. Only a few of the men, those that had been working nearest the road, threw down their tools and ran toward Brad, calling out to attract his attention.

Brad sized up the situation instantly. Whirling away, he raced over the rice banks, nimble as a mountain goat. His long legs barely broke stride as he vaulted over canal after canal, closing the distance between himself and the road. Faith dropped her heavy sack on the ground and scrambled up the bank to get a better view.

The scene that met her eyes hardly seemed worthy of such an uproar. A small procession of men, one black, the others white, all of them too far away to make out their faces, was winding slowly up the narrow dirt road toward the main house. There was something familiar about the man who reined in the lead horse when Brad approached to challenge him—something vaguely unpleasant—but other than that, everything seemed normal. It was a moment before Faith realized who the man was.

Eleazar Carstairs. But why on earth would he come calling at planting time? And why would he have a group of men behind him?

It was then that she saw the woman. Faith's hand slipped up to her breast, twisting and untwisting the fabric of her bodice. The woman had been bound like an animal, then attached with a long rope to the saddle of the last rider in line, the only black man in the group. Faith squinted into the distance, raising her hand to shield her eyes from the glare of the sun. But even before she made out dark features, she knew what she would see.

The woman being pulled at the end of the rope was Estee.

Now it was Faith who was running along the banks, her skirts hiked up to her knees, her feet tangling in the vines that sprawled across the earth. She did not hesitate when she reached the first canal, but leaped over it, landing with a clumsy thud on the other side.

Oh, please, God, she thought, trying desperately not to feel the violent thumping of her heart against her chest. Please let it be a mistake. A misunderstanding. Please don't let it be what it looks like!

But the minute she reached the road, the minute she stopped at the edge and looked up at the man seated tensely on the lead horse, she knew it was no use. Estee had met her lover once too often—and they had been caught. The look on Carstairs' face was enough to tell her the man at least could expect no mercy. Dark eyes burned against untanned skin, blazing with a hatred that transcended rage.

Faith was almost afraid to look at Estee, but she could not tear her eyes away. Her hair had come loose, hanging in shaggy tufts down her back, and her dress, once a gay calico, was now dark brown with dirt. Her arms were badly scraped and covered with blood, as if she had fallen and been dragged behind the horse, but her head was as high as ever, her body straight and tall. Even when Brad cut her cords, freeing her at last, she did not try to move, but stood alone, a little apart from the others.

Faith drew closer to the men, anxious to hear what they were saying. Carstairs' voice reached her first.

"I want the man Prince back, do you hear? Tonight!"

Faith caught the brittle tension in his tone. Surreptitiously, she threw a glance at Estee. So that was why she was so defiant! The man had escaped, and she still had hope for him.

But Brad's face was grim. "You'll have him."

"You're the captain of the patrol, Alleyn. Don't think you can go soft on us now. The man's a real firebrand, make no mistake about it. If we let him go, we'll have another Stono River on——"

"I said, you'll have him!"

Carstairs' face darkened, but he did not say anything. Setting his lips in a taut line, he turned his horse around, gesturing to the men to follow. He was several paces down the road before he stopped to give Brad one last telling look.

"Tonight, Alleyn! We'll be waiting for you."

Faith wanted to weep as she watched the men ride away, their horses' hooves stirring up a cloud of dust in the air behind them. Estee looked so small suddenly, so childlike, standing all by herself in the center of the road. Faith took a tentative step toward her, then drew back. It was such a fragile thing, this bond that had grown between them in the last few months. Could she really expect a slave to share her pain with a white woman?

Before she could decide what to do, another figure came into view, pushing everyone out of the way as she strode emphatically down the road. There was something wonderfully reassuring in the stern expression on Beneba's face, Faith thought as she watched her draw near. Something in that gruff, no-nonsense facade that almost made everything safe and familiar again. Estee seemed to sense it, too, for she leaned against the woman for a brief second before allowing herself to be led away.

Faith stared after them, the stout old slave, her back strong but bent, the slender girl, rigid and proud even in despair. The tenderness between them surprised her. It had never occurred to her that Beneba—tough, cantankerous old Beneba—might actually harbor a woman's softness in her heart. Yet there was in her mien now a sorrow that seemed timelessly maternal. A sorrow that spoke of love and resignation—and the need to comfort, even when no comfort was possible.

By the time they finally disappeared and Faith turned back again, she saw that the blacks had returned to their work, taking up tools and sacks of rice again, as if there were some comfort to be found even in routine drudgery. Only Brad still remained in the road, his eyes fixed blankly on the distant horizon.

"Brad, what—what's going to happen to Estee?"

His faced looked ashen in profile. "What do you think is going to happen? That I'm going to take her out and beat her? I'm not a monster, Faith."

Faith stared at him miserably. She should have trusted him, she realized now. She should have come to this man long ago and begged him to avert a senseless tragedy. Now she was too ashamed even to confess what she had done.

"But the man. What's going to happen to the man? What did Carstairs mean when he kept saying 'tonight'?"

"Tonight?" Brad tilted his hat back on his head, but he did not look at her. "Tonight, my dear, you are going to see Colonial civilization in full flower. Tonight, a bold band of men—the strongest and the bravest in the land—will mount the swiftest horses and take up the finest weapons money can buy. And all to track down one terrified, unarmed slave running on foot through the swamps."

At last he turned to her. His face was hard and cold, like a mask carved out of stone.

"And God help the poor devil when we get him."

Two

The dull *clop-clop, clop-clop* of horse's hooves against the soft dirt trail was a hollow, empty sound in the still night. Brad unhooked a tarnished brass lantern from the saddle and raised it to shoulder height, swinging the rays in a slow, even arc to illuminate both sides of the path. Dark shadows, heavy beneath low-hanging pine branches and thick, flowering shrubs, vanished in brief flashes of gold. A squirrel, startled by the sudden intrusion, stared at Brad with frightened eyes, then scurried away in a rustle of leaves and dry twigs. There was no other sound—no other movement. No sense of a group of men behind him, reining in their horses with impatient hands, willing to hold back only a moment or two while he scouted the darkness ahead.

The path turned away from the shore, climbing a low rise that separated orchards and cornfields from the marshy swampland along the river. Brad hesitated, then touched his heel to the stallion's flank. It was unlikely that a runaway slave would venture into open fields, but he couldn't overlook the possibility.

He paused when he reached the top, holding the horse back with a firm hand. There was no need for the lantern now. A full moon, round and white against a backdrop of deep, cloudless blue, cast a haunting, almost unnatural glow over rolling hills and long, flat rows of red-brown earth. No one could move out there without casting a shadow; nothing bigger than a mole could crouch in the furrows in the soil. Not even an owl could fly from pine to pine without being seen.

Damn the fool! Brad thought, surprised at the sudden feeling of empathy he had with the man. If he had deliberately set out to pick the worst possible night to flee, he couldn't have made a better job of it.

Brad leaned forward, running his hand along the stallion's neck, more to settle his own nerves than to reassure his mount. He could still see the look in Faith's eyes when she came into the hallway that evening and saw him in a dark jacket and riding boots.

"You mean you're going out there? With *them*?"

If he had been standing in front of her with an ax in his hand, ready to chop little children into bits, she could not have been more horrified—or more disgusted. It irritated Brad to realize how much he minded. It was not as if he cared about the woman!

"It's my duty," he replied stiffly. "As captain of the patrol, I have to go."

"But he hasn't done anything, Brad. You know he hasn't! Surely it isn't a crime to make love to a woman—even if you don't marry her first. You of all people ought to know that!"

There was no missing the sarcasm in her voice. Brad could not forget an afternoon when this same beauty had trembled in his arms—and he had been all too ready to take advantage of her passion.

"The man is a runaway slave, Faith, and a troublemaker at that. Someone has to bring him back."

Confound the bitch anyway, what did she want of him? He turned the horse with a flick of his wrist, heading him back down the low incline toward the clearing they had just left. Did she want him to stay at home and pretend all this wasn't happening? Who did she think would lead the patrol, then? Someone like Eleazar Carstairs? A sadist without a trace of conscience!

He pulled the horse to a stop at the bottom of the hill. The hell of it was, the bitch was right. He didn't want to be there any more than she wanted him to—and there wasn't a thing he could do about it! He raised his lantern, moving it back and forth over his head to call in the men.

Suddenly the darkness seemed to be filled with sound. The heavy plodding of hooves; a jangle of bridles and stirrups; hoarse, masculine whispers rising above everything else. Brad eyed the men warily as they filed one by one into the clearing. Dan Fraser. His father had come to the Colonies forty years ago without a farthing to his name, and he had died with his pockets still empty. Dan had done no better with their meager patch of land—but he would fight to the death to protect it. Jim Burden. A decent, hard-working man, compassionate to black and white alike—until last year when his pretty young wife decided to visit her brother and his family at Stono River. Not a child was left alive when the runaways finished with them. Jarvis Reid. A firm advocate of the "Ship 'em back to Africa" school, Reid had found an even more efficient way to thin out the slaves—whip them to death if they didn't stay in line. He had come out for every patrol as long as Brad could remember, and he would keep on patrolling until he was too old to hold his seat on a horse. Young Hugh Corbin, filling in for an ailing father. His eyes were dilated with excitement, his body alert and eager—he was a man among men for the first time in his life. How much of a man would he feel later, Brad wondered, when they had put an end to their mission?

Within minutes, the group in the clearing had swelled until they numbered nearly thirty, double the contingent that rode on routine patrols at least once a month. Leave it to the hunt to bring them out in full force, Brad thought dryly. One whiff of blood and they were after the scent, like hounds sniffing out a fox.

Brad made no effort to conceal his distaste as he turned, tight-lipped, toward the swamp that separated Havenhurst from Lord Warren's Oakwood plantation to the west. He didn't like the looks of the place, but then neither did the others, judging from the restless sounds in the darkness behind him. Too many streamers of gray moss dangled from cypresses and live-oaks, too many hollows provided hiding places in tall grasses—and a damn sight too many soft, treacherous spots in the earth threatened to catch a horse's hooves, drawing him into a deadly trap of quicksand.

Brad's face was taut as he turned back.

"All right, men, it looks as if he's taken to the swamps. I don't need to tell you, we can't afford to let him slip past us. Burden, take half the men and search the area closest to the shore. Spread out so you cover the whole territory—but don't spread yourselves too thin. I don't want a rabbit or a gopher to get between you without your knowing it.

Brad ran his eyes tensely over the rest of the group. Burden had been an easy choice. He might have a grudge against the slaves, but he was a fair, law-abiding man. It was appalling to think of sending the others out under Jarvis Reid, but there didn't seem to be any choice. The man was tough and experienced—and he was a natural leader.

"You, Reid—take the inland side of the swamp and do the same thing."

The men responded to the authority in his voice. Maybe it wasn't so bad, being known as a son-of-a-bitch, Brad thought with a grim smile. The men didn't like him—they sure as hell didn't trust him!—but they respected him enough to vote him in as captain. And they would never question his orders.

He watched with cold, assessing eyes as the two groups fanned guiding their horses in cautious, zigzag lines through the undergrowth. The pointed tips of their boots were sharp weapons jabbing into the shrubbery; their riding crops looked like sabres in their hands. It took Brad only an instant to see that the plan was flawed. Already Burden and his men had begun to hang back, working the area carefully, methodically, taking time to do the job right. Reid, the more impulsive of the two, moved ahead, covering the same ground in half the time. If the slave was cunning—and Brad had the feeling he was—he would stick close to the shore, waiting until Reid's men had passed. Then he would slip in behind them, doubling back on his tracks.

But if one man stayed behind—if one man crept stealthily through the brush, well to the rear of the others—the slave would fall into his trap!

Brad waited until he could no longer see the men, then prodded his horse slowly forward. The swamp looked more perilous than ever. Dammit, why had Adam been too stubborn to clear it away—and why had he been too swayed by Adam's judgment to do it himself? He almost hoped the man Prince would get through to Oakwood. It would be easier to pursue him there.

His ear picked up a sound on the trail behind him, an unexpected echo of his own hoofbeats. Whirling around, he saw Eleazar Carstairs rein his horse to a stop.

"What in God's name are you doing here? I thought I told everyone to move out."

The man didn't intimidate easily, Brad had to give him that. "You're not a fool, Alleyn—neither am I. I'll make a bargain with you. Don't pretend you don't know what I'm doing, and I won't pretend I haven't figured out what you're up to."

Brad shifted the lantern, aiming it deliberately at Carstairs' face. Dark eyes glittered with an ugly intensity. Blast the villain! Brad thought furiously. It excited him to track down an unarmed man—it actually excited him! Just as it must have excited him to stumble on a pair of lovers, caught in the throes of a desperate passion.

"You'll get your slave back, Carstairs. I guaranteed you that. But don't expect me to stomach you in the process."

Carstairs only laughed. There was a quick, almost buoyant animation in his manner as he turned back toward the swamp.

"You should have cleaned that mess up years ago, Alleyn. I always said so. If we're going to lose him anywhere, we'll lose him there. And there'll be the devil to pay if we do!"

Brad tensed. Carstairs was only uttering the words he himself had been thinking, but he was in no humor to put up with him.

"Preserving the swamp was Adam's idea. He wanted it that was. Wanted? Hell, he insisted on it! I'll defer to Adam any day. When it came to running a plantation, he knew what he was doing."

"Did he? Correct my memory, my friend, but isn't that the same Adam Eliot who later lost Havenhurst to debts and bad management?"

"Goddammit, Carstairs, I've had about as much of you as I can take! You know beastly well Adam ran a tight ship here. The plantation Jeremy got his hands on was efficient and profitable. Not the shambles I took over a year and a half later."

He stopped abruptly, angry at himself for his childishness. Outbursts like that only played into Carstairs' hands. Besides, much as he hated to admit it, the man was right. They *couldn't* afford to let Prince get away. Even at Havenhurst, the slave had already acquired a following. Solemn, humorless Toney, Cuffee's only son, had been seen talking with him more than once, as had Phillis, the most unobtrusive of the house maids, and even giddy little Fibby. And those were just the ones he knew about!

"All right, Carstairs—you win. But stay behind me. And for God's sake, try to be quiet!"

The earth changed subtly as the two men moved forward. The ground, firm only a minute before, was soft and muddy now, the vegetation so damp it smelled rotten. Brad felt the horse balk beneath him, and he tightened his grip on the reins. They were going to need all the strength they could muster, he and his mount both, if they were to work their way deep into the heart of this fetid marshland.

Trees loomed up on every side. Timeless cypresses with twisted limbs. Tall live-oaks, so thick with moss they looked like gray willows, weeping false tears into the earth. Brad scanned each tree as he passed, jumping when he caught a hint of movement beneath one of them. Something blowing in the wind? he asked himself tensely. Or just imagination?

Or the quarry he had set himself to catch?

The horse resisted, sidestepping gingerly as he forced its flank against a long tendril of moss, but Brad held him in place with a firm hand. Thrusting out his arm, he pushed the lantern forward, letting light play through a cavern of shadows at the base of the tree. Nervous eyes darted first to one side, then the other, searching the darkness around the trunk, rising to the lower branches. The tension did not drain out of his body until he had convinced himself there was no one there.

So it *was* imagination, he thought, hooking the lantern back on the saddle and steering his horse toward the path again. Imagination and nerves. He had the feeling it was going to be a long night.

Carstairs was a constant presence in the darkness behind him. Brad could not see the man as they pressed deeper into the swamp—he could barely hear the soft sound of his hoofbeats in the mud—but he did not for a second forget he was there. Watching, waiting, ready to laugh every time Brad jumped at a shadow that did not exist.

Blast it! Why was it taking so long anyway? They should have had the slave by now. He should have bolted into their arms long ago in a flight of panic. Unless, of course. . . .

Unless he was shrewder than Brad had anticipated. Unless he already knew one man was following behind the main group.

The horse shied suddenly, putting an end to speculation as skittish hooves dug stubbornly into the moist sand. Brad tightened his knees, holding his seat as best he could, and leaned forward. He was about to urge the stallion on again when the scent of water reached his nostrils. Squinting into the darkness, he was surprised to catch a glimmer of white moonlight on glassy black.

A pond. Brad could vaguely remember having seen it before. A shallow, insignificant puddle, barely worth noting. Now, in a spate of freshets from the mountains, it had swelled into a small lake.

Well, so much the better, he thought, waiting for Carstairs to catch up with him. This was just the opportunity he had been waiting for.

"We'd better split up. There's no telling which way he went. You take the low ground, toward the river. I'll cover the other side."

Carstairs reacted just as he had expected. "The hell you will! You know bloody well the bastard would never be fool enough to get caught between the pond and the river. *You* go that way—if you think it's such a good idea!"

Brad concealed a smile. A fugitive might very well risk the narrow stretch of marshland along the river—if he thought that was the last thing his pursuer would expect!

"Have it your way, Carstairs. But if you catch him, I want him taken alive—or shot cleanly! Any marks of abuse and you'll answer to me."

Brad watched with a grim sense of satisfaction as the other man picked a cautious path through the muddy bogs that edged the pond. Carstairs had not only swallowed the bait—in a way, he *was* the bait. If Prince did know what was going on—and Brad was more and more sure he did—the dull echo of a horse's hooves on the far shore of the pond would be certain to throw him off guard.

Brad dismounted, tying his horse tightly to a trunk of a nearby tree. He might not make as good time on foot, but at least he wouldn't be sending out audible signals to tell the slave where he was. He took down the lantern, throwing his jacket over it to hide its bright yellow beams. He did not miss the illumination. Every tree, every shrub, every blade of grass, stood out in the crisp light of the moon.

The ground was like a wet sponge, sinking with a slushy sigh every time he stepped on it. Brad tested each new spot with his foot, making sure there was a bottom to the oozing mud before he set his weight on it. He began to feel a disconcerting sense of affinity with his own horse. The last thing he'd want now was some insensitive dolt on his back, digging hard heels into his side every time he decided he didn't like the rotten mush under his feet.

He had gone no more than a quarter of a mile, perhaps less, when his leg rammed into something hard on the path in front of him. Reaching down, he ran his hand along a taut, slender object, stretched horizontally across the trail. A length of cord? he asked himself, puzzled. A leather thong? Then slowly, he realized what it was.

A vine. Someone had deliberately tied a vine across the path. At just the height of a horse's shin!

So the man did know he was there. It occurred to Brad that he had underestimated his adversary. The man not only knew he would lag behind the others, he knew which side of the pond he would choose. And he knew he would come alone!

But the advantage was still on his side, Brad reminded himself coolly. The trick with the vine told him that the man had made one miscalculation—and that was a bad one. He assumed Brad was on horseback. Raising his eyes, Brad scrutinized the terrain. Somewhere ahead, there was a small clearing—fifty, perhaps a hundred yards away. The slave would be there now, his body tense, his ears straining into the darkness, waiting for the crash that would tell him Brad had been caught in his snare.

Brad slipped a hunting knife out of his belt, slashing through the vine with one quick stroke. Cold moonlight glinted on a shiny blade as he tucked it back again. Sweat poured down his brow, but he did not take the time to reach up and brush it away with a brusque hand. This time, when he touched his belt, he was not looking for his knife. The cold metal butt of a dueling pistol felt solid and reassuring against his palm.

He had taken only a few steps when a sharp crack burst suddenly through the still night. Every muscle in his body tightened as he spun around, peering into the darkness in a vain effort to see what had happened. It took several seconds to realize that the sound had not come from somewhere *out there*—it had come from beneath his own feet. Looking down, he was dismayed to see the rough, jagged edge of a broken branch.

Damn! One dry branch in this soggy, stinking swamp, and he had to find it! He might as well have shot off a cannon to announce his approach.

The advantages were all on the other side now. He knew it—and the man he was stalking knew it, too. He shifted the gun in his hand, holding it cautiously in front of him as he began to inch forward. The slave could afford to wait. He could stay where he was, standing absolutely still, not moving an inch—not even drawing too deep a breath. Just letting Brad take all the chances.

Brad stopped after a few steps. A new idea had begun to take hold of him. He mulled it over in his mind, then turned and retraced his path, returning the way he had come. When he found a spot where the tangled vines and grasses were not quite so dense, he veered to the right, following natural breaks in the undergrowth whenever he could. It was a risky business, trying to circle around to the back of the clearing, but it was nowhere near as risky as staying on the path.

It took him a good half hour to work his way to the clearing, but he did not try to hurry. He knew the slave must be apprehensive by now, alerted to danger by the long delay, but carelessness would only make things worse. His hand was slow and steady as he pushed the last leaves aside and peered into the clearing.

Only the wavery shadows of moss-draped oaks, shivering in a cold night wind, met his eye. It was frustrating, but it was no more than Brad had expected. Prince was hardly a man to make things easy for his masters. Anyone who wanted to take him was going to have to be tough—and bold. Brad did not wait an instant longer. Letting out a loud cry, he leaped forward, pulling the cover off the lantern.

They saw each other at the same time. The white man was only a shadow, hazy and vague in the halo surrounding the light. But the black man, caught in bright, probing rays, made a striking figure, poised like a panther on the far side of the clearing. His bare chest glowed golden-brown, and taut muscles bulged until they seemed to have doubled in size. A thick pine branch looked heavy and menacing in upraised hands as he whirled to face his pursuer.

Brad tensed automatically. Leveling the gun in his hand, he watched the man warily, waiting for the first break in that rigid posture. His finger was tight on the trigger, his knuckles white as he gripped the handle, but still the slave did not move. Slowly, without breaking his gaze, Brad lowered the gun, easing it down, first an inch, then two. The slave responded, dropping the branch until it rested against his shoulder.

There was something in the man's bearing that fascinated Brad. A kind of arrogance he had not expected—a defiance that was almost a challenge. As if he did not know the game was over. As if he still thought he had a chance to win.

It was a moment before Brad understood that the challenge he had sensed was not an illusion. When he did, he felt his blood run cold.

Shoot me! the slave was daring him. *Go ahead and shoot—if you're man enough! You tracked me down like a wild beast. Now have the decency to put me out of my misery.*

And damn him, he was right! Every nerve in Brad's body was on edge as he raised the pistol again. There was only one thing he could do for the slave now. Only one justification for being there at all. Every man—even a man in bondage—had the right to an honorable death.

Not the unspeakable degradation Eleazar Carstairs had planned for him.

Brad aimed at the man's chest, trying to focus on it dispassionately, as if it were some sort of inanimate target on the practice field. Why the devil was it so hard? he asked himself angrily. Because the slave was unarmed. But that was no excuse. God help him, if *he* were the man on the other side of the clearing—if he were about to face Carstairs' vindictive wrath—he would want the mercy of a quick death himself.

Then, suddenly, the silence was shattered by a raucous medley of shouts and hoofbeats, and Brad realized that the moment of choice was over. He could not shoot the slave now, even if he wanted to. Men and horses erupted into the clearing, filling the space with frenetic motion and whoops of jubilation. Blast it, he thought bitterly. He should have hidden his horse better. He had set them on the trail himself.

The slave reacted with a burst of fury. Howling out his rage, he whipped the pine branch over his head, hurling it into the mass of men with a force calculated to wrench from them the bitter triumph Brad had denied him. But he had misjudged his captors. The man who rode into the clearing was not hot-tempered Jarvis Reid, but Jim Burden. Cool and level-headed, he held his horse steady, calling out to the men to hold their fire, even as he leaned to one side, ducking the deadly missive that whizzed past his head.

It was all over in a matter of seconds. Men leaped from the saddle, swarming over the ground like a colony of ants with a crumb of bread. The slave put up a good fight, but he was badly outnumbered, and they had him in the dirt before he knew it. Dan Fraser threw down a rope, and they tied his hands behind him, holding him flat on his stomach until they finished the job.

Brad sat on his horse, watching impassively as they pulled the man to his feet again. He was like a caged beast, immobile but tense, ready to explode at any second with the savage anger trapped inside him. Only when he looked up and saw Brad did he finally move. His lips contorted, his head turned to the side, and he spat contemptuously in the dirt.

Brad winced as if the spittle had struck him in the face. He knew only too well what those silent, scornful lips were saying.

Coward! the man accused him. Spineless, hypocritical coward! You shoot a horse when he breaks a leg. You shoot a dog when he's old and suffering. Where is your compassion for a human being?

Where, indeed? Brad thought wearily as he turned away, barking out the orders the men expected to hear. He had had one chance for compassion that night—he would not have another in the long hours that lay ahead. All he could do now was take the end of the rope that bound the man and tie it to his own saddle, holding his horse to a slow, easy gait as they moved out of the clearing.

Salve for the conscience? he asked himself with a bitter half smile. As if conscience had anything to do with the things that were about to happen. It was all empty gestures now—but empty gestures were all he had. At least he could make sure the trip to Cypress Hill would not be painful and degrading. At least the slave would not have to suffer the final indignity of being dragged through the mud behind his horse.

At least he would walk to his fate like a man.

Brad sprawled uncomfortably on the narrow bed, feeling every lump in the crude mattress beneath him. Sweat drained off his naked flesh, drenching dried gray moss until it smelled as sour as decaying ferns in the swamp. The door was open, and a biting wind whistled across his body.

Don't think about it, he warned himself sharply. Just don't think about it, and you'll be all right!

He sat up restlessly, swinging his feet over the side and bracing them against the floor. The woman had moved across the room. She stood beside the fire now, a long cotton robe covering dark ocher skin. Thick smoke dimmed her features, making her look younger, softer, as she picked up a long stick and dipped it into a heavy iron cauldron on the flames.

Probably a potion of some sort, Brad thought with a grimace. Something to make him feel more like a man!

"Put that damn thing down, Eva, and come here. I don't need any of your blasted witchcraft—or Beneba's herbs either. I need a woman's body next to mine."

Eva braced the stick against the wall and turned toward him, but she did not move. Something in that dark inscrutable gaze made Brad uncomfortable, as if he were some kind of bug that had just crawled out from under a rock. Was she contemptuous of him because he had not been able to prove his masculinity just now? Or had she already learned what happened earlier?

"Dammit, I said come here!"

He did not wait, but jumped up and strode across the room, thrusting out rough hands. His body was ready for her now, hard and strong, the way a man was supposed to feel.

He didn't give a damn what she thought anyhow! He wanted her, and by God, he was going to have her!

However she felt, she did not try to resist. She came toward him, her arms opening obediently, as they always did when he demanded it of her. She was nearly touching him when she stopped abruptly, taking an unexpected step backward. Angrily, Brad grabbed her wrist, jerking her toward him.

The first queasy twinges of apprehension touched him when he realized she was staring not at him but the open doorway behind him. He released her slowly, barely noticing that she rubbed her arm as she pulled it away from him. Even before he turned, he knew what he was going to see.

Faith stood in the doorway. But this was not the Faith he knew. This was a different Faith. A brooding, fiery Fury, pale hair flying around her face, green-gold eyes snapping like lightning in a summer storm. Brad felt his mouth go dry as he stared at her.

She knows, he thought, ignoring the beads of perspiration that stood out on his forehead. *She knows—and she despises me even more than I despise myself.*

A surge of anger swept over him, and he clung to it, yearning for the safety of an emotion he could understand. How dare she come in here, unwanted, uninvited? How dare she call him to account with his own conscience?

"What the hell do you think you're doing?"

Faith swayed against the doorframe, fighting a sickening wave of dizziness as she stared into the dingy room. This was not what she had expected when she raced impulsively into the darkness, searching for the one man she was sure would share her concern. Not this filthy pigsty, with kindling and wood shavings littering the floor. Not rumpled, graying sheets on an unmade bed in the corner. Not a man she thought she knew, standing stark naked in front of her, every hair on his body gleaming with sweat, the rigid proof of his gross appetites jutting out at her like an obscene joke.

"What am *I* doing? I could ask you the same thing."

"Could you, my dear?" His nonchalance was infuriating, as if he stood naked in front of young women every day of the week. "That hardly seems necessary. I would have thought the answer was perfectly clear."

The insolence in his voice was too blatant to ignore. Faith didn't know what disgusted her most, the vulgarity of his manner or the dark-skinned woman standing brazenly in front of the fire.

"I see you seek your carnal pleasures in the same foul hovels as my father. No wonder you got along so well. But don't worry, I haven't come to interrupt your coarse amusements. I only want to know one thing. What happened tonight?"

Brad felt a tremor of tension run through his body, but he was careful not to let her see it. So she didn't know, after all. Blast it anyway! What the hell was he doing without his britches? A man was at a definite disadvantage without his britches!

"Eva, get me my pants. Do you want me to stand around with my balls hanging out?"

If Eva minded his crudity, she did not show it. Her expression did not change as she knelt beside the bed, picking up his trousers where he had cast them carelessly on the floor.

"Confound it, woman, don't take all night!"

Faith struggled to conceal her distaste as she watched Brad grab his pants from the woman and begin to put them on. They were just like a married couple, these two, so used to each other's moods they took them for granted. Not that she was jealous, of course—she didn't give a fig for any of Brad's mistresses, black or white!—but this creature's boldness was an affront to every decent woman.

She fixed the slave with an icy stare, noting for the first time her odd coloring: the yellowish tinge to her skin, the way her hair turned almost red in the firelight.

"Don't tell me you're another of my father's brats?"

The minute the words were out of her mouth, she regretted them. Brad paused, his trousers half fastened, to give her a surprised look, but the woman barely seemed to notice. Her eyelids did not so much as flicker as she looked at Faith.

"I am a white man's daughter—but not your father's. I was born to a free woman in a settlement of free blacks in Virginia."

Good for her! Brad thought with a silent cheer. Eva might look like a peasant, but she had the composure of a queen. Why was it, he wondered, in all the months he'd known this woman—all the times he'd used her body again and again for his own purposes—he'd never once thought to ask her about herself?

Faith did not give him time to contemplate the revelation she herself had caused. She dismissed the woman without a shrug, or even a backward glance. He could see that she was troubled as she turned to him again. He dreaded the words he knew were coming.

"You didn't answer my question, Brad. I asked you what happened tonight."

It gave him a sick feeling in the pit of his stomach to look at her face. All quivering and misty, as if she thought she could hide her fear from him. Damn! What he wouldn't give to look her right in the eye and say, I shot him, Faith. He tried to attack, and I shot him down. It was a dreadful, beastly thing, but it's over now and the poor bastard's at peace.

"We caught him."

Her eyes were wide. "What did you do with him?"

"We turned him over to Carstairs. We had no choice. That's the law. The man is his property—to dispose of any way he likes."

"And how—how did he . . . dispose of him?"

There was no hiding the fear now. Her face was ashen with it. God, how he wished he could say, I shot him.

"He had him castrated."

Three

"Whoa! Easy, girl. Steady now."

Faith laid a gloved hand on the mare's neck, trying to make the gesture firm and masterly, the way it looked when Brad did it. It was so frustrating, not being able to handle a horse. It hardly seemed fair, all those years she never had a chance to ride, just because Fleur didn't think it looked feminine.

"Easy, now—easy!" She tugged at the reins, pulling the spirited mare to a stop on a shallow ridge overlooking the river valley. "Here, girl—you're all vinegar and pepper today, aren't you?"

There must be something in the air, she thought, gazing down at the blacks in freshly drained rice fields below. The days immediately following the capture of the slave Prince had been marred by an ugly undercurrent of tension, but it had seemed to her that everything had been getting back to normal again. Now, watching the restlessness in dark hands as they plucked weed after weed from rows of bright green sprouts, she was not so sure.

Even Beneba did not seem to be her old self nowadays.

Faith could not forget how surprised she was when she walked into the dining room that morning, long after Brad and Alexandre had breakfast, and saw a stout, familiar form standing at the sideboard. She had seen all sorts of expressions on Beneba's face in the past few months, ranging from grudging approval to irritation to outright anger—but she had never seen her look tired before.

"Where's Cuffee?" she had asked, more to make polite conversation than anything else. "I don't think he's missed serving a meal since the day I arrived. I hope he's not ill."

Beneba mustered enough of her old spirit to give Faith a sharp look.

"Now what yo' fussin' fo' chile? Ain't I got 'nough to do wi'out I listen to yo' fussin'? And doan' yo' let them eggs git cold! Where's yo' manners? Cook gits hustlin' a'fore sunup to fret over yo' food, and what yo' do? Yo' sits there an' picks at it lak' a bird!"

Faith could only stare at her in astonishment. Any other day, Beneba would have scolded her with a stern, "Yo' stuffs yo' face lak' that, Miz Faith, yo' ain't gonna fit into that new dress Fibby made fo' yo'." Sometimes it was hard to figure out what was going on in that amazingly complex mind.

It was not until later, when she had had the stableboy saddle up the horse Brad had given her to ride, that Faith remembered she had once seen Toney, Cuffee's sullen-looking son, talking to Prince at the edge of the woods.

The horse threw back her head, letting out an impatient snort, and Faith forced herself to concentrate on the reins, gripping them in hands that had not yet figured out the technique. The frisky mare was right! She ought to be flying like the wind across the meadows, daring a lively mount to teach her to ride, not sitting in a hot spring sun, brooding on things she could not change. And imagining things that hadn't even happened!

"All right, girl—come on!"

Faith let go of the reins, giving the mare her head. The feel of rippling muscles beneath her body was surprisingly smooth, the breeze generated by the movement a cool kiss against her cheeks, and for the first time in her life, Faith understood what it was to share that moment of communion when horse and rider blended into one.

She did not tighten her hold again until they had reached the top of the hill. Even then, the mare rebelled, shaking her head as if to say, Why are we stopping here? I could run on for hours.

The fields that meandered across the sloping hill and over its crest made a lazy contrast to the activity in the rice paddies below. Tall golden oats, already more than half grown, billowed in undulating waves against a dense blue-green pine copse, and dark rows of freshly plowed soil formed long rectangles, angling off occasionally to avoid a jagged outcropping of rock or a tree stump that had not been cleared away. Only a handful of slaves still squatted in a corner of one of the fields, patting down the dirt with their hands as they planted the last of the potatoes and summer corn. On the far side, near the oats, almost in the shade of the tallest of the pines, Alexandre stood alone. His back was half turned toward Faith, his brow furrowed as he checked out the acreage that had just been finished.

Faith held the horse steady and watched him. From a distance, he looked deceptively young, like a boy just grown to manhood. Yet there was in his mien nothing of the gawky uncertainty of adolescence. Long legs looked hard and lean in tight pearl-gray britches, and the graceful flare of a loose cambric shirt, immaculate even after a half day's work, emphasized a *bon ton* that was at once both studied and innate. It made Faith's heart ache to gaze at him. She had almost forgotten how handsome he looked, that day less than a year ago when she stepped out of Brad's study and saw him for the first time.

Was it her fault, she asked herself now, this rift that had grown between them? It surprised her to realize she had never thought about it before. It was so easy to blame everything on him. So easy to remember the pain she felt when she heard her sister's name on his lips. So easy to say—my husband is obsessed with another woman, and he will never love me.

And so hard to say—but he did care about me once. He felt close enough to ask me to marry him. Where did I fail him, then? What did *I* do to make him turn away?

You cheated him, my dear.

Brad's words—and, oh, how furious she had been the day he dared to utter them! Yet, even then, she knew he was right. She had coaxed a proposal out of Alexandre with a coy imitation of Fleur's sensuality—and then she had turned it all off the minute he married her!

Impulsively, she guided her horse around the edge of the fields. Alexandre was so deep in thought, he did not see her, even when she drew to a stop beside him.

"How industrious you are, husband! I don't think I've ever seen you so intent before."

He glanced up, a faraway look clouding his eyes. For an instant, Faith had the feeling he did not even see her.

"What on earth is so fascinating, Alexandre? Did the field-hands dare to sow one of the rows a quarter of an inch askew? Or are you contemplating all sorts of nasty little vermin, crawling around in the soil and nibbling your precious seeds?"

He smiled then, a vague, distracted smile that only half acknowledged her words.

"Faith! I had not expected to see you here. But should you be out in the midday heat, *ma chère*?"

Faith twisted in the saddle, adjusting the full scarlet skirt of her new riding habit to cover her discomfort. How like Alexandre to be concerned with her needs. When was the last time *she* had worried about *him*?

"How else could I see my own husband?" She tilted her head to the side, throwing him what she hoped was an enigmatic smile. Thank heaven, she had had the good sense to tuck a gay red feather in the brim of her black tricorne. "You've been so devoted to these tiresome chores, you hardly have time for me anymore. I decided if I wanted to have a minute alone with you, I'd have to come out in the fields like one of the darkies."

To her delight, he seemed to enjoy the repartee. "Come now, Faith, I haven't been as bad as all that. Surely, when you lured me to the altar, you didn't think I was going to spend every second of my time with you."

It took so little to please him, Faith thought with a twinge of guilt. Why had she been so stubborn all these months, holding back the outrageous flirtation he loved so much? Because her pride was hurt when he slipped and called her by another's name?

"Every second of your time? Why, Alexandre Julliard, whatever are you talking about? Here it is—well, it must be past noon anyway—and you haven't spent so much as a single second with me yet. Do you wonder I feel neglected?"

"Be fair, Faith. You know how busy we are at planting time. Cousin Brad oversees the rice and I take care of the rest of the crops. That's our agreement."

"Agreement, indeed! It seems to me 'Cousin' Brad stacked all the chips on his side of the table. You don't have any stake in Havenhurst. Where's *your* profit for all those extra hours you put in?" Faith stopped abruptly, hearing irritation creep into her voice at the thought of Brad and the way he used everyone. The last thing she wanted now was any note of unpleasantness between herself and her husband. "Besides, my love, what's more important, this silly old plantation, or me?"

The look that greeted her words was enough to tear at her heart. Alexandre seemed every bit as entranced with her as he had been that first afternoon when he turned and watched her glide down the steps from the piazza. Only then he had thought she was Fleur.

Suddenly, unbidden, another image leaped into Faith's

mind. A dark, slender form, proud in the fraying cords that bound her. Still daring to hope because her lover had escaped. What would Estee give now to spend the rest of her life with the man she had chosen? *She* would never waste precious time on hurt feelings or false pride.

With a sharp flick of her wrist, Faith slapped her reins against the horse's neck, as eager to dispel unwanted reflections as she was to attract Alexandre's attention. On a sudden whim, she steered the spirited mare out into the field, listening in fascination to the sound of prancing hooves plopping against the earth. Mud spattered indiscriminately across the field. The spontaneity of the gesture was so unfamiliar, she did not realize what she was doing at first.

Fleur! The thought was sudden and stunning. This was exactly what Fleur would have done—if you could ever have coaxed her up on a horse! Only Fleur would have thrown herself wholeheartedly into the prank. Fleur would never glance uncomfortably over her shoulder, watching blacks in nearby fields and wondering how they felt as they saw their morning's work being undone.

"Faith, for heaven's sake!"

Faith heard Alexandre call out behind her, but she did not slow down until she had reached the center of the field. He caught up with her then, laughing out loud as he pulled the reins out of her hand and forced the horse to stop. The little mare mimicked the sound, tossing back her head and whinnying, as if she knew what a good joke she had played. Faith giggled with them, then caught herself, pursing her lips into a pout.

"There, now, Alexandre—see what you made me do! It's all your fault, you know it is! It drives a woman to distraction when her husband ignores her."

"Enough, enough!" Alexandre conceded. "I promise, *chérie*, I will never neglect you again. I will give you all the attention you want. Only please—*please!*—get out of the cornfield."

Faith did not protest, but folded her hands demurely on the saddle in front of her as Alexandre led her out of the muddy field, back toward the waving river of oats that ran along the base of the pine forest. She knew she had won, much more easily than she expected, and every nerve in her body tingled with triumph. Rather the way Fleur must have felt, she thought wrily, every time *she* had twisted Alexandre around her little finger.

Well, so be it! If she had to evoke memories of her sister

to keep her marriage alive, then she was going to do it. A marriage was worth fighting for!

Alexandre's body brushed against hers as he lifted her from the saddle and swung her down to the ground. Faith was conscious of the warmth of him, the closeness, and she longed to throw her arms around his neck, clinging to him with the very possessiveness that would be certain to disappoint him. Reluctantly, she held back. She had promised herself she would play the game his way this time. She would give him what *he* wanted.

"How hot it is, my love." She whimpered a little as she twisted away from him. Pulling a lace-edged handkerchief from her pocket, she daubed at moist curls nestled against her forehead. "I don't think I can bear it a minute longer. Have mercy on me, sweet husband, and find a nice cool shade tree where we can be alone together."

"A shade tree?" Alexandre laughed as he looped the horse's reins over a fence rail. "You don't ask for miracles, do you, *chérie*? Why didn't you come to me yesterday when I was working in the orchards? We plant remarkably few oaks and maples in the cornfields."

"Don't you dare make fun of me. I didn't ask for an oak tree, and you know it! Or an apple or a nectron for that matter." Faith picked up her skirts, careful to show only an inch or two of ankle, and began to cut through the oats. "A plain, old-fashioned pine copse is good enough for me, thank you very much."

And a much better choice than an orchard! she added silently, smiling at the thought. Tall trees, dense enough to hide behind; the fragrance of pine and wild flowers; a stolen kiss to whet the appetite—and he wouldn't fail to come to her room that night!

She was barely halfway across the shallow field when she heard footsteps trampling the earth behind her. She was startled to feel Alexandre grab her arm, whirling her roughly around.

"Don't go in there, Faith!"

"What?"

The words were so sudden, so unexpected, Faith did not know what to make of them. She glanced toward the edge of the forest, half curious, half apprehensive, but she could see nothing to justify his alarm.

"The blacks," he said tersely. "The rebels."

"The rebels?" But the rebels were at Stono River—and that

was more than a year ago! Even if some of them had eluded capture, surely they would be far away by now.

"The runaways, Faith."

At last she understood. It was all so clear now. She could still hear the sound of his voice, the deep melancholy of his words. *Our way of life isn't feasible, Faith. It doesn't work. It's going to destroy us all in the end.* He had always been afraid of the slaves. Deathly afraid. Only she had been too insensitive to notice.

"Oh, my dear, there are no runaways. Only *one* runaway—Eleazar Carstairs' man, Prince—and they brought him back again."

"And put him in a little cage on the front lawn, not even high enough to stand in. That was Carstairs' idea—he thought it would do the others good to see him there. Only he didn't make the damned thing strong enough. The man got away."

"He got . . . away."

"Some time last night. A bunch of them got past the security at Cypress Hill and set him free. Two of Carstairs' guards were killed."

He paused, his expression puzzled as he stared at her.

"My God, Faith! The look on your face. Almost as if you're glad he got away."

"I *am* glad!" Faith blurted out the words, not even stopping to think how they sounded. She saw the pallor that drained his features, and she knew she should be frightened, too—but all she could feel was a tremendous surge of relief. "I don't care what you think! I'm glad he's free. I hate what they did to him. I hate it!"

"So do I! So does every sane man in this colony. Atrocities like that only stir up more trouble."

"But you're not glad he escaped?"

"Of course not! How could I be? Don't be naive, Faith. If this thing gets out of hand, it will be as bad as Stono River—maybe even worse. Innocent people will suffer. Black and white alike."

"But *one* man, Alexandre? Even a few men——"

"There weren't a few men last night. There were at least a dozen. And a dozen men can become a hundred in a day."

Faith tried to ignore the thumping of her heart against her chest as she listened to him. A dozen men last night. And this morning, Cuffee hadn't been in his place at the serving table.

"Oh, that's ridiculous, Alexandre!" She was letting him infect her with his own silly fears. Cuffee was no rebel. Not that faithful, dignified old man. "I think you're the one who's naive. Even if there were a hundred rebels—and I don't for a minute believe there are!—they're not lurking behind the pines in that one little copse. You can stay here as long as you want, quaking at the sight of your own shadow, but I'm going in there where it's cool and pleasant."

The tall grasses caught at her hem, but Faith barely noticed as she flounced stubbornly toward the woods. Fleur again! she thought, and wondered why the idea bothered her so much. It was uncanny how like her sister she could be sometimes. Fleur had never been afraid of danger, not a day in her life. She would have thrived on the challenge!

The copse was nowhere near as inviting when Faith approached. It had not occurred to her the trees might grow so close together, or the darkness beneath them be so somber. Barely a ray of sunlight filtered through thick branches to illuminate a mantle of pine needles on the forest floor. Faith shivered in the sudden chill, but she knew she could not turn back. Not when she had set out to prove she was as exciting and irrepressible as her sister!

It was a relief to glance over her shoulder and see that Alexandre, for all his trepidations, was too much of a gentleman to let her wander into the woods alone. She smiled, stretching out her hand.

"There, my love, you see. There are no. . . ."

Her voice dwindled off as she caught sight of the look on his face. Dark. Bitter. Much too angry. As if she had done some awful, unspeakable thing. But she had just been flirting, trying to tease him a little.

He stepped closer, but he did not touch her. His lips seemed to curl with contempt as they parted slowly.

"This excites you, doesn't it?"

Faith caught her breath, trying to make sense out of words that meant nothing to her. What on earth was wrong with him? she asked herself, more bewildered than frightened. Why was he so furious all of a sudden? If his masculine pride had been piqued—if he had snapped at her for baiting his fears—she could have understood that. But this reaction was all out of proportion.

"Oh, Alexandre, it's cold and the ground is soggy—and gnats are flying around my face and catching in my hair. What's so exciting about that?"

"The daring, *chérie*? The danger? The fact that I hate it so much? That's all part of it, isn't it? You'd love to see some black brute leap out from behind those trees—preferably with a cudgel in his hands. *Mon dieu*, how it would excite you, watching a lover defend your honor with his life."

He paused, fixing her with an icy gaze.

"Or would it excite you more if I didn't defend you?"

Faith closed her eyes, fighting off a sickening wave of faintness. She had only seen Alexandre like this once before, that terrible night she went to his room and tried to pretend she was as free as Fleur. Only then she had deserved his fury. Now she didn't even understand the accusations he was hurling at her. That was not her, that creature he was describing. That was not her at all!

When she finally opened her eyes, his face was so white it seemed to glow in the shadows.

"I—I want to go home, Alexandre. I don't want to stay here anymore."

She was not surprised when he grasped her arm and dragged her forcefully forward. She had known, even before he moved, that this time he was not going to let her off so easily.

"That's not the way the game is played, *mon ange*. You know that—you made the rules yourself. And we always play by the rules."

Always. The word went right through Faith, sending a chill down her spine. *Always. . . .*

"Please, Alexandre. I don't understand."

"Don't play me for a fool, *chérie*. We both know what you lured me in here for. And we both know what I'm going to have to do to get it."

For an instant, Faith still did not understand. Then, slowly, realization began to seep into her consciousness. He thought she wanted something sordid from him. Some wanton sexual charade that needed discomfort and danger to give it spice.

And there was only one reason he could think that. Because that was just the sort of thing Fleur would consider an adventure!

"Oh, no! Believe me, I wasn't . . . I would never——"

"Damn you, *vache!*"

The thin thread of his patience snapped. His movements were abrupt, almost convulsive, as he clutched her, holding her trembling body against the hard pressure of his chest. One hand tangled in her hair, arching her head back, turning her face upward; the other groped at her breast, seizing her bodice until it gave with a hideous ripping sound.

Instinctively, Faith pulled back, tugging the torn remnants of her dress across her naked breast.

"Oh, Alexandre! My new riding habit!"

The cry no sooner escaped her lips than she realized what she had done. How could she have been so careless? So foolish? He wanted her to be like Fleur now—he *insisted* she be like Fleur. And that was the last thing Fleur would have said.

Fleur would have loved the feel of fabric tearing away from her flesh. She would have exulted in the final proof of her power over him.

Faith did not try to struggle, but let herself sink limply into his arms. She sensed the brutal force of the compulsion that held him, and she knew it was beyond his control or hers. Whatever he had planned for her, whatever anger or pain he needed to work out on her body, it would only go harder with her if she resisted.

Her acquiescence did not mollify him as she had hoped. Taking her by the shoulders, he shook her until her head ached.

"Dammit, get it over with, will you? Play the game to the end and be done with it! Pull away from me the way you always do! Fight with me! Force me into what has to be done!"

The way you always do! Faith bit her lips to keep from crying out in fear. There it was again. *Always*. Only this had never happened before.

Slowly, rigid with terror, she forced herself to look up. She could no longer deny the truth she saw in his eyes.

He was mad. God help them both, he was utterly, hopelessly mad. Somewhere in the last few minutes, he had slipped over the brink, and there was no sense, no reason, left in him. He was so wrapped up in his obsession—so tortured by dreams of the love he had lost—he could no longer separate reality from fantasy. Faith was not a substitute for Fleur anymore. She *was* Fleur.

He stopped shaking her, but his hands still gripped her shoulders, slipping upward until they rested against the smooth white skin of her throat. Every muscle in his face was taut, his eyes were burning. Faith knew he hated her, almost as much as he loved her.

"I could kill you when you do this to me!"

His hands tightened around her neck, squeezing until she could barely breathe. Faith stood absolutely still, trying desperately not to provoke him. There was not a bit of her sister in her after all, she thought, fighting back an insane urge to giggle. Fleur would not have been frightened now—she would have been exhilarated. This would have been a contest to her. A test of his will against hers.

And she would not for a moment have doubted she was going to win!

Then, just when Faith was sure her body would snap with strain, Alexandre released her throat. His arms were warm, surprisingly tender, as he held her, clinging to her with the hungry possessiveness she had longed to feel for him. His voice, when he cried out, was low and piercing, the plea of a madman trapped in his own twisted nightmare.

"Why do you do this to me, Fleur?"

At last it was over. He pulled her clumsily, urgently to the earth. All the tension, all the anger, flooded out of his body, and he buried himself with a sigh in unresisting flesh.

"Ah, Fleur, Fleur, Fleur. . . ."

A single oak rose in lonely splendor from the bluff, its thick, gnarled trunk almost black with age. The man who stood beneath wide, sweeping branches was as dark as the tree itself—and as silent. His feet were firmly planted on the ground, his back straight, his shoulders broad and powerful. Anger seemed to shimmer in the heat around him.

"How did you find me?"

The woman did not flinch. She had expected no gentleness from him, nor had she wanted it. Rage was his only refuge now. She would not deny him that.

"I know you so well, Rodrigo. Where else would you go?"

Where but the grassy knoll at the base of the hill where they had first come to each other? Not because there was sentiment in his memories. Not because of his love for her. Simply because it was the one place he felt free.

His anger did not abate. "What did you come here for? There is nothing between us now. You know that. There will never be anything between us again."

Estee held her head high, her spine as rigid as his. He was a proud man, but she was proud, too.

"I have come to join you."

"What? Do you mock me, *mujer?* What do I have to give you now? Words as sweet as kisses? A handclasp for an embrace? Conversation all night long? Will that quench the fire between your thighs?"

The mockery in his voice spurred a wave of indignation. "Was that all it was for you? Everything between us?" She understood his pain, she felt it as her own—but she would let no man talk to her like that! "Do you think my love for you was only passion? To be satisfied in the thighs alone? I shared your heart with you, Rodrigo. Your spirit. How dare you tell me I cannot share your dreams?"

"My dreams? What do you know of my dreams, light-skinned girl who sleeps between sheets in a room in back of the main house? How do you know what it is to be black?"

Estee did not move, but stood absolutely still, letting his bitterness flood over her until she seemed to be drowning in it. He had taunted her with her fairness often enough, but always before he had been teasing.

"I am black, too, Rodrigo, whether you accept it or not. Whether you let me join you or not. I am as black as you. And I have dreams, too."

"But not my dreams! I was born with the taste of freedom in my mouth. I was as free as the wind in the sails on the high seas. And I tell you this—a man who has tasted freedom cannot die a slave!"

"And I was born in utter squalor on one of the most miserable sugar plantations in the Islands. Does that make me inferior to you, Rodrigo? My mother was a slave. God alone knows who my father was, but at least he was black! No white man would defile himself with the scum from the cane-fields. I have never tasted freedom. Not one day, not one hour of my life. Do you think it is less important for me to die free?"

The eloquence in her voice confused him, as she had known it would. Eloquence always swayed him, touching the feelings he could not put into words himself. His eyes were still hard as he stared at her, but he was less sure.

"There can be nothing between us. No reminder of the things that were."

She nodded her silent agreement. She had known when she came that this would be his condition. She was ready to accept it.

"I have twenty people with me already. Maybe twenty-five. Even some from your own plantation—did you ever think they would come to me? They are all fighters. Are you? Do you remember I said to you once, What will you do if I put a gun in your hand? And you said, I will do what you ask. Did you think then I did not know you were lying?"

The faint flicker of a smile on his lips surprised her. She had not known that humor could be so dark or so frightening.

"I was not lying, Rodrigo. Putting off the inevitable, perhaps, but not lying. I think I have known from the minute I saw you that one day it would come to this."

"Then you will take the gun?" There was barely a hint of question in his inflection.

"I will take it."

"And point it at the white man? And pull the trigger?"

"Yes."

Steady eyes seemed to bore through her. The question in their depths was clear. Can I trust her? Is she lying again?

"Even the man who owns you? The white man who gives you food and puts the clothes on your back? The man who treats his slaves so well you say?"

"Even him, yes."

"And the girl?" His eyes narrowed, his lips tensed. He was watching her closely now. "The white girl who sits on the lawn with you? And talks with you and laughs with you?"

For the first time, Estee wavered. The rest she would concede. But Faith? She had never had a friend before.

"The white girl? Will you point the gun at her? Will you dare?"

His sharpness warned her there was no more time. The choice was plain, and it was hers alone to make. Turn and walk away, or accept his terms.

"Yes, her, too."

The question was still in his eyes. Is she lying again? But now the answer was there, too.

"You will join us."

She tilted her chin up, facing him squarely. "And I have the right to die free?"

White teeth gleamed in a sudden grin. "Damn, you are stubborn, *mujer!* Die then, if you are so set on it! Die free!"

Faith huddled miserably at the edge of the pine grove, wrapping the torn pieces of her skirt tightly around her legs. It was late, and afternoon shadows muted the vivid hues of wild flowers on the hillside, but she did not dare go home. Not yet. Not while there was still enough light to pick up the ugly rents in her dress or the drying blood where pine needles had scratched her limbs and shoulders.

Oh, dear God, it had been terrible, that moment when he had finished with her and their eyes met. He had looked at her, then, and he *knew*. He knew he had called her Fleur—and he knew she hated him for it. Nothing would ever be the same between them again.

It's one thing to put on a white dress and say a few words in front of the minister. It's quite another to spend the rest of your life regretting it.

Brad's words again. Why did she keep remembering what *he* said? And why did he always have to be right?

She rose slowly, making her way toward a young pine at the edge of the copse. It made a comfortable shield, and she stood behind it, peeking out at empty, silent fields. Dusk was heavy now, and even the tidy, symmetrical paddies in the distance had begun to fade into mists of gray.

Had she really seen madness in his eyes? she wondered. Or was that only a fancy of her own, spawned by fear and confusion? When did a man's obsession cease to be an obsession and become insanity? And what happened when it did?

Mad or not, there was no denying his was a tormented soul. Not evil, Faith thought sadly. Only tormented. A misfit in a world too turbulent to understand. He belonged on a country estate somewhere, just outside of London, with a swift horse and a pack of hounds at his heels—and a doting wife who adored him. Not here on a rough frontier with nothing but violence around him. And a woman who brought out the violence in his own heart.

Sighing wearily, Faith tucked the loose ends of a badly ripped riding coat into her bodice, trying vainly to make herself look presentable. The fields were almost dark, and she knew if she did not go soon, she would have trouble groping her way through unfamiliar terrain. She hoped someone had at least had the good sense to untie her horse and bring it back to the stable.

I could kill you.

The words rang in her ears, as blazing and brutal as before. She could still feel strong hands on her throat, pressing into the cartilage of her larynx. He *could* have killed her, then—he could have done it so easily. He hated her enough.

No, not *her*, she reminded herself, shuddering.

Fleur. . . .

It all came back to her then. A study in the lamplight. A tall, golden-haired man leveling a gun against her breast. The excitement, the sheer thrill of it all—the certainty that passion would stay his finger.

A study. A plain, nondescript chamber. A desk. A lamp. French doors opening onto the piazza. Brad's study? She had thought so once. But Alexandre's room looked almost the same.

And Alexandre's hair turned to gold in the lamplight.

She reached out her hand, resting it unconsciously on one of the pine branches. Sharp needles resisted, then broke, as her fingers closed around them. Alexandre. Why hadn't it occurred to her to wonder about him before? He had had as much opportunity as Brad to kill Fleur.

And he at least had had a motive.

She let go of the branch, feeling pain in her fingers where the needles had gouged her skin. All this time, she had hated herself for daring to be attracted to Brad. For wanting to like him in spite of herself. All this time, she had been so sure he had murdered her sister. Had she fled from him only to run into the arms of the real killer?

The fields were cloaked with the shadows of encroaching night when she finally stepped out of the copse. The sun had already set; the moon was still a dream somewhere on the distant horizon. She did not even feel the chill in the air as she began to walk slowly down the hill.

Four

Faith turned the small, leather-bound volume over in her hands, staring down at a trim, masculine binding. Funny, she thought, the way things turned up when you least expected them. She hadn't even been thinking of the past when she came to the attic an hour ago. All she wanted was some kind of diversion: an old ball gown of her mother's to try on, a piece of jewelry perhaps—a delightfully outmoded bonnet, so quaint and funny she would burst out laughing when she set it on her curls and peeked into the mirror. Anything to take her mind off the painful events of the last few days.

Like an ostrich with its head buried in the sand, she told herself with a wry grimace. Trying to pretend the rest of the world didn't exist.

Not that it worked that way! Sighing, Faith laid the book on her lap and leaned back against a rough oak beam. An ostrich might be able to hide his eyes, but he couldn't keep the wind from blowing on his tailfeathers. Just the way she would never be able to forget the terrible madness she had seen in her husband's eyes. Or the look on Estee's face the day they dragged her back from Cypress Hill.

Faith shook her head, brushing away thoughts too troubled to dwell on. Picking up the book again, she ran her fingers along the worn edges of the binding. It had come as a shock to open a battered trunk in the corner and pull out coarse woolen garments and the crude navigational tools of a sea captain. In all the time she had been at Havenhurst, she had taken the plantation for granted, accepting it as something that was simply there. Now for the first time, it occurred to her to wonder how Adam Eliot, the second son of a man of relatively modest means, had acquired the fortune to build it up.

She started to open the book, then hesitated. There had been a number of other volumes in the trunk: an official log; a handful of philosophical treatises that looked as if they had seen heavy duty on long, dull evenings; a technical description of navigation and seamanship, so complicated it was almost indecipherable. But this was different. This was personal, more like a diary than a dry, cold record. Faith was not at all sure she wanted to know what was inside it.

Her own timidity irritated her. Really, it was idiotic, the way she was letting everything frighten her nowadays. All it took was something simple, like Cuffee's not showing up for three days in a row, and she started to conjure up all kinds of dark, sinister conspiracies. And when she couldn't find Fibby in the sewing room that morning—well, her imagination absolutely went crazy! The slaves were all banding together, she told herself hysterically. Any hour now—any minute—they were going to march down from the hills with torches in their hands, and Havenhurst would go up in a blaze of red and yellow flames.

As if a pack of rebellious slaves would even consider taking a witless little Fibby with them!

Faith forced her attention back to the book, opening it randomly somewhere in the center. Bold, black handwriting leaped out of yellowing pages, an undisciplined scrawl, yet surprisingly legible. She laid her hands on the paper, trying to capture some sense of warmth and life beneath her fingertips, but she could feel nothing save the smooth, dry texture of aging parchment.

She turned the pages slowly, taking care not to damage the crumbling corners. How old was the journal now? she wondered. Twenty years? Twenty-five? It must have been written around 1715 or 1716. Certainly not much later than that, for it had to be sometime before she was born.

She found the first page and began to read.

21 March

Liverpool. As foul a hellhole as I've ever seen, though not, I admit, without an undercurrent of raw excitement. Went to the shipyards first thing in the morning to see the vessel I want to buy, but the highway robber who has it up for sale wasn't there—or so his man told me. Jes' set 'is foot out the door, not 'arf an 'our ago, ain't that a shame, Cap'n?

Captain, indeed! As if anyone here thinks I've ever commanded a vessel before. They don't care if the bloody thing sinks, crew, cargo, and all, right in the middle of the Atlantic. Just as long as they get their money up front!

At least it gave me a bit of a chance to see the town, and in spite of myself, I must confess a grudging fondness. Like an old whore, with her face painted on and her breasts hanging out of her dress, she makes no secret of what she is, and that is both her allure and her disgrace. She is frankly a seaport, rough and brash, new in the trade and not the least bit fussy what she has to do to get a bigger bite of it. There are only two kinds of men on the streets near the docks, avaricious merchants in long black coats with threadbare cuffs, and yellow-eyed, sunken-cheeked sailors. And only one kind of woman.

If it weren't for *her*, would I be here I wonder? I sit in a cheap waterfront bar, drinking bad whiskey out of a dirty glass, and I think of the way Madeira shines in cut crystal when she lifts it to her lips. Or the lightness in her laughter as she touches the keys of a clavichord, faking the chords when her hands are too small to reach. And I know then I would do anything—dare anything—to win her for my own.

29 March

Liverpool again. Saw the ship at last, after a week's wait, and a filthier vessel you'd be hard pressed to find anywhere in England. It was smaller by half than the bastard had claimed, not that that surprised me, and so unseaworthy you could see light seeping through the bows under the decks. They call her the *Esther*. God, what a misnomer! Don't they know Esther is a queen in the Bible? A woman of pride and majesty? This tub would better have been dubbed the *Sukie* or the *Nancey*, after some little tart on the streets.

The hell of it is, I can't afford to turn it down, not at that price. I could find a better ship in Bristol (they're heavier in the trade there) but the cost would be double, more than my purse would bear. We haggled bitterly, and I brought the price down, though not, I daresay, any more than the crafty beggar had intended all along.

I demanded repairs, and he agreed, though it's a wonder we didn't both choke on the word. Repairs, hah! As if paint and nails and glue could make a penny's worth of difference. Still, I am to come back next week for a final inspection—with the final payment in hand, of course. The work will be done by then, so he says. Would I lie to you, Cap'n? A man of my integrity?

Well, we shall see.

4 April

Returned to the shipyard yesterday, as agreed, and had my faith in human nature restored. Or should I say my faith in human cupidity? That wily old scoundrel, eager for his thirty pieces of gold, had made all the specified modifications, at least to the letter of the agreement. Not for him the chance of losing the sale at the last minute!

We went over the vessel together inch by inch, and as near as I can tell, the damned thing will stay afloat, at least as long as I need it. Barring a typhoon that is, or some other disaster, and what ship wouldn't founder then?

The hold seemed unnecessarily cramped, but when I pointed it out, the man assured me that was the custom. More'n five feet high'd be a waste, Cap'n.

Distasteful as it sounds, I suspect the bastard knows what he is talking about. You load the cargo in two layers, he tells me. After you have the first layer in, directly on the floor, you build a shelf halfway up to the ceiling and stack the second layer on that.

Ah, pretty girl under the magnolia tree, with your pink dress and petals falling on your hair, do you know what I am doing for you? And will you love me when I come back?

Faith looked up from the book, surprised at how deeply it had engrossed her. *Pretty girl . . . with . . . petals falling on your hair. . . .* Had the tall, strong man who smelled of horses and tobacco when he pulled her up in his arms really penned those tender words? And had he written them about her mother?

The *Esther*. Faith glanced down, scanning the text to make sure she had not read it wrong. Yes, there it was, plain as anything. The *Esther*. It had to be more than coincidence that one of her favorite names was also the name of her father's first command.

This time when she lifted the book again, Faith's eyes were no longer reluctant to search its pages. The past she had stumbled on was not an intimidating past at all; it was a past that was both familiar and exotic, and she was eager to explore it further. How dashing and romantic he seemed, this young adventurer, risking everything for the love of a beautiful woman. That he was also her father only added zest to the tale.

By the time April drew to a close and Adam Eliot had finished his business in Liverpool, Faith was almost as impatient as her father to run up the sails and head for the open seas.

21 April

Put the last of the trading cargo in the hold yesterday, and an odd assortment it is, too. I just finished entering it in the official log, but I couldn't resist putting it here, too. Will anyone believe me when I get home (How strange to write the word *home* and know I mean that sultry colony where I spent only a few weeks) and try to tell them about it?

50 boxes of soap
2,000 pounds of ham
100 tin buckets
50 barrels of coffee
50 dozen men's half hose
400 pounds of lead
1,000 brass kettles
£500 worth of chintz and muslin
20 kegs of nails
7 dozen silk umbrellas
100 barrels of powder
20 boxes of Spanish cigars. . . .

Faith thumbed through the next few pages, barely glancing at the list that ran on and on, until it numbered several hundred items. Her father was right, she thought, strangely uncomfortable, though she couldn't for the life of her figure out why. It *was* an odd assortment. Umbrellas and white lead, tin buckets and Spanish cigars—how on earth could he hope to make a fortune from such a peculiar ragbag of goods?

She skipped ahead, skimming the routine notations of position and weather that comprised the bulk of the journal now. Something still bothered her, something about that strange accumulation of cargo, but she couldn't quite put her finger on it. It was almost as if she had heard it all before, though that of course was ridiculous. Where would she ever have run across a list like that?

She was well into the entries for May when something suddenly struck her. It seemed so ordinary at first, she almost missed it.

> The air has grown quite warm, the breezes balmy, even at night. The sweet perfume of flowers wafts in on salt winds from the shore. We have had good fortune so far. The sea has been calm, though always with enough wind to swell the sails, and we have seen no more than a few gentle drops of rain. Pray God our luck will hold on the Middle Passage.

Balmy air at sea? In early May? Faith tightened her brow, pinching up her entire face as she reread the words. The scent of flowers on salt air. If she hadn't known better, she would have thought he was somewhere off the Carolinas. But how could he have crossed the Atlantic in two weeks?

Where was he, then? Down the coast toward Spain? Or the Mediterranean?

Or . . . ?

Faith blocked the word out of her mind even before she could form it. She tensed her fingers around the book and pressed it, still open, against her breast. Five hundreds pounds' worth of chintz. Seven dozen umbrellas. Now she remembered where she had heard such things before.

She was dragged out of her home like a jungle animal and loaded into the hold of a ship by her own people—seduced by chintz and brass pots and a dozen silk umbrellas.

Only Adam Eliot wasn't that kind of a man! Brad had said he wasn't!

Faith's hand was trembling as she laid the book flat on her lap. She barely dared to breathe, but she forced herself to read on, searching for the one thing she prayed was not there. She found it on the 21st of May.

> 21 May
>
> The Guinea Coast. Not quite the glamorous spot little boys envision as they soak up pirate tales around the fireside on cold winter's nights. After the first trip ashore (more from curiosity, I am sure, than anything else), most of the captains elect to stay on board with their crews and leave the actual trading to local representatives. "Factors," they are called here, and while I have seen only three or four of them, I would warrant a guess that they are generally an unsavory lot. Local legend has

it (and I wouldn't be surprised if it were at least half true) that they are immune to the diseases that strike white men in this unhealthful clime because pure alcohol flows in place of the blood in their veins. Where they get the wretched, half-starved specimens they sell is a question I have been warned one never asks here.

Some, I suppose, are obtained legitimately: criminals, after all, have to be punished; prisoners of war require some sort of disposal; and wealthy Africans might be persuaded to part with excess household help for a few material advantages. But most, I daresay, have been brought in by one of the unscrupulous gangs that continually roam the interior. These ruffians, oddly enough, are usually black, though one occasionally hears of a white crew operating nearer the coast where the heat and insects (and the irate natives!) are less likely to finish them off.

Of course, if you come during a famine, you have no trouble at all, one of the older captains told me, a rather nasty-looking man with most of his teeth missing. With a little luck, you can fill your ship the day you arrive and set sail with the dawn.

Luck, he calls it! I started to ask, How can a man stand by and watch another man sell his parents or his children—or even himself—for food? But I thought better of it. Things are bad enough here without quarreling with my peers.

Instead, I looked him right in the eye. But what would you do with all those silk umbrellas then? I said. The man didn't even chuckle.

Ah, well, I don't suppose I'll have a sense of humor myself when this whole sorry business is over.

23 May

My first trip ashore, and God willing, my last! I managed to pick up more than three dozen men and women, most in relatively good condition, so I suppose I should chalk it up as time well spent. Anything that gets me out of this damnable place a day sooner is worth whatever it takes.

Against the advice of other captains, I went to one of the local "factories" hoping to speed things up a bit. It is run by a man named Piet Masters. At least that is what he calls himself, though one name is as good as another here. He might be Dutch, he might be German, he might be almost anything for all I know. He's been here so long, even his accent is blurred and indistinguishable. He lives in what he calls a house (I would term it a shanty myself) with a native mistress and a patrol of armed black mercenaries. Not a flower, not a shrub, not even a scraggly tree, breaks the monotony of his parched yard. Nothing but piles of rotting rubbish and dozens of empty whiskey bottles.

I have always considered myself a strong man, but today I realized how naive one's opinion of oneself can be. When I saw the thing Masters called the "pen" (the place where he keeps *them*), I came close to swooning like a faint-hearted woman. It was afternoon. The heat and the stench were unbelievable, and flies swarmed around my head, thick as grains of grit in a sandstorm.

At first glance, it looked like a corral, built to hold cattle or horses. A narrow wooden structure, no more than a roof on stilts, had been erected in the middle. Down the center ran a rusty chain, anchored to stakes at either end, and to this, men and women had been secured at intervals. Had there been children under the age of ten or twelve, Masters told me with a self-righteous smirk, they would have been allowed to run free within the pen.

I wanted to retch as I watched the miserable creatures. An old man, so frail his bones seemed to stick out of his ribs, sat on the ground, staring blankly at oozing ulcers on his legs. A young girl (his daughter, I was sure) strained against her chain, struggling unsuccessfully to get closer to him.

It struck me as I watched her that she was uncommonly attractive. Not pretty and vivacious, the way I have always liked a woman to be, but imbued with a dark, strong-featured beauty that is every bit as compelling in its own way. I found it hard to look at her, knowing what I was about to do.

Masters saw my face, and he seemed to think it was funny. I suppose he's seen that same expression often enough before.

It isn't like they was human, Cap'n, he told me with a grin. Not like you an' me. They looks like it, doesn't they?—but I seen monkeys in the jungle, cute little things, that chatter just as lively as these. They isn't Christians or nothin' like that. Not with souls to worry about.

I heard his words but I could not bring myself to look at him. The girl was standing at the edge of the pen, not far from us. At the sound of our voices, she glanced up. For just an instant, I could have sworn she understood.

Oh, I know! It was only fancy. Good God, I had a dog once that looked at me just like that. As if he knew every word I was saying. And horses many times. It doesn't mean they were human, "like you and me, Cap'n."

But dammit, I wouldn't keep a dog or a horse chained up in a foul pen like that!

Faith glanced up, barely noticing that the sun had moved away from the window and the attic was bathed in shadows. Slaves! She could hide from the truth no longer. Adam Eliot had made his fortune running slaves. Havenhurst had been purchased with the suffering of that beautiful girl in the corral.

She didn't have a soul, he had said. Like his dog or his horse, she didn't have a soul. Dear God in heaven, that was like saying Estee—beautiful, proud, tortured Estee—didn't have a soul.

Faith turned back to the book with a kind of compulsive fascination. The last thing in the world she wanted now was to read on, but she could not tear her eyes away. This was her past, her heritage. No matter how sordid it was, she had to face it.

28 May

There are two ways of packing the cargo, "tight pack" and "loose pack." I suspect I would have thought the others were putting me on had I not already heard the terms before.

"Tight pack," one of them told me (and in all seriousness, damn him!) was by far the most efficient use of space. He had it all down to a formula: 6′ by 16″ for a man, 5′10″ by 16″ for a woman, 5′ by 14″ for a boy, 4′6″ by 12″ for a girl.

Of course, you can stow even more if you put them in on their sides, he boasted. Cram 'em in "spoon fashion." You lose a few more that way, but you still get more to port. And if some of them are too weak, you can always fatten 'em up at a slave yard in the West Indies.

One of the other captains took almost immediate exception. We had met at the "castle," a fortress on an island off the coast controlled by the English, although it had been occupied briefly by the Dutch. "Loose pack" was more practical, he assured me. To say nothing of more economical. You buy fewer slaves in the first place, and if you do well, you might get them all across. Besides, there's less chance of trouble on the voyage.

And not a word through all this of decency or humanity! What system are you going to use? one of them asked me. I remembered the girl in the pen, and I thought of her lying on the bottom layer in that stifling hold, with urine and vomit dripping down from above, and I started to say, "loose pack," but the words stuck in my throat. They sounded so callous. I could not bring myself to utter them aloud.

11 June

Seven days at sea, and it seems like seven years. They say you can smell a slaver ten miles away, and I believe them. The stench of human excrement is so strong, it's almost unendurable.

The days are already growing monotonous. At eight o'clock, I have my crew take the slaves out of the hold and bring them up on deck. The men are fastened by leg irons to chains on the bulwarks. The women and children are allowed to move about freely.

At nine, they have their first meal. Millet and salt beef, and occasionally stewed yams, an orange-colored root they seem to savor. Oh, yes, and half a pint of water.

The rest of the day slaves remain on deck, getting what exercise they can. Some of the captains believe in "dancing the slaves," which as near as I can make out means forcing some of them to sing and play crude instruments while the rest are prodded into hopping in their leg irons by a liberal use of the cat o' nine tails. I cannot find any justification for calling such a thing beneficial. To me it is cruelty, and I do not allow it.

While the slaves are on deck, the crew cleans the hold as best they can, swabbing it down and "perfuming" it with vinegar. It is hardly a task they relish, and I cannot say I blame them. I think a little less of myself as captain, but I do not see what I can do except tighten my discipline and force them to do their job. I have always said I would never ask of my men anything I was not willing to do myself, but I'll be damned if I'll set foot in that stinking hold.

At four o'clock, the second meal is served, millet and salt beef again, and then the slaves are stowed away for the night. It is a relief when the hatches are finally closed and battened after them, and we do not have to look at them for another day.

Sometimes, in the night, sounds drift up from below. Strange, melancholy wails that swell the empty darkness. They are dreaming, an old sailor tells me, a man who has made the crossing many times and seen all these things before. They are dreaming they are in their own land, and when they wake up and find themselves on the slave ship, they go out of their minds with grief.

13 June

I watch her sometimes, the girl with the old father, and it touches me, the way she is so gentle with him. He is very ill now, and I have had him taken off the chain, but he cannot walk and I think she knows he is going to die.

Some of the other girls have brightly colored kerchiefs knotted around their waists. They are presents from the sailors who did not have to beat them to get what they wanted. One girl, not the prettiest at all, but a lively, sassy creature, even has a golden ring in her ear. I wonder if she knows she will not be allowed to keep it once we get to port. I suppose it is better that she does not. At least it seems to make her happy now.

Still, I am glad *she* does not have a kerchief, too. I do not know why it matters, but it does. I do not want that degradation for her.

20 June

He is near death now, and she does not leave him for a minute. She sits beside him on the deck and croons to him. Soft, tender lullabies, like a mother to her babe. Her hand is as strong as a man's as she takes his head and presses it to her shoulder.

What makes one being human, I ask myself as I think of her, and another not worth redemption? What is it that marks the measure of a soul?

Is it Christianity? But what is Christianity, then? A touch of water? A few words spouted over a dripping head? If I threw them all in the ocean, this whole dark cargo of mine, and said a prayer over them and pulled them out again, would they be Christians then? And could I let them go?

Oh, hell, it's past midnight, and the darkness is full of eerie wails. A man's mind is bound to turn to morbid fancies.

25 June

They sing sometimes on deck. Sad, haunting songs that remind me of their cries in the night. I cannot make out the sound of the words, if in fact there are any. They speak many languages, these dark creatures, and they cannot understand each other any better than they understand me. But they all seem to know the melodies.

What are they singing? I ask the old sailor, the one who has made the Middle Passage before. Their death song, he tells me. They are afraid of the ocean. Many saw it for the first time when they were dragged out of the interior and forced onto broad, open beaches with waves crashing like thunder against the shore. They look at the water now and it seems to stretch on forever, and they think they are already dead.

He is making it up, of course. He does not speak the native tongues, and he knows no more than I. But at that, I think he is not far wrong. They sing of their loneliness, that much I can hear in their voices. They sing of pain and illness. Of their fear of the sea and their longing for the homeland they know they have left forever.

And when I listen to them, I am lonely, too. And I wonder if I will ever see my home again.

27 June

He died this morning. He made it through the night, and he seemed almost alert when they brought him up on deck, but then he simply laid his head in his daughter's lap and gave up. I wanted to weep for her, she was so brave. She stood quietly beside his body, watching the men wrap him in strips of dirty linen, and I knew she sensed we were going to throw him into the sea. I would have given half my profit for this whole miserable venture if I could have offered her the comfort of a few more hours with him. But I dared not leave a decomposing body in the hot sun.

I made the men carry him all the way to the stern of the ship. A pointless gesture, I suppose, but I had nothing else to give. I hoped the girl would see her father's body drift through the water behind us, and like a simple, superstitious child, think he was returning to the shores from whence he had come. It was a futile hope. I could see at once she was too knowing for that. She thought her father was going to spend his eternity in the cold, uncomforting arms of a sea he had always feared. And of course she was right.

That night I let her stay on deck. I tried to tell myself she would feel closer to him that way, but I knew even then she wouldn't. Her father was in the sea now, and she would never feel close to the sea. But at least for one night she would be free of that foul hold and its vile stench.

I went out on deck about midnight. The moon was full, and I could see her clearly, sitting at the railing with her back to the water. She saw me approach, but she did not seem frightened. At least she did not try to run. I wanted to talk to her, but I knew she could not understand. Impulsively, I pulled the kerchief from my neck and held it out to her.

Her eyes widened, turning into big black circles of fear, and I realized what I had done. I hated myself for being so clumsy.

No, I said quietly, though I knew the word meant nothing to her. No. And I laid the kerchief on the deck and stepped back a pace. No, I am not asking you to do anything for this. I just want to give you something. I want to make you feel less alone.

She seemed to understand. Her eyes were still wide, but they softened, and her lips curved up in a smile. She reached down and picked up the kerchief, tying it not around her waist as the other girls had done, but around her neck, the way I wore it.

And I knew then the thing that will haunt me the rest of my life. That girl is as human as I.

God help me, she does have a soul.

Horrified, Faith let the book drop, not even noticing when it slipped from her lap onto the floor. There were more words, more writing that went on for pages and pages, but she could not bear to look at it any longer.

A soul! The girl had a soul, he said—as if he had made some unique, clever discovery all his own. Dear God in heaven, what kind of a monster was he, this man who had fathered her?

She did not even feel herself get up, pushing boxes and trunks out of her way as she hurried toward the door. She was aware of her own movement only when she found herself on the stairway, taking the steep steps two and three at a time in her eagerness to get down. Even then, she did not know where she was going, nor did she care. She knew only that she had to get away from there. Away from the heat and the stale smell and the cobwebs. Away from everything that reminded her of a man whose only legacy to his daughter was a chronicle of his atrocities.

The breeze outside felt like a hot breath in her face when she flung open the front door and raced out onto the wide veranda. She opened her mouth, taking in deep, painful gulps of air, but she did not try to stop. Somehow, somewhere, she had to find the strength to escape from it all. Dust swirled around her, burning her eyes and catching in her throat as she followed the dirt road away from the house.

She was halfway to the river before she finally realized where she was going. The thought was so startling, she stopped where she was, gasping to catch her breath. Brad! She was running toward the rice fields—and Brad!

What a fool she had been! All these months, all these long, bitter months, she had quarreled with him, resented him, tried to blame him for her sister's death—and not once had she stopped to think that every time she had a problem or a question, it was always Brad she turned to. She had no loving family to take care of her, no husband able to comfort and cherish her, not even a kindly old servant with plump, sheltering arms, but she did have Brad. Surely he would not fail her now.

She found him at the edge of the rice fields, bending down to pull a weed the workers had missed. He ran a hand across his brow, brushing back an unruly lock of hair, then straightened abruptly as he saw her approach. One look at her face was enough to tell him something had happened.

He was beside her in a second, drawing her swiftly into his arms. His body was strong and warm with sweat, his voice soothing in her ear.

"It's all right, Faith. Shhhh! It's all right. Don't be frightened. I'm not going to let anyone hurt you. Don't you know that? It's all right."

Faith longed to believe him. She longed to sink into his arms, accepting the solace her heart hungered for, but his words held her back. It's all right, he kept telling her over and over. It's all right.

But it wasn't all right!

"Liar!" The word burst out of her mouth. All the tension that had been building inside her suddenly seemed to explode. Angrily, she pulled away from him, her fists turning into raging hammers, pounding against his chest. "Liar, liar, liar!"

He was too astonished to do anything more than catch her wrists in his hands, holding her awkwardly at arm's length. All he could see was a pink-and-white hurricane, all ruffles and lace and tumbling golden hair.

"For God's sake, what's wrong? What the devil's gotten into you?"

"How could you lie to me like that? You know I trusted you!"

He shook his head slowly. "I never lied to you, Faith. I don't lie."

"But you did! You told me my father hated slavery."

He stiffened at her words, but she was too preoccupied to notice. He eased his hold on her wrists; then, when she showed no signs of renewing her tantrum, he let her go.

"And so he did, Faith. More than any man I know."

"Of course he did! He hated it so much he made a fortune off it. He captained a slave ship, Brad! Don't try to tell me he didn't. I know. I read his diary."

Brad gave her a sharp glance, catching the clues he had missed before. The wrinkled skirt. The smudges of dust on her nose and forearm. Damn! Those old trunks in the attic. Why hadn't he taken the time to go through them?

"Listen to me, Faith. I don't expect you to understand what I am going to tell you. Just try to listen. Then later, when you've had a chance to think about it, maybe you'll be able to put it all into perspective."

"Perspective?" Faith was so incensed the word came out in a squeak. Perspective? "Do you really think everything's going to be just fine after I've had a chance to sleep on it?"

"You do me an injustice, my dear, if you think I'm that much of a fool. No, I don't think it will ever be 'just fine.' But is it so hard for you to understand how young Adam was when he went to sea—and what an adventure it must have seemed to him? Never underestimate the lure of adventure for a young man."

"Adventure? Is that what you call it? Stowing human beings into the cargo hold of a ship, 'tight pack' and 'loose pack'? Spoon-fashion?"

"Yes, I call it just that. Do you think Adam knew any of the shabby details when he left Liverpool? To him, the whole thing was exciting, daring—a chance to pit his strength against the wind and the sea in an old tub that would barely float. What would you have had him do when he reached Africa and found out what a despicable business slaving really is? Turn back and leave those poor wretches to be transported by a less scrupulous captain? Or maybe you think, when he got out in the center of the ocean and was wracked with horror at what he had done, he should just have jettisoned the lot of them and washed his hands of the whole thing!"

Faith glared at him furiously. How could he try to make rational excuses for such an—an irrational thing! Besides, he didn't understand at all. She had wanted to like Adam Eliot when she opened that book and began to read about him. She had wanted it desperately. All her life, she had watched everyone else dote on Fleur—her mother, her aunt, even her uncle. It would have been good to think *she* was someone's favorite once. Papa's little diamond. Only now "Papa" was a man so heinous she could not bear to think of him.

Tears misted her eyes, but she blinked them stubbornly back. It was enough that Brad had betrayed her when she came to him for comfort and sympathy. She was not going to suffer the final humiliation of letting him see her cry.

Brad watched her trembling lips, and he knew the only reason she wasn't hurling angry retorts at him was that she didn't trust her voice not to quiver. His hand was gentle as he cupped her chin, tilting her face upward.

"I'm not trying to say what your father did was right. He would be the first to tell you it wasn't! But he lived with his guilt the rest of his life—isn't that punishment enough? He could never forgive himself for what he did. I had hoped he would find more mercy at the hands of his daughter."

Faith could hold back the tears no longer. She hated the way they felt, wet and revealing on her cheeks. "That's not fair, Brad. I want to understand. Really I do. But——"

"But you can't forgive? Is that it?"

Dammit, she was Adam through and through. What else did he expect? And what else would he want?

He laid his hands lightly on her shoulders. When she did not resist, he drew her into his arms. "I'm sorry, Faith. I can be a clumsy oaf sometimes, can't I? I tell you how young Adam was when he set sail, and I forget you are even younger."

He cradled her in his arms, feeling her tears soak through

his shirt and moisten his chest. Blast it, he had never been able to resist a woman's tears. Especially this woman's. There were a dozen reasons why he should not hold her now. A hundred. And only one why he should. Because she felt right in his arms.

Faith sensed the potency of his tenderness, and in spite of herself, she could not help being drawn to it. There was security in the closeness of a man, even if that man was as maddening and arrogant as Brad. Besides, much as he infuriated her sometimes, he could be kind, too, when he wanted. She slipped her arms around him, holding on to him with all the aching loneliness in her heart.

Neither of them noticed they were not alone until a new voice cut through the stillness.

"What a tender scene! It warms the cockles of my heart—whatever the hell they are."

Faith looked up to see her husband mounted on a chestnut gelding in front of her. His face had never seemed so hard and cold. His skin was flushed, but his eyes were like ice.

"Is this what they call *droit de seigneur*? The right of the master to the vassal's wife? How positively feudal of you, Cousin Bradford."

Faith gaped at him in amazement. Did he really think that was what she was doing? Dallying in Brad's arms?

"Oh, Alexandre, it . . . it isn't what you're thinking. I was just upset about—about something I found in the attic."

Alexandre gave a short, brittle laugh. "Something you found in the attic? How novel, *chérie*. You haven't tried that one before."

I haven't tried anything before, Faith started to say, then stopped herself abruptly. Alexandre had never found *her* in Brad's arms before—but he might well have found her sister there! Unconsciously, her hand slipped to her throat, rubbing the place where his fingers had bruised her flesh.

The touch of a hand on her arm made her jump. She relaxed a little when she realized it was only Brad. He stepped closer, tightening his hold protectively.

"You're an asshole, Juilliard."

Alexandre's eyes snapped from ice to fire in a single second. Leaping from his horse, he stood in the middle of the road and glowered at Brad.

"*Bâtard*. I find you with your arms around my woman and you call *me* names. It seems to me I'm the one who——"

Brad did not let him finish. "Did you find out what I sent you for?"

All the color drained out of Alexandre's face. Faith stared at him in fascination. He had been so red before—so angry. Now he was deathly pale.

"Yes, I found out."

"And?"

"It's just as we feared. They hit Egan's store about eight o'clock this morning. Fortunately, Egan was warned in time, and he managed to get his wife and children away. But they caught his father-in-law coming out of the necessary house out in back. Chopped him into bits with an ax."

Faith shuddered as she listened to him. The words were ugly, unthinkable—but there wasn't a trace of expression in his voice. Confused, she turned toward Brad, but he seemed to have forgotten she was there. All his attention was centered on Alexandre.

"How many were there?"

"Forty. Maybe fifty. I ran into Carstairs on the way back and he said——"

"Thirty, then. Carstairs likes to exaggerate. Maybe less. There are only three or four from Havenhurst, not many more from the other plantations. If we can stop them before they gain any more strength . . ."

Faith shook her head dizzily, trying to take in all the words that were bouncing back and forth between them. Egan's store. Wasn't that the general store in town?

"What are you talking about?" she cried, breaking into their conversation. "What happened at Egan's store? What do you mean, someone 'hit' it?"

Brad paused to glance down at her. Faith did not like the glint in his eyes. It looked suspiciously like pity to her.

"I don't want you to be frightened, Faith."

"Frightened?" That what he had said before, when she came running down from the house. *Don't be frightened, Faith.* Only she had been too distraught to notice. "Why should I be frightened? Brad, *please*—please—tell me what's going on?"

"I guess there's no point in keeping it from you. You'll find out soon enough as it is. Some of the slaves have been banding together. We've known it for several days, but we haven't been able to ferret out their hiding place. This morning they finally made their move."

He didn't add that there was an ample supply of guns and powder at Egan's store. No need making the thing sound worse than it already did.

"You mean, they're runaways? That man Prince and a few others?"

"More than runaways, Faith. I think we have to face that. This is a full-scale rebellion, and if we don't crush it quickly, it could turn into a massacre. The hell of it is, some of them are from Havenhurst."

Havenhurst. The saliva turned all funny and salty in Faith's mouth and she could not bring herself to swallow. Three or four from Havenhurst, he had said. Cuffee. That *was* why he wasn't at breakfast. And Toney—Toney would be there, too. And Fibby.

But that was only three. Who else? That strange, very dark housemaid, Phillis? She was so quiet Faith never knew whether she was there or not, but she had heard the others whispering about her. Yes, Phillis would make four.

Not Estee. Please God, don't let Estee be with them.

"Oh, Brad. . . ."

She wanted to ask him, but she was afraid. She did not even remember her husband was there as she took his hand and held it tight. All her own problems seemed so insignificant now—the loss of her sister, the deterioration of her marriage, even the shameful secret she had just learned about her father.

And yet it was all part of the same thing, she thought sadly. Adam Eliot had sailed his ship on the Middle Passage a little more than twenty years ago. The rebels threatening Havenhurst today might be the very slaves he had brought from Africa in chains. Or their children.

"It had to happen, didn't it?" she said, her voice soft and reflective. "It had to happen."

Five

"I'm going with you."

Faith stood in the stable and stared at powerful muscles rippling through the back of Brad's shirt as he tightened his horse's cinch. Only when he had finished did he turn to scowl at her.

"The devil you are!"

Faith's heart sank, but she was determined not to let him see it. "You can't leave me here, Brad. Not with all the terrible things that are going on. I wouldn't be safe."

"You'd be a damn sight safer here than out in the open with me. Blast it, woman, this isn't a game! I may have a well-organized army to contend with, and the hell of it is, I won't even know until I get out there. If worse comes to worst—if I have to make a stand someplace—the last thing I need is a simpering female on my hands."

"I don't simper. And I wouldn't be in the way—you know I wouldn't." Faith made no effort to hide the tremor in her voice. If firmness failed to move him, perhaps a show of helplessness would. "Oh, Brad, I—I'm afraid. I don't want to stay here alone."

He fixed a cool gaze on her face.

"Not exactly *alone*, my dear. You do have a husband to look after you. . . or have you forgotten?"

Faith glanced down at splinters jutting out of the rough plank stall in front of her. "Alexandre isn't . . . he can't. . . ."

She stumbled on the words that were so hard to say. The change in Alexandre, right from the moment the slave rebellion started, was so dramatic, it was uncanny. It was as if that final stroke of violence had been too much for him. He had simply gone back to the room that had once been his and without a word to anyone, positioned himself in front of the window. He was there now, eyes staring sightlessly into the distance, face turned outward, like a blind man drawn by the heat of the sun.

"Alexandre can't help himself, Brad—much less me. I don't think he'll ever be the same again."

Brad turned away, busying himself with the horse. She had a point, he had to admit that.

"You don't need Alexandre to look after you, Faith. I've already organized the defenses of the house, under some of my most capable slaves. And don't worry—they're all loyal to me."

"To you, perhaps. But to me? A stranger—and a white woman at that? Oh, Brad, how do you think those men are going to feel when they look down the road and see their own people marching toward them?"

"I've asked myself that same question," he admitted reluctantly. "If I were a black man, would I be able to load a gun and point it at some poor bastard who only wanted the same freedom and dignity I hungered for myself? I'll be damned if I know the answer."

"There, you see! I *wouldn't* be safe here. You have to take me with you."

Brad hesitated. The woman was right—he *couldn't* guarantee her safety. Besides, they still had three or four hours of daylight left. With any luck, they'd get to one of the other plantations before then. Sam Hardin's place perhaps, or Eleazar Carstairs' Cypress Hill.

"All right." He covered the distance to the other side of the stable and took down a second saddle. "I don't like it, but I guess I haven't any choice. Only we're not going for a romp across the meadows, is that understood? I want you to stay beside me at all times—and do exactly what I tell you!"

Faith eyed the saddle warily. It was a dark well-worn piece of equipment, much too heavy for the frisky mare she usually rode, but she did not dare protest. Not when he could still change his mind and leave her behind.

The minute she saw the horse he led from a stall at the rear of the stable, she realized what he was up to. This was not her friendly little mare at all, but a massive Arabian gray, almost as pale as his own stallion, only half a hand higher and much stockier in build.

Faith took a step forward, then stopped. The horse watched her approach. His eyes rolled upward, and he lifted his lips, revealing the most enormous set of teeth she had ever seen in her life.

It was almost, she thought with a shudder, as if the beast knew she was afraid and was laughing at her.

No, not laughing—sneering.

"I—I don't think he likes me."

"He doesn't like anyone. But he won't try to throw you, if that's what you're afraid of. What he lacks in personality, he makes up in instinct. If we get in a tight spot, just give him his head and hang on like hell."

Faith studied the horse dubiously. He seemed awfully stolid and plodding to her.

"What do you mean, if we get into a tight spot?"

Brad paused, his hand resting on the saddle. For the first time, Faith noticed he had tucked a gun in his belt.

"Those runaways are armed, Faith, and dangerous. If they see us before we see them, we may have to do some fancy riding. A horse that knows what he's doing can mean the difference between life and death."

Faith felt the warmth drain from her cheeks, but she did not flinch or pull away. If she wanted this man to take her with him, she was going to have to be his equal, in coolness as well as courage. Disdaining his offer to help, she pulled herself up on the horse. Hard leather chafed the inside of her thighs through sheer muslin pantalettes as she forced herself to straddle the broad back. Keeping her chin pointed defiantly upward, she urged the unfamiliar steed toward the door.

Brad lingered a moment beside his own horse, watching her. Damn, she was a fiery little witch! So terrified she was ready to burst into tears, and there she was, sitting as tall and straight in the saddle as if she had been riding all her life. If only she could hold onto that magnificent spirit a little longer, maybe the next few hours wouldn't be so bad after all.

The sun was shining in Faith's eyes when she rode outside, and she barely noticed a solitary figure beside the gate that separated the stableyard from the road. As she drew nearer, she was startled to recognize Beneba's dark features. Somehow, standing all by herself, with no one next to her, the woman looked smaller, less imposing, than she had before. Her shoulders were stooped, and mercilessly bright light picked out every strand of gray in her hair.

Brad pulled at the reins, drawing his mount to a stop in front of her. His eyes were guarded as he gazed down. His voice was low and troubled.

"I cannot force you to stay. You know that as well as I.

All I can do is warn you—it will go hard on those who leave. Even if I want to, there is nothing I can do to protect them."

The words sounded ominous to Faith, but to her surprise, the old woman only chuckled softly.

"Now where I gonna go, heh? Yo' tell me that, Mist' Brad."

"I thought you might feel you had to join them. Because *she* is there."

The emphasis in his voice sent a cold chill through Faith's flesh. *She*. There could only be one person he meant—yet, oh, dear heaven, she prayed he was wrong.

Beneba shook her head slowly. "I ain't neber gonna leave this house. Not as long as they is a breath left in my body. *She* wouldn't want it no other way."

She again. The word rolled off Beneba's tongue with much the same emphasis it had had when Brad uttered it a moment ago, yet Faith had the distinct feeling it did not mean the same thing.

Faith threw a quizzical glance at Brad, but to her horror, she saw that he had already passed through the gate and was beginning to move down the road toward the river. Forgetting the old slave, Faith touched her heel to the horse's flank, prodding him into an easy trot. Brad had made his terms perfectly clear, right from the start. If she wanted to go with him, she was going to have to keep up.

She reached him just where the road turned to wander along the riverbank. One look at the grim set of his jaw was enough to tell her his mind was preoccupied and he would not thank her for a stream of nervous prattle. Taking her cue from him, she rode beside him in silence.

The river was a burst of beauty, with cascades of lush spring greenery tumbling over the banks. Gaily colored petals, blown by the winds, touched the shimmering water with their pastel brightness. It was almost, Faith thought, watching the ripples drift lazily by, as if they had just gone out for a ride. As if all the ugliness and violence of recent days had been nothing more than a bad dream. They followed the river, turning occasionally inland, until at last the cloying perfume of the gardens dissolved into the mingled fragrance of pine from the forest and sweet jessamine from the rice field banks.

Wherever Faith looked, everything seemed so commonplace and routine, it was almost frightening. Black women with baskets balanced on their heads scampered nimbly over the banks, clinging resolutely to everyday chores. Beside them, their men, knee deep in mud, struggled to repair the canals and clear away roots and fallen trunks from the edges of the fields. The planting had been finished the day before, and the seed rice was covered with several inches of water.

They had been riding together for more than an hour before Faith at last dared to speak.

"Brad, what did you mean when you asked Beneba if she was going to join the runaways?"

From the sharp glance he threw her, Faith could not tell whether he was irritated or not.

"Did anyone ever tell you you have a bad habit of asking questions when you don't want to hear the answers?"

"Yes, you. But I do want to hear them! Well, not *want* to, maybe—but I know I have to."

Brad stopped unexpectedly, reaching out to catch her reins and hold her beside him a second.

"Let it go, Faith," he urged. "Don't push."

"You might as well tell me, Brad. I'm going to find out sooner or later. She is with them, isn't she? Estee?"

"The man was her lover, my dear, what did you expect? She was bound to follow him."

Faith gripped the saddle to keep from swaying. Though he was telling her no more than she already knew, still it hurt to have her fears confirmed.

"But Beneba said something strange, Brad. Something I didn't understand. She said—'*She* wouldn't want me to go.' Was she talking about Estee?"

"Not Estee—Katherine."

"Katherine?" Of all the things he could have said, that was the one she expected least. "What on earth does Katherine have to do with all this? She's been dead for years."

"Try to understand, Faith. Katherine was still a child when they dragged her off that slave ship in the Islands. And she was probably already pregnant, perhaps by one of the sailors—that kind of thing is appallingly common—perhaps by one of the slaves to whom she was chained in the hold. Beneba had buried her own children long before in the harsh, unforgiving soil of the sugar plantations. When she saw Katherine, young, helpless, no doubt terrified, she simply crushed her to that ample bosom of hers. And there she remained, figuratively speaking, to the end of her days."

"But Brad—" Faith's eyes narrowed skeptically. "You aren't making sense. If Beneba was so devoted to Katherine, why on earth would she want to stay at Havenhurst?"

"Ah, yes, your father's house. The site of poor Katherine's

shame and degradation. My dear child, when are you going to——"

The break in his voice was so abrupt, it was startling. Only when she looked up and saw that his eyes fixed on something behind her did Faith remember where they were—and what they had come for. Her heart beat wildly against her chest as she eased her mount slowly around.

On the road in front of her, just at the top of a low hill, a group of thirty or forty men and women, their skin ranging in tone from deep brown-black to a soft golden hue, had begun to straggle down the slope. Faith held her seat on the horse and stared at them, more in wonder than in fear. This was not the bold, disciplined band of rebels she had both dreaded and secretly admired. Here were no makeshift banners hoisted defiantly to the wind, no polished muskets clenched in readiness in ruthless black fists. This was a motley crew of vagabonds, no more, no less. Their clothes were rumpled and dirty, as if they had slept in them for weeks, and what few guns the men possessed were slung carelessly over their shoulders. Their hands were occupied with heavy crockery jugs they passed back and forth.

"The poor devils!"

Brad's murmur was so intense, it drew Faith's attention. Seeing her puzzled look, he gave her a wry half smile.

"They must have gotten into someone's private cache. Probably Lord Warren's. He keeps his liquor in an outbuilding, away from the main house. It's a damn fool thing to do—I've told him that often enough—but there's no getting a man to listen when his mind is made up."

Faith stared at him with wide, uncomprehending eyes. "You sound almost—angry. As if you mind about the liquor more than the guns."

"I am angry! Dammit, all he had to do, that arrogant bastard, was keep his men away from the whiskey. He'd have had a band to be proud of then."

"Brad!" Faith was horrified. She had been sympathetic toward the slaves, too—but that was before they took up guns and began killing people. "How can you say that? Surely you don't want them to beat us."

"Beat us? By God, woman, do you have any idea what you're saying? Everything I care about—everything I've worked for—is right here on this plantation. Beat us? Hell, no! I want to beat them, and soundly too! But I don't want to take away every shred of their dignity in the process."

Dignity? Faith turned to watch the slaves' erratic progress

down the hill. It was a funny choice of words. They were barely a quarter of a mile away now, but they were so absorbed in their own progress, they had not yet noticed a pair of riders in the center of the road. There was nothing even remotely akin to dignity in their appearance.

"Oh, Brad. . . ."

Faith clutched his arm as she caught sight of a small figure, wandering off vaguely, first to one side of the road, then to the other. She looked almost comical, like a little bird with a wounded wing, half hopping, half fluttering, as it struggled to keep up with the rest of the flock.

Brad nodded grimly. "I know. Fibby."

"But she's just a child! She can't do anything but sew and embroider. Why would they want to take her with them, for God's sake? And, oh, Brad, someone's been giving that witless little creature whiskey!"

Brad pulled away, laying a hand on the horse's neck to steady it. "There's nothing we can do about it," he reminded her evenly. "We can't get her out of that mob now, and we haven't got a snowball's chance in hell of convincing anyone to go easy on her when the shooting starts. Just pray someone at least has the decency to shoot her cleanly."

"Oh, my God. . . ." For the first time, Faith truly understood what was happening, and it sickened her. There was nothing romantic about the idea of rebellion now. Nothing glamorous. Not when helpless little children like Fibby were caught in the middle of it.

Brad did not let her dwell on the thought.

"Listen carefully. Here's what I want you to do. They haven't spotted us yet, and I don't want them to. Just turn your horse around, nice and easy, and walk him back down the road. When you get past that clump of shrubbery at the bend, give him a slap on the rump and ride like hell. And don't make the mistake of thinking a drunk can't get off a straight shot!"

Faith was surprised at how calm she felt. There was no time for doubt now. No time for fear. No time for anything but coolly, deliberately, following his orders. She turned her horse and began to move cautiously down the road. She had just looked up to see how far she was from the shrubbery when she saw a sight that took her breath away.

They must have been there all the time, she thought helplessly. Hiding in the bushes, waiting . . . biding their time. Now they leaped out and, following their leader, Prince, fanned across the road. There could have been no more than a dozen, but they were strong and sober—and every one of them had a gun.

Faith yanked at the reins, startling the horse into a backward step. She was aware of a strange sense of unreality, as if she were watching everything from some detached place far away. This wasn't really happening to her, this terrible, frightening ordeal. It was happening to someone else, some character she had read about in a book or made up in her own head. Not to her at all.

Then her eyes picked out the only woman in the band, a dusky, slender beauty standing just behind the leader, and suddenly the whole thing became devastatingly real.

Estee. Her friend *was* with the rebels, just as Brad had told her. And she was there not to drink and carouse like some of the others, but to hold a deadly musket in her hands.

Faith longed to leap from her horse and run up to her, but instinct warned her that any show of friendship would be unwelcome now. Whatever fragile thread had once bound these two young women together, it had snapped in the savage events of the last few days. Estee had chosen up sides, just as she herself had done, and neither of them could go back now. Faith was white, and her place would always be with the white men who lived in white houses high on the hill, just as Estee was black and would live or die with her own kind.

"Stay where you are, Faith."

Brad's voice was even and steady. Faith glanced over at him. His profile told her nothing, but the knuckles that gripped his reins were white with strain. He did not turn his head so much as a fraction of an inch, yet his eyes were constantly in motion, searching the terrain on both sides of the road.

Faith followed with her own eyes. On one side of the road, she saw nothing but rough, uncultivated fields, much too tangled for a horse to get through; on the other, a rushing river, swollen by spring floods. That left only two directions they could ride—straight ahead, into that tight, armed band—or back toward the drunken mob.

"All right. . . ."

Brad's voice was so low Faith could barely hear it. Tense with anticipation, she sat absolutely still, waiting for him to continue.

"Don't make a move until I give the word. Don't even shift your eyes to let them guess what you're thinking. Wait until I say 'Now!' then turn your horse around as fast as you can and drop the reins."

Turn the horse around? Faith started to lift the reins, then remembering his warning, forced herself to remain immobile. Turn around? That meant they were going back—toward the mob. But how were they going to get around them? The undergrowth was impassable there, and the river——

"Now!"

Then the time for thought was over. Faith spun her horse around, then tossed the reins away, letting him bolt. It was all she could do to grab at the front of the saddle, hanging on for all she was worth. For an instant, she did not even realize what was happening. When she did, her body went rigid with terror.

They were not going around the mob at all. They were riding right into the heart of it!

Everything happened so quickly, it was only a blur of action and color. Faith saw startled men and women leap hastily to the side, but the movement was so chaotic she could not pick out faces or individuals. Even in her fear, she recognized the boldness of Brad's plan, and she could not help admiring it. The slaves in the mob, surprised by the swiftness of the charge, had time only to clamber out of the way of the horses' crushing hooves, and the disciplined band behind dared not shoot for fear of hitting one of their own comrades by mistake.

Faith's heart jumped with excitement when the last of the slaves scampered away and she saw empty road stretching out in front of her. They had made it! They had actually made it! And without sustaining so much as a single scratch.

She was so swept up with exhilaration that the sound of the first shot was a brutal shock. Her body jerked convulsively, as if the bullet had hit her, and she crouched low in the saddle, trying instinctively to merge her body into the protective strength of her mount. Brad's words echoed menacingly in her ears. *Don't make the mistake of thinking a drunk can't get off a straight shot!*

She felt something catch at her skirt, and glancing down, was surprised to see that she was nowhere near the brambles and branches at the edge of the road. Not until she saw a jagged tear, ripping through both her skirt and petticoats, did she realize a bullet had missed her leg by less than an inch. Terrified, she flung herself forward, clinging to the horse's mane and praying she would not fall off.

She was not aware of the moment the sound of gunfire finally faded behind her. She knew only that she listened for it, and it was gone at last. But she was still so frightened, she could not force herself to sit upright and grip the horse's reins again. She barely saw Brad pull ahead of her, positioning his stallion in front of hers to slow the horse and nudge it gently off the side of the road.

He did not waste time on words, but gave her a sharp look to make sure she was all right. Then, handing the reins back to her, he prodded his horse forward, moving out in front of her. Faith followed, grateful for his reticence. She had disgraced herself badly in his eyes; she was determined not to do it again.

Dusk had already begun to fall, but Brad did not slacken his pace. The riverbank was eerie and quiet, with only the gentle lapping of current against the sand to provide a background for dual hoofbeats. The land had begun to take on a marshy smell, and deep green shadows spread, vibrant and translucent, across the earth.

It was almost dark when Brad stiffened suddenly, pulling his horse to a stop. Behind him, on the path, Faith did the same thing. In the silence that followed, she realized the duet of hoofbeats she had heard was only an illusion. In reality, there were not two horses on the path that night, but three. And the third was drawing closer every second.

Her body tensed with fear as Brad whirled around, aiming the barrel of his pistol into the shadows. Slowly, a figure began to emerge from the darkness.

The instant she made him out, Faith felt a sudden, almost irresistible, urge to giggle. No one could have looked more incongruous on a night like that—or more comforting. A slender man, trim and boyish, he looked like a dandy in immaculately tailored burgundy velvet, with silver braid trim. A long, curving white plume gave his black tricorne a rakish air.

If he was alarmed at the sight of a gun in Brad's grip, he did not show it. Breaking into a grin, he raised a careless hand in protest.

"Hold your fire, lad. What did you think? That I was a highwayman come to rob you?"

Brad did not quite succeed in looking stern. "Damn you, Warren. That's a good way to get yourself shot!"

"Oh, come, come, dear boy. I have always had complete faith in your good judgment. I can't imagine your shooting a man without at least checking to see who he was."

"And, of course, you were absolutely sure it was me you were sneaking up on in the dark. It couldn't have been some other damn fool, caught outside, skittish and half scared to death."

"Of course I was sure." Lord Warren tipped his hat with a bawdy wink at Faith. "Who else would be out on a night like this?" His face grew serious again as he turned back to Brad. "There's a whole passel of them back there, drunk and rowdy, but I suspect you already know that. I think they're only a decoy. I nearly ran into a smaller band, eight or ten strong, under your man Toney. I daresay there may be more."

"There are. At least one more—under Prince himself. They seem to be headed this way."

Lord Warren peered thoughtfully into the darkness. "So did the band I saw. Does that, perchance, strike you as odd?"

"You mean, they're going the wrong way if they want to get to Florida."

"They'll never make it to Florida. Not in the shape they're in. Oh, Prince has managed to hang onto a few of his men, but how long do you think that will last? Sooner or later, they'll stop in some field and finish my good liquor, and the militia will pick them off before noon. You know that and I know that—and Prince is too intelligent not to know it, too."

"So you think he's planning to make a stand. A good tough fight to sober them up. Give them a sense of purpose again."

"Or go out in style, so to speak."

Brad nodded grimly. "If they're headed this way, there can only be two places they're aiming for. Dan Fraser's homestead, or the Hardin plantation. Fraser's the logical choice, of course—that shack of his will be poorly defended—but with a man like Prince, there's no telling what he'll do. If he knows it's the end, he might just decide to go out in a blaze of fury."

"My conclusions exactly. I was on my way to warn them both."

"Well, now there are two of us. I'll head for Fraser's and see what I can do for him. You give the word to Sam Hardin. And for God's sake, stay there, at least until dawn."

"Stay there?" Lord Warren rolled his eyes up in a gesture of mock horror. "Fie, lad! That's hardship beyond reason, and well you know it. I have a hankering for a nice feather bed with linen sheets, and old Sam has never been noted for his hospitality. No, I think I'll head on to Charles Town and see what the local hostelries have to offer."

"You think that's wise?"

"Ah, so it's wisdom you want, is it? Someday, my boy, you

will understand that it is not wisdom an old man's heart craves, but a glass of wine in front of the fire—and a pretty wench to share it with."

He turned to Faith with a smile. His hat was in his hand, and she thought he was about to offer her a farewell salute. Instead, he glanced quizzically at Brad.

"But I would be glad to escort the woman there if you like."

Brad hesitated. Common sense warned him Faith would be safer at Sam Hardin's plantation, but the way was long and treacherous and he could not trust Lord Warren to be as cautious as he might be. Beside, knowing Prince as he did, the man might as well attack one place as the other.

"No," he said quietly. "The woman stays with me."

Lord Warren grinned agreeably. "A wise choice, lad. Never trust a beautiful woman with an old lecher like me." He dipped his hat with a gallant flourish, and without another word, vanished into the darkness.

Brad turned to Faith with a worried look. Damn! Why had he let her talk him into this? If he had an ounce of sense in his head, he would have left her at Havenhurst.

"This wasn't exactly what I had in mind when I said you could come along."

She managed a weak smile.

"It wasn't what I had in mind either. But don't worry. Whatever happens, I can handle it."

Six

A foul-smelling grease lamp hissed and sputtered on a table in the center of the one-room shack. Faith wrinkled her nose in distaste as she looked around at the crude furnishings. Really, this place was every bit as mean as a slave cottage at Havenhurst. Not a trace of whitewash could be seen on any of the unfinished siding boards, and gaps in the wooden floor were so wide the earth showed through in places. A wattle-and-daub fireplace was centered on one of the walls, but even though the night was chill, no fire had been laid.

"It ain't what you're used to, I'm afraid. We be but simple folks here. But I do keep it as clean as ever I can."

Faith turned guiltily to face the speaker. Sally Fraser had been a pretty woman once, but now her blond hair was dulled with gray, and deep lines in her face made her look older than she was.

"Of course you do. I noticed that right away. And please don't think I'm used to being mistress of a luxurious manor like Havenhurst. Why, in England I was nothing but a poor relation."

"But you didn't live like this, I'll warrant," a youthful voice cut in. "You ain't never once got down on your knees to scrub a floor. Not with hands that look like that."

"Josh!"

Dan Fraser's tone was enough to silence his eldest son, but Sally blushed with embarassment.

"You must excuse Young Josh, Mrs. Juilliard. He don't usually forget his manners like this."

"Please don't apologize. The boy is right. I *haven't* ever scrubbed a floor in my life. And don't call me Mrs. Juilliard. My name is Faith."

She saw instantly that her attempts at friendliness were ill-advised. For a woman like Sally, used to keeping her place, overtures from someone she considered a "lady" were not only awkward but downright unseemly. Determined to avoid any further gaucherie, Faith settled down in a plain wooden chair in front of the cold hearth and watched the others rearrange the room with brisk, efficient motions.

She could readily see why Brad had thought the Frasers would need help. The couple had three sons, but the oldest, the boy who had spoken out before, could have been no more than fifteen. The other two, Ben and Daniel, appeared about twelve and ten respectively. There was only one other occupant of the room, a short, stocky black man who seemed almost as wary of Faith as she was of him.

The preparations were quickly finished. Within minutes, the furniture had been cleared away, with beds upended in every available corner and chairs piled in a hasty heap in the center of the room. Heavy wooden shutters were bolted over unglazed windows, and one by one, the men tested them to make sure they were secure.

When everything had been accomplished to his satisfaction, Brad picked up a bulky, blanket-wrapped bundle that had been lashed to his saddle and laid it out on the floor beside the fireplace. He unwrapped it carefully, peeling away a double thickness of wool from a lethal accumulation of pistols and long-barreled muskets. Although the others gathered around eagerly, curious to see the weapons he had brought to add to their defense, Faith pulled away, unable to look at them. Nothing brought home the reality of the danger they were facing more keenly than the sight of that small arsenal on the floor.

Brad looked up to see the pallor on her face.

"Do you know how to load a gun?"

For a minute, Faith could only gape at him. The question was so absurd, she almost forgot her fears.

"Good heavens, Brad! Where on earth would I learn something like that?"

"Well, it's time then. Come here and let me show you."

Faith started to rise, then held back, half hoping he would tell her he was only joking. Surely he didn't expect a gentle, properly bred young Englishwoman to pick up one of those dreadful-looking guns and take it in her hand?

But the look on his face warned her that he did. Well, she had only herself to blame, she thought miserably, dragging her feet as she went over to him. She had insisted on coming along—now she would have to live with the consequences.

Tucking her full skirt close around her legs, she squatted on the ground beside him.

"There will be four of us firing the guns," he told her. "One on each side of the house. Sally will take the window that faces the river. The terrain is more exposed there, and I doubt she'll see much action. The three men will man the other sides."

The *three* men?

Faith glanced doubtfully around the room. Brad and Dan Fraser were the only men there. Unless of course. . . .

Brad saw her consternation. "A black man can be a good fighter," he reminded her coolly.

"Yes, but can we—can we trust him?"

"I would trust that man with my life."

Faith stared at the pile of guns on the floor and hoped fervently that Brad knew what he was talking about. If the worst happened, it would not only be his life he was entrusting to a black man, but the life of everyone in that room.

Brad spent the next hour explaining the various guns to her and showing her how to handle them. She would be responsible for loading for Sally, he told her, while the three boys would tend to the needs of the more experienced marksmen. Faith ran through the procedures again and again under his tutelage, feeling a little clumsier each time, and she prayed he was right when he said Sally would not see much action. If things happened too quickly, she was sure she would let them all down.

She was nearly in tears at the end of the hour, and Brad made her stop.

"That's enough for one sitting. If you push too hard, you'll make yourself so tense you'll be no good to anyone."

Dragging a three-legged stool out of the jumble in the center of the room, he set it beside one of the windows and motioned for her to sit down. The light was faint enough to risk opening a shutter, and a welcome breeze freshened the sweaty room. Outside, a tree, dense with spring foliage, provided an effective screen against watching eyes.

Brad stood directly behind her. He did not try to touch her, but he was so close, he could feel the trembling of her limbs.

"It doesn't have to be here, you know," he whispered reassuringly. "They might just as well be heading for Sam Hardin's place. If they're planning to attack anyone at all."

Faith rested her elbows on the window ledge and cupped her chin in her hands. She saw what he was trying to do, but it was no good. Nothing he could ever say would make her forget that somewhere out there, dozens of unseen black figures were creeping through the darkness.

"Brad, what. . . ." She glanced back into the room, bitterly aware of the black man crouched at a window on the other side. "What makes you think you can trust him?"

Brad pulled away irritably. Just when he thought he was getting to know her, she went and pulled something like this.

"Dammit, Faith, is your vision so narrow, your heart so self-centered, you can't find it in you to trust a man because his skin is a different color?"

"That's not fair, Brad. I wanted to trust the blacks, truly I did. And I *did* trust them. I trusted Cuffee and poor little Fibby . . . and Estee."

He relented, sensing not only her confusion, but her pain. "It's different with Black Josh, I promise you."

"Black . . . *Josh?*"

"He was named for Dan's father," Sally Fraser broke in. She had been checking to make sure the boys were loading the guns properly, and now she paused beside Faith's stool. "His father, Cud Joe, was with Old Josh since he was a boy. When it come time for Joe to get married, Old Josh had to scrape some to get the money to buy him a wife, but he done it. It only seemed natural Joe would want to call his firstborn after him."

"But you gave your own son the same name?"

"Of course. There'd of been the devil to pay from the old man if we hadn't. 'Sides, Black Josh is a fine, hard-workin' man. My son don't have no cause to be ashamed of the name." She hesitated, searching for the words to make Faith understand. "See, Black Josh, he ain't like a slave. Not really. He's more like—like one o' us."

"That's not uncommon here in the Colonies," Brad explained after Sally had retreated to the other side of the room. "The large landowners have dozens, often hundreds of slaves, and it makes sense to maintain them in separate quarters. But most of the farmers and small planters can afford only one or two slaves. They sleep under the same roof with their masters, and they eat at the same table; they toil side by side to bring in a good harvest, and they tighten their belts together when the yield is poor. After a while, it's hard to remember which is the master and which the slave."

Faith stared out the window, catching an occasional glimmer of distant stars through the thick foliage. It was hard to imagine a world without all the comfortable distinctions she had been taught to rely on. A world where the words *master* and *worker* no longer had any meaning. Or even *freedom* and *slavery.*

Brad leaned over her, intoxicated by the sweet floral fragrance that wafted up from her shoulders and breasts. She seemed at that moment utterly tantalizing, a wonderful, bewitching union of everything that had always intrigued him. Half little girl, helpless, vulnerable, crying out for his protection—half knowing, sensual woman.

He let his fingers toy with a stray curl that had twisted out of her coiffure to lie against her neck. It was so soft and silky, it felt like the hair of a babe.

Faith was conscious every second of the feel of his hand against her skin. There was, in those tender fingers, a masculinity more potent than any virile show of strength she had ever known. No man had touched her like that before, or made her feel so intensely feminine.

His fingers were still gentle as he tucked them under her chin, teasing it slowly upward.

"Do you have any idea how beautiful you are? Or how my blood boils when I look at you?"

Faith did not miss the low tremor that gave substance to his words. For the first time with this man, she sensed he was not merely flirting with her, but saying things he truly meant.

"You—you shouldn't talk to me like that."

"Why not?"

"Because . . . I'm a married woman."

To her surprise, he began to laugh. It was a soft sound, deliberately low and private.

"All this time, and we still can't be honest with each other. Surely, you know, you calculating little creature, that I was completely captivated the minute I laid eyes on you. I wanted you, even then, more than any woman I have ever known. And that, my pet, is an admission a man like me does not make easily."

She could not bring herself to look at him. "The first time you laid eyes on me, Brad Alleyn, you didn't see me at all. You saw only Fleur."

"Fleur?"

Brad's voice was sharp enough to draw her gaze upward. He looked annoyed, almost angry for a second. Then, shaking his head, he started to laugh again.

"How the devil do you come up with things like that? I didn't see Fleur at all when I looked at you."

"Oh, yes, you did! I saw your face that afternoon. You looked at me, and you thought I was Fleur."

"Maybe at first," he conceded. "But when you spoke, when you moved, when you smiled—then there was nothing reminiscent of Fleur in you. Then you were totally Faith. And totally enchanting."

He lowered his voice until it was no more than a sensuous whisper. His lips were barely inches from her own. Faith had the terrible, frightening feeling he was going to kiss her—and that she wanted him to.

"Oh, Brad, please . . . please. . . ."

"Please what, my darling?"

"Please. . . ." She was painfully conscious of vague figures moving back and forth in other parts of the room. "Please . . . what will they think of us?"

"Does it matter so much? What other people think?"

"Yes." She did not know why, but it did. She would never be like her sister, able to thumb her nose at the world and all its conventions. "Yes, it matters desperately."

Brad was wise enough to pull back. He had never wanted her more than he did at that moment, but she was not ready for him yet. Planting a light kiss on her cheek, he stepped over to the sputtering lamp.

"I think it's time to put this out. Just in case."

The darkness was complete, but strangely, it seemed more enveloping than frightening. Faith leaned her head against the window frame and stared out into the night. A single golden light flickered occasionally through the branches, like a little yellow star fallen to the earth. There was a friendly feeling about it, as if it were a torch in the hand of——

A torch! Faith jumped up, kicking over the stool in her haste.

"Brad!"

He was beside her in a second. The light went out almost immediately, but he had had a chance to get a quick look at it. Reacting instinctively, he thrust out an abrupt hand and slammed the shutter closed.

The darkness, mellow and comforting only a moment before, was suddenly terrifying. Faith groped along the wall until she managed to find one of the windows that faced the road. Crouching down, she pressed her eyes against it, peering through chinks in the rough boarding. The road was a ribbon of white in the dim moonlight, stretching off into the distance; on either side, bushes and trees quivered in a light breeze from the river. Faith could not make out any trace of the rebels threading their way through thick undergrowth toward the house, but she knew they were there. And she knew they would not wait long to make their move.

She stayed at the window as long as she dared, then forced herself back into the room. The darkness did not seem quite so forbidding now. She still could not make out the pile of furniture in the center of the room, but at least a deeper pattern of shadow gave her a hint where it was, and she got around it without stumbling. Sally was already at the window, and she took her place beside her.

Not a sound filled the great empty pit of night outside. Not a whisper could be heard, not a footstep, not even a cracking twig or rustling shrub to tell them what was happening. Faith sat with the others and listened, but all she could hear was the short, controlled rasping of their own breath, and she knew every hand that rested on a gun was as taut and trembling as her own.

It was the waiting that was hardest, she thought, trying in vain to catch at least a glimpse of the others in the darkness. The waiting . . . and wondering. It would almost be a relief when it finally began.

Yet, the first shot that splintered the silence brought with it an impact that was both stunning and unexpected. Faith felt her body jump with shock, and she crouched closer to the wall. From around her in the darkened room, she heard the grating of gun barrels against wooden sills and the ominous creaking of rusty hinges as shutters slid open a cautious inch or two. There was no other sound for an instant; then the fighting began in earnest.

Faith stayed close to Sally, holding one of a pair of loaded pistols out where she could grab it whenever she needed it. Sally kept her eyes fastened on the broad expanse of moon-drenched riverbank. She did not waste ammunition shooting at shadows, but held her hand steady. When at last she squeezed the trigger, a cry of pain outside told Faith the bullet had found its mark.

Faith pushed a new pistol toward her with one hand and grabbed for the spent weapon with the other. The barrel singed her fingers; the smell of smoke was hot and acrid in her nostrils. She felt awkward and inept, like a little girl just learning to buckle her shoe, as she juggled the unfamiliar weapon, trying desperately to reload it before Sally could call for it again. She was glad now that Brad had forced her to go through the routine over and over again. But why—dear heaven, *why?*—hadn't he made her do it with her eyes closed? It was so much harder when she couldn't see what she was doing.

Faith quickly lost all sense of time. She had no idea how long the fighting went on. It might have been hours, it might as well have been only a few minutes—either way, it felt like eternity. To her surprise, her hands seemed to have found a will of their own, completely separate from her fear-numbed brain, and she cleaned and loaded the gun barrels with a skill she never dreamed she possessed. Perhaps, after all, everything was going to be all right. Perhaps they would be able to hold off their attackers until the first light of dawn drove them away.

She had just begun to let herself hope when a sharp, feminine cry rang in her eyes. It was followed almost immediately by the dull thud of a gun dropping to the floor.

"Sally?" She thrust out her arms in the darkness. "Sally, are you all right?"

Catching hold of the woman, Faith drew her down, laying her on the floor beside the window. Something warm and sticky coated her hands, and she had the horrible feeling it was blood.

"I'm all right," Sally reassured her weakly. "It's only a scratch. The bullet just grazed my arm."

Brad hurried across the room, stooping low to stay out of the range of partially opened shutters. Ripping open Sally's sleeve, he examined the wound with his hands.

"No bones broken, thank God, but it's more than a scratch. Faith, tear your petticoat into strips and bind the wound. That should stop the bleeding, at least for now. But she's not going to be able to handle a gun."

Faith caught her breath at the sound of his words. What was he telling her? That she would have to take up a pistol in Sally's stead? She who had never so much as held a gun in her hands before?

"Let me take her place," a boyish voice chimed in. "I can do it. I know I can."

Faith hesitated. Young Josh was just a boy, much too young to know about death and killing, but she was not at all sure she could point a gun at another human being and actually do that terrible, irrevocable thing they were asking of her.

To her relief, Brad settled the question before she could speak.

"All right. But keep your head, boy. I don't want to hear

you wasting ammunition. Faith, come here. You'll have to load for me."

Faith was so grateful not to have to take Sally's place she was not even nervous as she took up her new post. She was more confident now, and she loaded and reloaded each weapon deftly and surely, staying well ahead of Brad and his needs. The force of the original onslaught had abated, and while sporadic bursts of gunfire still erupted from time to time, they were punctuated by periods of eerie silence.

Faith took advantage of one of the respites to stretch her legs out in front of her and lean against the wall. It seemed lighter now, though she suspected that was only because her eyes had adjusted to the darkness. She glanced around the room, picking out hazy forms: Dan Fraser, a lank, tense figure, the long barrel of his gun propped against the window ledge; Young Josh, his jaw set like his father's, his eyes shining as if it were all a game and he was winning; Sally, sitting quietly beside her son, showing none of the pain she must be feeling as she patiently loaded his guns for him.

In the darkness outside, the sounds were comforting and normal. Crickets chirped in shadowy fields; frogs teased each other in the marshes; a distant owl mimicked the low wail of the wind. And somewhere near the house, a horse whinnied his petulant protest into the night.

The sound had an immediate effect on Dan Fraser. Whirling away from the window, he caught Brad's eye.

"The stables! Damn the black bastards!"

"And damn us for being such short-sighted idiots! Of course they're going for the horses. They have to."

The angry tension in Brad's voice frightened Faith.

"But what difference does it make? I know you value your stallions, Brad, but isn't it better to lose a couple of horses than our own lives?"

"Lose a couple of horses? Do you think that's what this is all about?" Even in the darkness, Faith could see that his eyes were flashing. "If they get those horses, my dear, they stand a good chance of outrunning the militia in the morning. And if even a handful of them get away, they can put together a new band of rebels and. . . ."

He left the sentence unfinished, but Faith filled it in for him.

"And then the whole thing will begin all over again."

Brad rose. His body was taut, like a coiled spring. "I'm going out there."

"It's too dangerous," Fraser objected. "Let them go!"

"No! Dammit, man, we've got to put an end to this whole blasted thing once and for all. Before it turns into another Stono River."

He tucked a gun grimly in his belt; then, picking up a pair of dueling pistols, grasped one in each hand. Not that it would do any good, he thought ruefully—he'd never been much of a shot with his left hand—but it was better than nothing.

He was conscious of feeling ridiculous, like some kind of swaggering, two-fisted highwayman as he headed toward the door, but there was nothing he could do about it. Ridiculous or not, he had a job to do, and he'd better get out there and do it.

He braced his foot against the door and shoved it open. The air outside was cooler than he had expected. Moisture lay in a heavy mantle on the earth, seeping through the thick soles of his boots and chilling his feet.

Dew. He wondered why that should surprise him. The siege had been going on for several hours; it was bound to be near morn by now. No wonder the poor devils were going for the stables. It was their last chance.

He slid cautiously down the length of the house, pressing his back against the rough siding. Every second counted, but he dared not let himself move too quickly. One false step, one stumble, one branch snapping under his feet, and it would all be over for him.

He rounded the corner of the house and saw the stable in front of him. It was barely a blurred outline in the faint gray light of encroaching dawn. As he watched, the door swung slowly open and a man emerged, leading several horses behind him. Brad sprang forward, away from the cover of the house.

The man saw him. Breaking his stride, he spun around.

Moonlight caught on a thatch of white hair, turning it into an impromptu silver halo. Brad's stomach contracted, as if someone had smashed him in the gut with an iron fist. For a second, he had the idiotic urge to point his gun downward, aiming only to wound, but he forced himself to hold it steady as he released the trigger.

He did not wait to see the man fall. Tossing the smoking gun aside, he leaped over the crumpled corpse, lashing out with an open hand to slap the rump of the nearest horse. The startled beast, whinnying with fear and anger, bolted toward the hills, taking the others with him. Brad grunted his satisfaction as he watched them scatter. In a matter of seconds, they would be too far away to be a threat to anyone.

His body tensed as he turned back toward the house. The most dangerous part of his mission was ahead of him. Every man and woman in that rebel army knew someone was out there now, and they would be gunning for him. He slipped the pistol from his belt, balancing a weapon once again in each hand. His weight was well forward, on the balls of his feet; every muscle in his calves strained as he moved slowly forward.

He spotted the enemy right away. He was in reality a smallish man, but he seemed a massive skulking figure, silhouetted black against the pale glow of the river. Brad reacted quickly. Raising his right hand, he got off a deadly shot.

Even as he watched the man take the bullet, Brad heard a sound somewhere behind him. He could smell his danger in that instant, the way an animal scented the threat of the hunter with upraised nostrils. Spinning around, he was just in time to catch sight of a husky, barrel-chested black man approaching him from the barn. Pulling his left hand up, he fired.

And missed.

Damn that left hand of his! With a burst of fury, he hurled the gun at the man. It bounced ineffectually off that broad chest, like a child's rubber ball, ricocheting to the earth.

Every muscle in Brad's body was taut as he stood and faced the anonymous black threat in front of him. There was nothing he could do to save himself now, no bold move he could make, no last gamble to dare—and both he and his adversary knew it. The man took his time. Raising his gun slowly, he pointed it at Brad's chest.

The sound of the shot came almost instantly. Brad's chest contracted, and he could taste saliva in the corners of his mouth, but the explosive surge of pain he had expected did not materialize. Stunned and disbelieving, he watched the man jerk suddenly backward, his body twitching violently in one last futile struggle with death.

Glancing toward the house, Brad saw that one of the shutters had been flung open. Black Josh was leaning out, his musket still braced against his shoulder. His torso was stretched so far into space, he looked like a court acrobat preparing for a garish stunt.

Damn! the man had guts. Brad had never seen anything like it before. The boldness of the act! The audacity! He sucked his breath between his teeth, waiting for Josh to pull himself back into the safety of the house. Praying for him to make it.

But the act had been too bold. From somewhere in the darkness, Brad heard the sharp report of a gun. Though he spun around, he could not pinpoint the location of the assassin. By the time he looked back, Josh had already dropped his musket and begun to slump over the window sill.

Inside the beleaguered hut, the shot sounded no different from all the others. Only a low, hoarse moan, escaping involuntarily from Black Josh's lips, drew Faith's eyes to the spot. Horrified, she watched the slave's body slide precariously forward. Her limbs were rigid with fear, her knuckles white as she clenched the gun she had been loading, but she was so terrified she could not move.

It was Sally who found the courage to help her slave. Ignoring both her own pain and the danger of the open window, she threw her arms around Black Josh's body and dragged him inside. Blood oozed out of the bandage on her arm, mingling with the red stains that saturated his shirtfront. She eased him gently down on the floor, settling him in a corner away from the window.

The shutters were still open. The wind, which had been rising steadily all night, flapped them against the outer wall with a harsh, relentless beat. Faith could hear the rhythm echoed in the thumping of her own heart as she stared, terrified, at the gaping space between them. Someone had to close them—someone had to reach out and pull them back again before the rebels outside noticed—but everyone else was watching the wounded man in the corner.

It took all the strength she could muster to crawl across the room, but somehow she managed to do it, still clutching the loaded gun in her hand. She tried not to see the bloodstains on the floor in front of the window as she wrapped her fingers around the ledge and pulled herself up. When at last she dared to peek over the sill, she was horrified to find herself staring into the features of a black man.

She tried to scream, but she was so frightened, she could not force the sound out of her mouth. The man had a gun raised in his hand. At any moment, Faith was sure he was going to turn around and jam it into her face. It was only after a second of sheer terror that she realized, incredibly, he had not seen her.

She watched him, fascinated and horrified all at the same time. His eyes seemed to be glued on something on the far side of the yard, and he was so engrossed he did not see anything else. Cautiously, Faith leaned out just far enough to follow his gaze. When she did, her body went cold with shock.

The man at the other end of that gun barrel was Brad.

She did not take an instant to think. She did not question, she did not even truly feel. She simply reacted. Pointing her gun at the man's head, she pulled the trigger.

The blast was deafening in her ears. The recoil of the gun threw her back into the room, and she huddled, shivering, on the floor beneath the window. She was still there, seconds later, unable to move or look up, when Dan Fraser, drawn by the sound of the shot, scrambled across the room and drew the shutters in at last. She was conscious of no further movement, no sound, until the door rammed suddenly against the wall and a welcome figure reappeared in the hut.

"Oh, Brad. You—you're all right."

He came to her and knelt at her side. The haunting pain in her eyes told him only too well what it had cost her to give him back his life, but he sensed it would only hurt her to dwell on it now.

"Did I tell you I didn't want to bring you with me tonight, pretty lady?" he said lightly. "Remind me one day, in gentler times, what a fool I was."

The siege was not over, but the momentum, once lost, was not to be regained again. Only an occasional gunshot here and there gave notice that their black assailants were still with them. It seemed strange, almost unreal, to sit in the gray half-light of dawn and listen to a lone gunshot from one corner of the yard, followed by utter silence, then minutes later by an isolated shot again. Finally, even those were gone, and only the stillness remained.

Dawn came with a dazzling burst of blue, barely tinged with streaks of pink against the horizon. Through the cracks in the shutters, the sky sparkled with maddening gaiety, and breezes from the forest and gardens brought with them the sweet, aching promise of spring. Faith looked down at her hands, smudged and blistering with powder burns, and thought how wonderful it was to feel the morning again.

She turned her head, catching sight of Sally beside her in the corner. Guiltily, she realized how thoughtless and self-absorbed she had been. All the time she was sitting there thinking how lucky she was, Sally had been patiently nursing the pain in her arm and tending to the wounded Josh without so much as an offer of help!

She started to crawl toward her, when something in the

other woman's face stopped her. Sally's eyes were open, but she was staring straight ahead. Not with the relief Faith would have expected, but with a strange, glassy emptiness. Her cheeks were streaked, as if she had been crying, but if the tears had been there, they had dried long ago.

"Sally . . . ?"

Sally looked up slowly.

"Dan offered him his freedom, you know. More than once he offered it to him. 'Ye've served the family well and faithfully Black Josh,' he told him. 'Ye've earned the right to be a free man.' But Josh always refused. I think the idea frightened him. 'Where's I gonna go?' he said."

Slowly, Faith began to understand. No one had offered to help Sally with Black Josh because there was no help they could give.

Sally ran her hand across her forehead, brushing the hair out of her eyes.

"It got to be a joke between us. A thing we teased each other with. 'I'll have my freedom one day,' Josh said. 'When I is old and ready fo' t' take my rest. Doan' got no use fo' it now.' "

She looked down at the man on the floor beside her. The wound in his chest was covered with a threadbare blanket, and his eyes were closed, as if he had just dozed off.

"Now he'll never be free."

Sensing her need for privacy, Faith rose and went over to the window on the far wall. She did not ask permission, nor did anyone object when she threw open the shutters and let in a blinding spate of sunlight. Why did it hurt so much? she wondered. The loss of this intangible thing called freedom? Obviously, it was a concept that meant less to Black Josh than it did to her. And yet, it touched her deeply to think that he had lived and died and never once been able to call himself a free man.

They remained inside the house another hour, waiting until Brad was certain the attackers had all gone before anyone ventured outside. Even then, he insisted on making the first trip alone. Faith felt an unexpected renewal of fear as she watched him slip one gun in his belt, then sling another over his shoulder.

"You're expecting trouble?" she asked nervously.

"Not the way you mean it, no."

"Then why all the guns?"

Dan Fraser had stepped up behind her. "Ye'd do best to

leave well enough alone, missus. Don't ask questions 'bout things ye don't want t' know."

The remark was so exactly what Brad would have said, Faith almost burst out laughing. Nerves, she told herself, biting her lip to stifle the unwelcome sound. Just nerves.

"What's wrong?" she insisted. "You think it's a trap, don't you? You think they're out there somewhere waiting for you."

"No. I think they're gone."

"But you're not sure?"

"Yes, I'm sure."

"Then why do you need the guns?"

He paused, setting his jaw in a resigned grimace. If what he feared was true, she was going to have to know anyway.

"They may have left their wounded behind."

Faith knit her brow, perplexed. Then, slowly, she began to understand. "You mean they might be dangerous." Of course! A wounded man would fight every bit as fiercely as a cornered beast. "You're afraid they're going to shoot you."

"No. I'm afraid I'm going to have to shoot them."

The cold finality in his words was unmistakable. Faith leaned wearily against the wall and watched as he stepped through the open doorway. Why in the name of all she held dear did she have to be so contrary? Dan Fraser had been right. There *were* questions better left unanswered. And yet, if she had been realistic, she should have realized all along. It would be no mercy to a wounded slave to spare him for the hangman. Or worse.

Faith kept herself busy for the next half hour helping Dan Fraser and his sons tidy the house again. They did everything quickly and efficiently, setting the beds up against the walls and positioning tables, chairs and benches back in their appointed places. They did not speak as they worked, they did not even look at each other, but Faith knew they were all thinking the same thing. They were thinking that Brad had been gone longer and longer every minute—and still there was no sound outside.

Was it a relief, Faith wondered, that great empty silence out there? Or would it have been easier to hear at last the terrible sounds they were all waiting for? She could not bear to think of Brad's shooting helpless, wounded slaves as they lay on the ground and looked up at him—but she could not bear to think of their being taken alive either.

She had just set the last wooden stool beside the table when Brad finally reappeared in the doorway. He looked exceptionally tall and broad-shouldered in the low, narrow frame. They waited, but he did not speak.

It was Fraser who finally broke the silence.

"They took their wounded with them?"

Brad's eyes hardened. "Those that were ambulatory, perhaps. But they couldn't take the others, you know that. They couldn't afford to be slowed down."

"Then . . . ?

"Those must have been the last shots we heard. Just before they pulled out."

"Aye. It makes sense. The man Prince is a firebrand, but he's no fool. He'd not be wanting us to take his people alive."

"No, he wouldn't." Brad could still see the contempt in dark eyes when a black man had dared his white oppressor to offer him an honorable death—and the white man had failed to find the courage. "And he wouldn't trust us to take care of it for him."

Faith had been standing silently in the center of the room. Now she stepped over to the door and looked out.

"Brad, was there . . . was there anyone from Havenhurst out there?"

His face clouded over. A burst of white hair, silver in the moonlight, flashed across his memory. He knew he would see it at odd and unwelcome moments for the rest of his life.

"One," he said softly.

"One . . . ?"

He caught the hope in her voice, and it angered him. Dammit, didn't she know she should be praying that the girl was lying out there? Praying the pain was over for her? Oh, hell, of course she didn't. She was still too innocent for that.

"No. Not her."

Seven

"It all seems so far away. As if it never really happened."

Faith withdrew from the window with its exquisite view of the hills on the other side of the river and glanced around the small summerhouse. Nothing could have been farther from the brutality and ugliness of the slave rebellion they had just experienced. The rococo daintiness of a bygone era permeated the airy chamber with an aura of feminine elegance. Delicately carved Italian nutwood chairs, gilded to an extravagant sheen, were upholstered in deep rose, matching the faded silk brocade panels on the walls. Shell-shaped niches, set with ornate baroque statues, added various tones of enameled pink to the setting.

"It is a different world," Brad agreed. "I've only been here once before, but I remember having the distinct impression then that it was something out of a fairy tale. Not part of the real world at all."

"Did you really? I see it more as a pavilion on the grounds of some grand palace in Europe. Versailles perhaps. But then, I suspect it's the same thing. Great kings and queens do lead a fairy tale existence, don't they?"

"I daresay you're right." Brad looked exceptionally large as he settled his tall body on one of the fragile chairs and propped his feet out in front of him. "Certainly there's nothing in the lifestyle of a palace like Versailles that enables royalty to keep in touch with the everyday realities of normal existence." He was glad now he had brought her to the summerhouse. He had stopped only because Faith's mount had not yet been recovered and they had been riding double on his stallion, but seeing the color in her cheeks, he realized it would have been a wise decision in any case.

Faith was too restless to sit down. Stepping over to a

marble-top console table on the window wall, she ran her finger through a thick layer of dust.

"What was this place used for originally?" she asked. "It's so feminine, it must have belonged to a woman, but I can hardly imagine it was my mother's."

"Ah, but it was. Adam had it built for her shortly after the main house was constructed. And at great expense, I might add. Though I doubt that made a whit of difference to Adam. Nothing was ever too good for the lovely Desirée."

"But it seems so far away from everything. So—so isolated. Why, it must have taken an hour's ride to get here, maybe even two. From what little I remember of my mother in those days, she wanted gaiety and laughter all around her."

"It *is* odd," Brad admitted. "All the more so because Desirée was never partial to riding. But perhaps she liked the place simply because it *was* isolated. Here she could be queen of her private realm—a little Versailles all her own—and none of the real world could intrude. At any rate, I doubt she came here alone. It would have been easy to cajole her younger brother, Olivier, into coming with her."

Faith caught a note of disapproval in his voice. "You didn't like my Uncle Olivier, did you?"

"I didn't know him. He was already dead by the time I came here. But no, you're right, from what I heard of the man, I didn't much approve of him. It seemed to me he could have taken his lily-white fingers off his lute strings every now and then and helped Adam with some of the work around the plantation."

"But, Brad, that's not fair. Uncle Olivier was a cripple."

"He had a limp, which I gather was barely noticeable. A slight limp hardly constitutes a cripple. But then, Desirée would have made a great deal of it. She always indulged Olivier the way Adam indulged her."

Faith set her lips in a pout. "Why do you always sound so disapproving when you talk about my mother? You didn't know her any more than you knew Olivier."

"Probably for the same reason you always wrinkle up that pretty nose of yours every time I bring up the subject of your father. Because we are two of the stubbornest, most opinionated human beings who ever walked the face of the earth."

Faith could not resist a smile. It was funny, the way he had of being so gentle with her sometimes, she almost forgot how terrified she had once been of him. She turned back to the window, marveling at how serene the river seemed as it flowed through banks of vibrant spring greenery.

"It just doesn't look right," she said softly. "There should be wild winds raging through the trees. Or thunder and lightning all around. How can anything look pretty and calm on a day like today?"

He was at her side in an instant. "Don't think about it," he told her. "Don't let yourself remember."

"I can't help it. I wish I could, but I can't. You don't erase a picture like that from your mind just because you want to."

It had been, she thought with a shudder, the most agonizing thing she had ever experienced, even worse than the terror of the night that preceded it. Brad had tried to spare her, but they had come on the open field outside of town too quickly, and there was no way he could shield her from the awful sight that met her eyes.

It had been a terrible, ignoble end for a rebellion that began with the thirst for freedom. As Lord Warren had so accurately predicted, the slaves, weary and frightened, had gathered with the last of his liquor in an empty field. There the militia, composed about equally of terrified landowners and disreputable adventurers spoiling for a fight, had caught up with them. The carnage was savage and complete. Tall green grasses, red-brown with drying blood, sheltered the bodies of men and women who had been arbitrarily shot down or run through with sharp swords. Those few who escaped the general massacre were hanging from nearby trees.

There had been only one sign of movement in that whole silent field. Faith's stomach still turned as she thought of it. Sweet heaven, it had been horrible! A pile of corpses had started to stir, as if of its own accord. Suddenly, from underneath, covered with blood and vomit, a dazed, terrorized face had appeared.

Brad had been as sickened as she to recognize the little seamstress from Havenhurst. Leaping from the horse, he raced into the startled mob of militia surrounding her. All the tension, all the frustration that had been building inside him burst in a violent explosion.

"She's just a child! You can't hold her to account for this!"

"Can't we?" A surly woodsman stepped forward. "She's a black African, ain't she? I say, death to the lot of 'em!"

"Damn you, you bastard! Have you no spark of decency in your soul? The child was born with only half a wit in her head. She had no idea what she was doing. I'll not let you punish her for that!"

The men hadn't liked it, of course. They had alternately defied and reasoned, blustered and threatened, but in the end they had backed away from the towering rage they could not understand, and Brad had sent Fibby back to Havenhurst with a man he could trust.

Faith glanced up at him now, standing beside her at the window, and thought how proud she had been of him at that moment.

"At least I have one consolation," she whispered musingly. "At least Estee wasn't there."

Some consolation, Brad thought, but he did not speak the words aloud. For himself, he was grateful that he could account for the rest of the slaves from Havenhurst. Cuffee, cleanly shot the night before; Phillis, victim of a swift thrust of the sword; Toney, hanging from a tall cypress at the side of the road. He wouldn't have liked to wonder what the patrols would do when they caught up with them.

"I think, my sweet," he said gently, "you have two choices now. You can continue to dwell on what happened and it will surely drive you mad. Or you can let yourself forget it." He laid his hands on her shoulders, drawing her slowly toward him. "And I am just the man to help you forget."

The low fervor in his voice left no doubt to his meaning. Confused, Faith turned away. She had been through so much in the past twenty-four hours, she was not sure she could find the strength to hold out against him now.

He laughed as he tightened his hold. "Don't tell me you're going to give me that tired old line about being a married woman?"

She allowed herself an ironic smile.

"It's easy to put on a white dress and say the right words in front of a minister—and a damn sight harder to spend the rest of your life regretting it. Didn't you tell me that yourself?"

"Regret is an emotion for fools. And you, my pet, are not a fool. Your marriage to Alexandre has no more substance now than it did the day you uttered those foolish vows. Surely by this time even you must admit that."

"I know." She let her head sink to the side, resting against his hand, and closed her eyes. "I thought when we made those promises that they really meant something. Only they didn't, because Alexandre wasn't making them to me at all. He was making them to Fleur."

Fleur. How very far away her sister seemed now. Faith could barely remember the horror that had flooded her heart at the realization of Fleur's death. And the hatred she felt for the man she was sure was her killer.

The touch of Brad's lips was a soft temptation, first on one closed eyelid, then the other. Even before she opened her eyes, the warmth of his breath on her cheeks told her how near he was.

"Why do you fight me, sweet Faith? You know you desire me, as much as I long for you. I think you have wanted me from the beginning, though you were too stubborn to admit it."

"Oh, I admitted it—at least to myself." Faith was surprised to hear the laughter in her voice. "Do you know what I thought the first time I saw you? I thought you were the most arrogant, vulgar, infuriating man I had ever laid eyes on!"

"And still you wanted me?"

Her laughter deepened to a rich, throaty sound. "I wonder if it is the fate of every woman to want the most impossible, infuriating man she sees."

He smiled, lowering his lips to hers. "Or for a man to want the most impossible, infuriating woman."

Faith did not try to resist. The burning ardor of his kiss was not a promise, but a fulfillment, answering the unslaked hunger that had too long lain dormant in her breast. This man might be the very devil to her—he might threaten her security, her peace of mind, even the sanctity of her soul—but she could think only of the way his hands seared her skin as he urged her down on a narrow day bed in the center of the room. There was more passion in her heart now than will, more longing than reason. She had said no to the needs of her body too many times; she could refuse no more.

He lifted off the layers of her clothing with slow reverence, like a high priest unveiling the goddess of love on a temple altar. It seemed to him an unexpected miracle, the way each sheer, lacy undergarment fell away to reveal some new, sweet aspect of her beauty. Had ever shoulders been so soft and white? he wondered, as he untied her chemise and gazed at flesh so milky it seemed translucent. Her breasts were round and ripe, yet firm, even without the support of her corset; her waist so slender it seemed almost childlike; her legs enticingly long and slim. He leaned over the bed and looked down, and his body ached with need for her.

She saw the longing in his eyes and smiled up at him.

"How intently you are looking at me. What are you thinking?"

"I am thinking how ravishing you are. And how I love to drink in your beauty with my eyes."

That was not quite accurate. He was thinking, too, that he wanted her. Desperately, urgently, with the burning thirst of a man trapped in a blazing desert. But not this way. Not carelessly in an abandoned summerhouse. Not when she was so exhausted she barely knew what she was doing.

His qualms surprised him, for he had never known qualms with a woman before, but he could not bring himself to take her like this. Sitting beside her, he took her hands and held them lightly in his own.

The reticence she did not understand confused Faith. Thinking she had done something wrong, displeasing him perhaps with her passivity, she raised her hand, resting it lightly on his shirtfront. She did not think she could bear it if he pulled away from her.

"Come, let me help you with this. You are wearing far too many clothes, my love."

The gesture excited him, and for an instant he longed to surrender to the urges of his body. Fighting the impulse, he lifted her hands to his lips.

"Not today, beautiful temptress. I want you and I will have you, but not today."

Today, he would show her another face of love, sweeter and more selfless than she had ever imagined. Today, he would submerge his own desires in her feminine needs.

He touched his mouth to her hair, teasing the edge of her forehead with tender kisses. Little tendrils of gold tasted like silk against his lips as he followed the soft contour of her brow and cheeks to nuzzle at last in the warmth of her neck. His own restraint aroused him, bringing with it not the frustration he had expected, but only a heightened sensation of passion. He had not realized until that moment that it could excite him almost as much to please her as to seek pleasure for himself.

He did not try to hurry, but let his hands slide slowly, sensuously down her body. His fingers were scouts for the greedy lips that would soon follow, exploring every inch of her throat, her shoulders, the rich swell of her bosom. Ripe flesh spilled out of cupped hands, tempting him until he could hold back no longer. His mouth was ravenous as he played with her nipple, circling it provocatively with his tongue.

His touch sent waves of longing through Faith's flesh. The faded upholstery on the bench beneath her felt as smooth and soft as a feather bed, the body above hard and savagely demanding. Sighing softly, she tangled her hands in blond hair, pulling him tighter and tighter against her breast.

His fingers were both suppliants and invaders, now pleading their cause with aching gentleness, now so bold they took her breath away. She felt their lingering presence on her belly, her hips, her thighs, and she knew that whatever power she had had to deny this man was gone forever. Her body quivered with longing for him; her thighs were moist and warm with her need.

She had not known a man's touch could do such devastating things to the body of a woman. Had Alexandre had the skills to arouse even half these tameless passions, she would have surrendered willingly to any violence, any depravity, he demanded of her. This man who challenged her now was excitement, he was passion, he was love itself! and she exulted in the tumultuous new sensations he awakened in her flesh.

She did not even notice when his head slipped down to repeat the path his fingers had taken. She took his mouth for granted, welcoming the provocative pressure of its boldness. Only when he buried his lips in the soft down nestled between her thighs did she come back to reality with a jolt.

"Brad!"

She was aware of the muffled sound of masculine laughter. Dimly, she realized she ought to pull away—surely no decent woman would allow a man such perverted liberties!—but the responses he evoked in her body were too compelling to resist.

"You shouldn't do that," she whispered feebly. "You mustn't!"

"Mustn't I? Oh, but I think I must."

His lips and tongue grew more daring, demanding the answering emotions her flesh was only too ready to offer. It no longer mattered whether it was right or wrong, whether tender or sinfully debauched, these things he was doing to her body were as exhilarating as they were tempting, and she could not give them up.

Twining long legs around his neck, she pulled him hard against her body. His lips were no less skillful than his fingers had been, his tongue no less tantalizing, and she gave herself up to surging raptures that swelled at last into peaks of frenzy.

And, oh, it was sweet! The longing and the surrender, the tenderness and pain. Sweeter than anything she had ever known, or ever dreamed of knowing. This was love, the way love was meant to be, and she was drowning in its sweetness.

He did not desert her when her passion was spent, but continued to kiss and caress her until she let him know with a hundred little sighs that she was ready to let him go at last. Drawing away, he saw that her eyes were soft and misty.

"I didn't know," she whispered, "that it could be like that."

"I know."

That fool Alexandre had never tapped her deeper passions, nor had any of the other men she had known. The idea pleased him. He wanted to be the first with her. Not the first to possess her body, for that was not important, but the first to touch her heart.

She raised her hand, running it lightly along the rough stubble on his cheek. Her expression was puzzled.

"And you . . . ?"

He knew what she was asking. Leaning forward, he touched his lips teasingly to the tip of her nose.

"I told you before. Not today."

"Don't you . . . want me?"

"Want you?" His laughter was soft, but deep and full. "Oh, God, yes, I want you. More than I've ever wanted anyone in my life."

He took her hand, guiding it gently between his legs. Whatever doubts she had had vanished as she felt him, hard and throbbing, beneath her fingers.

"Then come to me, dear heart. Let me give you at least a small measure of the joy you have given me."

He was sorely tempted, but he forced himself to hold back. This moment had been intended as a gift for her, not a gratification of his own physical desires.

"I will come to you soon," he promised. "And when I do, when I touch you as a man is meant to touch a woman, then you will belong to me."

She smiled up at him. She was sure of herself now. Sure of his need for her.

"Oh? I will belong to you? Is that how it works? And you, of course, will never belong to me."

"No." His voice was low and somehow sad. "No, I am not the kind of man to give myself to any woman."

She hesitated, her lower lip trembling for a moment, then she let herself smile again.

"No, of course not. That wouldn't be 'masculine,' would it? Tall, strong men have to be tough and independent."

He indulged her with an answering smile. "Quite the contrary. There are many men, even the tall, strong ones, as you so charmingly put it, who are capable of giving their hearts away. I am simply not one of them."

He bent over her, laughing a little as he gazed into her eyes.

"Just as there are women, some as beautiful and fiery as you, who can never truly belong to a man. You, thank God, are not among them."

She gave him a teasing look. "You're sure of that?"

"I'm sure. You are one of those soft, generous, bewitchingly feminine women created by nature to give herself totally to her man."

"And you, I suppose, are that man?"

He looked down at her for a long time before he spoke.

"I am that man."

Eight

The summerhouse was cold and curiously quiet after Brad left. Faith pulled her riding coat tighter around her shivering limbs and stared down into the empty river valley, Only the faint sound of the wind, whining through cracks in the old-fashioned windows, broke the heavy silence. Below, the air seemed still. The river was a sheet of dark green glass, the barren sand along its banks a seemingly endless stretch of golden tan, broken only by an abandoned raft, crudely crafted of logs and leather thongs.

Faith ran her fingers lightly along her forearm, marveling at the sensitivity of her skin, even through the fabric of her coat. What an amazing thing it was, the human body, capable of an incredible range of impressions and sensations. Even now, even hours later, she could still feel the touch of Brad's hands, his lips, the warmth of his breath on her cheek, and she knew that somewhere in her sensory memory a part of that magic moment would stay with her forever.

It frightened her a little, the hold this man had over her. *When I come to you,* he had told her, *when I touch you as a man is meant to touch a woman, then you will belong to me.* Could he have been right?

Sighing, she turned away from the window. An iron wheel-lock pistol, lying in the streaked dust of the marble console table, caught her eye, and she paused to stare at it. It was, in its way, a pretty piece, with an engraved silver butt and elaborate inlays of staghorn, but she could not help remembering the terrible chill that had come over the room when Brad put it there.

"Not that you'll need it," he had said reassuringly. "There are only a handful of rebels still at large, and they won't be hanging around here. But I think you might feel better if you have it."

Feel better? Faith scowled at the deadly contraption and wondered how he could say such a thing.

"The only thing that would make me feel better is to go with you."

"Not two on a horse. I have a lot of ground to scout before nightfall, and it's too late to take you back to Havenhurst now. Besides, how could I keep my mind on what I was doing if I felt your arms around me?"

He turned suddenly serious, giving her a solemn look.

"I expect to be back in three or four hours. But if I'm not, there's an old raft beached on the shore. It doesn't look it, I'll grant you, but it's as sound as they come. It will get you to Havenhurst."

Faith shook her head dubiously. "I don't know the first thing about boats."

Brad only laughed. "From what I've seen of you in the past twenty-four hours, my dear, I doubt there's anything you can't do if you set your mind to it." Putting an arm around her waist, he drew her over to the window. "Do you see that pine tree, there on the hill? If I'm not back by the time the sun dips to the top branches, I want you to go on without me."

And now he had been gone at least three hours, and there was no sign of his return. Faith stepped back to the window, staring restlessly at open fields and dark, moody hills. Her eyes could pick up no motion save the rustle of leaves in the breeze.

Where could he be? she asked herself nervously. What could be taking so long? A stop at small, neighboring farms, a check of the seldom-traveled roads linking plantations and villages together—how much time could that require? She was acutely aware of the boat on the shore, and for the first time she found herself wondering if she would have the strength to pole it all the way to Havenhurst.

Not that it would come to that, she reminded herself soothingly. Brad would almost certainly be back in a few minutes. Ten minutes, twenty at most. She threw another anxious glance at the window, seeing just what she had seen before—absolutely nothing. And she asked herself the same question she had asked at least a hundred times in the last half hour.

Where could he be?

Brad sat motionless on his mount at the edge of the narrow

forest path. Burgundy velvet splashed in an artlessly graceful pattern across the earth. A jaunty white plume, caught in light breezes, waved up at him with mocking gaiety.

Some day, my boy, you will understand that it is not wisdom an old man's heart craves, but a glass of wine in front of the fire—and a pretty wench to share it with.

"Damn!"

What the hell had Lord Warren done to deserve such an untimely end? A good glass, a pretty woman, a hearty laugh with a friend—that was all the man had ever asked. He had not come to the Colonies to wrest a fortune from the wilderness, only to secure a modest inheritance for his infant nephew. Now all Brad could do was sell the land for whatever it would fetch and send the gold to the boy as full measure of his uncle's life.

"Damn!"

The utterance was inadequate, but it was all he had. Dismounting, he knelt beside his friend and wrapped the modish velvet cloak around his body. Later, he would send a party to bring him back to Oakwood; for now, he would rest easily enough in the soft green grasses that edged the road.

At least, Brad thought grimly, trying to salvage what he could from the whole sorry business, he had had the good sense not to send Faith with Lord Warren last night. He could not even begin to imagine how it would feel to stand in this place and look down at frilly feminine petticoats and golden curls, dulled by the dust of the road.

Faith. He was surprised at the surge of longing that swelled through his body at the thought of her. Soft, womanly Faith—how he ached to be with her now. He had told himself he was a man who did not need women, but he realized now he was nothing more than a fool. Any man who had known the things he had—any man who had experienced ugliness, killing, wanton violence—was a man desperately in need of the sweet solace of a woman's heart.

He took hold of the reins, pausing only long enough to cast one last glance at his friend's body. He had done everything he could; there was no point lingering any longer. He still had one task to perform, one final area he had promised himself he would search, then he would be free to go back to his woman.

Back to his woman . . . he smiled at the image. *His* woman. Had he really thought it enough merely to tantalize her today, reserving for tomorrow the perfect joy that came only from shared rapture? But if he had learned anything these last terrible hours, it was that there was no tomorrow, and you had to capture joy where you could.

He swung easily into the saddle. In less than an hour, he would return to the place where he had left Faith. And there, in that small, airy summerhouse where he had touched her, teased her, taught her the secret fulfillment of being a woman, he would make her his at last.

Prodding the stallion lightly with his heels, he began to ride down the road.

Faith dug her pole into the muddy river bottom, urging the raft steadily toward shore. The crude vessel hovered in the shallow water, then with a rasping shudder, grated onto the sand. Dense vegetation tumbled over the ground, and the air smelled damp and fetid. Lengthening shadows warned of approaching evening.

Faith picked up the pistol Brad had left for her and, holding it gingerly in her hand, stepped onto the bank. Had she been a fool to pole the boat so impulsively to shore? she asked herself uncertainly. It had seemed a good idea a few minutes ago when she looked up and recognized, on the rolling crest of a low hill, the secluded hollow where she once stumbled on Estee and her lover. Surely, she had told herself then, that was the logical place for her friend to hide. Now she was not sure the whole thing wasn't a wild goose chase—and a dangerous one at that.

Even if she was right, she had the feeling Estee would not thank her for meddling. The dark fire smoldering in black eyes the last time they had met was enough to tell her that. Not that it mattered, she thought with a burst of defiance. No matter what happened between them, no matter how coldly or angrily Estee might greet her, they were still friends. She could not turn her back on a friend in trouble.

The foliage along the riverbank was so thick and tangled, it was nearly impassable. Faith searched it for several minutes, despairing of ever getting through, when she finally discovered a break in the matted vines and branches. It was narrow and ill defined, more a vague impression than a path, but at least it was something, and she pressed eagerly to it. Her skirt caught on the shrubbery, and stout roots, twisting out of the earth, stubbed her toes, but she barely noticed as she hurried forward, moving as fast as the terrain would allow. The vegetation grew denser, rising so high in places that it was over her head. The shadows were so heavy, sometimes she could not see where she was going.

She had not realized it would be so frightening. Green leaves, moist and pungent, grazed her cheek, tempting her eyes to scan the impenetrable darkness behind them. Shuddering, she realized a whole army of slaves could be hiding not ten feet away and she would not be able to see them. Gripping the gun tightly in her right hand, she used the left to brush aside branches that impeded her way.

A sound behind her made her jump with fright. Whirling around, she saw a frog staring up at her with baleful eyes. The creature seemed as startled as she, for he gave a low belch of protest, then hopped away again. Faith could only stand and gape at the spot where he had been—and wonder what on earth she was doing there.

Only when the hill began to slope upward did the tangled greenery fall away at last, and the path opened out into a broad meadow, resplendent with spring wild flowers. Faith found the going easier, but still she was panting as she reached the tall pines that rimmed the grassy hollow. It was not until she paused beneath them and dared her eyes to look down that she realized how much she had counted on finding her friend there.

But the hollow was empty. Blue-green pines stood out against the sky like silent sentinels, but they were guarding nothing.

Faith stepped forward slowly, moving down the slope. If Estee was there, mightn't she be hiding beneath the sheltering branches of one of the pines? Cupping her hand around her lips, she gave a soft cry.

"Estee . . . ?"

It was barely a whisper, but it was all she dared. She waited a moment, then when she heard nothing, called out a little louder.

"Estee!"

The wind carried the word away, wafting it through the pines, but though Faith stood absolutely still and listened, she could hear no answer. Bitterly, she realized no answer was forthcoming. Estee was not going to respond because Estee was not there.

Furiously, she berated herself for being such an idiot. There hadn't been a chance in a hundred—no, not a chance in a thousand!—that she would find Estee there, but she had had to grab at it anyway. Now she would never be able to find her way back to the spot where she had left the raft. She would have to venture the rest of the way to Havenhurst on foot. And it would be well past dark before she arrived!

She had moved only a short distance up the hill when her ear caught a faint rustling sound somewhere in the hollow behind her. Her heart quickened, but she forced herself to remain steady. Only a rabbit, she told herself as she turned. Or a squirrel scampering through dead twigs and fallen pine needles.

But the sound had not been made by an animal. Faith's eyes widened with disbelief as she stood and stared across the sloping hollow. How could she have been so foolish? So careless? How could she have forgotten that there was more than one runaway with cause to remember that spot.

The slave Prince looked like a statue carved of black marble. His legs were spread out to form a solid brace against the earth, his hands were jammed defiantly on his hips. He was easily forty yards away, yet Faith could see his face clearly. His eyes were devoid of expression, but his lips were open, and he almost seemed to be grinning.

It was a minute before Faith remembered the gun. When she did, she raised it cautiously, praying he would see it and back away from her. She was trembling so badly she had to hold it with both hands.

But the man did not move. The grin on his face broadened into a grotesque parody of mirth. Faith gaped at him in horror, unable to tear her eyes from his face. Was he laughing, she wondered, because he saw that she was afraid and thought she would not have the nerve to pull the trigger? Or was it only that life had grown so bitter, even death was no more than an obscene joke?

He remained where he was for what seemed to Faith an eternity. Then, slowly, mechanically, he began to move toward her. Terrified, she realized that the time had come. She could hope neither to reason with this man nor to outrun him. All she could do was point the gun at his chest and close her eyes as her finger tightened on the trigger.

But the trigger did not move!

Opening her eyes, Faith glanced down at the gun in horror. Desperately, she tried it again, using all her strength. It seemed to release for a second, then caught again.

"Oh, God!"

The gun was not going to fire. The trigger was stuck, and it was not going to fire!

The slave began to run toward her. There was no time to recover now, no time to throw the gun aside and flee. With a suddenness that was terrifying, he was upon her, lunging forward with the savage fury of a wounded tiger. Faith cried out in pain as iron fingers clamped her wrist.

Wrenching away, she tried to pull her arm free, if only for a second. The gun, precarious as it was, was her only chance now. Tears of pain dimmed her sight, but she did not let herself give up. His fingers were a relentless vise, clenching her wrist so brutally she was terrified the bone would snap in two.

If only she could find the strength to twist her arm around, she thought frantically. If only she could get the gun between their bodies and turn the barrel toward him.

And if only the blasted thing would work this time!

Writhing to one side, she flung her body as far back as she could, trying to throw him off balance. If she could just catch him off guard——

The sound of a gunshot was sudden and unexpected. The man seemed as surprised as Faith, for he eased his hold, letting her pull away. Bewildered and confused, she stood and gaped at him. She had not even felt her finger move on the trigger, yet here he was, wavering unsteadily in front of her. His eyes were dull and empty; his body slumped heavily to the ground.

She had killed him. Faith stood and stared down at him, but she was too numb to feel or understand. She had looked into his eyes and seen the moment of death, and she had not even felt her finger move on the trigger.

It was only slowly that she became conscious of a movement on the slope opposite her. Glancing up, she saw a tall, fair-haired man standing just in front of the pines. Lowering the musket from his shoulder, he let it drop to the earth.

"Brad!"

She was not even aware of picking up her skirt and racing toward him. She knew only that somehow she was at the bottom of the hollow and he was there in front of her. His arms were strong and protective as he swept her off her feet, drawing her tightly against his chest.

"It's all right, darling. It's all right. I was there all the time. I saw what happened, but I didn't dare shoot for fear of hitting you. Thank God you pulled away when you did."

Faith felt her body begin to tremble, but she made no attempt to hold herself back. His embrace was so warm, so succoring, she dared give in to her fear at last. She barely noticed as he eased the gun out of her fingers and slipped it into his belt. She felt only the strength of masculine hands against her back, the tenderness of masculine lips on her hair and brow.

They were both so engrossed in each other, they did not notice at first that they were not alone. When they finally drew apart, they were equally startled to see a slender, dark-skinned woman watching them from the opposite slope.

Estee stood as tall and straight as the pines, and as silent. In her hand she held a small, deadly pistol.

Brad was the first to recognize their danger. He was bitterly aware of the gun at his waist, just inches from his fingers, but he did not dare reach for it. Thrusting Faith behind the broad shield of his back, he began to walk slowly forward. He stopped a few feet away from her.

"He had to die," he said softly. "The pain was too great. He could not have lived with it."

She met his gaze.

"I know. That is why I did not shoot when I saw you standing on the hillside with a musket against your shoulder."

She stood and faced him in silence for a moment. Then, holding the gun steady, she began to move across the slope. Faith wanted to weep as she watched, but she sensed that tears would somehow rob the other woman of her dignity. She did not stop until she reached the spot where her lover's body lay. Keeping the gun trained on the two white intruders, she knelt mutely at his side.

There was a quiet resignation in her bearing. A kind of majesty Faith had never seen before. The legacy of royal African ancestry perhaps, or perhaps only the mark of personal dignity in the face of years of bitterness and frustration. Suffering and loss had not marred the effect of her incredible beauty. There was about her an aura of tragedy, more theatrical than real.

She did no more than lay her hand briefly on the man's cheek. It was a simple gesture, but in it, Faith sensed the passion of kisses she could not give. The sorrow of tears she could not shed.

Her eyes were flashing as she rose to face them. Defiance and pride were all that sustained her now.

"He was born without chains on African soil, and when he fell, there were no manacles on his hands or feet. He died as he longed to live—a free man!"

"Yes," Brad agreed quietly. "He died free!"

"And I shall *live* free!" She jerked the pistol up to threaten him. "What are you looking at, white man, with your smug, self-satisfied ways? Did you really think I would be fool enough to hand over the gun and let you take me back?"

"I did not think you would shoot to stop me."

"Why not? Tell me that? Do you think they will show me mercy because I surrendered? Or are you going to play the big, strong hero and protect me? Are you going to stand up to them and say, 'This woman is under my protection. I will not let you hurt her!' "

"I cannot. And you know it. It has gone too far for that."

"Then why should I go back?"

"There are worse fates than hanging. Especially for a beautiful woman. God help you when one of the patrols catches up with you."

She seemed to falter. Faith watched from where she stood, and for the first time, she realized her friend was afraid.

"I don't care!" she cried out suddenly. "I'll take my chances. I am going to live!"

She slipped her hand unconsciously to her belly, feeling the soft roundness that was still barely a hint. For two weeks, she had guessed the secret her body held, but only in the last few days had she been sure.

She had made the gesture too obvious. Brad saw it, and he realized instantly what it meant. "Damn!" he muttered under his breath. It was one thing to take in a rebellious slave. It was quite another to have the blood of an unborn infant on his hands.

"You'll never get away," he said cautiously. "Sooner or later, they're bound to catch you."

"Just as long as it's later. I only need a little while."

"Nine months? You won't make it that long. Not with everyone scouring the countryside for you."

The corners of her lips tilted up ironically. "*Seven* months. Seven and a half. After that, I don't care what happens to me." The smile turned into brittle laughter. "Don't look so worried. I'm not going to ask you to hide me in your barn."

"I'd offer it myself if I thought it would do any good. But half of Havenhurst would know you were there in five minutes, and the other half would have it figured out by the end of the day. How long do you think it would be before one of your own people turned you in for the reward?"

He hesitated grimly. It wouldn't do her any good to run, but hell, what choice did she have? He'd do the same thing in her place. He jammed his hand into his pocket.

The movement startled her. "Hold it!"

"What? Do you think I have a gun? Don't be a fool. My pocket isn't big enough."

He took out a few meager coins and eyed them ruefully. Palm open, he held them out ot her.

"It's not much, but it's the best I can do. I'm not in the habit of carrying cash in my pockets."

Her expression hardened as she realized what he was saying. "Damn you, white man! Who asked for your pity? Or your charity! I don't need anything from you. I have a gun. I can get whatever I want."

"Blast it, woman! Take the money, and to hell with your pride! It can mean the difference between life and death. You're in no position to turn down charity. Or pity!"

He continued to hold out the coins. When she did not take them, he tossed them on the ground in front of her.

Faith stood a short distance away, watching wide-eyed and frightened. The coins seemed so pathetically few. She wished she could add to them, but all the money she possessed was at home in her room. As it was, the only thing of value she had with her was the locket around her neck.

She took it off and held it in her hand. What little she had left of her sister seemed inexorably tied to that one small trinket, and it made her feel bereft to think of parting with it. But Fleur was memory now and Estee was alive, and memories could never stand in balance against a human life. She stepped forward, setting the locket beside the coins on the grass.

She had no sooner done so than she knew she had made a mistake. The look Estee threw her was not one of gratitude, but sheer hatred. Her pride, already wounded, could not bear to accept help from a young woman who might claim her as a friend, but never an equal.

Faith stepped back uncertainly. Brad waited until she was several paces away, then began to move toward Estee. His left hand was empty as he held it out.

"I can't let you take the gun with you."

"What?" Estee's voice rang with contempt. "You think I would give up my only protection? Never!"

"I can't take the chance. There's been enough bloodshed as it is. I won't have the death of an innocent man on my conscience."

"Innocent? You call the blackguards and scoundrels who hunt down helpless slaves innocent? They deserve whatever they get!"

"And what about the farmer who comes out too early in

the morning and catches you stealing his vegetables. Or the unfortunate wayfarer who just happens to stumble across you on the road? Do they deserve what they get, too?"

She did not try to answer. "It does not matter, white man. I will not give you the gun, and you cannot take it from me."

"Can't I?" His hand hovered pointedly in the air, just above the butt of his own weapon. "I'm fast, Estee. And I have more experience with firearms."

"You talk a good bluff. But you still have to draw your gun, and I only have to pull the trigger on mine."

"Oh, you'll get off a shot all right. You might even hit me. But I'll still be able to raise my gun the six inches I need. And I promise you, my bullet will find its mark."

Her eyes narrowed as she assessed him, gauging her chances. He knew what she was thinking, and he knew that he had won.

"Besides," he added, "you don't want to kill an innocent man any more than I want you to."

She lowered the gun barrel a fraction of an inch.

"I have your word? You will let me go?"

"You have my word."

"You will not break it?"

"I have never broken my word to anyone—black or white."

She held on to the gun a second longer. Then with a wry smile, she pitched it to the earth at his feet.

"There's only one bullet anyhow. That wouldn't do me much good, would it?"

Brad did not speak as he bent down and picked up the gun, slipping it into a pocket that turned out to be big enough to hold it after all. He went over to Faith and, placing a firm hand on her waist, led her toward the clump of pines where he had left his horse.

Faith resisted the urge to turn at the top of the hill. Estee had lost enough of her pride as it was. At least she deserved a moment of privacy as she stooped to pick up the white man's bounty where they had cast it on the earth. Only the wind, wailing through the pines, bade them farewell as they rode away.

Nine

They buried Cuffee at sunset in the black cemetery beside the river. Dark figures formed a solemn ring around the grave as the body was lowered into the earth. None of the last comforting rituals was denied him. His head was placed to the west, as it was meant to be, so he would sleep forever crosswise to the world. The objects he would need rested beside him: a small canoe to aid him in the journey back to Africa, a primitive bow and a set of arrows to protect him on the way.

Faith stood beside Brad, watching as dark hands scooped up sandy soil and cast it into the grave. They were the only whites among the mourners.

"It seems so final," she whispered softly.

"It *is* final." Brad took her hand and clasped it tightly. "Nothing brings home the reality of death quite so poignantly as that moment when the grave is closed. Yet the Africans make much of grave dirt in their burial rituals. Perhaps the very finality is a comfort to them, helping them accept what they cannot change."

Faith clung openly to his hand. She did not even care if anyone noticed.

"I can't help thinking about the others."

"I know," Brad agreed. "Nor can I."

It has been appalling, after all the bloodshed was over and it was time to clear that disgraceful field at the edge of town, to realize that mounting public hysteria would not let landowners claim the bodies of their slaves. A common, unmarked grave—that was all the hated rebels would ever be allowed.

Brad could still see the horror on Faith's face when she had realized what was happening.

"Can't you do something?" she had pleaded.

"Not with all the bitterness," he had replied. "Can you really blame them, Faith? These people have been terrified half out of their wits. Some have lost friends or relatives in the fighting. Their fear and frustration has to find an outlet somewhere. Let them take it out on the dead; at least the dead can feel no pain. The living will suffer enough in the months and years to come."

They waited together in silence as the grave was filled in. Then, slipping an arm around Faith's waist, Brad drew her closer. The men had piled the loose earth into a mound, tamping it down until it was firm and compact. Now the women were beginning to decorate it with bits of broken earthenware and shiny glass.

Faith was conscious, as she looked up at Brad's profile beside her, of a subtle change in their relationship. It was almost as if they were not two separate individuals, anymore, but an acknowledged couple. Brad had come to that cemetery at dusk as master of the manor, paying his last respects to a faithful servant; he had brought her with him, not as his guest, not even as his friend, but as the woman whose place it was to stand at his side.

That feeling, she realized, as they strolled together toward the house, was more than an idle fancy. It was exactly the feeling that Brad had intended her to have. Circumstances would never permit him to marry her, even had he been so inclined, but neither did he intend for her the shoddy role of a backstreet paramour. She would be, as far as he was concerned, his woman, open and declared. She would live in his house and share his life, and be, if she wanted, mistress of Havenhurst in everything but name.

It was on those terms that he came to her that night. He did not slip stealthily up the back stairway, avoiding the watchful eyes of gossipy servants, not did he pause to tap discreetly at her door, humbly begging admittance. He simply flung it open, as if he had every right to be there, and came in to her.

She was not truly surprised to see him standing on the threshold. She had been seated at the dressing table, running a silver-handled brush through long, loose tresses. Now she laid it down, smiling as she caught sight of a wine bottle and crystal glasses in his hand. In that mute offering, she recognized a tender attempt to compensate her for the wedding feast that would never be theirs.

"I do not think," she said softly, "we will need that."

"No." Brad set the glasses down beside the brush on the table. "I don't think we will."

The wine was forgotten as he drew her slowly, longingly into his arms. He was thirsty, as was she—but not for the stuff of which wine is made. And they were already intoxicated with the madness of love.

The gentle strength of his embrace was sweet perfection. Faith felt as if she were floating on a current of air as Brad lifted her in his arms and carried her over to the bed. When, at last, he fulfilled their mutual passions, coupling his body to hers, she was more than ready to abandon herself to the ravenous force of his assault. There were no doubts in her heart now, no fears, no inhibitions—only an all-consuming hunger for this man who had long since stolen her heart. And in that final moment, when longing flooded into ecstasy, she knew that he had not lied to her. She *did* belong to him.

In the quiet time that followed, after they had searched each other's bodies again and again and been sated at last, Faith was filled with a contentment she had never experienced before. She lay beside him, luxuriating in the warmth of his nearness, and wondered how she could ever have thought she was a woman before. When the altered pattern of his breathing told her he had drifted into sleep, she pulled herself up on one elbow to gaze at him.

How different a man looked in sleep, she thought wondrously. All the lines eased away from around his eyes and lips, and he looked touchingly young, like a lad just grown to manhood. She had not realized before that vulnerability might be a masculine trait, or protectiveness a need of the feminine heart, and it confused her now.

He stirred in his sleep, tossing fitfully, and she realized that her restlessness was contagious. Not wanting to disturb him, she threw on a wrapper and went over to the window.

The night, dark and moonless, turned the glass into a mirror of polished ebony. Faith starred at her reflection in fascination. High cheekbones picked up the shadows, giving her face a striking beauty she had never noticed before. Her lips, parted breathlessly, were soft and sensuous; her eyes, deep, fluid pools of translucent green.

She touched her hand tentatively to the glass. It felt strangely cold beneath her fingertips. It was almost, she thought, shivering, as if that were not her at all. As if it were not Faith's features trapped in a dark night mirror, but Fleur's.

Only Fleur was dead.

A noise behind her broke into her thoughts. Turning, she say that Brad's eyes were open. In the hazy candlelight, she could barely make out the smile on his lips.

"What are you doing all the way over there?" he teased.

She longed to respond to the tenderness in his tone, but the sense of Fleur was still too much with her.

"I was just thinking."

"Of me, I hope."

"I was thinking . . . of Fleur."

The change that came over him was subtle, but unmistakable. His lips tightened into a thin line, and his brows contracted. Faith felt a wave of nausea sweep over her as she watched him.

What a fool she had been. What a terrible, terrible fool! Would she never learn her lesson?

"You were with my sister, weren't you? Here, in this room."

"Don't be ridiculous," he parried. "Fleur didn't even sleep here. She asked to be given a chamber at the end of the hall."

"You know what I mean. This room or another, what does it matter? You shared a bed with my sister."

Brad pulled himself up, propping the pillows behind his back. His broad shoulders looked even tanner against the white linen. He studied her in silence for a moment.

"I'm not going to lie to you, Faith," he said at last. "And I'm not going to evade your question if you insist on asking it, though God knows why you'd want to. I haven't exactly been a saint all these years. Or pretended to be. I've been with many women. Are you going to dredge up all the sordid details about every one of them?"

Faith could not deny the logic of his words. She wished desperately that she had the good sense just to let it go, but she could not.

"You *were* with her, weren't you? Like . . . this."

His eyes were moody, but he did not flinch.

"Yes. I was with her. Like this."

Faith had not realized it would hurt so much. It was childish, of course—she had known all along her sister would never have been able to resist this ruggedly handsome man—but still it was painful to hear it in words. It all came back, all over again. All the rivalry. The jealousy. The aching fear that wherever she went, whatever man she chose, her sister would have been there before her.

"Did you—did you love her?"

"Love her?" He spit out the words. "Is that what you're afraid of? I told you once, I am not one to love any woman. Especially not a woman like your sister. Fleur wasn't the kind a man could love."

"Oh, Brad!" Faith did not know what hurt most, his cool admission that he had lain with her sister, or the fact that he was lying to her now. "I think every man who knew Fleur was a little bit in love with her. She had a way of dazzling them until they couldn't see straight anymore."

"And you think that's love? Hardly, my dear. Obsession, yes—I'll grant you obsession. But not love."

Obsession? Shivering, Faith pulled the wrapper tighter around her body. The word had an ominous sound. Alexandre had been obsessed with Fleur, and it had destroyed him.

"And you?" she asked quietly. "Were you obsessed with my sister, too?"

His eyes dilated, turning almost black. For an instant, Faith thought he was either going to lash out at her or get up and stomp out of the room. Then, suddenly, with an abruptness that startled her, his mood changed and he began to laugh.

"Am I obsessed?" He reached out, catching her by the wrist and pulling her onto the bed beside him. "By God, yes, I admit it! I *am* obsessed. Obsessed with your fire and your sensuality—and that devilish way you have of getting under my skin."

Horrified, Faith realized he meant to have her again.

"Oh, no. Brad. No!"

Not while the memory of Fleur was still in his heart. Not while he was thinking of *her!*

But he would not let her go. Pressing his body down on hers, he gazed deeply into her eyes.

"Give up your sister, Faith. Let her go. I am not with Fleur now, I am with you. Isn't that enough?"

His lips were hard and demanding on her mouth. Faith struggled frantically, trying with all her strength to push him away. But all too soon, her body turned traitor, remembering the raptures he alone could offer, and she fought him no longer. It did not matter now whether he had been with her sister, it did even matter if he loved her, all she could feel was the savage power of masculine passion, unleashing tameless longings in her heart. Cries of protest turned into cries of longing, and to her shame, she heard her own voice calling out to him, begging him to make her his again. He did not deny her.

Only later, lying awake in the warm enclosure of his embrace, did Faith feel her doubts return. Only then did she at last force herself to admit the one thing she had been afraid to face before.

Fleur had been with her that night not because of her own jealousy—though heaven knows, that jealousy was real enough—but because Fleur was a tormented soul, unable to find rest. God help her, as long as her sister's murder was unsolved, as long as her death went unavenged, Faith would see her image every time she looked into a mirror—and feel her pain every time she made love to the only man she wanted.

And when the passion was over, she realized sadly, when the kisses and caresses and cries of love were ended, there would always be a moment when she turned to the man lying beside her and said to herself: Did you kill my sister?

There was only a single candle in the room, a sputtering stub, but the light it cast illuminated Brad's features with surprising clarity. Faith tried to study him objectively. Had those same features really looked boyish before? she wondered. Innocent? Now they seemed closed and secretive.

Were you obsessed with Fleur? she dared to ask again.

His choice of words—obsession, not love. Had it been an unconscious confession? Alexandre's obsession had driven him to madness.

Had Brad's driven him to murder?

The next evening, Faith sat alone in the library, listening as the last sounds of the day's activities died away and the house was bathed in silence. Outside the circle of candlelight, the darkness intensified until it was a deep, mystical blue-black. The hands of the clock pointed, as they always did, to six o'clock, but the night stillness told Faith it was much later. Brad would long since have come to her room and found it empty—and gone away again.

She could not help wondering if he had taken her absence gracefully, leaving without a second thought, or if he had lingered a while, waiting for her to come back. She hated herself for hoping he had waited.

She rose from her chair and wandered over to the clock. She had not been curious about it before, but now she took the time to examine it. It was an odd timepiece, constructed like the wag-on-the-wall clocks in the other rooms but with its pendulum enclosed in rosewood panels. Rather like a tallcase clock, she decided, only shorter and squatter. It was obviously one of a kind, yet there was about it a comfortable feeling, as if she had known clocks like that all her life and come to take them for granted.

Was she being foolish about the whole thing? she thought, her mind drifting back to that empty room upstairs. Was she exaggerating everything out of all proportion? After all, she had only one reason for suspecting Brad of Fleur's murder, and that was a dream, so vague and long ago she could barely remember it. Surely Alexandre, already teetering then on the brink of madness, was a better suspect. Or perhaps, as she had sensed in that fleeting vision the morning after her dream, Fleur had dared to cross the swamps alone at dawn and run into a desperado or runaway slave.

Was she using it all as an excuse? A way to hide from her growing involvement with Brad? A way to keep from having to trust too deeply?

Sighing, she let her hand run down the front of the clock. She had a feeling the panel opened, though neither catch nor hinges were visible to prove her theory. Well, so much the better, she thought with a smile. If she opened it up, she would be tempted to see if she could repair it. Time had stood still too long in this room to try and change it now.

She was still there, curled up in a high-backed mahogany chair in the corner, when Brad found her an hour later. When she did not notice him in the doorway, he tapped on the frame to get her attention.

"What, only six o'clock?" he quipped, glancing at the clock. "Here I thought you were avoiding me, and it was only impatient ardor that made me long to find you in your room so early."

Faith looked up, confused to see him. She had been so sure his pride would not let him search for her.

"Hardly six o'clock," she replied awkwardly. "That's what it always says. I thought about trying to fix it, but it seemed silly. I mean, it's said six o'clock all these years, what difference can it make now?"

Her nervousness was more apparent than she realized. Brad leaned against the doorframe and smiled indulgently.

"I've thought of fixing it myself," he said easily. "But your father always insisted on leaving it as it was. And such was the force of Adam's personality, no one dared to touch it, even after his death."

"Oh, yes. God forbid anyone should go against my father's wishes."

Brad regarded her thoughtfully. "I'm sorry, Faith. I was trying for a little lighthearted banter, but I seem to have stuck my foot in my mouth. I keep forgetting how much it upsets you when I mention Adam."

"No." Faith shook her head distractedly. "No, I wasn't thinking about my father. Not really."

"No? But it's obvious there's something on your mind. If not Adam, then what? Me?" His voice was teasing, but husky, calling up feelings that were distinctly disturbing. "I can cure that, you know, if only you'd let me. Come upstairs with me, darling. It's much too lonesome down here by yourself."

"No, Brad, I—I can't."

"You can't . . . or you won't?"

"I think this time—honestly—I can't."

He set his jaw in a tight line. "You still have qualms about Alex?"

"No, it's not Alexandre. . . . Well, yes, maybe in a way that's part of it." It *wasn't* Alexandre, of course, but it was so much easier to blame things on him than try and face the truth. Especially when the truth was the one thing she dared not talk about with this man. "He *is* my husband."

Brad resisted the urge to go over and kneel beside her chair.

"I just passed your husband's room, not ten minutes ago. Do you know what he's doing right now? He's sitting at his window, the way he always does, staring out at absolutely nothing. Oh, my dear, he'll be there tomorrow and next week—and next year. There is nothing left of him—he is only the shell of a man. Surely you can't have any feeling for him."

"Not even pity, Brad? Don't you see? Alexandre's such a gentle, sensitive man. In another place, another time, he would have been all right. He just couldn't bear the terrible violence around him."

"Sensitive? Alex? Hell, Faith, your husband is about as sensitive as a dead mackerel." He caught himself, hearing what he sounded like. "How's that for a jealous lover? Sorry. I didn't mean to sound petty. I daresay you see a side of Alex I've never bothered to look for. But to be honest, it always seemed to me he was attracted to violence, or at least the idea of it. It seemed to hold a warped fascination for him."

"Well . . . maybe." Faith could not deny that violence had excited Alexandre, at least sexually. "I suppose it's possible to be fascinated by something and afraid of it all at the same time. That would account for—for a lot of things."

There was a softness in her voice that made Brad's body

ache. How could she be so warm and womanly, he wondered—and so damned unapproachable? So close last night and so far today?

"And still you feel tied to him," he said bitterly.

Her eyes were troubled. "No, I don't feel tied at all. Not anymore. I just need time to . . . well, to think. To sort things out in my mind."

He longed to go to her and catch her up in his arms, playing on the needs of her body to still the doubts of her mind, but he held himself back.

"All right, Faith. I won't try to push you. I'll wait for you to come to me."

He paused, smiling as much at his own uncharacteristic restraint as at her.

"And you will come, you know. Whatever madness this is that draws me back to you time after time is in your blood, too. You will come to me—and it will be soon."

You will come to me.

Faith mused on his words often enough the next day, and the day that followed, and she wondered how long it would be before they came true. It was easy enough to control the passions of her body during the daytime, when she could wander up on the hillside and watch the fieldhands thresh the early oats or drain turpentine out of pitch-pine trees. Or peek curiously into the cookhouse, where the women had already churned cream into butter early in the morning and lowered it in buckets into the well where the heat could not curdle it. But the nights were long and increasingly sultry, and all she could think about then was what it would be like if Brad were lying asleep beside her and she could lean over and wake him with a kiss.

Finally, on the third night, she could bear it no longer. It was especially hot, and she had retired early, bringing a book upstairs with her. She tried to tell herself, as she set it aside and slipped on a sheer silk wrapper, that she was only bored and restless. That she needed no more than someone to talk to for a while. But even as she opened the door of her room and stepped out into the empty corridor, she knew she was lying to herself.

She encountered no one as she made her way to the other side of the house. She had never entered Brad's rooms from the inner hallway before, and she was surprised to find that his dressing room opened onto a small antechamber, furnished only with a table and a pair of three-legged stools. A large copper bathing vessel had been set up in the center of the room. Brad stood on one side, a towel knotted carelessly around his waist. Opposite him, her back turned toward Faith, Beneba was pouring hot water from a kettle into the steaming tub.

Brad saw her instantly, but he did not speak. Faith took advantage of the moment to appraise him with her eyes. She had not had a chance to stand aside and study his body before, and she marveled now at what a powerful physical specimen he was. His body was sinewy, a dynamic contrast of powerful arms and shoulders and lean masculine hips. His skin glowed with a deep tan, making the thick hair on his chest look so fair it almost seemed to be touched with gold.

Beneba turned suddenly and saw Faith standing in the doorway. Her features contracted in a dark scowl, then eased as she brought her surprise under control. She said none of the things she must have been thinking, but simply set her kettle on one of the stools and walked out of the room. Only as she passed Faith did her eyes betray her, flashing out a look that might have been anger or disappointment—or anything in between.

And no wonder, Faith thought, averting her eyes. What a pitiable sight she must be! A young married woman, so lonely she had to go to another man's rooms in the middle of the night.

Brad waited until Beneba was gone, then crossed the room to come to her. He lifted his hand, letting it play with the neck of her robe.

"What perfect timing. The water's warm and waiting for you."

Faith smiled. "I've already had my bath, sir. Or are you saying that, on such a warm and sweaty night, I am not fit to be with?"

"You think a bath is only for cleansing the body. Ah, my poor, sweet innocent, what a lot you have to learn."

He ran his hands along the wrapper, slipping it teasingly from her shoulders. A tremor of longing coursed though his body when he saw she was wearing nothing underneath. Lifting her up, he carried her over to the tub and knelt beside her.

The water was wonderfully warm, just as he had promised. Faith let herself slip down until she felt tiny waves lapping against her chin. Steam rose around her head, making her feel sleepy and sensuous all at the same time.

She reached out her arms, trying to coax him closer.

"Come, my love. Aren't you going to share my bath with me?"

He held back teasingly.

"What a greedy little thing you are."

"And you aren't?"

He laughed. "I am not a man of infinite patience, I will admit that. But there are times when it has its rewards. And lovemaking is one of them."

He dipped a bar of soap into the water, swishing it around until the smell of bayberry filled the air. Rubbing it between his hands, he raised a lather of suds, then began to run it up and down her limbs. Her arms delighted in the smooth feel of soap against warm skin. Her toes tingled as he toyed with each one individually, working his way up to her ankles.

She had never felt anything like it before. Turning over, she rested her chin against the edge of the tub and let him lay his hands on her shoulders, massaging tense muscles until they relaxed beneath his touch. Sighing, she felt his fingers move downward, giving the same sweet ease to the muscles in her back, her buttocks, her calves. It seemed to her he had found new parts of her body, places she barely knew existed. Her knees, her arches, the small of her back, the baby-smooth skin on the inside of her elbows—surely none of these had ever seemed so exciting before. Or so sensitive.

The feel of his hands on her thighs was a sweet temptation, their lingering presence on that adjacent center of desire a burning agony. He had raised her longing to a fever pitch—now it was time to satisfy it. Reaching out with hungry arms, she drew him toward her.

This time he did not resist. Slipping off his towel, he slid into the water beside her. His body felt hard and muscular against the soft resilience of her flesh. Daringly, she let her hand slide down, resting in between his legs. When at last it was time to claim each other, it was she who guided him into her body.

The moment of their union was urgent and intense. Faith met the forward thrust of his hips with an eager movement of her own, and they came together with a force as painful as it was exhilarating. Floods of rapture swelled her body. She tried desperately to hold them back, making the moment last as long as she could. But the passions he had awakened were too powerful, and she could not control them. They surrendered at the same time, he erupting with a stifled cry inside her, she accepting the proof of his desire and her own sweet need with equal joy.

The water was barely tepid when he finally released her, but the glow of lovemaking still warmed their bodies and they hardly noticed. Brad drew back to look at her. Her cheeks were flushed, her eyes shining with the misty residue of her passion for him. Her hair had slipped into the water and floated, long and golden, around her.

He was painfully conscious that he had never felt like this before. No woman had ever satisfied him so deeply on one level—or left him so unsatisfied on another. He realized now that mere physical possession would never be enough with this woman. He had a deep hunger to own every part of her as well.

Jealousy was a new emotion for him, and he did not recognize it now. He knew only that he thought of Alexandre—pale, weak, pretty Alexandre—and hated him with a passion.

"I'd like to kill every man who ever touched you," he said with feeling.

Faith smiled up at him. She was still too enveloped in the sweet enchantment of love to be frightened yet by the devastating power he had once again exhibited over her body.

"There haven't been any other men. Don't you know that? Except Alexandre, of course—and he never made me feel like this."

For an instant, he half believed her. Perhaps, he thought wryly, because he wanted to so much.

"Alexandre—and all the lovers you had before him."

"No other lovers, my darling. No lovers at all until now."

Her voice was too sincere to be doubted. Slowly, the truth began to dawn on him.

"You mean . . . that afternoon in the study . . . the first time I. . . ."

She smiled at his confusion. "That afternoon, I was as untouched—and heaven help me, as innocent—as a newborn babe."

It took him a moment to realize what she was saying. When he did, he was sick with self-disgust. God, what a boor he must have seemed! And how he must have frightened her! No wonder she had run straight into Alexandre's arms.

He looked down at her and saw what he should have seen all the time. A loveliness that was gentle and pure.

"Do you know how——"

He caught himself just in time. It was funny, how words could slip out when you weren't paying attention. He had almost said, Do you know how much I love you? But that of course, was a thing no woman would ever hear from his lips.

"Do you know how beautiful you are?" he whispered instead. "The most beautiful woman in the world."

He drew her into his arms and slowly, tenderly made love to her again.

The next morning Faith sat in the midst of a pile of trunks and boxes on the riverbank, waiting for the boatman to tug the barge up on the shore. She had sat up half the night trying to get things straight in her mind, but it wasn't until the first streaks of red colored the horizon that she realized at last what she had to do. She would never be able to live with herself if she lay night after night in the arms of a man who might be her sister's killer—and she would never know for sure if she continued to let passion blind her reason. She had to get away, somewhere where she could think.

Besides, she had the feeling she was approaching the whole thing from the wrong direction. Fleur had not intended to come to the Carolina Colonies when she left London. She had been heading for New York. Something must have happened there to lure her southward. If Faith could somehow retrace her sister's steps—if she could find out what the something was—perhaps she could finally learn the truth.

Brad saw her first from the top of the hill. He reined in his stallion and sat for a long time watching her. By the time he rode down to the shore, his face was set and composed.

He eyed the bundles around her with a sarcastic look.

"I see you're leaving with a few more worldly goods than you had when you arrived."

If he had slapped her in the face, he could not have hurt her more. Of all the reactions she had feared—surprise, fury, pain—this was the worst.

"Shall I have my uncle send you money to cover the dresses I've taken?" she said tartly. "Or perhaps you'd prefer I return them when I get to New York and locate the luggage I lost."

"Spare me, please. Fashions go out of style so quickly nowadays. I doubt they'd suit my next mistress, even if she happens to be your size."

Faith bit her lip to keep it from trembling. She was a fool to match wits with him—he was a master of the cutting barb!—but she wasn't going to let him see how badly he had hurt her.

"Dare I hope your rude temper means you will miss me,

sir? Or is your masculine ego only wounded because I'm not throwing myself in your arms?"

The remark hit home. Brad glared at her angrily. Damn the little bitch! She had gotten just what she wanted out of him. She had quivered in his arms, and whispered sweet endearments in his ear—and he had come as close to saying "I love you," to her as he would with any woman. Now she was bored.

"So you're just like your sister after all."

"Like . . . my sister?" The words caught Faith off guard. "What do you mean?"

He shrugged nonchalantly. "If you don't know the answer to that, my dear, I don't suppose there's much point in telling you."

Faith's heart sank. She had hoped he was trying to say that her impetuous departure recalled her sister's—and, oh, how she longed to believe him! Now she realized he was only reminding her how capricious Fleur had been with other people's feelings.

She stared at him miserably and wondered how things could have gotten so out of hand. All she had wanted was to make him understand. Instead, they were at each other's throats.

"I did try to tell you before I need some time to myself. Some time to think."

He studied her coolly, as if he were still trying to make up his mind about her.

"Take all the time you want, madam. Just don't expect me to be waiting for you when you get back."

He turned and, leaving his stallion behind, strode down the bank. Faith wanted to weep as she followed him with her eyes. She cared for this man so deeply—she longed at least to make their parting a moving memory—yet there wasn't a thing in the world she could do about it. Even if he never forgave her for it, still she had to go.

It would be, she thought bitterly, the final irony if she proved his innocence only to find it was too late.

She waited a few minutes for him to turn and look at her. When he did not, she climbed onto the boat and sat down in the center, letting the slaves pile her luggage around her. The air was hot and still as the boatman propelled the craft away from the shore. The river current made a gentle splashing sound against the sides.

Brad did not turn until she had gone. He stood alone on

the shore, long after the slaves had returned to their chores, and watched the boat disappear around a bend in the river. Even then he did not move, but stayed where he was, a tall, solitary figure, staring moodily into the distance.

IV

TORCHES IN THE NIGHT

One

The Colony of New York, Faith decided after she had been there a few days, was a far cry from what she had expected. More than once since her arrival, she had questioned the wisdom of her impulsive decision to come here. Now she was beginning to ask herself if it made sense to stay.

The air was stifling in the small attic bedroom of Jakob Howe's townhouse, a narrow wooden structure on a quiet, if none-too-fashionable side street near the bustling Commons. Faith threw the window open as far as she could, and even left the door a few inches ajar, but she could not raise the slightest crosscurrent in the overheated room. Unfastening the bow of her cotton powdering robe, she let it fall open over a corsetless chemise.

Jakob Howe had been a complete surprise to her. When she stood alone, bewildered and uncertain, on the rough, brawling dockside of New York, she had had only one thing to cling to. A piece of torn notepaper with five words in her sister's handwriting—Jakob Howe, Merchant of Manhattan. A few judicious inquiries had located the man easily enough, and as she settled back in the hired carriage, she tried to picture what he would be like. Classically handsome, that was for sure. Dashing, but a bit of a rogue. Charming. Unscrupulous. More the type to cadge a living from wealthy relatives than try and make it on his own. His wife, of course, would be plain in appearance—Fleur never tolerated the rivalry of other beautiful women—but witty and sharp-tongued. And every bit as unconventional as her husband.

But the man who had stepped out of his front door to greet Faith when her carriage pulled up to his house was not the Jakob Howe she had imagined at all. She recognized his type instantly. He was the sort people always described, a bit patronizingly perhaps, as a "pillar of the community." Decent, hardworking, conservative, modest—in other words, more than a little dull. As for his wife, she had died many years before, leaving him a childless widower, and the woman who kept his house was his sister, Temperance.

Temperance Howe was no less a surprise to Faith than her brother had been. She had already been well past the age where a woman could safely be termed a spinster at the time Jakob's wife died, and more than a few skeptical brows must have been raised when she gave up a comfortable existence in England to join him in the Colonies. She was perhaps, by the standards of the age, a daring woman—after all, how many of her peers turned down marriage proposals from respectable young men on the rather illogical grounds that their company was not particularly pleasing?—but "bold" and "independent" were among the last adjectives that would ever be ascribed to her. She and Jakob made comfortable partners. She got from him that one intangible asset usually denied an unmarried woman—a social position—and in return she brought a touch of color, even eccentricity, into a life that would otherwise have been hopelessly drab.

All in all, Faith decided, sighing in the heat, Jakob and Temperance were the last people in the world she would have expected her sister to stay with. She picked up a small folding fan, handpainted with a scene from Ovid, and flipped it open. Fleur had always thrived on noise, gaiety—outrageous boldness. What could she have found to excite her in the home of the quiet Howes?

Or in the city that surrounded it? Surrendering to the heat, Faith snapped the fan shut and glanced toward the window. New York had been the biggest surprise of all. She had expected, in the narrow, twisting lanes of that English Colony, to find something reminiscent of the London she had left behind, but she was quickly disappointed. Tossing the fan on the bed, she stepped over to the window and looked out on a discordant sea of gables and sharply slanted tile roofs. When Henry Hudson sailed his *Half Moon* up the river in 1609, acting on a commission from the Dutch, his crew had consisted of both Hollanders and Englishmen, and the city had retained an international character ever since.

Not that that would have been altogether displeasing, Faith had to admit, if only she had managed to arrive at a less unfortunate time. It had been hard for her to believe that the northern Colonies, with their heavy dependence on indentured labor, could be as crippled by the effects of slavery as the plantation-oriented south, yet obviously it was so. By the year 1741, nearly twenty percent of the City of New York was composed of slaves, and the white majority was so terrified of the black seed of Cain in their midst that they enacted stringent laws to keep them in their place. No slave would be allowed to make purchases of any kind; no black man could bear witness against a white; whenever three or more slaves were found together, they would be punished by forty lashes on the bare back.

Yet for all their rigidity, the laws did not work. Black men still gathered in groups, no matter what the risk, and rumors of rebellion began to spread. By the time the city sweltered in its first heat wave, panicky citizens were so frightened that they fled in droves, paying exorbitant prices for even the flimsiest cart or wagon.

Only, unlike similar rumors of rebellion in the south, these seemed to have been cut from whole cloth. Faith shook her head in amazement, wondering how people could be so gullible. A series of fires had broken out in various locations, starting with one in the lieutenant governor's residence, caused by a careless plumber who had left a fire burning in a gutter between the house and the neighboring chapel. Tales of arson soon surfaced, and a nervous city began looking for answers. When an indentured servant named Mary Burton, prompted by an offer of freedom and a hundred pounds from the Common Council, claimed the whole thing was a conspiracy among the slaves, terrified citizens were only ready to believe her. In the hysteria that followed, dozens of blacks were arrested and imminent hangings threatened. Not that it would come to that, of course—cooler heads were bound to prevail on the Council—but the mere fact that such an unreasoning madness could engulf the entire city was enough to make Faith shudder with revulsion.

And the worst of it was, she thought unhappily, with all those rumors and counterrumors flying around, no one could think of anything else. Everywhere she went, everyone she talked to, Faith could find no one who wasn't obsessed with the "conspiracy" and what they ought to do about it. To a young woman who only wanted to turn the conversation around to her sister and what she had done in New York, it was hopelessly frustrating. Sometimes she thought she might as well just pack up and go on back. . . .

But back to what? She was aware of a deep sense of bitterness as the words crossed her mind. Back to Brad? But Brad had made it perfectly clear the moment of their parting that he would not welcome her back. Not in his life, not in his heart—perhaps not even in his bed. Tears stung her eyes as she recalled the magic perfection of their last hours in each other's arms, and she wondered if she would ever feel that same sweet fire raging through her veins again.

Impatiently, she brushed aside her tears. What on earth was she doing anyway? There was no point dwelling on the past. No sense in weeping over things she could not change. She had come here to find out what had happened to her sister, and that was just what she was going to do!

On impulse, she threw off the dusting robe and began to riffle through her wardrobe, picking out something to wear. In the end, she chose a fashionable walking dress, one she had had made a few weeks before she left London. She might not be able to do anything to trace Fleur's actions that afternoon, but that didn't mean she had to sit around and brood. At least she could see a bit of the city.

She finished dressing and descended the steep, narrow staircase that led to the ground floor. She was halfway down the last flight when she heard a flutter of movement in the entry hall beneath her. Looking down, she saw Temperance Howe standing in front of a mahogany side table. The drawer was open, and she was searching through it.

"Oh, dear, dear," she murmured agitatedly. Faith could see no one else in the hallway, so presumably the words were meant for her own ears. "Now where *did* I put that letter? I know it's here somewhere. I finished it yesterday afternoon, and I'm sure I put it here first thing. Otherwise I'd never remember to send it off."

Faith could not resist an affectionate smile. For all her primness, Temperance was rather a fanciful creature. White hair, piled in outdated splendor on top of her head, would have looked like a powdered wig had it not been tinged with pale lavender, reflecting the deeper lavender of her dress. The roses in her cheeks were several shades pinker than nature had intended.

"Miss Temperance, I swear you'd leave your head behind if the good Lord hadn't fastened it securely to your neck." Faith laughed as she glided down the last few steps. "Can I help you find whatever it is you're looking for?"

"Oh, would you dear?" Temperance turned dazzling blue

eyes on Faith's face. "How sweet of you to offer. My, it is nice to have another of dear Adam's daughters with us again. Jakob was so fond of your father, you know. He looked on him almost as the son he never had."

Faith frowned as she rummaged through the papers and paraphernalia in the drawer. Somehow it had surprised her to learn that the Howes were her father's friends and not her mother's. Fleur had never seemed to take any interest in Adam before.

She had just opened her lips to ask Temperance about it when a yellowing corner of parchment caught her eye.

"Here, what's this?" she cried, tugging it out from beneath what looked suspiciously like the remains of an old corsage. "Can this be what you're looking for?"

Temperance regarded the letter dubiously.

"Oh, I hardly think so, dear . . . No, this is a letter I wrote to Frances Jennaway three or four months ago. Or was it longer . . . ? Oh, my, will you look at that? September 1738! No, no, the letter I'm looking for is the one I wrote to Cousin Julia Simms yesterday."

She refolded the letter neatly, taking care to make no new creases and tucked it back in the drawer. Faith tried not to laugh as she watched, but she could not help herself.

"Don't you think you could bring yourself to part with that after three years, Miss Temperance? It is a little out of date."

"Oh, no, dear." Temperance gave Faith a mildly surprised look. "That would be terribly wasteful, now wouldn't it? It's just a chatty little letter, nothing very timely. Rather the way I talk, don't you know? I'll just wait until Julia writes again, then I'll change the date and send it off to her. Won't she be impressed when she sees how promptly I have answered!"

"And that, young lady," a new voice boomed from the shadows at the side of the hall, "is a perfect example of my dear sister's logic. Now you see what I've had to put up with all these years. But don't let it worry you. Not unless it starts making sense, of course."

Faith turned to see Jakob Howe standing in the doorway of the small front salon. He was a quiet, portly man, well suited to the browns and tans that made up his habitual garb.

"Oh, hello, Uncle Jakob. What a pleasant surprise to see you here. I had not realized you were in this afternoon."

"And you, it appears, are on your way out. Unless, of course, my eye for female fashion has led me astray, which my sister informs me it often does."

Faith rewarded his banter with a grin. Jakob's gray eyes might look sleepy, but they didn't miss much. Her dress, an isabella-colored cotton, as stylish today in the Colonies as it would have been last spring in London, was hardly a garment intended for lounging around the house.

"How observant you are, Uncle Jakob. Yes, I thought I would go for a walk. You and Miss Temperance have kept me so busy the week I've been here, I've hardly had a chance to see anything of the town."

To her surprise, Jakob's brows contracted in a disapproving frown.

"Go for a walk, dear girl? I don't think I can allow that. Not with all the unpleasantness that's been going on these past few weeks."

Faith stared at him in dismay. "But that has nothing to do with me, Uncle Jakob. You know it hasn't. If I were a black serving maid, I could understand your not wanting me to go out. Heaven knows, I doubt if any black is safe on the streets of New York today. Nothing's going to happen to a white woman in broad daylight. Surely you don't expect me to stay inside all the time I'm here."

"Not at all, not at all. By all means, go out whenever you wish. We have no desire to keep you prisoner in the house. But at least let me have the coachman bring the carriage around for you. And let me arrange a suitable escort."

Temperance hastened to agree. "Mercy, child! What can you be thinking? Well-brought-up young ladies simply do *not* go out by themselves. What would the neighbors say? What would your dear father have said?"

"Oh, Miss Temperance. . . ."

Faith had to bite her lip to keep from laughing out loud. Dear Temperance. She tried so hard to sound like a strict chaperone—and she failed so dismally! No wonder Fleur had chosen to stay in her house.

"I promise I won't go far," she compromised. Their fears were groundless, of course, but she did not want to worry them, not after they had been so kind. "A block or two at most. And I promise to behave with perfect, ladylike decorum! But I will *not* be cooped up in a stuffy carriage on a hot afternoon. And I won't be stuck with some boring young man who's no more interested in my company than I am in his."

The words couldn't have been bolder if Fleur herself had uttered them. Faith was pleased with her bravado as she waved a cheerful goodbye to her hosts and closed the door firmly behind her. But once in the street, with the noise and stench of the city around her, she began to wonder if what she had taken as a spirited show of female independence had not been more akin to plain, old-fashioned pigheadedness.

Certainly there was nothing appealing in that dingy setting. Late spring rains had clotted the yellow dust of the road until it was the same consistency as the cakes of dung nestled in its ruts. Only a few passers-by could be seen: sweaty workmen in stained leather aprons; crudely clad youths with britches of coarse linsey-woolsey and hand-knitted stockings; gaunt-faced women, drab as sparrows in brown and gray, who looked as if they had never owned a proper bonnet in their lives. The air was hot and steamy. Faith's curls hung limply in her eyes, and little beads of perspiration prickled her skin.

If she hadn't been so stubborn, she thought, grateful that she at least had the humor to laugh at herself, she would have hiked up her skirts and petticoats to keep them out of the mud and marched right back to the house. But the thought of Jakob and Temperance still fretting in the entry hall held her back. If she wanted to be treated as independently as Fleur, she was going to have to act like her. Squaring her shoulders resolutely, she forced herself to take a good look at the city around her.

The Colony of New York, or New Amsterdam as the Dutch still preferred to call it, had been built on the lower tip of a small island. Faith had been amused when Jakob told her that the entire area had been purchased from the Manhattan Indians more than a century ago for the equivalent of a small sum of cash. That the Colonials had no more faith in their dealings with the redskins than they did in the pacts they made with each other was evidenced by the fact that they had erected a sturdy wall at the edge of the settlement to keep the marauding savages out. In actuality, that wall, together with the rivers that flanked the island, proved as much of a constraint to the settlers themselves as to the hostile Indians. With no space to expand, each succeeding generation of merchants and sea captains had nowhere to built their houses but in between those that were already there, and soon the city was so crowded, it was barely livable.

It was no wonder, Faith thought, stopping to look at tall, skinny buildings, crammed one against the other, that the arson story had gained such credence. Black involvement might have been exaggerated, but the fear of fire was genuine enough. With so many wooden structures in so close a space, all it would take was a good blaze and a windy day to turn the whole thing into a fiery inferno.

Faith paused at the corner, then headed down Ann Street toward the Commons. She had seen the large central square of the city only once, from the window of a closed carriage, but she knew it was bounded not only by Ann, but by Nassau, Broadway, and Chambers streets as well. From it, the Post Road led to an area known as the Vineyard, a place of public amusement that doubled on occasion as the site of public executions.

The neighborhood she found herself in now was more fashionable than the one in which she was staying, and the houses showed it. Immaculate white curtains peeked out from leaded sashed windows, and brass knockers on the heavy wooden doors were so highly polished they gleamed in the sunlight. A profusion of brightly colored tulips in front of one of the houses marked it as the residence of a Dutch family. Faith smiled as she caught sight of an elaborately decorated white pin cushion on the door knocker. No doubt it had been set in place by a proud grandmother to announce the birth of a child. Such ornaments were treasured by the Dutch and handed down as heirlooms from generation to generation. The color told Faith the new arrival was a girl; had the child been a boy, the pin cushion would have been blue.

The street around her had grown more crowded as she walked. Faith barely noticed at first, taking it for granted, until slowly she became aware of a surly, restless atmosphere in the air. There was nothing tangible about it, just a kind of tense anticipation that should not have been there. Slowing her pace, she peered into the faces of the people passing by to see if she could figure out what it was.

A stocky man, hurrying up from behind, nearly ran into her. Thrusting out a rude arm, he shoved her roughly out of the way. Faith barely managed to keep her balance as she stumbled into a recessed doorway at the side of the road. She stayed there for a minute, trying to catch her breath.

Shadows darkened the doorway, but the air was so stagnant it felt even hotter there than in the bright sunlight. Faith shook the mud off her skirt as best she could and was about to step out again when a pair of men stopped in front of her. One of them seemed quite young, though he was so filthy it was hard to tell. The other was older, with a scraggly gray beard and hair so matted it looked as if it were crawling with lice.

Faith pressed deeper into the shadows. The men had turned their backs, but she could hear their voices distinctly.

"Damn them nigger bastards!" The speaker spit out the words with feeling.

"Aye," the other agreed. From his rasping tones, Faith judged he was the older of the two. "The black mark of Cain, that's what they call 'em, and that's what they be! You mark my words, boy, ain't none o' us gonna sleep safe in our beds, not while there's any o' them niggers left alive!"

"Hang 'em, that's what I say. Beat 'em first to git the truth outa 'em, then string 'em up on the gallows!"

"Hanging's a damn sight too good for 'em!"

"Well, burn 'em then. Beat 'em first, an' burn 'em at the stake."

"Beat the *men,*" the older man chuckled. "But fuck the women!"

His friend laughed. "Only if they's purty."

The men moved on, but Faith remained where she was, grateful for the darkness that hid her blush. It was not their masculine crudeness that shocked her, but the intensity of the hatred they bore the blacks. She had not until that moment realized how deeply public sentiment ran. Of course, they were only a pair of low-class ruffians, and the most slovenly ones she had seen at that, but still it was frightening to think that anyone could actually be excited by the idea of taking a black man's life.

Or brutalizing a helpless black woman.

Unbidden, the image of Estee leaped into her thoughts. Beautiful, tormented Estee. It was foolish, she knew. Her friend was nowhere near New York—she had nothing to do with all these terrible things. Yet still her heart ached to think of all the other Estees who would be caught in the madness that day.

By the time she finally stepped out of the doorway, there were only a few people left on the street. Their faces were pinched, their pace hurried, as they struggled to catch up with the others. A young boy, a youth of perhaps sixteen or eighteen, rounded a corner at the end of the street and loped forward. His clothes were faded and patched, but at least they were clean, and he looked reasonably well-mannered. Faith reached out impulsively to catch his sleeve as he passed.

"What's happening? Where is everyone going?"

The lad's dark eyes shone with excitement. Now that she

could see him better, Faith realized he was younger than she had thought.

"They're hangin' 'em," he said breathlessly. "Them niggers what burned John Murray's stable, down to Broadway."

"Hanging?" Faith's fingers tightened on his sleeve. "They're . . . *hanging* them?"

"You'd better hurry, missus, or you'll miss it all."

The boy jerked his arm loose and, without a backward glance, raced off down the street. Faith made no attempt to stop him.

Hanging? Were they actually hanging those men? All because some serving maid had figured out a sly way to make a hundred pounds and get her freedom in the bargain? It had been horrifying enough to stand in a darkened doorway and listen to a pair of loutish churls vent their vindictiveness aganst the blacks. But to think that sober-minded judges and citizens of standing actually agreed with them—that was intolerable!

She wished now she had not been too stubborn to listen to Jakob and Temperance when they urged her not to go out. She would have found out about it all sooner or later—the whole town would be buzzing with the story by nightfall—but at least she would not have had to see it with her own eyes.

The street emptied quickly. Only an old man in a gray coat and pants, so baggy they hung on his gaunt frame, still sidled crablike down the street. His eyes were as bright as the boy's, and he was limping in his haste. Deliberately ignoring him, Faith began to walk in the opposite direction.

The sound of a horse's hooves drew her attention, and she looked up just in time to see a closed black carriage pull to a stop in the center of the street. The coachman cursed soundly, applying a liberal whip to the horse's back as he turned the vehicle around. Faith glanced at the window, curious to see the passenger inside. Was he as appalled as she at what was happening ahead, or was he simply in too much of a hurry to get caught in the crowd?

Bright sunlight shimmered on the glass, turning it into a silvery mirror. Behind the reflected image of dirty wooden buildings and clean blue sky, Faith caught only a sketchy glimpse of masculine features. She was about to turn away when she realized that something in that vague profile looked familiar.

Just at that moment, the man opened the carriage door she got a good look at him. No wonder he had seemed famil-

and stuck out his head, calling to the driver. Faith gasped as iar, she thought with a rush of horror. She would recognize those dark eyes and that wavy brown hair anywhere.

The man was Rolfe Stephens.

For an instant, she could only stare at him in stunned silence. Rolfe Stephens was the last person in the world she had expected to find in New York. Never once had it occurred to her that he might still be here a full year after his arrival. Only when he moved again, pulling back into the carriage, did she suddenly realize what she was doing. Raising her hand to screen her face, she turned away from him.

Fortunately, he did not seem to see her. A narrow lane, a few yards away, beckoned enticingly, and Faith slipped into it. If she never had to face Rolfe Stephens again after the shameful way she had treated him, it would be all right with her! She waited until the sound of carriage wheels faded in the distance before she stepped out again.

The streets were quiet and subdued as she made her way back to the Howe house. It was a relief to step into the cool hallway and pull the heavy door shut behind her. What an idiot she had been to go out in the first place. Fleur was the one with the spirit of adventure, not she. Fleur would have been fascinated by everything she saw, no matter how horrible or terrifying it was. From now on, she would be well advised to concentrate on being Faith and leave the imitations of Fleur to someone who could handle them.

She walked slowly up the narrow staircase toward her room. When she reached the second floor, she saw that the door to Jakob's study was open, and she headed toward it. Perhaps, if she was lucky, she would find him poring over his business papers, the bowl of his pipe clutched absent-mindedly in his hand. After the things she had seen and heard that afternoon, it would be good to have someone sympathetic to talk to.

But when she got there, she saw to her surprise that Jakob was not alone in the smoke-filled room. Two men were with him. They seemed to be engaged in animated conversation.

Faith recognized the angular, middle-aged man sitting opposite Jakob as his cousin, Nathaniel Howe. He was singularly unattractive, with bushy black brows and hawkish features, and his lean frame looked oddly incongruous on a dainty, slipper-footed Queen Anne sidechair. The second man was a stranger to Faith, but she thought she saw in his youthful features a softened, handsomer version of the man in the chair.

She was about to step inside and greet them when the young man turned suddenly. He had been leaning carelessly against the mantelpiece. Now he strode into the center of the room, his hands jammed into his pockets.

"By Jove!" he said excitedly. "Those two must be dancing in the air this very minute. And about time, too! Now maybe this whole blasted thing will come to an end."

Faith was so stunned she could only stand there with her mouth open. This was hardly the kind of talk she had expected to hear in Jakob's study.

Nathaniel Howe seemed wryly amused.

"So you think that's all there is to it, eh, Crawford? Good God, have I spawned a simpleton? It will take more than a hanging or two, dear boy, to quell the madness that has caught the city in its grasp."

"But it's a beginning, sir—you must grant me that. And once begun, there'll be no stopping us. We'll ferret those bastards out of every hole and hiding place, and feed them to the hangman."

The intensity in his voice sent shivers up and down Faith's spine. He sounded exactly like those two men on the street—only they at least had been bred in poverty and ignorance. What was his excuse?

"Has it ever occurred to you," Jakob broke in, "that those 'bastards,' as you put it, might be innocent? Where is the evidence against them? Who is their accuser? A serving wench who stands to gain a hundred pounds for her trouble? Hardly a reliable witness, I'd say?"

"Blast it, Cousin Jakob! Those men are proven thieves. Don't expect my heart to bleed for them. They were caught with stolen goods on them."

"Thieves, perhaps. And if so, they deserve to hang for that. But arsonists? Leaders of a diabolically clever conspiracy? Lord help you, lad, you don't seriously believe that?"

Crawford shrugged nonchalantly as he turned to his father. "It seems our cousin thinks slaves don't have the wit to be plotters. Tell me, how do you feel about that? Are they witless dolts, the lot of them?"

"Don't put words in my mouth, Crawford. You know perfectly well I agree with Jakob. Oh, not that the blacks are witless—I've known more than a few who are half again as clever as they ought to be—but I hardly think they arranged all this. That fire in the lieutenant governor's residence was caused by carelessness, and——"

"And the next was a common chimney fire in Captain

Warren's house. Yes, yes, father—I've heard all that. I daresay you're right. Those first few fires probably *were* accidents. But there have been a damn sight too many now for the whole thing to be freakish coincidence. Maybe the blacks didn't start it all. Maybe it didn't even occur to them to take up the torch until they heard all those hysterical white idiots running around screaming, 'The blacks are setting fire to our buildings!' 'The blacks are destroying the city!' But they're sure as hell doing it now!"

Nathaniel laughed obligingly, but Jakob looked troubled.

"I wish I could fault your reasoning. But the power of suggestion is a frightening thing. Accuse a man of something often enough and, like as not, you'll drive him to it in the end."

Faith backed slowly out of the doorway. She had already heard more than she wanted, and she had no intention of staying for any more. Even Jakob, even kind, easygoing, fair-minded Jakob, actually believed that the slaves were guilty. The men's voices were just a blur of sound as she reached the staircase, but the masculine odor of smoke still evoked their presence.

And the worst of it was, she thought sadly, he might be right. The blacks, already embittered by years of inhumane treatment, must have been terrified when the new accusations sprang forth. Mightn't they, in their desperation, have found it a fitting vengeance to make the white men's nightmares come true?

But *might have* and *did* were two different things. And *might have* was a sorry excuse to take a man's life on the gallows.

Unaccountably, she found her thoughts drifting back to Estee again. It was strange, the way she couldn't seem to get her out of her mind today. Was it simply that the plight of other blacks brought back memories of her suffering, she wondered, or was it some kind of premonition, warning her that her friend was in trouble?

Premonition?

She stopped halfway up the stairs, startled at where her thoughts were taking her. Premonition, indeed! She had had that kind of feeling sometimes with Fleur, but Fleur, after all, was her sister, and her twin at that. The next thing she knew she'd be letting her imagination tell her that Estee was in New York and in desperate need of her help.

Which was, of course, patently ridiculous. Faith gripped the railing firmly in her hand and forced herself to march the rest of the way up the stairs. Never in a million years would

Estee have been foolish enough to head north. She would have gone south, cutting through Georgia on her way to Florida. There was no point imagining anything else!

Still, she thought, turning to watch clouds of smoke drift up from the landing below, she would feel a lot better if she knew where Estee was right now.

Two

The packed-earth floor was damp and smelled of dung and rotting straw. In the next stall, an animal stirred restlessly, filling the darkness with its plaintive lows. Estee lay on her back, ignoring the waves of pain and nausea that flooded her body, and listened to the hoarse cries of an angry mob outside the stable. Her skirt was warm and sticky with blood.

It was all over, she thought bitterly. Over at last. She had put up a desperate fight, but she had lost.

She could hardly remember how it all began. Could that really have been her, that fiery young slave standing in a grassy hollow and watching her white master ride away? So she didn't have a chance, did she? she had thought defiantly. Well, she would show him! What man would ever understand the fierce determination of a woman fighting for her unborn child?

Gold coins, scattered across the earth, had insulted her eyes, and she longed to leave them lying beside Faith's locket in the tall grasses. Why should she take anything from them, those arrogant, patronizing whites who robbed a black man of his dignity with one hand while they doled out alms with the other?

But then she thought of the new life beneath her breast, and she knew she could not afford to refuse them. She would suffer no humiliation for herself—she would let no man or woman abase her again!—but for her child she would grovel in the dirt, crawling on her hands and knees if she had to.

There had been no decisions at first. She had gone the only direction she could, toward the south and the promise of St. Augustine. It was not that she believed the Spanish made kinder masters—she knew, in truth, they were rumored to be brutal to their own slaves—but she prayed that, in their eagerness to incite violence in the English Colonies, they would honor their offer of freedom to all escaped slaves. At any rate, it was her only chance and she had to take it.

The first few days proved far easier than she had dared to hope. She was cautious enough to travel primarily under cover of darkness, resting during daylight hours in whatever secluded spot she could find. The earth proved a fertile helpmate, providing an abundance of sweet wild berries and cool water from gurgling spring streams.

Only at midday did she sometimes grow discouraged. The heat would be sweltering then. Bees would drone overhead, and a sudden breath of jessamine, blowing from across the fields, would bring back memories too poignant to bear.

"Oh, my love. My Rodrigo. . . ."

How bold he had looked, leaping out onto the path of her master's garden. And how his eyes had danced with laughter! *Come to me, querida. Come to me tonight. You will not say no to me.*

Oh, God, how it hurt to remember. Sharp blades of grass pricked her bare arms, and she could feel again the ground against her skin as he pressed her down beneath him. The scent of jessamine had been sweet in the air then, too. If it weren't for the child, she thought wearily, she would curl up like a wounded tiger and let herself die in the bushes.

But there *was* the child. *His* child. And his child must have a chance to live.

As the days passed, the terrain became more and more inhospitable, and Estee found it increasingly difficult to make any progress at all. At first, she managed to stay close to the seacoast, but soon the land grew so marshy, it was impossible to penetrate and she was forced to turn inland. Now, without the sea to guide her, she could only look up at the stars in the night sky and try to memorize their patterns. And pray that she was not misreading them.

She quickly learned it was not exhaustion, or even fear, that would prove her greatest enemy, but hunger. The wild berries that had seemed so succulent those first few days soon ceased to be satisfying, and she knew her body craved the kind of nourishment she could not give it. The realization frightened her. That she was starving herself was a thing she could accept, but that she was also starving the child inside her body was unthinkable.

She decided on a bold plan. Previously, she had avoided human habitation as much as possible, circling small towns and solitary dwellings with equal caution. Now she deliberately ventured nearer, checking out each farm and plantation with an assessing eye. She knew exactly what kind of place she needed. Not too large—for she dared not risk the sharp eyes of roving watchmen—but not too small and mean either.

She found what she was looking for early the second night. It was a modest farmhouse, rudely constructed of logs, with a wattle-and-daub chimney, but it was neatly tended and bright flowers bloomed in the yard. Behind it loomed a larger structure, gray and weathered, with a fenced area to one side. No light showed in any of the windows.

Estee cast a hungry eye toward the barn. She had a feeling there were chickens inside—the place seemed substantial enough for that—but it would be a risky matter trying to steal one. Even if she could wring its neck quickly enough, the rest of the flock would start squawking and flapping their wings, and someone inside the house would be certain to hear.

But if they had chickens, they might have a cow, too. And where there was a cow, there would be plenty of warm, nourishing milk.

She waited a full hour to make sure no insomniac still thrashed sleeplessly on a straw mattress inside the house. Then, staying out of the moonlight as much as possible, she approached the barn. The door was partially open, and a reassuring animal smell drifted out.

She slipped stealthily inside, groping through the darkness. She had not gone more than a few steps when her foot slammed into a metal bucket, left carelessly on the floor. The sound was enough to set off the chickens, and soon the screeching cacophony she had feared filled the air. Cursing angrily at her own clumsiness, she flung herself through the open door and out into the yard.

She barely had time to hurl herself on the ground behind a scrawny bush when she saw a middle-aged man shuffle irritably out of the house. He was carrying a candle, and he cupped one hand around the flame to protect it as he headed for the barn.

He stayed inside only a few minutes. Estee waited, her heart in her throat, until he emerged again. Muttering under his breath, he made his way back across the yard. He did not put out the candle until he reached the door.

Estee moved up to a copse of trees on a nearby hillside, but she went no farther than that. She was still there the next morning, peering down at the farmer and his family as they finished their chores and headed for the fields. She hated the idea of showing herself in daylight, but if she wanted to get something to eat—eggs, a chicken, even a cup of milk—she knew she couldn't do it while anyone was in earshot.

There was little cover on the hillside, and the best she could do was move as quickly as possible. She had seen the farmer's wife store what looked like a small wooden bucket in the cool shadows underneath the house, and she headed for that now. If she was right, it might well be sweet heavy cream, skimmed from the morning milk preparatory to making butter.

She reached the house easily. Sinking to her knees, she peered anxiously into the dark crawl space. The outline of the bucket was distinct, even in the shadows. Her mouth filled with saliva, and she could almost taste the sweet cream on her tongue.

The opening was so shallow, she had to drop on her belly to crawl into it. The scent of the cream was in her nostrils now, rich and warm, and she forgot everything else as she stretched toward it. She had nearly reached it when suddenly, to her horror, she felt something grip her ankles and pull her out from under the house. Terrified, she looked up to see coarse masculine features grinning down at her.

"Well, lookee what I got here. Dammee, if it ain't a little blackie. Whatcha doin', girl? He'pin' yourself t'sumpin' w'at ain't your'n?"

Estee choked back her fear. The man's coat and waistcoat were filthy and torn, but they were hardly the garb of a working farmer. Besides, his horse, a tired old nag tied to a nearby fence, was loaded down with what looked like a roll of bedding and a few crude utensils.

She decided to risk a bluff.

"You have no right to questions me, sir. I belong here. You don't."

He eyed her skeptically. "You tryin' t' tell me them folks here has got slaves t' work fer 'em? Shoot, girl! It don't rightly look t' me as tho' they could afford a sturdy bitch the likes o' you. Less o' course, you's tryin' t' say you's the daughter o' the house."

Estee cringed at the lewd insinuation in his tone, but she stood her ground.

"It's no business of yours if I am."

"Or if you ain't," he agreed complacently. "Only I'm bettin' you ain't. You wouldn't never o' rushed the house like that, if'n you had a right t' be here. Torn down that hill, you did, like you's scared o' your own shadow. No, missee, what I got me here is a runaway."

"No!" The word came out too sharply, and she knew it. "No, you're wrong. I do belong here. I'm just not allowed to touch the cream, that's all."

The man's grin broadened. Darkened gaps showed between brown teeth. Leaning forward, he caught her wrist in a painful grip.

"Don't you worry none. I ain't gonna tell on you. Not if you're smart like you look. You be nice t' Ol' Tom, you hear, an' Ol' Tom, he'll be right nice t' you."

The leer on his face was unmistakable. Estee felt her stomach tighten until she was sure she would vomit. Summoning all her strength, she wrenched her arm away.

"You bastard!"

He was too startled to react for an instant. Whirling away, Estee began to run as fast as she could up the hill.

If only she could make it to the woods where she had spent the night, she thought frantically. The man had a horse of sorts, but even a decent mount would never be able to get through that thick undergrowth. And on foot, she was sure she could outrun him.

She almost made it. She was only yards from the nearest trees when she heard hoofbeats close in behind her. Gasping with terror, she redoubled her pace, but it was no good. He wheeled his horse in front of her and leaped from the saddle. Rough hands clutched her arms, and she felt herself being dragged into the woods.

He was stronger than he looked. With savage force, he thrust her painfully to the ground. Estee gave a sharp cry as her knee jammed into the earth. She did not even notice that her apron had fallen to the side, revealing a kerchief-tied bundle beneath. But Tom spotted it instantly. Reaching down, he ripped it from her sash.

His eyes lit up when he opened it and saw what was inside.

"Well, well, well. . . ." He whistled through his teeth at the gold coins on his palm. "Will you lookee here? Seems like it must be Ol' Tom's lucky day. Looks like you gonna bring me more'n jest a bit o' fun, girl."

Estee pulled herself to her feet and glared at him furiously.

"Damn you!"

Those coins were all she had! Her only chance to buy her way to freedom! With a cry of fury, she lunged forward, sinking her teeth into his arm.

He yowled in pain, but he did not let go. Raising his other hand, he struck her smartly on the side of the head.

Estee reeled from the blow, but she managed to hold her balance. Her knee jerked upward, searching for his groin, but he was too fast for her, and the attack glanced harmlessly off his thigh. He retaliated brutally, smashing his fist into her bosom.

Her breasts were swollen and sore, but the low moan that escaped her lips was more a sob of fear than pain. The assault had been savage and random. His fist might just as well have landed a few inches lower, where it would surely have been too much for the tiny fetus inside her body.

"Please—" she begged hoarsely. "Please don't hurt me."

"You wanna fight, missee, you gonna git beat sure."

"It's all right. I—I won't fight anymore. I promise."

"You better not, you know what's good fer you. I ain't bin lyin' t' you, girl. You be good t' Ol' Tom, he'll be good t' you. But you keep on fightin' the way you bin, an' ain't nobody gonna answer fer w'at happens t' you."

Estee did not reply, but she did not try to move again. She knew only too bitterly that there was but one thing she could do if she wanted to save the life of her child. She closed her eyes when she saw him reach down to unfasten stained gray britches, but there was no way she could block out the smell of sweat and rotting teeth as he came closer. Biting her lip to keep from crying out in disgust, she let him push her down to the ground. He needed no preliminaries to heighten his excitement. A simple matter of pulling her skirt out of the way was all it took. He did not take the time to undress her or he would have noticed a gold and diamond locket around her neck.

When he had finished with her, he simply rolled off her body. Drawing himself up to his knees, he casually did up the front of his pants. Estee pulled away as far as she dared and lay on her back, staring up at the sky.

She had never felt so dirty or defiled in her life. Only one man had ever touched her, and he with love and joy. Never before had she understood how degrading it could feel for a woman to have her body used like that. For an instant—a single, insane instant—she almost wished she were not carrying the child so she could have forced him to kill her instead.

It was not until he had gone over to check on his horse that Estee suddenly remembered the locket she was wearing beneath her dress. She reached up surreptitiously, feeling it with wary fingers to make sure it was still there. How ironic it seemed that she had not wanted it when Faith offered it to her. Now it was the only hope she had. The only thing she could convert into the cash she needed.

She threw a sly glance at Tom, making sure he was too busy with the horse to see what she was doing. Then, when she convinced herself it was safe, she undid the clasp and took it off. She could think of only one place to hide it. Removing a pin from her hair, she twisted the chain around it, then used it to secure the locket in thick, dark curls. As a last precaution, she tied several long tresses in a painful snarl around it.

Tom turned around just as she was finishing. Something in her manner caught his eye.

"What are you doing?" he asked suspiciously.

"Nothing."

"Nothing?"

"I was just fixing my hair. It got all messed up."

She resisted the urge to raise her hand again. The locket was safe where it was. She would be a fool to try and touch it. All she could do now was force herself to be docile and even-tempered—and do whatever she could to keep from arousing Tom's suspicions.

That turned out to be easier than she had feared. Old Tom, while he was hardly as "nice" as he had claimed, was in reality not unkind. Once she stopped resisting him, he was almost good to her, at least in his own fashion. She soon learned that he required only two things of her—to prepare his meals over an open campfire, and to lie down and pull up her skirts whenever he told her to. As long as she did that, he treated her in a manner that bordered on gentleness.

Estee had learned enough of the stars by this time to realize that they were traveling in a northerly direction. At first, the idea alarmed her, but slowly she grew reconciled to it. She had been foolish, she realized now, to head toward Florida. That was the way every runaway went, and that was where they would be looking for her. She would be better off moving north with Tom, biding her time until they came close to some community of free blacks. Then she would try to escape.

But when they reached the outskirts of Charles Town she learned that Tom had other plans for her. He had reassessed the situation, he told her bluntly, and much as he regretted it, he could no longer afford to keep her. She was pretty, of course, and he enjoyed having her around, but he was, after all, not a rich man, and the few coins she had brought were hardly enough to keep them both. With a show of reluctance that was at least in part genuine, he brought her to a local merchant and traded her for three pounds of English money.

The merchant, more sophisticated in the ways of the world, saw instantly what Old Tom's eyes had missed, that Estee was pregnant and would soon begin to show. He was shrewd enough to know what that would do to her price. A slave was an investment, and no slaveowner wanted to see nine months cut out of his work schedule, to say nothing of feeding and clothing a child who wouldn't begin producing for years. He kept Estee only a few days, using her much as Tom had, though not nearly as gently, then took her into town and sold her for double his original investment to a Barbadan sea captain, sailing with a cargo of slaves from the Islands to Virginia.

The minute Estee laid eyes on Captain Francisco Flood she knew that the pain she had already suffered was only a taste of what was yet to come. He was a strange-looking man, with a short, peculiarly shaped body and a large, squarish head. His skin was swarthy, as if he shared the negroid blood of his cargo, and he had a neatly trimmed black beard and bushy black hair.

For the first time in her life, Estee truly understood what it was to be a slave. Rodrigo had told her often enough, sometimes taunting, sometimes teasing, that she did not know the first thing about it, but she had not realized until today that he was right. Serving a master like Brad Alleyn, and before him Adam Eliot, had left her as innocent of the bitter realities of slavery as white-skinned, golden-haired Faith.

The weight of chains at her wrists and ankles frightened her, and she was surprised to feel how quickly the iron rings rubbed raw spots on her skin. They took her from the slave market where she had been sold to an open yard nearby. It was a filthy place, strewn with trash and garbage, where anyone with the stomach for it could stop and watch what was going on. There they stripped her, tossing her discarded garments in a heap on the ground, and began to examine her like some kind of farm animal up for sale.

Ordinarily, a slave trader would send for a surgeon to check over potential purchases and give his expert opinion. But Francisco Flood was a man with no time for such niceties, and no inclination to pay the fee involved, so the job was done by a pair of common sailors. They did their work thoroughly. Calloused hands probed her flesh, patting, pinching, insinuating themselves into every opening of her body.

Their manner was cold and impersonal, but by the time they were through with her, Estee felt more violated than if they had pulled down their pants and raped her.

They were searching, or so Flood told her at least, for signs of yaws, "or any other filthy disease you blacks carry!" But all the time, Estee had the terrible feeling that they knew about the locket and were looking for it. Perhaps she ought to be grateful for those two crude sailors, she thought bitterly. A trained surgeon would almost certainly have searched her for head lice.

They did not return her clothes, but gave her instead a loose brown dress that hung awkwardly on her body. She was taken to an area near the docks and placed in what they called "the pen," a narrow, confined space about half the size of a small corral. A low, stout rail ran through the center, and to this a score of wretched blacks had been chained, each by one ankle. Estee did not try to resist as she was forced to take her place among them.

She saw her own despair mirrored in every face around her. At her side, a woman was weeping silently. She simply sat in the dirt, patiently holding the iron ring away from festering sores on her ankle and let the silent tears flow down her cheeks. A young man at the far end of the rail, naked save for a filthy rag around his loins, strained against his bonds until every muscle stood out in his legs and shoulders. The whites of his eyes gleamed against black skin, making him look wild with rage and terror.

The chain that bound Estee was short, and she could move only a few feet. She had to stretch it to the limit to peer into the next pen. To her surprise, she found that it was nearly empty. There was only one slave there, a black man sprawled in an awkward position on the ground. Looking closer, she saw that long, crooked stakes had been driven through his limbs, nailing him to the earth.

"Tha's a mean one," a voice beside her said. "Ain't been here from Africa but two, three month. Doan' speak a word o' no language a man kin understand, but already he done bashed in the head o' one o' them sailors."

Estee turned to see an elderly man beside her.

"He killed a sailor?"

"Killed 'im? Faugh, no! That sailor ain't dead. They doan' go easy lak' that on a killer."

"Easy?" Faith shuddered as she stared at the man on the ground. "You call that easy? Staking a man to the earth and leaving him out in the noonday sun."

"The cap'n, he's from Barbados," the man said, as if that explained it all.

"And that's what they do in Barbados?"

"Oh, no. In Barbados, they'd o' put a fire to his feet an' hands, an' moved in real slow to the heart. Here, they'll only whup 'im 'til his skin ain't there no more an' rub in salt and pepper."

Estee turned away, unable to bear the sight of the man on the ground any longer. If she had not known before what it was to be a slave, she thought miserably, she certainly did now. Was this to be her lot for the rest of her life? And the lot of the unborn child she was struggling so desperately to bring into the world?

She was destined to remain in the pen only two days before the slaves were rounded up and herded on board ship for the journey north. Had she not been beautiful, she would have been put in the hold with the others, there to be confronted with the same cruel choice that faced every female slave; stay in that foul, stifling hellhole for the entire voyage, or venture out for a breath of fresh air and become an easy prey for every sailor on deck. But because she *was* beautiful, she was garbed in a revealing red gown, becoming, if a trifle gaudy, and brought to the cabin of the man who purchased her.

Estee had ample opportunity in the days that followed to reflect on how appallingly accurate her first assessment of Francisco Flood had been. The demands he made on her body were not the demands of the other men who had forced themselves on her, and she quickly realized that he intended to initiate her into a world where no appetite was too perverse, no whim too cruel, to be indulged. Only the thought of the child—Rodrigo's child—gave her the courage to go on.

The experience was utterly dehumanizing. She was, she thought with a wave of bitter resignation, not truly a person any more. Not a human being with rights and feelings. Not even a woman to be used and abased by the men who owned her. She was merely a vessel now, a container for the precious life that dwelled within her, and nothing else had any meaning.

They had been scheduled to disembark in the Colony of Virginia, where the captain had been promised a good market for his slaves, but the winds were unfavorable and they made poor time. Deciding frugally not to throw good money after bad, Flood opted to put into a small town on the coast of North Carolina. It was almost a relief to Estee when she saw land approach at last. She dreaded what lay ahead, but anything was better than staying on the ship. Besides, one place was as good as another to be put up on the auction block and offered for sale.

Flood put on a good show. Even Estee could not deny that. He was an Islander, and as such, he knew how to make a slave auction dramatic and colorful. Filling the air with the sound of pipes and drums, he attracted a large crowd to the parade of slaves that moved down the main street of town. Stopping in the public square, he displayed his goods with a flair, offering one and all the opportunity to step up and examine the strong young buck or lusty wench of his choice. The circus atmosphere accomplished just what he had intended. By midafternoon, the square was flooded with curious onlookers.

The auction proper did not begin until late in the day. Ordinarily, it would have been held in the open square, but no sooner had the men begun to set up than gentle drops of spring rain fell on surprised, upturned faces. Amid laughter and shouts of encouragement, the event was moved to a nearby tavern.

It was a fitting setting for the sale of one human being by another. Indifference had left it remarkably filthy and rundown. The tables were no more than rough planks, with wooden stools wobbling on uneven legs beside them. The air was sour with the smell of rum and ale.

It had been agreed that the auction would be held by "inch of candle." To Estee, watching with the rest of the slaves from the back room, it seemed a barbaric custom. The first slave was brought out, a powerful young man with broad shoulders and a barrel chest, and a murmur of expectation ran through the crowd. The captain set a candle in a crude earthenware holder, and marking off an inch of tallow, touched a flame to the wick. Bidding was quick and spirited. By the time the alloted amount had burned down, one of the local aristocrats had a new field hand and Captain Flood was thirty pounds richer.

When Estee's turn came, she was placed on a hogshead in the center of the room so the men could see her better. Her beauty brought out their baser instincts, and they vied with each other to see who could call out the bawdiest comments. Raucous laughter burned her ears, but she pretended not to hear it. Fixing her eyes straight ahead, she stared at a spot on the wall behind them.

The bidding began slowly. Flood was not surprised, for he

knew his audience well. A man might enjoy an obscenity or two with his cronies, but when it came time to put his money on the line, he was more likely to think: What will my wife say if I try to bring a beauty like that into my house? Hoping to stimulate interest, he called out that the girl could read and write. Instantly, he realized he had made a mistake. The men might have been doubtful before, but they were downright suspicious now. The candle burned to within a hair's breadth of the mark, and still the bidding had barely reached twelve pounds.

There were only seconds left when a new voice called out from the back of the tavern.

"Fifty pounds!"

An audible gasp rose from the crowd. Fifty pounds? Francisco Flood turned toward the doorway that led out into the muddy street. In his wildest dreams, he had not hoped to get more than twenty pounds for the woman. Twenty-five at most. This was unheard of.

A stunned hush had fallen over the room. Estee glanced up apprehensively, but she could not make out the features of the man who stood just inside the door. The tavern light was dim, and a sudden spate of sunlight, glaring off the rain-drenched street behind him, turned him into a dark silhouette. Not until he had paid for her and taken her outside did she get a good look at him. Then she saw a tallish man, unusually thin, with a gawky, angular body. His eyes protruded slightly, and dark, thinning hair was brushed back from his face. His features were sharp and decidedly ugly.

He looked vaguely displeased as he studied her.

"I suppose you'll clean up well enough," he said dubiously. "But we'll have to find something more suitable for you to wear. I've been looking for a girl to read to my wife—she has long been an invalid and her eyesight of late is failing—but I doubt she'd approve of you as you are."

He caught himself with a look of mild surprise. His voice, as he continued, was unexpectedly kind.

"But I haven't told you who I am, have I? Since I am to be your new master, I daresay it is of more than passing interest to you. My name is Nathaniel Howe, and I reside in the Colony of New York."

A cold draft swept across the stable floor, chilling the sweat that coated Estee's body and drenched her dress. The sound of the mob outside had grown louder, rising to an angry roar, but she barely heard it. Why hadn't she had the sense to stay in Nathaniel Howe's house? she berated herself bitterly. The man might be ugly, but he was kind, and she would have been safe with him. If only he hadn't made things so easy for her, leaving his doors unlocked, as if he actually dared to trust his slaves.

But she *couldn't* have stayed, she thought suddenly, surprised that she had forgotten so easily. She curled into a fetal position, trying in vain to ease the pain that wracked her body. She had known she couldn't stay the instant she saw Nathaniel's son.

Crawford Howe had been standing at his mother's bedside the first time she entered the room. If the poor woman noticed her son's peevish impatience, she did not show it as she reached up to pat him fretfully on the hand. It was funny, Estee thought, watching the two of them, the way some women barely seemed to notice their devoted husbands, yet they always had time for a pampered, selfish son.

But then Crawford had looked up and seen Estee across the room, and she had forgotten everything else.

There was no misjudging the look in his eyes. It was a challenge and a declaration both, as bold as it was vile. Crawford Howe was very obviously a young man used to getting everything he wanted—and Estee knew exactly what he wanted now.

He had wasted no time following up the lewd insinuation of his eyes. He was waiting for her when she came out of his mother's room, balancing a heavy tray in her hands. She had tried to get around him, but he was too adroit for her. Side stepping quickly, he set himself squarely in her path.

"Well, what have we here? A comely wench? In my father's house? Will wonders never cease? Tell me, are you dear old pater's exclusive property, or can a hot-blooded son hope to share in your favors?"

Estee stiffened with revulsion.

"I am certain, sir, that your father would not appreciate hearing you speak like that. He is too much of a gentleman to allow any woman, even a slave, to be treated vulgarly under his roof."

Crawford had only laughed. His hands were deliberately insulting as he pinched her on the breast.

"You have one thing to learn about my father. He does whatever my mother tells him to. And my mother has never denied me anything."

No, Estee thought, retching at the nausea that welled up in her stomach again, she could not have stayed in that house.

Not with a man like Crawford Howe. She had had no choice but to flee into the darkness. She closed her eyes against the pain and sank deeper into the straw.

She had been so sure, when she took shelter against the chill of the night in a cow barn across town, that she would be safe, for the time being at least. But when her eyes grew accustomed to the darkness, she had been horrified to see a group of men huddled together under an open window. Moonlight glinted on heavy plate and silver candlesticks in their hands, and she knew they were thieves.

She tried to turn and run, but one of them had seen her, and he leaped up with an angry cry. She backed away, but he was between her and the door and she had no place to go. She was about to scream in terror when he came closer, and she saw that his skin was black like hers. Waves of relief flooded through her body.

"It's all right," she blurted out. "You don't have to worry about me. Don't you see? I'm a slave, too."

But they did not seem to understand. They were all on their feet now, surly and snarling as they surrounded her. She turned from one to another, trying desperately to convince them.

"You have nothing to fear from me. Truly you don't. I am a fugitive, too. Would I be here if I were not? I couldn't tell on you even if I wanted to."

Their expressions did not change. Slowly, she began to realize. It was not fear she had seen in their eyes at all. Not the dread of discovery. It was another, more frightening expression. One she had seen all too often.

"Oh, please . . . please. . . ."

These were her own kind. Her own people. Surely they could not do this terrible thing to her.

They did not hear her pleas. One of the men grabbed her and thrust her down on the floor. Another lunged forward, ripping her skirt away from her body. It was only seconds before the others followed. There was more anger than passion in their assault, and they battered her mercilessly, continuing to beat and kick her even after their sexual hungers had been satisfied. All the fury, all the frustration, of their twisted souls exploded in a savage burst of violence.

The first terrible pain cut through her body with blinding force. Even then, even in that fleeting moment, Estee knew what was happening. The tiny life inside her seemed to cling for an instant, making the moment of surrender even more agonizing. She let out a hoarse cry of despair as she felt warm blood hemorrhage onto her legs.

The child was dead. Rodrigo's child was dead. And with that death, she sensed the death of everything that had been good and pure in her. Everything that had given purpose to her life.

She took no comfort in the angry mob that milled outside. Their early shouts frightened the men away, just as later roars of excitement proclaimed that the thieves had been caught, but all that meant little to her. The respite, she knew, would be a short one. Soon the raging citizens, hungry for vengeance, would comb the area in a search for confederates.

They would find only one. A lone black woman on a stable floor. When they searched her, they would find a gold locket beneath the high neck of her dress, and then they would know she, too, was a thief. Blacks were hanged for less.

And the terrible thing was, it did not matter. Estee listened to the sound of the mob swarming outside the door, and it seemed to her as distant and detached as waves crashing against the shore. The man she loved had lived a few weeks longer inside her body. Now she had lost him forever.

Nothing would matter again.

Three

Faith woke up in the morning with a vague sense of uneasiness. She felt her body rebel as she forced herself out of bed, and she realized she had slept only fitfully all night long. At first, she could not figure out what was troubling her. Then slowly she began to remember.

Estee. She was worried about Estee.

She sat down at the dressing table and picked up a small silver-framed mirror. The image she saw in the glass did little to reassure her. Her skin was so pale she looked ill, and there were dark circles under her eyes.

Estee. It was heartbreaking to think of her friend and not have the slightest idea where she was or what was happening to her. She could have been captured by now or tortured—or God help her, even killed—and Faith would have no way of knowing. It was infuriating to feel so helpless.

She pinched her cheeks, trying to coax some color back into them. Infuriating or not, there was nothing she could do about it, and she might as well admit it. Besides, she had other, more urgent things to think about. She had already been in New York more than a week now, and still she was no closer to finding out about Fleur than she had been the day she arrived. Sighing, she cupped her chin in her hands and tried to figure out what to do.

One thing at least was clear. The subtle approach was not working very well. She had the feeling she could sit around for the next twenty years casually dropping Fleur's name into the conversation and never learn anything at all. If she wanted to discover the truth, she was going to have to be more direct, even if it meant arousing a few suspicions in the bargain.

She decided to tackle Temperance first. Her hostess was

just vague enough not to notice the drift of her questions, and somewhere in that idle prattle, she might find the clue she was looking for.

She waited until early afternoon when she knew Temperance would be in the small front room that served as her salon. As Faith had expected, she found her seated beside a round tilt-top table, set with a full silver tea service and porcelain cups. Dear Temperance, how childlike she was—and how obvious. Her blue eyes sparkled with expectation as she looked up at the door, hoping that one or another of her neighbors had come to call. Though in all that heat, Faith suspected, the other ladies were probably at home, too, sitting in front of their own tables and hoping exactly the same thing.

"What a charming room, Miss Temperance," she said graciously. "I believe it's my favorite place in the house."

"Do you really think so, dear? You know, I've never been quite sure. Sometimes I think I ought to have it painted red or yellow or something like that. Maybe one of those lovely, artistic marble effects."

"Heaven forbid. The natural walnut is much nicer. And it shows off the damask wall hangings from Lyons to perfection."

"Yes, I suppose it does." Temperance glanced around doubtfully. "But do you think it's quite fashionable?"

Faith laughed. "I think it's lovely and tasteful. And it smells absolutely divine."

"You like my potpourri, then? How nice, dear. I keep it in that India jar over there. Now where did I get the recipe? Oh, yes, from one of the Dutch housewives. So clever, the Dutch. You stick a Seville orange all full of cloves, then you cover it with rose petals and bay salt, and add cinnamon, lemon peel, and just the right amount of powdered musk——"

She broke off, her eyes twinkling.

"But you're not interested in trading recipes with an old lady. Not a pretty girl like you. Young people have so much more exciting things to think about nowadays. Come and have a cup of tea with me and tell me how you are enjoying our city."

Faith accepted a dainty Oriental cup from her hostess's hand and took a sip of the warm, fragrant liquid. She rather liked the exotic taste of tea, though judging from the tentative way Temperance approached her own cup, she was sure the older woman served it only because it was so wonderfully *à la mode*. Until recently, the prohibitive cost of imported tea had made it a beverage only for special occasions. Even now, it was a sign of affluence to be able to drink it every day.

She had barely had a chance to take a second sip when Jakob stuck his head in the door. Temperance, delighted at the prospect of filling her salon after all, invited him in. Faith had the feeling Jakob would infinitely prefer a cup of coffee in the masculine atmosphere of his club, but he was much too good-natured to disappoint his sister. He looked a little like a trained bear, perching on the edge of a Queen Anne chair with a cup and saucer balanced on his knee.

Faith was tempted to wait for him to leave before broaching the subject of Fleur, but she decided against it. If she kept letting circumstances get in her way, she would never accomplish what she had come for. Taking advantage of a lull in the conversation, she pitched her voice on what she hoped was a casual note.

"I can't tell you how much my sister enjoyed staying with you. She wrote several times and told me how happy she was here."

It was a lie, of course—Fleur never put pen to paper unless she wanted something—but Faith doubted the Howes would know that.

Temperance reacted much as she had hoped.

"Yes, I really think she did, dear. She was such a charming girl. We did love having her here, didn't we, Jakob?"

"Certainly, certainly. She livened up the house, I must say." He turned gallantly to Faith. "Just as you do, my dear."

"I do think New York was a good place for her," Temperance added. "So lively and fun. All the parties and balls. Do you know, I think Fleur could have gone to a different ball every day and never once have grown tired of them?"

"That's what I don't understand." Faith laid her cup on the table and leaned forward. "With all the excitement in New York, why would Fleur want to go someplace as dull as Havenhurst?"

"Havenhurst?" Jakob sounded genuinely surprised. "I can't imagine she would."

"Certainly not," Temperance hastened to agree. "Whatever put an idea like that into your head? Such a rough place. They say the people there are no better than peasants. Fleur would never associate with peasants."

Faith looked from one to another, puzzled. "You mean my sister never mentioned Havenhurst to you? She never expressed any curiosity about it?"

"Why should she?" Jakob asked. "After all, it's not in the family anymore."

"Oh, but it is. When my father lost the plantation, it was taken over by a distant cousin of my mother's, Jeremy Alleyn. His brother has it now. His half brother, actually."

"Oh, yes, Jeremy." Temperance's nose wrinkled visibly. "We had occasion to meet him more than once. Not a very nice man. I am sorry to say that, since he is a relation of yours, no matter how distant, but not a nice man at all."

"Now Temperance," Jakob interjected soothingly. "The man is dead, after all. There's no point harping on the past." He turned apologetically to Faith. "You see, my dear, we didn't hear about your father's tragic death until long after it had happened. By that time, Jeremy was already dead himself. Shot, I understand."

"Yes," Faith agreed. "A hunting accident."

"Ah?" Something in Jakob's tone told Faith he shared his sister's opinion. "Knowing Jeremy, we thought. . . . Well, that hardly matters now. I daresay we were remiss not to have looked into the disposal of Havenhurst at the time. But since your father left no male heirs and you girls were so young. . . ."

"Oh, please, Uncle Jakob. Don't trouble yourself about that. Fleur and I had no claim on Jeremy Alleyn's estate. Besides, even if my father hadn't lost Havenhurst, we could hardly have expected to inherit it. It would have been different if we were older, with husbands to look after our interests. But as it was, how could we possibly have managed a large plantation? Oddly enough, I suspect Jeremy would have gotten it anyway. He may have been a distant cousin, but he was the closest male relative my mother and Uncle Olivier had. And Havenhurst was originally theirs, you know."

"And now the younger brother has it?" Temperance interrupted curiously. "What was his name, Jakob? Do you recall? Oh, yes—Bradford."

"Judith Bradford's son," Jakob agreed. "A fine woman, Judith. I remember her well. I daresay young Bradford is cut from a different cloth than his brother."

Faith rose and stepped over to the window. Sunlight coming through leaded-glass panes cast diamond-shaped patterns on the floor, and she stared at them in feigned interest. Young Bradford. The words sounded comfortable and reassuring on Jakob's lips, but then Jakob had never known Brad. Was he really cut from a different cloth than his half brother, or were they more alike than she cared to guess?

When she finally turned back to Jakob and Temperance, her head was spinning, but she was careful not to let them see it. Incredible as it seemed, the elderly couple obviously had no idea that Fleur had gone to Havenhurst after she left them. Faith was more certain than ever now that that fateful journey had been prompted by something her sister learned while she was staying in the Howe house.

And whatever it was, she had gone to great lengths to keep it to herself.

Her head was still spinning later that evening as she rode alone in a closed carriage through twilight-darkened streets. The gala balls that Fleur could have gone to every day "and never once grown tired of them," were already beginning to have the opposite effect on Faith, but she dared not turn down any invitations, not when the young people her sister had associated with were likely to be there. And this promised to be the event of the season.

The day's heat still lingered, intensifying the smells of the city: the odor of dung and mud, of horses and human sweat, and slops tossed out of upper windows into open flowing gutters. Faith reached into her *étui* and, pulling out a small silver pomander, pressed it to her nose and took a deep whiff of sweet floral perfume.

No wonder Temperance had been just as glad to stay at home. Faith smiled as she remembered the brief confrontation they had had. The poor woman had tried so hard to do what she considered her duty, but when Faith held her ground, insisting on the right to go out alone, she had not been able to keep a sigh of relief from slipping through her lips. It was, Faith thought, exactly the reaction one would expect from the chaperone Fleur had chosen for herself.

Dusk had already deepened into night by the time she alit from the carriage. Flickering golden lanterns, dangling from passing coaches, danced like fireflies in the darkness. The house was properly impressive, a substantial brick structure, larger than any of its neighbors, with a handsome Palladian window above the central entrance. Two young black boys, dressed like footmen in coats of crimson with shiny silver buttons, flanked the door. Blazing torches in their hands sent sputtering sparks into the night.

And people thought that arsonists were setting fire to the city! Faith shook her head in amazement. With carelessness like that, it was a wonder the whole place hadn't gone up in flames long ago.

The entry hall was shimmering with light. Candles

twinkled in brass sconces on the walls, and a dark hardwood floor picked up the glow of the chandelier. The women in their dresses of damask and brocade, lutestring and silk, were a rainbow of color; the young men looked dashing and gallant in the fashionable buffs and burgundies of the season. The first strains of music were already beginning to drift down a sweeping circular staircase from the floor above.

Faith was halfway across the hall before she noticed a familiar figure descending the stairs toward her. Without thinking, she stepped over to a portrait on the wall and pretended to study the morose features that gazed out of an oval frame.

She had not liked Crawford Howe the first time she saw him, and she had found no reason to change her opinion later when Jakob introduced the young man to her and she felt dark eyes frankly assessing her face and figure. She had absolutely no desire to make small talk with him now.

A group of girls, plump and pink-cheeked, giggled as they passed, their full skirts brushing briefly against Faith's. When they had gone, a hush settled over the hall, and she could hear the sound of Crawford's voice.

"Well, Bob Jamieson! I never thought I'd see you come late to a ball. Aren't you always the first to arrive?"

In spite of herself, Faith turned around, curious to see the newcomer. Bob Jamieson turned out to be a lanky youth, homely but likeable looking.

"And the last to leave," he agreed, laughing. "But not today. Not with all the excitement."

There was enough of an edge to his voice to pique Crawford's interest.

"Why today?"

"They caught another gang of those blasted blacks. Caught 'em red-handed in a stable by the waterfront. Good God, man, don't tell me you haven't heard? I thought you'd be the first to know."

"I came straight here from the house. Know what?"

"One of your slaves was with them. The little blackbird that flew the coop."

Crawford sucked in his breath between his teeth. "The little bitch that ran away? The one my father just imported from the South?"

"None other. But what's this bitterness I detect in your voice? I thought the girl was supposed to be a beauty."

"What does that have to do with it?"

"Come off it, Craw. When you call a beautiful woman a

bitch, it only means one thing. She wouldn't let you touch her without a fight. Don't tell me that's why she ran away from your father's house? To keep you out of her petticoats?"

Crawford blanched visibly. "She's just an ungrateful bitch, that's all. I warned my father not to pick up a slave who can read and write. They never know their place."

Faith stood to the side, listening to the two men. She tried not to dwell on the implications of their words, though not with much success. A slave from the South, she kept thinking over and over, a beauty who could both read and write—how many black women fitted that description? For the first time, she admitted to herself that the terrible premonitions she had been feeling for the past few days might be more than fancy after all. Estee *might* be in New York.

She took all her fear and channeled it into a burst of anger. She had had about as much as she could take of Crawford Howe and all the men like him. Men who thought they could do anything they wanted with their slaves and no one would dare speak up! Forgetting her reservations, she flounced over and looked him straight in the eye.

"Crawford Howe, you are the stupidest, most pompous man I have ever met in my life! That poor girl is probably terrified half out of her wits, and here you are, trying to make her look like some kind of arsonist. Or a thief, for heaven's sake!"

Crawford looked more amused than annoyed. "Isn't she?"

"No, of course she isn't! It's amazing the lengths some men will go to just to save face. That girl only committed one sin. She wasn't as overwhelmed as you are every time you look in your mirror!"

If she expected a responsive spark of anger, she was quickly disappointed. Crawford only broke out laughing.

"By George, what a spitfire! Tell me, Bob, would any man hanker after blackbirds with a temptress like this around?"

That was more than Faith could take. "I find it a wonder, sir, that any well-bred young ladies are willing to live in this filthy city of yours. Or attend your gaudy balls. You Colonials are such boors!"

The sound of male laughter followed her up the stairs. Honestly! she thought, almost as surprised as she was irritated, it was incredible the way Crawford Howe's mind worked. When Bob Jamieson insulted him, he was furious. When she did the same thing, he only took it as some kind of flirtatious gambit.

She resisted the urge to turn at the top of the stairs and see if he was still staring at her. She knew only too well that he was. It astonished her to think that he actually believed a woman might fancy him. To her, he seemed everything that was unappealing in a man: hard without being strong; sharp without being clever; sarcastic without the saving grace of humor.

The ballroom, glimpsed through open double doors at the end of the hall, was a burst of light and color. Faith mingled with the others, letting them sweep her along on a wave of laughter and good spirits as they hurried forward. The instant she stepped inside, she understood why they had been so eager.

The decorations were exquisite. The ball was a "Posey Dance," a custom inspired by the Spanish Colonies, and the entire room had been turned into an arbor. Spring flowers in pretty pastel hues twined up tall white pillars, and garlands of blood-red roses dangled from overhead trellises. Hundreds of twinkling candles cast a seductive golden glow over perfumed petals, giving the chamber the enchanted air of a palatial garden on a warm summer's eve.

Faith was so captivated by the loveliness of the setting, she did not even notice a young man standing a few feet away from her. When at last she sensed the intensity of his gaze, she turned, half curious, half flattered. A tentative smile died on her lips as she found herself staring into soft brown eyes.

"Rolfe . . . ?"

He must have been as surprised as she, perhaps more so, for he had not seen her when his carriage turned in the street yesterday, but he did not say a thing. Faith braced herself, waiting for the torrent of accusations she knew must come, and tried desperately to think of something to say. Some kind of excuse to make him understand. Then, just when her mouth grew so dry she was sure she couldn't speak anyway, he simply turned his back and, without a word, walked away.

Faith felt the blood drain from her face as he vanished into the crowd. If he had sat up all night thinking about it, he could not have found a way to hurt her more. Or humiliate her so deeply. She knew she deserved his disdain—heaven knew, she had treated him badly enough—but to cut her dead like that! Without even waiting to hear her side of the story! It seemed so unfair.

It was a relief when the background music paused at last, and the musicians adjusted the sheets on the racks in front of them. The dance floor cleared, the murmuring crowd fell silent, and the clear, pure tones of a clavichord filled the air.

Soon the flutes joined in, followed by recorders, violins, and hautboys, and an eager throng of revelers turned their eyes toward the center of the room.

There was a moment's pause, then the daughter of the house stepped shyly out of a group at the sidelines. It was her ball, her special night, but Faith had the feeling she did not know how to take advantage of it. They had dressed her in the height of fashion. Expensive green brocade swelled out in a full skirt, parted in front to reveal a petticoat flowered in crimson, gold, and blue, and her white silk stomacher had been embroidered to perfection. But all the money in the world could not conceal a gawky, big-boned frame, or soften a face that seemed more teeth than eyes.

In her hands she held a colorful bouquet, the "posey" of the dance. Looking embarrassed, though pleased with all the attention, she circled the ring of onlookers, offering the posey to one young man after another, then pulling it teasingly back again. When at last she stopped before her favored swain—the man she had chosen to be her consort for the dance—she thrust the bouquet at him with an awkward, childlike gesture.

Faith shook her head slowly as she stared at the man. And she had thought no woman would ever fancy Crawford Howe! Yet here was a girl gazing up at him with what could only be described as lovesick eyes.

Poor Crawford, she thought, suppressing a giggle. This was probably the only female who would every look at him like that—and he couldn't enjoy it because she wasn't pretty!

Crawford was a good sport about it, Faith had to give him that. With a smile and a bow he led his ungainly queen back into the center of the floor, beckoning for the other couples to follow. An attractive young man, several inches taller than Faith and at least as fair, appeared at her elbow. She answered his bow with a deep, sweeping curtsy of her own and, accepting his arm, stepped onto the floor. The musicians took up their instruments again, and it was only minutes before she lost herself in the complex pattern of the minuet.

The music, elegant and subdued, seemed strangely formal after the less disciplined exuberance of South Carolina, and Faith found that it required all her concentration just to keep in step. She wished now she had been more like Fleur, practicing the intricate movements over and over again in front of a mirror so she could dazzle everyone with her stylish perfection.

The rhythm was deceptively simple. Sweet, yet subtly enticing, it soon took hold of her, coaxing her into the dance with instinctive grace. She began to move automatically, no longer counting out the one-two-three, one-two-three of each step and turn. Her body swayed with unconscious sensuality; her toes looked pert and dainty as she pointed them against the floor. When the time came to dip one last curtsy to her partner and smile goodbye, she was ready to move on to the next man in line.

From across the floor, Rolfe was aware of her every movement, even after she had forgotten he was there. He had been enamored of his own partner, a willowy silver blond, when he first saw her that evening. Now he barely noticed as her hand slipped out of his and she left him for a new partner. He had eyes for only one woman in the room, and that woman was Faith.

It was uncanny how like her sister she was—and how different all at the same time. She was as devious as Fleur, she was as flirtatious, she was a woman who knew how to use men to her own advantage, yet she had a style, a *ton,* all her own. Where Fleur would have executed the dance with studied skill, Faith almost seemed to ignore the steps, letting her body flow instead with the rhythm of the music. And in place of the vivid emerald damask that would have drawn every eye toward her sister, Faith had garbed herself even more compellingly in virginal white, accented only by an embroidered silver échelle and silver buckles on her slippers.

Don't look at her, he warned himself. Don't let your eyes keep going back to her. That woman is poison to you, and you're a blasted idiot if you let yourself forget it.

Faith, for her part, was still unaware of Rolfe, even though the dance had brought them so close they were nearly side by side. The music was a part of her now, catching her up in its vibrant spell, and she could think of nothing else. Only when she twirled away from one last partner and found herself facing him did she suddenly remember he was in the room. She was so nonplussed, she could only stand there with her hand poised awkwardly in the air.

It was Rolfe who managed the social grace required of them both. Taking her hand, he bowed with exaggerated courtesy and drew her toward him.

"Well . . . Miss Faith Eliot."

Faith heard the brittle sarcasm in his voice with a sinking heart. Holding her hand steady, she forced herself to meet his gaze. If she was going to salvage anything of her pride, she would have to be as cool as he.

"It's Mrs. Juilliard now. Mrs. Alexandre Juilliard."

The brief flicker of surprise in his eyes told her that Uncle Andrew had not broadcast the news of her marriage.

"Ah, a husband. But of course, I should have known. What a pity it would have been to let those feminine wiles go to waste. I presume you found exactly the man you were looking for. Handsome, I daresay. And wealthy?"

"Why not? Do you think I am not attractive enough to snare such a paragon?"

He did not reply. The steps of the dance drew them apart in a welcome respite that ended all too soon. When they came together again, his eyes were cold and unfathomable.

"Not attractive enough, my dear Mrs. Juilliard? Oh, but you're very attractive, I assure you. On the outside at least. And to some men, that's all that counts."

Faith was so stunned, she could think of no reply. How deeply she must have hurt him, she thought guiltily, for him to be so cruel to her now. They did not speak again, but finished their part of the formal pattern in silence, waiting for the final bow and curtsy that would release them from each other.

It seemed forever, but at last the dance moved full circle and Faith found herself back with her original partner again. The final melodic bars had barely sounded when she murmured a hasty "Thank you" and began to push her way across the crowded floor toward the hall. She did not think she could bear to stay in that room a minute longer. Not when she knew that disdainful eyes would be following her wherever she went.

The wide stairway that curved up from the floor below was empty. Faith leaned against the railing and stared down into a candlelit entry. Why did she mind so much? she wondered. Why did it matter what one man thought of her when she knew the truth in her own heart?

A faint sound beside her warned her she was no longer alone. Glancing over, she was irritated to see Crawford Howe. His lank form was draped carelessly against the railing, and his eyes seemed to be laughing.

"What have we here? Don't tell me you're bored with the ball already? Or did you perhaps have some romantic tryst planned for the dim hallway? I hope I didn't spoil anything for you."

Faith felt her body stiffen with irritation. She had already suffered enough unpleasantness that evening. Putting up with an arrogant lout like Crawford was the last straw.

"You are absolutely the last man on earth——"

"Here, here. No fair. Don't dig your claws in again, you little she-cat. I was right, you know."

"Right? What are you talking about? Right about what?"

"About the girl. The one who ran away from my father."

The girl? Faith suddenly felt cold, as if an icy draft had blown through the hall. In the embarrassment of seeing Rolfe again, she had completely forgotten the girl Nathaniel Howe had brought up from the South.

"I don't know what you mean."

"I mean the girl was a thief after all. She was caught with the goods on her."

Faith could only stare at him for a moment. She hated herself for the tension that tied her stomach into a knot, but she could not help it. It was so farfetched, this thing she was thinking. So utterly implausible.

"I don't believe you. You're just saying that to make yourself look good."

A slow, satisfied smirk spread across his face. "Am I? But that would be foolish, wouldn't it? Ask anyone you like. They'll all tell you the same thing. The girl was caught with a valuable piece of jewelry."

"Of . . . jewelry?" Faith gripped the railing with her hand. Dear heaven, could it possibly be? This one terrible thing that seemed so remote only minutes ago?

"Jewelry indeed. And not just a bauble, I understand. They say it was quite a unique ornament. She was wearing it on a chain around her neck."

"What kind of an ornament?"

"A gold locket. With a diamond in the center."

Four

Faith stood at the head of the empty stairway and gazed in horror at the man in front of her. Soft strains of music, floating through the open ballroom door, filled the air with sweetness, but she barely heard them. A gold locket, he had said. The captured girl was wearing a gold locket with a diamond in the center.

How many slaves had a trinket like that?

Catching her skirt up in her hands, she began to race down the steps, taking them two and three at a time in her haste. She knew that Crawford must be staring after her, but she did not care. Let him make what he would of her bizarre behavior. Estee was in trouble, and she had to help her.

The night had darkened considerably in the brief hour Faith had been inside. In front of the house, the red-golden glow of twin torches, still guarded by a pair of costumed black boys, formed a circle of warmth in the deep blue shadows. The street was completely deserted. No groaning carriage wheels broke the heavy silence; no late-night strollers passed by to peer curiously into gaily lighted windows.

Faith left the security of the doorway and took a tentative step onto the cold pavement. If only there were someone she could turn to, she thought helplessly, throwing a last glance over her shoulder at the house she had left behind. If only there were some friend inside she dared to trust. But the only man she had ever been able to turn to was Brad—and Brad was too far away to help her now.

She squinted into the darkness, following the street as far as she could with her eyes, as if something in those murky shadows might tell her what to do. She had no idea where the jailhouse was located, or even if there was more than one, and she didn't dare raise suspicions by asking anyone inside. At last, she did the only thing she could. She simply picked an arbitrary direction and forced herself to begin walking. At least, she thought, taking solace where she could, the walled city was so compact, she could cover it in a single night if she had to.

The air had grown cooler, and a biting wind rose from the river. Casting a rueful eye down at her dress, Faith wished she had had the good sense to bring at least a thin mantle with her. Sheer white silk and a daring décolletage might look perfectly charming in the ballroom, but they were hopelessly out of place on city streets at night.

It took her longer than she expected to locate the area where the jail was situated, and she was so discouraged at times, she was tempted to give up. Only the thought of Estee and the fate that would surely be hers when the Common Council convened in the morning kept her going.

When she finally found the place, it was her ears and not her eyes that led her to it. She had been aware for several minutes of hoarse shouting somewhere in the distance, but she paid it little heed, thinking only that she had stumbled too close to some brawling dockside tavern or area of raucous public amusement. It was not until she ventured nearer that she recognized the sound for what it was. The angry howling of a mob.

And there was only one place a mob would gather on a night like this—outside the jail where black prisoners were being held.

If she needed confirmation, she got it when the narrow lane she was following opened suddenly onto a small square. A crowd of surly ruffians, perhaps eighty or ninety strong, swarmed around the entrance to one of the buildings, calling out threats and coarse obscenities at the top of their lungs. Faith shuddered as she watched them. The men were, for the most part, a filthy lot, clad in the rough garb of workmen or beggars; the few women among them were the crudest she had ever seen. It had not occurred to her, until that very moment, just how desperate—and how precarious—Estee's situation might be.

She dared not step out of the shadowy lane, for she knew only too well the kind of attention she would attract in her elegant ballgown, but at least she had a decent view of the jail from where she was.

It was, she was surprised to note, a small, nondescript

structure. Had it not been for the crowd milling outside, she was sure she would have passed it by without a second glance. Peeling paint gave it an incongrously flimsy appearance, although the heavy wooden door in the center of the front wall looked strong and secure. A dozen armed soldiers guarded the entrance.

Faith's heart sank as she watched them. She knew she ought to be grateful for the muskets on their shoulders—without that show of force, she doubted if anything could have kept the angry mob from storming the building—but she had the terrible feeling their presence was going to make it almost impossible to rescue Estee. Even if she could bribe or cajole someone inside into setting her free, how could she ever get her past so formidable a guard?

She stepped back into the lane and began to make her way around the buildings that surrounded the jail. It was too dangerous to use the front entrance—she didn't dare go in or out that way—but perhaps she could find a door in back. And perhaps it would not be so heavily guarded.

The alleyway that led behind the jail was more encouraging than Faith had dared to hope. It turned out to be a dingy path, so narrow a proper carriage would have trouble getting through. The only light came from the faint rays of the moon. The cries of the mob sounded muffled and far away.

Perhaps she was going to be lucky after all. Perhaps, if that raging mob had not yet thought of circling the building, she would find only a soldier or two covering the doors and windows in the back. And a soldier or two could be distracted, especially in the dark.

She stumbled on the building more by accident than design, for neither light nor markings appeared anywhere to tell her what it was. Even then, she had to go back and forth, checking the structures on either side to make sure she was in the right place. There was only one door, set in the center, much like the door in front, and no windows at all that she could see. To her surprise, there was not so much as a single soldier in sight.

It was a moment before she understood what was going on. When she did, a cold shiver ran down her spine.

There were no soldiers in back of the jail because no one was planning to defend it. All those guards in front were just for show. When that angry mob finally came hurtling down the alleyway, there would be nothing to hold them back.

The realization made Faith sick with dread. She had been so sure she would have all night to see where Estee was being held and form a plan to get her out. Now she knew she had only hours—perhaps even minutes—and then it would be too late.

She went up to the door and gave it a tentative shove. As she had feared, it was securely locked, and neither handles nor hinges showed on the outside. She had no tools to force it, and even had she hoped to find a sturdy boulder on the street, she would never have dared to smash it in. The sound would be certain to attract either the jailors within or the savage mob in front—and either prospect was equally alarming.

She stood alone in the alleyway, turning all the possibilities over in her mind. Slowly, she realized what she had to do. She didn't like it—the risks were too great, the chances of success far too slim—but she didn't see what choice she had.

The mood of the mob seemed to have changed when she found her way back to the square again. Were they really as sullen and restless as they appeared, she asked herself tensely, or was it only that fear had made her see them in a new perspective? She lingered in the shadows one last minute, then forced herself forward. If she couldn't get through the door in back, then she was going to have to go in the front. And there was no point trying to be discreet about it!

The mob was even uglier than she had anticipated. The smell of unwashed bodies and stale tobacco was bad enough, but her skin crawled as she thrust out bare arms, pushing past men so filthy they seemed to be infested with vermin. Curious eyes peered at her from all sides. Hands clutched her rudely, sometimes catching the fabric of her dress, but she brushed them aside.

She was only a few feet from the entrance when she felt stubby fingers curl around her upper arm, pulling her to a stop. She tried to shrug them away, as she had with the others, but she could not work them loose. Turning, she found herself staring into eyes that were no more than inky pits of darkness, sunk deep in puffy white skin.

"Well, if it ain't a proper little miss." The man's voice was as slimy as his appearance. "All decked out like a princess, it is. Heh, look a' that, mates! A right squirmy bit o' baggage, wouldn't ya say?"

Faith was terrified, but she dared not show it. This was the kind of bully who thrived on fear. And no one in that brutal mob would lift a finger to help her.

She drew her arm back as far as she could.

"Take your hands off me, you pig!" Swinging her arm forward, she struck him a sound blow on the side of the face.

The man gave a yelp of surprise and let go. That was all Faith needed. Pushing past the last group of ruffians, she ran up to one of the soldiers. The whole thing couldn't have worked out better if she had planned it that way.

"Is this how a lady is treated in your presence, sir? What kind of militia do we have in this Colony if a woman can't even feel safe in the presence of an armed regiment?"

The soldier was so surprised, he took a step backward. He was just a lad, barely old enough to shave, Faith judged.

"I'm s-sorry, ma'am," he stammered awkwardly. "It all h-happened so fast, I didn't know what to do. We were told not t-to leave our p-posts."

"Not to leave your posts? Now, really, do you expect me to believe a story like that? You were told you could not move so much as a few paces? Even to aid a defenseless woman? Those were your orders?"

Faith almost felt sorry for the boy. He was so nervous, his Adam's apple bobbed up and down.

"N-no, ma'am. Of course not, ma'am. It won't h-happen again."

"Well, I should hope not. It would be a sorry state of affairs if it did. Now young man, I would appreciate it if you would step aside. I have been told one of my slaves is inside and I want to see for myself."

The boy looked confused, but he held his ground. Faith was about to tackle him again, when one of the other soldiers stepped out of line to back him up.

"I'm sorry, madam. I appreciate your position, but I cannot allow you to go inside."

Faith was dismayed to find herself staring into the features of a hardened veteran. This was no green recruit to be bluffed so easily. Still, she had to try.

"*You* cannot allow me? And who, pray tell, are you?"

"Just a soldier. But I have my orders. No one is to go in or out of that building."

"Just a soldier, you say? Well, not much of one if you ask me. First you allow a woman to be molested right in front of your eyes, then you tell a slaveowner she has no right to check on her own property. That doesn't sound reasonable to me."

"Sorry, madam. The matter is out of my hands."

Faith stared at him helplessly. Had she come so far only to be turned away at the last minute? She could not let that happen.

"Well, this is a fine kettle of fish, isn't it? I wonder what my uncle, the lieutenant governor, will have to say when I tell him about it."

She did not even know if the lieutenant governor had a niece, but apparently neither did the soldier. He looked uncomfortable as he searched her face with his eyes.

"The lieutenant governor sent you here?"

"Of course he did. My uncle expects me to look after my slaves, as well he should. Now, sir, are you going to step aside or aren't you?"

To her surprise, the answer seemed to be in the affirmative. The man did not look happy about it, but he made no move to stop her as she squared her shoulders and marched up to the door.

She did not feel quite so brave when she stepped inside. The door opened directly onto a room that was as rough and ill-tended as any she had ever seen in her life. A tallow candle cast its feeble rays over walls that must once have been gray or tan, but now were darkened with grime. Only a single jailor could be seen, seated at a rickety table in front of an open doorway leading to the rear.

Faith took a step forward, then hesitated.

"Good evening, sir. I wonder if you could help me."

The man did not reply, but looked up dully as if she had awakened him from a sound sleep. He was, she decided as she studied him, not at all what one would expect of a jailkeeper. A smallish man, with thinning white hair that straggled to his shoulders, he looked more fragile than wiry. His eyes were a benign gray and his clothes comfortably rumpled.

She decided to try again, more forcefully this time.

"I understand you are holding one of my slaves here. Without my permission, I might add. I don't claim it's your fault. I am sure the capture was none of your doing, and I do not hold you accountable for it. Nonetheless, I must insist that you fetch the slave to me at once."

Brashness worked no better than courtesy. The man raised a hand, scratching his head with dirty fingernails, and simply ignored her. Faith stared at him in frustration. Could it be that what she had taken for benignity was only dull-wittedness?

"I said, fetch the slave, sir. Now! Or if you are not willing to go yourself, send one of your men."

The man sighed, as if she were some kind of nuisance that would not go away. Leaning back in his chair, he let his vest fall open over a coarse homespun shirt.

"I ain't got no men here. Don't need 'em. Not tonight. And I ain't about t' do yer fetching fer ya."

"Give me the key then. I'll fetch the slave myself."

The man shook his head slowly. One side of his mouth twisted up in a lopsided grin.

"I don't give that key t' nobody."

"Well, why not? I only want to check through your prisoners to see if my slave is there. What harm could that do?"

"Prob'ly none," he admitted complacently. "But wouldn't do no good neither. I ain't got but one slave in there. They hanged th' others this afternoon. An' that one ain't your'n."

Faith's heart caught in her throat. "The slave that's left, is it a woman?"

"Oh, she's a gal all right. One of them snippy things what thinks she kin read an' write. Don't see as how she's much worth fussin' about. I reckon she was purty once, but she ain't anythin' t' look at now."

His words shocked Faith. She had been so preoccupied with all the dangers that lay ahead for Estee, it had not occurred to her that she might already have suffered deeply.

"That *is* my slave!" she insisted. "You're given a perfect description of her, though she was in better condition when I had her. That will teach her to run away from me, the foolish girl. Now if you will just——"

"I told ya, lady. She ain't your'n. She b'longs to a man name o' Nathaniel Howe, and I ain't gonna turn her over to ya."

"But she is mine! Nathaniel Howe has no rightful claim on her. Listen to me—I can prove what I'm saying! The girl was wearing a locket when she was taken. A gold locket with a diamond in it. Well, that locket is mine! She stole it from me. That's why I want her back, so I can arrange suitable punishment myself."

The man gave her a curious look. "How do I know you're tellin' the truth? Ain't much o' anybody in this town hasn't heard o' that locket by now. Half a hundred people could make up a story ever' bit as good as that."

"Maybe they could." Faith paused to give her words effect. "But how many of them can tell you what's inside the locket? Only I know that. It's a golden curl, cut from my sister's head. My twin sister. Her hair was exactly the same color as mine."

The man's expression changed. He stared at her hair for a long time, then dropped his gaze to his hands as they played with the edge of the table. When he looked up again, he was chuckling.

"Well, well, don't that beat all. So ya wasn't makin' it up, huh? Not that it means nothin', mind ya. Even if I wanted t' let that gal go, them folks outside'd never let her past."

Faith thought of the door in back, but she was careful not to say anything. If the man turned out to be shrewder than he looked, she did not want him to realize how much she knew about the place.

"I'm sure you could think of something if you wanted to," she said slowly. "A clever man like you. I doubt there's much you can't do."

She had not expected him to respond. The words were merely a ploy to buy time. Yet, to her surprise, he seemed to puff up in front of her eyes.

"Well, I don't know. . . ."

"Oh, but you *do* know!" If she couldn't bluff him into giving her what she wanted, maybe flattery would work. "It would take a lot of daring, of course. But surely you aren't a coward. And I could make it worth your while."

His eyes lit up with a greedy glint.

"You didn't say there might be sum'pin in it fer me."

"I don't have any money with me. But my uncle is rich. Very rich. Just tell me what you want——"

"An' I'll git it t'morrow, is that it? Oh, no, I ain't such a fool as that. Pay up tonight or it's no deal."

"But I told you. I don't have anything with me. If you'll just wait——"

"No. I ain't waitin'." His eyes had an unnatural glimmer as he rose from his chair and came around the table. "If ya ain't got no money, mebbe we kin work out sum'pin else."

"Something . . . else?" Faith stared at him in revulsion. Could he really be suggesting what she thought? "I—I don't know what you mean."

Instinct made her back away, even without realizing it. Suddenly, she was painfully aware that she was alone in the room with him.

He seemed aware of it, too. "C'mon, lady, don't play dumb with me. It ain't such a bad idea, now is it? I got sum'pin you want, an' you got sum'pin I want. Why don't we jes' make a little trade?"

He began to move toward her. Horrified, Faith felt the wall against her back, and she knew she could retreat no farther.

"Don't come any closer! If you do, I'll scream my head off."

"Go ahead. Scream all ya want. Even if they hear ya, what with all that racket, they'll jes' think its that slave gal settin' up a fuss over sum'pin or other."

An ugly grin distorted his features as he came to a stop a few feet away from her. He was so near Faith could smell his breath.

"Ya want that blackbird in there, ya better stop actin' so uppity. It won't do ya no good nohow, one way or t'other, so ya might as well git sum'pin fer yer trouble."

Faith gaped at him in disgust and anger. Did the old lecher really think she would let him use her like that without a fight?

"I'll see you in hell first, you son of a bitch!"

Lunging forward, she grabbed hold of the flimsy table and shoved it at him in a desperate effort to throw him off balance. She needed only a second, just time enough to get to the exit, but the man was wilier than she thought. Pushing away the table, he threw himself not at her, but at the heavy wooden door. Terrified, Faith realized there was no way she could get past him.

They stood and eyed each other in wary silence. The man was small, Faith thought, sizing him up, and not in particularly good condition. She might be able to take him in a fight.

But she might not, either—and she didn't dare risk it. Not when guile would work so much better. Lowering her lashes, she let the tears she had been holding back slip down her cheeks. Her lips parted to emit a soft whimper of fear.

He reacted just as she expected. With a gloating laugh, he began to lumber toward her. She let him get halfway across the room, then raised a trembling hand to stop him.

"Wait! Please . . . Just—just give me time to think."

"To think?" he snorted incredulously. "Hell, lady, thinkin' ain't got nothin' t' do with it."

Oh, but it does, Faith thought grimly. Thinking had everything to do with it. The only way she was going to get away from this man was to outwit him.

"Do you promise to let the girl go?" she asked tremulously. "If I do what you want?"

Suspicion dissolved into smug amusement. "Sure. Jes' roll up them lacy white petticoats, an' I'll give ya anythin' ya want."

Liar, Faith thought bitterly. Filthy, rotten liar! He had no intention of keeping his word. He would use her brutally, then laugh in her face when she demanded Estee's freedom.

Only she wasn't going to give him the chance!

"All right," she said coolly. She tilted her head at a cocky angle, as if she were in control of her emotions again. "If you promise me the girl, I'll do it. Only don't rush at me like some bull out in the fields. I can't abide crudity. If you want me, you'll have to treat me like a lady."

The remark was so unexpected, it threw him off guard. His eyes glazed over with a dull, bewildered expression. If she had not been so frightened, Faith thought, she would have laughed at him, he was such a fool.

She timed her next move perfectly. Waiting until he had just recovered from his confusion, she raised her hand to the neck of her dress, slipping sheer white silk off her shoulder. The man began to quiver almost uncontrollably as he caught sight of smooth, milky skin.

Slowly, tantalizingly, Faith eased the fabric down, inch by inch, revealing the soft, full swell of her bosom. Then, when the feverish brightness in his eyes told her he was at the breaking point, she let it go, exposing her breast to his view.

It was more than the man could endure. Surrendering the last shred of caution, he staggered forward. Faith waited until he was inches away, then brought up her knee, jabbing it sharply into his groin. A howl of pain and shock burst out of his lips.

Thrusting out her hands, Faith pushed him away. He tried to grab her, but all his clawing fingers could catch was the silk of her bodice, and the fabric gave with a loud ripping sound. Grunting like a barnyard beast, he fell to his knees on the floor.

Faith clutched torn silk over her naked breast as she stumbled frantically toward the door. She had just caught hold of the handle and was about to pull it open when a menacing roar rose from the mob outside. Shivering, she drew back. Those were not men out there anymore, they were animals. If she let them see her with her hair in wild disarray and her dress half ripped from her body, a dozen soldiers with a dozen muskets would never be enough to protect her.

She hesitated only an instant, then made for the gaping doorway that led to the rear of the jail. She did not know if the back door opened with a bolt or a key, but she did not waste time thinking about it. It was her only way out, and somehow she had to get through it.

The hallway was surprisingly narrow. Faint candlelight, filtering through from the front room, was just enough to pick up vague outlines. The exit door was only a shadow at the end of the hall. Two other doors, constructed of thick wooden planks, led off to either side.

Faith cast a nervous glance over her shoulder, making sure the man was still writhing in pain on the floor. Those must be the doors that led to cells where the prisoners were being kept. If Estee was there—if she was behind one of those stout wooden barriers—Faith might still be able to get her out.

She tried one of the doors. It opened easily, but a quick look inside was enough to tell her the cell was empty. The other door, the one that led to the right, resisted her efforts. Flinging herself against it, she began to beat on it with her fists.

"Estee! Are you in there, Estee! Can you hear me?"

She pressed her ear to the door, straining to hear something inside. She thought she detected a faint rustle of movement, but there was no answering call.

If only she had something to break the door down, Faith thought frantically. Some kind of battering ram. She turned tensely toward the front room, wondering if she dared to go back. The chair the man had been sitting on seemed sturdy and well built.

But just at that moment, the one thing she dreaded above all else happened. The man, pulling himself together, managed to get to his feet and work his way to the door. He was crouching grotesquely, like some barbaric ape, but that did not stop him from coming toward her.

Crying out in fear, she raced down the hall, throwing her body at the outer door in a frantic effort to jolt it open. When it held fast, she began to grope desperately around the handle, praying that she would find an iron bolt. Yet the bar that greeted her fingers brought no relief, for try as she would, she could not make it budge.

Behind her, she heard the man's footsteps shuffling painfully down the corridor. Every muscle in her body tensed as she tugged at the bolt again. For a single, agonizing second, she thought it was going to hold fast. Then, with a harsh, rasping sound, it gave, sliding back so suddenly it nearly threw her off balance.

She could feel the heat of the man's breath on her neck as she pushed the door open and leaped outside. Her hands reacted automatically, catching hold of the door and swinging it back again. There was a sickening crunch of wood against bone as it slammed into his face.

Faith stood where she was for a second, too terrified even to breathe. Then she began to run, irrationally, she knew, for the man was in no condition to follow her, but she could not help herself. She simply ran and ran, stumbling through the darkness until she barely knew where she was anymore.

Only when she reached the main thoroughfare did she finally stop to catch her breath. Torchlight spilled out of the square, making the dark street look even eerier and more deserted than ever. Helpless and discouraged, Faith forced herself to face the truth at last. She had thought she could save Estee by herself, but she had been wrong. If she was going to do anything for her friend, she had to find someone to help her.

But where could she turn? It seemed a question without an answer. To Uncle Jakob? But Jakob Howe was a deeply conservative man, awed by the law and not at all inclined to antagonize his neighbors. Besides, she reminded herself grimly, Jakob thought the slaves were guilty. Nathaniel Howe then? After all, he was the one who had brought Estee up from the South. But Nathaniel, she suspected, was every bit as conservative as his cousin, and as reluctant to risk the wrath of his neighbors. Crawford would help her, of course—Crawford had nothing like qualms or scruples to stand in his way—but she could well imagine the price he would exact for his aid.

A solitary carriage rumbled slowly around the corner and headed toward her. Faith could not see it distinctly until it was halfway down the street. Even then she studied it only idly. It was a simple vehicle, plain black with neither adornment nor insignia to set it apart, and she would have paid it no further heed had not the rays of the coachman's lantern fallen on his features. Faith had seen the man only once before, but she recognized him immediately.

Was the party over already? she thought, surprised. She had not realized it was so late. Or perhaps she had simply spoiled Rolfe Stephen's evening as thoroughly as he had spoiled hers. She moved deeper into the shadows, not wanting him to see her as he passed.

Rolfe Stephens. She wondered why his was the one name that had not occurred to her a moment before. Was it because she could not bear the humiliation of facing him again? But Rolfe was the only person in the Colony who could help her now. He was conservative, true; he was honorable and law-abiding; but he was a fair man and a decent one. And he was not a coward.

She stepped out of the shadows and began to walk slowly down the center of the street.

Five

Rolfe Stephens sprawled out uncomfortably on the seat of the moving carriage. Propping one leg up on the bench opposite him, he stared gloomily into the darkness. Blast! The last thing in the world he had wanted tonight was to run into Faith Eliot again.

No, not Faith Eliot, he reminded himself wryly. Faith *Juilliard*. She had made that perfectly clear. The little minx! She hadn't wasted any time catching a husband, had she? And one who no doubt had more to offer in terms of wealth and status than a British merchant's son.

He shifted his weight restlessly, planting both feet on the floor again. Well, more power to the poor devil. Whoever he was, he'd learn soon enough what lay beneath those wide hazel eyes and that sweetly innocent smile.

The carriage slowed down and groaned to an unexpected stop. Opening the door, Rolfe stuck his head out to see what was the matter. He was about to chide the coachman when he caught sight of a slender young woman standing alone in the middle of the road.

She lingered just outside the beams of the coachman's lantern, but Rolfe had no trouble identifying her. There could hardly be two pretty partygoers defying the bold colors of fashion that night to garb themselves in simple white and silver. His eyes took in everything at once—the rent in her dress, the way her hair tumbled to her shoulders, the hint of a tremor on full pink lips—and for an instant, he had a reckless urge to leap out of the carriage and catch her up in his arms.

Damn! he thought furiously. What kind of man let himself be taken in by the same female twice? So she had gotten herself into trouble, had she? Well, what the devil did she expect, running around like that? She had probably had a tryst with some disreputable adventurer on midnight streets and gotten exactly what she deserved.

His hand hesitated on the half-open door. If he had an ounce of sense in his head, he told himself irritably, he would shut it in her face and order the driver to move on. But even as the thought crossed his mind, he knew he would not do it. It was not in his nature to go off and leave a woman helpless and alone, no matter how much he despised her. Besides, for all her faults, Faith was still the niece of his father's friend and long-time associate. For Andrew Devereaux' sake, if for no other reason, he had to offer her assistance.

He flung the door wide with a brusque gesture.

"All right," he said gruffly. "Get in. I'll take you home."

His grudging kindness made Faith even more uncomfortable than the scorn he had shown earlier that evening. Miserably, she climbed into the carriage and sat on the seat across from him. It frightened her to realize that somehow she had to find a way to win this man's trust again.

"Rolfe, please. . . ."

To her embarrassment, her voice broke so badly she could not go on. She could barely make out Rolfe's features in the darkness, but she sensed they were hard and disapproving, and she hated herself for having to beg for his help. But if she wanted to save Estee, she knew she could spare herself nothing.

"I think," she said at last, "I will have to tell you the truth."

It was painful, but somehow she forced herself to go through with it. She did not begin quite honestly, for she dared not, even now, hint that Fleur was dead, but she told him everything else. The dream that warned her her sister was in trouble, the difficult journey that took her to Havenhurst, the cold reception she received when she arrived—even the disastrous infatuation she formed for the man she should never have married. Rolfe did not interrupt, even to ask questions, but Faith sensed in his silence none of the cold disdain he had shown her before. Gathering up her courage, she told him at last about Estee and the terrifying events of that evening.

By the time she finished, Rolfe was leaning forward, attentive and concerned.

"I wish you had trusted me before. Why didn't you tell me what was going on right from the beginning? If I had known Fleur was in danger, don't you think I would have helped?"

Faith's lashes glittered with unshed tears. "Oh, if only I could have! But I was afraid you wouldn't believe me. Besides, you never liked my sister. You told me so yourself."

"That isn't fair. I may not have been overly fond of Fleur, but I would never willingly stand by and let her come to harm. And I certainly wouldn't let you go off searching for her by yourself."

Faith settled back in the corner of the carriage and let her head rest against the window. Was he right? she asked herself wearily. Should she have trusted him that fateful day so long ago? What would her life be like now if she had?

"Oh, my dear, does that really matter? The past is over and done with. I couldn't change it even if I wanted to. What matters now is Estee—and the terrible things that are going to happen if we don't get her out of that place."

Rolfe did not waste time arguing. "You're right."

Sticking his head through the door again, he began to bark out orders in crisp, decisive tones. Faith did not recognize the names of the streets he ordered the coachmen to follow, but she did not try to question him. Rolfe was in charge now—strong, capable Rolfe—and she was ready to leave everything in his hands.

What a relief it was to lean back and let someone else make the decisions for a change. Faith had not realized how heavily the responsibility weighed on her own slender shoulders, and she was grateful to have someone to share it with now. She caught occasional glimpses of Rolfe's profile in the moonlight as the carriage lurched forward, and she could not help wondering what there was in this man that allowed him to be so generous and forgiving.

"Why are you doing this for me?" she asked. "Heaven knows, I've done nothing to warrant it. You don't even know that the girl is innocent. You only have my word for it."

"And you think I ought to suspect you of lying?" Faith could not see his features clearly, but she had the feeling he was smiling. "Oh, yes, my calculating little friend, I know perfectly well you're capable of the most outrageous fibs if it suits your purpose. But I don't think you're lying now, not about the girl at least. I haven't exactly been blind these past few weeks. I've watched fear and suspicion grow into mass hysteria, and I never once believed that the blacks were anything but scapegoats."

"And you don't think it's strange? The fact that I have a black friend?"

"Why should I?"

"I . . . I don't know. Because everyone else does, I guess. Because the slaves are . . . well, they're not like us. They're different."

"You mean, they're not human the way we are? They're some lower form of animal life? Come on, Faith, you don't believe that drivel any more than I do. You wouldn't have chosen a black woman for a friend if you did."

"No," she said softly. "No, I wouldn't."

She wished she could see him better in the darkness, but she could not. The carriage clattered on the cobbled pavement, jolting her roughly from side to side as the coachman steered it into a dirt lane. She could not keep her mind from turning back to the same fleeting thought that had crossed it before. Where would she be tonight, she wondered again, if she had had the courage to trust this man a year ago?

It was only a minute before the carriage wheels creaked to a stop in the narrow, unlighted side street. Not until Rolfe leaped to the ground and helped her down beside him did Faith recognize the place as one of the rutted lanes that led into the alley behind the jail. Shivering, she stepped closer to Rolfe, taking comfort in the reassuring warmth of his nearness. The gesture caught his attention, and taking off his coat, he slipped it over her shoulders.

"We haven't got much time," he said tensely. "I want to get everything clear before we make a move. When you were there before, how thoroughly did you check out the building?"

Faith pulled the coat tighter around her body. The urgency in his voice was as chilling as the wind.

"You mean the outside of the building?"

"Yes."

"Thoroughly."

"There was a door in front, you said—and another in back. Did you see any more?"

"No. And I would have seen them if they were there."

"What about windows?"

"None. . . . No, wait. There might have been some in front. High up, toward the roof. With bars on them."

"But none in the back?"

"No."

"And none on the sides?"

"No."

Rolfe took a step away from her. His hands on his hips, he peered into the darkness, as if he were trying to see through stone structures that blocked his view of the jail. When he turned back, he took hold of Faith's shoulders and pulled her close.

"Now, think very carefully. When you left the building, did you shut the door behind you?"

"Yes, I——" Faith caught her breath. As long as she lived, she would never forget that terrible crunching sound. "I slammed it."

"But you didn't lock it?"

"I couldn't. The bolt was on the other side."

"Try to remember." His voice was quiet, but strained. "Did you stand there? By the door? Even for a moment?"

"I think so. Not for long, but yes . . . I think so."

"Did you hear anything in the darkness behind you? Like the sound of a bolt being drawn?"

"No . . . No, I don't remember anything like that."

"Then maybe it's still open." Rolfe kept his voice steady as he put a firm hand on her waist and guided her into the alleyway. "It's worth a try anyway. Let's go."

They did not speak in the brief time it took them to reach the jail. Even then, they simply stood there, staring at a door that looked ominously sturdy in the dim light. When at last Rolfe raised his hand, Faith was so nervous she caught his wrist and held him back.

"Oh, Rolfe, what if—what if it's locked?"

"Then we'll have to think of something else. But let's not borrow trouble until we have to."

The wooden planks that formed the door were solid, but one of them had warped slightly, and Rolfe managed to get a grip on it. Faith watched tensely as he began to pull it slowly outward. It resisted for an instant, then swung noiselessly open.

They stood in the darkness outside, listening for anything that would tell them their intrusion had been discovered. When they heard nothing, Rolfe stepped cautiously inside, motioning for Faith to stay behind him.

The hallway was unexpectedly bright. Glancing over Rolfe's shoulder, Faith was surprised to see that the tallow candle had been moved from the front room and now rested on the floor beside Estee's cell. To her horror, she saw that the door was open.

"Oh, Rolfe——"

Rolfe raised a hand to silence her, but he was too late. A man appeared suddenly in the doorway, drawn out of the darkened cell by the unexpected sound. He had a long black whip coiled loosely in one hand.

Faith was too stunned to do anything more than stand there and stare at him. If it hadn't been for his clothes, she doubted that she would even have recognized him. His jaw was dark brown with drying blood, and livid circles had already begun to form around both eyes. A crouching posture gave him the deformed look of a hunchback.

Rolfe reacted swiftly. Hurtling his body at the startled jailor, he wrenched the whip out of his hand and hurled it with savage force across the floor. With a yelp of fear, the man raced down the corridor and into the front room. Rolfe was after him in a second.

By the time Faith managed to follow, the man had already reached the writing table and dragged it over to the side of the room. Flinging open one of the drawers, he began to claw through it in a desperate frenzy. When she saw his fingers close over the hilt of a knife, Faith realized what he was up to. Terrified, she let out a shrill shriek of warning.

Rolfe did not need her scream. He saw the knife as quickly as she and acted with sure instinct. Lashing out with his hand, he caught the man's wrist in a deathlike vise. His opponent gave a hoarse grunt of pain as Rolfe pinned him from behind and twisted the blade out of his grasp.

A sudden sound from the other outer doorway froze them all in a tableau of surprise. Horrified, Faith watched as the handle turned and the door moved slowly inward. Too late, she realized what had happened, and it was all her fault! What a fool she had been to believe the jailor when he told her no one would come if she screamed.

The soldier who stepped into the room had only a split second to blink in astonishment at the scene that met his eyes. Rolfe, knowing he could not take on both men at once, aimed the tip of his blade at the jailer's chest and gave it a sharp inward thrust. Yanking it out again, he threw his body against the startled soldier.

The man stumbled awkwardly under the impact. Faith did not wait to see what happened, but raced over to the door, slipping up from behind to close it before anyone could see inside. By the time she turned back, the struggle was already over and Rolfe was holding the man's gun on him. He had jammed the bloody knife into his waistband.

The soldier stood absolutely still, making no attempt to move. With a sinking heart, Faith recognized in him the older man who had challenged her outside. She had a feeling that any one of the other eleven soldiers would have been easier to handle.

If Rolfe had any such misgivings, he did not show them. He held the musket steady as he eyed the man.

"Just keep your hands up and everything will be fine. We only want the girl in there. We don't want to hurt anyone."

The man cast a glance at the bloody corpse on the floor, but he was shrewd enough not to say anything. Raising his hands, he let them rest lightly on top of his head.

"All right." Rolfe tilted the gun barrel toward the candlelit corridor. "In there. Nice and easy. No fast moves."

The three of them made a strange procession, the soldier first, his hands above his head, then Rolfe with the gun, and finally Faith. The man slowed after a few paces and threw a quizzical look over his shoulder. Rolfe jerked his head wordlessly toward the open side door.

Faith's heart skipped a beat as she watched the two men walk slowly into the room. She started to follow, but her feet grew heavy and she could not force herself to cross the threshold. It surprised her to realize that her palms were coated with sweat, and she knew suddenly that she was afraid to go inside.

Angrily, she squared her shoulders and forced herself through the doorway. Estee was her friend. She could not let Rolfe bear the burden of helping her alone.

The room was so dark, Faith could see nothing at first. Even when her eyes finally became adjusted and she made out a faint outline in the corner, she thought only that it was a pile of old rags someone had cast away. It was a moment before she realized the brown-clad figure huddled on a heap of matted straw was human.

Kneeling slowly, she looked down into features so empty they might as well have been carved of stone. Estee's eyes were open, but Faith could see no expression in those dark, haunting depths. Only the faint golden echo of flickering candlelight touched them with hints of life.

"My poor, poor Estee. What have they done to you?"

Leaning closer, Faith saw that the girl's skirt was not brown, as it had looked from a distance, but soft gray cotton, stiffened and stained with blood. In that terrible instant, she realized what had happened. Swaying faintly, she pressed her hand to the floor to steady herself. She had sensed when she stepped into that room that she would see things there she could not bear. But she had not known how agonizing they would be.

"Oh, Estee. . . ." Her heart ached for the pain she could

not ease. "I have come to help you, my dear. I'm going to get you out of this dreadful place."

Estee raised her head with an effort. Her lips moved, but her voice was so faint Faith had to bend over to hear it.

"I did not ask for your help."

The cold denial in her tone confused Faith. "I know you didn't, Estee, but I had to come. You don't understand. They'll kill you if we don't——"

"No, it's you who don't understand! You've never understood me, not from the day we met. I don't want you to get me out of here, and I won't thank you for it. If you have any mercy in your heart—if you have any trace of affection left for me—just go away and leave me here."

"And let you . . . die?"

Estee let her head sink back into the straw. "Why not? What's left but pain and regret? I don't want to live for that."

Faith faltered uncertainly. If she had learned anything these past bitter months, it was that death was not always the cruelest course for a slave. Still she found it abhorrent to give up.

Leaping to her feet, she turned to Rolfe. "I don't care what she says. She's too ill to know what she wants. We've got to get her out of here."

Rolfe nodded briskly. Still keeping his gun trained on the soldier, he crouched beside Estee. His eyes were worried as he studied her.

"Do you think she can walk?"

It was a futile question, and Faith sensed he knew it. "I doubt she can even move. I know it will make things harder, but we're going to have to carry her."

"Well, then, we'd better find something to wrap her in."

Faith searched the shadows with her eyes. "I don't see anything."

"There's a blanket in the corner," a rough, masculine voice broke in.

Faith was so startled, she jumped nervously. In her concern over Estee, she had completely forgotten the soldier. It was a relief to see that Rolfe still had the gun aimed at his chest.

"There's a blanket in the corner," the man repeated. "It isn't much, but it's all there is."

Faith stared at him in fascination. Was he being kind? she wondered. Or was he just biding his time, waiting for them to make a mistake?

Rolfe was asking himself the same question, only in his

case, it was more than idle curiosity. He had already figured out the one thing Faith had not yet considered—that they would be especially vulnerable when he had to lay down the gun to lift Estee in his arms. If the man was willing to stand aside, they would have no trouble. If he wasn't——

If he wasn't, there'd be the devil to pay. And there was only one way to find out.

Lowering the gun, Rolfe flipped it over and tossed it to Faith. She was startled, but recovered quickly. Catching it deftly in her hands, she pointed the barrel at the soldier.

"If he makes a move," Rolfe told her coldly, "you're going to have to shoot him. Can you do that?"

Faith nodded. She was not at all sure she could, but she sensed this was not the time to let her weakness show.

"Yes, I can do it."

"Then you'd better have this, too." Rolfe pulled out the knife and handed it to her. He would have liked to hang onto it himself, but common sense warned him it would only get in the way. "Put it in one of the coat pockets. I want you to keep your hands free for the gun."

He found the blanket just where the man had said it was, in a corner of the room. He picked it up and shook out the dust and filth as best he could. Dropping to one knee beside the slave girl, he wrapped it around her.

Estee gave a soft whimper, like the cry of a small animal in pain, but she was too weak to resist him as he drew her up in his arms. His body stiffened with anticipation when at last he turned his back on the soldier and began to move toward the door. If anything was going to happen, it would happen now.

Even though he was expecting it, the sound of the man's voice made him jump.

"You aren't gonna leave me here, mister? Not like this?"

Rolfe turned steadily to face him. This was the moment he had been waiting for, he was sure of it, but he still couldn't figure out what the man was up to.

"What do you expect me to do?"

"They'll string me up, sure as anything, if they think I let you go like this."

"And how am I supposed to convince them? Write out an affadavit for you? Swear you put up a good fight?"

"Naw." A slow grin spread across the man's face. "They're so dumb, they couldn't read it even if you did. Just rough me up a bit. Or let me have a scratch or two with that knife."

So that was it, Rolfe thought, drawing in a deep breath. He

couldn't risk getting close to the man, and the son-of-a-bitch knew it. But what else could he do? Give him the knife so he could draw blood himself? Could he trust Faith to react quickly enough if he tried to pull something?

But, dammit, what were the alternatives? Turn his back and walk out of there, and let the bastard holler his head off the minute they were out the door? Or shoot him in cold blood simply because he *might* betray them? What if he was telling the truth? What if he really was willing to risk his life for a suffering black slave?

"Oh, hell, Faith, give him the knife. Don't go near him. Just toss it on the ground at his feet."

Faith threw him a startled look, but she did not say anything. She had seen enough of Rolfe Stephens that night to know she trusted his judgment, no matter how dubious it might seem to her. Taking the knife out of her pocket, she slid it across the floor.

The man stood absolutely still, waiting for the weapon to come to a stop in front of him. Then, without a word, without so much as a change of expression, he bent down and picked it up.

Only then did he allow himself to grin again. It was, Faith thought, a maddening look, impudent, yet completely unfathomable. Lifting the knife slowly, he stared at the tip of the blade, as if he had not quite made up his mind what to do with it. Then with an abrupt movement, he drew it upward and slashed it across his cheek. Swinging his arm out, he tossed it into the hall.

"You better lock the door behind you. I wouldn't want anybody to ask why I didn't come after you, even grievous wounded like I am."

Faith did not wait to acknowledge his words. Rolfe was already in the hallway, and she followed as quickly as she could. It was all over, she kept telling herself again and again. It was over and they had saved Estee! Slamming the door behind her, she let herself lean on it for a second, shaking with fear and relief.

She had one last moment of panic when she reached down to turn the key in the lock and discovered it was not there. Horrified, she realized what must have happened. The jailor, when he opened the door and went in to Estee, had slipped it back in his pocket.

And if she was not going to betray the brave soldier who risked his life to help them, she was going to have to get it back.

Candlelight seeped through the hall doorway, illuminating the center of the front room, but the corner where the man's body lay in a crumpled heap was heavy in shadow. Faith had to grope with her toe to find the corpse in the darkness. Squatting down beside it, she forced herself to stretch out her hand.

She had expected the body to be cold, but it was not. The flesh that greeted her fingertips was warm and disturbingly lifelike. Choking with revulsion, she jammed her hand against her mouth to keep from retching. She could weep and swoon all she wanted to later, she told herself firmly. There was no time for feminine frailty now. Searching first one pocket, then another, she found what she was looking for.

Her legs were weak as she stood up, but her feet served her well, carrying her back down the corridor and toward the door again. The key turned so easily in the lock, it almost felt as if it had been greased. Faith did not wait to pull it out again, but left it where it was and made her way outside.

She felt free and exuberant as she joined Rolfe beside the carriage where it waited in the narrow side street. He had just settled Estee on one of the seats with the aid of the coachman and was turning back to find Faith when he saw her racing toward him. Even in the faint moonlight, he could tell that her eyes were shining with excitement.

"We did it, Rolfe," she cried out. "We really did it!"

"Yes, we did it."

He did not remind her, as he made a step out of his hands and boosted her into the carriage, of the price they had paid for their victory. Climbing in beside her, he put a reassuring arm around her. Time enough tomorrow for her to remember that they had had to kill a man to free her friend. Perhaps then she would remember, too, that he was a man who had earned his fate. He hoped so.

He shifted his arm, drawing her closer. She did not resist, but let herself sink into the shelter of his embrace.

Six

Faith snuggled into the corner of an oversize settee in Temperance Howe's front salon and tried not to think how tired she was. It was well into the early hours of the morning, and not a sound could be heard anywhere in the house. Rolfe was standing by a small table under the window, staring absent-mindedly at the *bric-a-brac* that cluttered its surface.

Faith kicked off her dancing slippers and tucked her feet underneath her. Thank heaven Rolfe was the kind of man she could feel comfortable with. She did not think she could have found the energy to sit up like a proper lady, or worry about whether her bare legs were showing.

"Rolfe, do you think we did the right thing?"

Rolfe looked older as he turned to face her. She could see deep creases in the skin around his mouth, and the candle-light cast dark shadows under his eyes.

"I think we did the *only* thing we could."

And, of course, Faith thought with a sigh, he was right. They had taken Estee immediately to the harbor and hidden her aboard Thomas Stephens' ship, lying at anchor just off the shore. But even then, they had been uneasy about her safety. It could be as long as a month before Rolfe was ready to return to England, and in that time, the black girl's presence would be difficult to conceal. It was Rolfe who had suggested that he order the captain to sail south, delivering the girl to Charles Town and the man who legally owned her.

Faith had agreed at the time. Now she was not so sure.

"It seems so risky."

"No riskier than keeping her here."

"I suppose not," she conceded reluctantly. In truth, perhaps she was making overmuch of the whole thing. When the captain docked in South Carolina, he would send Faith's hastily penned note to Havenhurst, and then it would be up to Brad. If he felt enough time had elasped since the ill-fated rebellion, he could smuggle Estee home and keep her there. If not, the captain would simply bring her back to New York, arriving just in time to embark again for England.

Brad. Faith ran her hands across her forehead, lightly massaging her temples. Why did it always seem to come back to him? Why was it he she always relied on? She began to wonder if she hadn't agreed to Rolfe's scheme only because it gave her an excuse to contact Brad again.

Rolfe did not miss the pallor in her cheeks. "Are you worried about this man? This Alleyn? Are you afraid you can't trust him?"

Faith glanced up, startled. "No, of course not. Brad can be trusted. With Estee's safety at least."

"But you are concerned about something."

"Am I?" Faith smiled wearily. "How do you know me so well, dear friend? Yes, I am concerned, but not about the way Brad will receive Estee. I was just trying to picture the look on his face when he opens that note and sees whom it's from. I'm not exactly the most popular young lady in the Colonies, you know. If I treated you abominably in New York, can you imagine the way I behaved when I got off at the dock in Havenhurst and saw that Fleur wasn't there? I was half out of my mind with worry, of course, but . . . well, Brad is not as forgiving as you."

Rolfe's eyes did not leave her face. "And you're still worried, aren't you? About Fleur?"

Faith looked down quickly. He was getting too close to secrets she was not ready to share. Not even with him.

"No, not really. I—I don't know where she is, of course. But that isn't unusual. My sister has always been casual about her comings and goings. Anyhow, wherever she is, I am sure she is not in trouble now. I would know if she were."

"Yes, I suppose you would. It's uncanny, that bond you and Fleur always had. I suppose it makes me nervous because I can't understand it."

He reached down idly and, picking up one of the curios on the table, turned it over in his hands. Faith got up, stretching out her legs, and went over to him. As she drew near, she saw that he was holding a miniature of a laughing, blue-eyed girl in a jeweled frame.

"What a lovely girl!" she said, genuinely entranced. "I wonder who she is."

"Miss Temperance, I suspect. When she was young. Funny, it never occurred to me she might have been pretty."

Faith took the portrait from his hands and studied it pensively. Could this really be the same sweet, elderly, slightly frivolous face she had seen over the tea table only the afternoon before? What a cruel thief time was.

"I wonder why we struggle so," she said softly. "We rail against the gods, we fight our fates—and we try so desperately to make something of our lives. And everything only fades in the end."

Rolfe took the picture from her and set it firmly on the table again.

"What's this? Are those tears I detect in your voice? Don't tell me I've made you sad. That's the last thing in the world I wanted to do."

"No, it's not you. It's not you at all. It's just that. . . ." She turned away, unable to bear his eyes on her face. "Oh, Rolfe, it hurt so much, seeing Estee like that. If you'd known her before, you'd understand. She had a kind of—I wish I knew how to describe it—a kind of dark fire blazing in her eyes. I know that sounds silly, but it's true. It's a terrible thing to see all that fierce pride broken."

Rolfe laid a gentle hand on her cheek, easing her face toward him again. When Faith looked up, she saw that his eyes were questioning.

"What about you? Your pride? Has that been broken, too?"

"My . . . pride?"

"You didn't tell me much about your marriage, but it's obvious that it's been a painful experience. One that has left your heart badly wounded. What about your pride? Your self-esteem? Are they wounded, too?"

He had hit too close to the mark. Faith tried to pull herself together, but she could not keep a single tear from slipping down her cheek.

"I—I'm sorry. I don't know what's wrong with me tonight. I didn't mean to——"

"Shhhh."

He touched his fingers lightly to her lips. Placing a firm hand on her waist, he led her over to the settee. He waited until he was sure she was comfortable, then sat beside her and took her hands in his.

"It might help if you told me about it."

"Oh, my dear, I wish I could! You have no idea how awful it was. How humiliating."

She drew away, pulling her hands back into her lap. The silver lace that edged her skirt felt soft and delicate as she twisted it in her fingers.

"It wasn't always bad. I wouldn't want you to think that. Alexandre is the handsomest man I've ever seen in my life. And he was very charming, at least at the beginning. I could hardly believe he was really interested in me. And that, of course, was the whole trouble. He *wasn't* interested. He never loved me at all."

"No?" Rolfe kept his voice light, trying to tease her out of her melancholy. "What a cold, unfeeling man he must be, not to succumb to such sweet charms."

"Not cold at all. Or unfeeling. He simply didn't care for me."

"He must have cared, Faith. He asked you to marry him."

"No, not *me!*" The words burst out of her mouth in a torrent of pain and anger. "Not me at all—Fleur! He loved Fleur from the very beginning. He only proposed to me because he couldn't have her."

Rolfe leaned back against the arm of the settee. He remembered Fleur too well to doubt what Faith was telling him. Sly little vixen that she was, she would have known exactly how to keep a man from forgetting her.

"Do you know, I've often thought young women shouldn't be allowed to marry men they find devastatingly handsome. A head filled with girlish daydreams—that's hardly fertile ground for good judgment, is it?"

Faith tried to smile, but she did not succeed. "If that were all there was to it, I wouldn't mind so much. I'm not the first woman whose husband didn't love her on their wedding day, and I'm sure I won't be the last. I know I could have won him over in the end if—if. . . ."

She paused long enough to take a steadying breath. It was funny how hard it was to force the words out of her mouth.

"You see, Rolfe, my husband is mad."

Slowly, painfully, she related all the sordid details of a relationship that had moved gradually from the promise of heaven to the reality of a private hell on earth. By the time she had finished, she was so drained of emotion, her voice was barely audible.

"Now he just sits there, beside the window in his room. The room that used to be his before we were married. He just sits and looks out, and never says a word to anyone."

The despair in her tone was more than Rolfe could tolerate. Rising from the settee, he paced agitatedly toward the window. His hands were clasped behind him, his head and shoulders thrust forward as he stared into the inky darkness.

"With God as my witness, Faith, I had no idea things were like that. If I had——"

He broke off abruptly, clenching his hand into a fist and ramming it against the wall in frustration. When he turned to her again, his face was set and determined.

"I'm going back to England in three weeks. Four at most. I want you to come with me."

Faith shook her head. "There's nothing in England for me now. I can't impose on Uncle Andrew anymore, and I have no one else to turn to."

"But you do have someone. Haven't you figured that out yet? Surely, you didn't think I was going to let you get away again." Rolfe paused, smiling at the confusion in her eyes. "I am offering you marriage if we can arrange some kind of annulment for you. If not, then the closest thing to marriage we can have."

"Oh, Rolfe. . . ." Faith wished he were not quite so sweet. It only made things harder. "Do you know what kind of life that would be? For you as well as me? They have names for men who throw their lives away on women beneath them, and they are not at all complimentary."

Rolfe did not flinch. "I hope it won't come to that, but if it does, I am prepared to face it. I love you, darling. I want to live with you and share the rest of my life with you. If that's all I can ever give, won't it be enough?"

Faith could not bring herself to look at him. It was tempting, this tender devotion he offered her now. It would be so easy to let herself give in.

Rolfe sensed both her yearning and her fear. "Trust me, sweet Faith, I will always take care of you. I will build a home for you and love the children you bear me and cherish you until the day I die. I will never fail you or desert you."

Oh, yes, it would be incredibly easy just to let go. If only he would touch her the way he had touched her once before, kiss her the way her lips longed to be kissed, all her fears, all her doubts would be no more than memories.

She looked up, meeting his gaze at last.

She whispered, "Come and hold me in your arms and make me forget everything else."

But this was no Brad Alleyn, ready to play on her sensual needs. "No, Faith. Not like that. I love you dearly—and I want you very much—but this is the rest of our lives I'm talking about. It has to feel as right to you as it does to me.

You are confused now and, I think, frightened. I would be an unspeakable cad if I took advantage of that."

He crossed the room to stand beside her. Bending down, he took hold of her hands again.

"I'm confusing you even more, aren't I? I'm sorry, I hadn't meant to do that. I'm not going to press you to make up your mind today. Or tomorrow. You have a whole month before I'm ready to set sail . . . and longer if you need it."

He touched gentle lips to her forehead in a farewell salute. Then, letting go of her hands, he turned and walked out of the room. His footsteps sounded soft and far away in the hallway. The front door opened, then closed again, and all that was left was the silence.

Faith sat alone, long after Rolfe had gone, trying to piece together her thoughts. The darkness began to soften, so subtly at first she barely noticed hints of gray showing at the window. It was a pretty picture, she thought wistfully—the one that Rolfe had painted for her. A comfortable home in her beloved England, children to love and take care of, a man at her side who would adore her the rest of her days. Could anyone blame her for wanting to accept that?

And would it truly be so wrong?

She got up restlessly, wandering over to the table beneath the window. Picking up the dainty miniature, she ran her fingers up and down the frame. Would it truly be wrong to forget Fleur and the mystery she had not been able to solve anyway? Wrong to abandon a husband who had never loved her? Perhaps Rolfe was right. Given the bizarre circumstances of her marriage, she might be able to get an annulment. And if she could——

If she could, then what? Brutally, Faith forced herself to face the truth. Annulment or not, it wasn't going to make any difference. Not when Alexandre wasn't the problem.

Sighing, she looked down, surprised to see that she was still holding the miniature portrait in her hands. Lovely Temperance. So vivacious—and so young. She wondered if she would be like that one day, too. A girl in a miniature that people looked at and said, "Was Faith Eliot ever that pretty?"

Setting the picture down, she stepped back to the window. There was just enough light to make out faint details of the quiet morning street. No, Alexandre was not the problem, she thought sadly. He was not the problem at all. She touched her fingers to the glass, tracing out the diamond shapes of the panes, and remembered that day more than a year ago when the hot Carolina sun beat down on her back as she stepped out of a dugout canoe onto alien soil. If she closed her eyes now and looked into her memory, she knew she would still see a tall, broad-shouldered man riding like a savage out of the hills, the wind whipping sun-streaked hair away from his face.

Turning back into the room, she stared at the comfortable, familiar furnishings and wished she could feel like she belonged there. At last she admitted to herself the one thing she should have known all along. There was no running away from Havenhurst. No running away from her sister's memory. Or from the man she dared not admit she loved. She would never be able to pick up the pieces of her life, not with Rolfe, not with any other man, until she had resolved her feelings for Brad once and for all.

And to do that, she was going to have to go back to Havenhurst.

Once the decision had been made, Faith was surprised how coolly she reacted. She went out into the hall and, pulling open the drawer of the sidetable, began to search for a blank sheet of paper. She had left Rolfe once before without so much as a word; she would not treat him so callously again. Besides, she had to leave a note for Jakob and Temperance, too.

She rummaged hastily through the drawer, pulling out papers and paraphernalia and scattering them on top of the table. If she had had any sense, she berated herself impatiently, she would have stayed on board ship last night with Estee. Still, if she hurried, it might not be too late. Surely the captain would not attempt to leave the crowded harbor before it was fully light.

A piece of paper caught her eye, and Faith pulled it out, scowling when she saw that it was only an old letter. The gossipy note to Frances Jennaway, no doubt, she thought, amused. It was amazing the clutter Temperance managed to cram into one small drawer. She was about to toss it aside when she got a better look at the address.

For all her haste, she could not resist pausing to smile. Not the letter to Frances at all, but the one to Cousin Julia. The one Temperance had been looking for so diligently yesterday. Faith propped it up against a silver pitcher where someone would be certain to see it and turned back to the drawer.

When another letter showed up a few seconds later, she glanced at it curiously, certain she had found the elusive missive to Frances this time. But the instant she saw the name scrawled across the surface, all thought of her hostess's idiosyncracies vanished from her mind. The color drained from her face as she stared down at it in silence.

It was addressed in Temperance's spidery hand:

To Adam Eliot
Havenhurst Plantation
The Colony of South Carolina

Faith did not know why, but suddenly her hand began to tremble, and she realized she was dreading the idea of having to open the letter and see what lay inside. It was silly, of course—it could be nothing more than one of those chatty notes Temperance kept around for years and years—but still, she did not like the looks of it. Turning it over, she noted the discolored appearance of the old wax on the seal. A crack ran down the center of it, a sharp, whitish line that made it look as if it had been broken recently.

Slowly, she opened it and began to read:

My dear, dear Adam—

Such a long way away, dear boy—I wonder if this will ever reach you. They do say the southern Colonies are rather primitive. Are you sure you want to stay there? But then, of course you are. You were always a young man to know your own mind.

We had Desirée's cousin, that odd Jeremy (now what is his last name? Ashton?) with us for a while. Frankly, dear, I can't say I like him at all. You know I don't like to speak ill of anyone, especially a relation of your wife's (though now you are estranged, of course, so perhaps it is not the same thing), but I really can't believe he is quite nice.

Do you know, I think he's plotting against someone. One of your neighbors, I daresay, for he seems to be spending most of his time in your part of the world these days. I overheard him talking with a rather scabby-looking gentleman in the study one night last week when he thought everyone was asleep. Jakob says I am probably imagining things (and I daresay he's right—Jakob usually is), but it definitely sounded to me like he was up to no good. He talked about having some papers made up ("forged" I think is the word he used, though Jakob says I don't always hear things right). Papers that would make it look as if he owned something or had bought something when he really hadn't, if you know what I mean.

And then he said (and I'm sure I heard this right), "When I get through with the beggar,"—only of course he didn't say beggar, but you know what I mean—"he won't be in any position to dispute my claim." Now what on earth do you imagine he meant by that?

Well, I suppose Jakob is right and I'm just a silly old woman, but I thought you ought to know anyway. I had better go now and see that Jakob sends this off, because if I don't, you know me, I never will, and it will just sit around for years gathering mildew on the corners.

All our love, mine and Jakob's both,
Your devoted friend,
T. Howe

For a minute Faith was too stunned to move. All she could do was stand there, staring down at the letter in her hand, and try to let it all sink in. It was a vague note, rambling and disoriented, as only Temperance could be, but there was no denying its import.

Slowly, all the bits and pieces began to come together.

Jeremy and Havenhurst. The thief and his plunder. How blind she had been not to see it before. Adam Eliot was not a man to lose a plantation through carelessness or poor management—even his enemies admitted that. But Jeremy was just the man to steal it from him! Faith thought of her father's death, a strong swimmer drowning in a river he knew like the back of his own hand, and she realized with a cold sense of finality just what Jeremy had meant when he said the beggar would never be able to dispute his claim.

Faith refolded the letter automatically and put it back in the drawer. At last she knew what Fleur had found in New York—and why she had gone to Havenhurst.

The thought made her feel sick inside. She knew her sister so well. She knew exactly what went on inside that devious mind of hers. If Jeremy Alleyn stole Havenhurst, she would have said to herself, then it was never really his. Not legally.

And Brad wasn't the rightful owner now.

That was a challenge Fleur could never have ignored. She would have gone to the Carolina Colonies determined to stake her claim on the vast lands that stretched along the riverbank, no matter how she had to do it. And there she would have found a man equally determined to stop her.

Adam Eliot had died trying to hold on to the plantation he had forged out of the wilderness. Had his daughter's life, too, been forfeit to that same lust for land?

V

THE PATHS OF YESTERDAY

One

Harvest season was the gayest time of year at Havenhurst. The air was crisp and cool, and the shimmering white light of summer had already begun to mellow into a soft, tawny amber. Faith sat on a low split-rail fence beside the narrow footpath that twisted down to the river and watched a long line of dark-skinned girls carry sheaves of rice up from the fields. They made a pretty picture. Patterned skirts of red, gold, and green billowed around their ankles, and brightly colored kerchiefs accented jet-black tresses. Bundles of grain were balanced on their heads, yet they moved with easy, graceful motions as if their burdens were too light to notice. The sound of laughter and song filled the air.

It felt strange to be at Havenhurst again. Everything was exactly the same, yet not the same at all. Sometimes, when Faith sat on the piazza at sunset and closed her eyes, taking in the smell of the gardens, the marshes, the fields, she could almost imagine she had never gone away. But the next morning, when she stepped into a silent dining room to get her breakfast, she knew the elderly man who stood at the sideboard ready to serve her would be a stranger. And a little, wraithlike figure, hunched over her table in the sewing room down the hall, would bear absolutely no resemblance to the giggling, half-witted child she had known before.

No, it was not the same at all, she thought with a sigh. The *things* had not changed, but the people had, and it was the people that gave a place its essential character. Cuffee, Fibby, Estee, Beneba . . . Brad.

Faith wriggled uncomfortably on the fence, feeling the rough rails dig into her legs. Brad. Of all the changes she had found at Havenhurst, it was the changes in him that hurt the most. If he had been furious with her when she came back, if he had railed and shouted, if he had glowered at her and made those horrible, biting, sarcastic comments he was so good at, she would have been able to deal with it. But Brad had done nothing of the kind. He had simply stared at her with the iciest eyes she had ever seen, made a few polite remarks about the weather, and mounted his horse and rode away.

It was, she thought miserably, almost as if he had to search his memory even to recall who she was. As if she had had absolutely no impact on his life one way or the other.

Sliding down from the fence, she fluffed out the ruffles in the skirt of her becoming, hyacinth-hued gown. Sometimes it seemed so unfair. She was the one with cause to be suspicious of him, yet here he was, making her feel clumsy and uncertain, like a spoiled child who had pulled one prank too many and gotten on everyone's nerves.

The procession of laughing slave girls had passed, and the river path was momentarily empty. Faith began to stroll down it, following its winding turns toward the fields that lay along the bank. Walking at a leisurely pace, it took her twenty minutes to reach them.

The rice paddies, tidy squares separated by high banks, were bustling hives of energy and vitality. The water had been drained several days before, and shining patches of mud alternated with dull, parched earth. Faith lingered for a few minutes and watched, marveling at how different the plantation could look at different times of year.

Everywhere she cast her eyes, the fields were alive with movement. Reapers with sickles, sharpened until their edges gleamed in the sun, swept methodically through the long rows of flowing grain. To Faith, the steady, rhythmic motion of their arms seemed as graceful as the soaring path of an eagle in flight. Groups of men followed, stooping to gather up golden heads of grain and lay them on the stubble to dry. For the next few days, Faith knew, everyone on the plantation would pray it would not rain, for the fragile rice crop was as vulnerable now as it had been in the earliest days of spring planting.

As the grain dried, the women bundled it into sheaves. Wrapping sturdy arms around each bundle, one of them would hold it while another tied it with a wisp of rice. As soon as they had finished, waiting girls caught up the sheaves and tossed them with a careless laugh onto their heads. Splashing bare feet through the last of the puddles, they clambered up on the banks and headed for the barn. Only in the far distant fields was it necessary to pile the rice on large, flat-bottomed boats and pole it up river.

Faith watched for a while and wondered how she could ever have thought the harvest was a simple process, when in reality it was made up of hundreds of complex details. Wearying at last, she turned and began to wander up the hill, leaving the path to cut through fields of half-tamed grasses and gaily colored wild flowers. She had just paused to catch her breath when she noticed a black woman standing under a lone oak overlooking the river. She was so still and silent, Faith almost passed without seeing her.

It was a moment before she recognized in the stooped shoulders and bowed head, features that had once been fiery and proud. It was, Faith thought sadly, heartbreaking to see her friend like this, yet she hadn't the vaguest notion what to do about it. Ever since Estee had returned to Havenhurst, she had been so subdued and unapproachable, she almost seemed a stranger.

Faith went up to her quietly, not wanting to startle her with too sudden a movement.

"It's pretty, isn't it?" she said softly. "The river this time of year. Isn't it fascinating the way the afternoon sun strikes it. It almost looks as if there were molten gold floating on the surface."

Estee did not move, but continued to stare at the river with expressionless eyes.

"My mother died there. Did you know that? In that same dark water."

A cool breeze rose from the river and swept across the open meadow. Faith could not help remembering the night Brad told her how Adam Eliot had died.

"Was she with my father? When he drowned?"

Estee turned, but her eyes did not focus. It was as if she were looking at Faith but did not truly see her.

"Yes. They died together."

Without another word, she bent down and, picking up a bucket half hidden in the tall grasses, began to walk away. Faith was conscious, as she watched her friend skirt the formal gardens and disappear behind the house, of a mounting sense of frustration.

It seemed to her nothing had gone right since the day she returned to Havenhurst. Not a single thing had worked out the way she had hoped. She was not one whit closer to proving what she already *knew* about Fleur; she could not begin to communicate with a husband who retreated farther and farther into madness every day; she was so estranged from her lover, she doubted they would ever share anything again; and now, as if all that weren't enough, she couldn't even find a word of solace for the young woman whose life she had saved at the risk of her own.

Gusts of teasing wind caught her skirts and whipped them up around her knees. With a startled laugh, Faith flung out her arms and pulled them down again. The distraction did her good, and she was wise enough to know it. If she stood there long enough, staring at the river and thinking how unhappy she was, she would end up every bit as moody as Estee. It seemed to her a foolish waste of a lovely day, especially with all the fascinating rites of autumn going on around her.

Besides, she reminded herself with a wry smile, if she was right, if Havenhurst really *was* ill-gotten Alleyn booty, one day this might all be hers. It would be improvident not to learn about it while she could.

Making her way across the hillside, she picked up a narrow footpath that led around a bend in the river. Sounds of merriment drifted up from the shore below. Looking down, Faith saw that a flat-bottomed barge had been tied to the dock. Hordes of half-naked children raced up and down the banks, laughing at the top of their lungs. The workers ignored them as they tugged sheaves of rice off a seamingly endless mound and tossed them onto the ground.

The flat was larger than Faith had expected. Fifty or sixty feet long, she judged, and no less than ten feet wide. She wished she had come early enough to watch them bring it in to the dock. There must have been at least a dozen sturdy black boatmen, propelling it with long poles on each side. The unwieldy craft was steered by an oar at the stern.

The grain the workers were heaping on the shore was June rice, planted late in the spring season. It had been a good crop, and there was an abundant supply to be carted up from the banks to the barn, where it would be left to dry for at least a month. Faith laughed aloud as she stood on the hillside and watched. Some of the bundles were so huge, they looked like golden haystacks with skinny brown legs and bare feet sticking out from underneath them.

When she reached the barn, Faith saw that it had been cleared to receive the new harvest, and the April rice had been spread out in a threshing yard at the side. The bulk of the work, she realized, was just beginning. The rice still had to be threshed and winnowed, husked and cleaned, before it was ready to be sorted into three groups: some to be used in the kitchens and slave cottages of the plantation, some to be sold, some to be set aside as seed for next year's planting.

Faith positioned herself at the side of the yard, taking care not to get in the way, and watched with fascination.

It was an arduous, primitive process. Black workers, cheerful despite the backbreaking work, sang and joked with each other as they picked up sheaves of rice, one at a time, and whipped them over a log until golden grains lay scattered on the ground. Across the yard, where the earth had been tamped down until it was as smooth as a clay floor, other slaves were busy beating the last grains of rice off the straw with long flails.

When they had finished with each batch, it was brought to the women to be winnowed. Some of the hands that clutched wide baskets, woven with strange African designs, were so old and gnarled Faith was sure they would never be able to manage. Yet they worked with an endurance that amazed her. Fanning their baskets back and forth, back and forth again, they patiently sifted the chaff from the rice.

The final task, cleaning the rice, would last well into the long winter months. This, too, would be women's work, for the male field hands would be occupied with more strenuous chores: clearing new fields for next year's harvest perhaps, or repairing sluices and canals. Faith stepped closer, watching the women scoop handfuls of rice into crude mortars, hollowed out of the ends of upright cypress logs. This they pounded with wooden pestles, using the sharp end to remove the husks and the flat end to polish and whiten the rice.

At the far side of the yard, partially blocking the gate to the road, stood a bulky farm wagon, bearing the oddest looking contraption Faith had ever seen. It was, she concluded after careful consideration, a machine of some sort, though what its purpose could be she hadn't the faintest notion. No one else seemed to know either, for apart from an occasional sidelong glance, the slaves in the threshing yard completely ignored it.

Faith went over to it curiously, stopping only when she caught sight of Brad on the other side. He was talking to one of the neighboring planters, a dour, uncommunicative man named Jim Burden.

Faith rested her hand on the gate and watched them. Burden was a perfect foil for Brad, his stocky frame and dark hair emphasizing the other man's lean, muscular good looks and golden vitality. When Faith saw her lover like this, his hair turning to fire in the sunlight, his strong features animated and full of excitement, she could not help feeling once again the same compelling magnetism that had drawn her toward him in the first place.

She was surprised to realize that her hand was trembling on the rough wooden gate. She was tempted to turn and walk away before the men noticed her, but she forced herself to hold her ground. She had let Brad Alleyn intimidate her far too much as it was. If she was ever going to accomplish her purpose at Havenhurst, she was going to have to come to terms with him sooner or later.

She called out to the men as she approached.

"What on earth is that? I don't think I've ever seen anything quite so ungainly. It looks like a madman's nightmare."

Brad looked none too pleased to see her, but Burden greeted her with an unexpected smile.

"Peter Villepontoux' new invention," he told her. "Yes, it does look like a nightmare, doesn't it? But it's an ingenious device, or so they say. I left my own harvest and rode all the way over here, hoping Brad would give me a demonstration. But as usual, he's too blasted stubborn."

"Not stubborn at all," Brad protested with a grin. "Just sensible. I've got enough on my mind right now without taking on something new. The confounded machine couldn't have arrived at a worse time if they'd planned it that way. But come back in three or four weeks, when the harvest is over, and I'll show it to you then. If I've figured out how it works, that is!"

Faith looked from one to the other, perplexed. "But what is it?" she insisted. "I'm sure the two of you know what you're talking about, but I haven't the slightest idea. What does that thing do, anyway?"

"It's a threshing machine," Brad explained. "An invention of the future, I daresay, though it certainly doesn't look like it. Still, clumsy as the thing is, they claim it can clean five thousand pounds of rice a day with the aid of two horses. If you use four horses, you can clean a thousand pounds an hour."

"Not a bad investment for sixty English pounds," Burden broke in.

Faith studied the machine skeptically. "I'm not sure I know what all those numbers mean. Is that a lot of rice to clean, a thousand pounds an hour?"

Brad laughed. "Put it this way—one woman with a mortar and pestle can clean three pecks a day. If she's fast."

Faith's eyes narrowed as she continued to stare at the machine. Invention of the future or not, it was hard to believe such a ponderous contraption could ever replace all those industrious slaves in the yard.

By the time she turned around again, the two men had ambled away, moving toward the fence post where Burden had hitched his horse. Faith waited until Brad bade farewell to his guest, then began to move toward him, running her hand along the rail as she walked. This was the first time she had caught him in an expansive mood since she had returned from New York, and she was determined not to let him go.

Brad remained where he was, waiting as she drew near, but a new tension in his bearing warned her he had hoped she would be gone before Burden took his leave. She cast about in her mind, trying to think of something clever to say, then gave it up as a hopeless cause. Besides, with a man like Brad, a direct approach was the best.

She stopped a few feet away from him.

"You're sorry, aren't you? That I came back?"

Her candor caught him off guard. "Sorry? Why should I be?" Propping one foot against the lower rail, he leaned on the fence and stared into the yard. "Your husband is here, such as he is. This is your home. Where else would you go?"

His coldness hurt more than Faith had expected. She paused for a moment, listening to the dull, rhythmic sound of pestles grinding grain against the gouged-out wood of tree stumps.

"Where indeed?" she said at last.

He caught the weariness in her voice and turned to her with a searching glance. "You should have come over five minutes sooner," he said in kinder tones. "If I had known you were around, I would have sent someone to fetch you. Burden brought some interesting news."

"News?" The sudden change in conversation confused Faith. "But I know so little about this area. What could he have to say that would interest me?"

"It wasn't about the area. He had a visitor recently. From New York."

"From . . . New York?" Faith caught her breath. Could Jim Burden possibly have found out where she had stayed in New York? Or what she learned while she was there? "What kind of news did this visitor bring?"

"Only one kind of news comes from New York of late," Brad said grimly. "But this time at least the news is good. It's all over, they say. The hangings, the burnings . . . the panic that threatened to destroy the city. They've put an end to it at last."

For a moment, Faith could not understand what he was talking about. "You mean . . . the arson conspiracy? But it can't be over! I was there. I saw it. Madness like that doesn't go away overnight."

"Ah, but it has. It was a moment of hysteria, my dear. A summer fever that came with the first hot days and left with the cooling touch of autumn. Trust me, it *is* over. The city is returning to normal. People are already talking about fashionable balls and the ridiculous price of imported tea. And whether they should send for a new carriage from the Continent or make do for another year with the one they have."

"But how? How did it end?"

"Much the way it began, I gather. With that girl. That indentured servant. Mary . . . uh. . . ."

"Mary Burton. The Common Council offered a hundred pounds to anybody who would expose the 'conspiracy' and she grabbed at it."

"Yes, well, I suspect the good gentlemen of the Common Council were only too glad to pay her off and be quit of her once and for all! It seems Little Miss Mary had rather a bolder imagination than they bargained for. When she saw how well she was doing with tales of black conspiracy, she decided to try pointing her finger at a few whites as well."

"At whites, too? But how could she get away with that?"

"She couldn't. She started with a clergyman, one suspected of being a papist—you know, an emissary of the Jesuits, sent to stir up violence in the English Colonies—so nobody paid her much heed. But when she started to take on men of substance, that, of course, was that. After all, a Jesuit is one thing. But good God! A prominent citizen!"

Faith shuddered. "You sound so cynical, Brad. As if you find it all amusing."

"Do I? Ah, the cold, heartless beast with no feeling for another's pain. Well, maybe you're right at that. Maybe I have gotten cynical of late. But I ask you, what the deuce is a man supposed to do when he's faced with nonsense like that except laugh at it?"

He fell into a moody silence. Faith took a step back and studied him with probing eyes. Sometimes, when he was cold and aloof, she could look at him and not mind so much that he might be her sister's killer. But other times, like now, when she caught a rare, fleeting glimpse of the man beneath that hardened facade, she could think only how deeply she cared for him.

He turned and caught her staring at him.

"What a strange look, Mrs. Juilliard. What are you thinking, I wonder."

"I was just thinking——" She caught herself with an ironic smile. What would he do, she wondered, if she looked him right in the eye and said, Did you kill my sister? "I was thinking about Fleur. You told me once you didn't like her. Do you dislike me, too?"

"If I said yes, would it make the least bit of difference to you?"

Faith looked away, hurt. "That's not fair, Brad."

"Isn't it? You and your sister are exactly alike. You seem to think that men are puppets to be pulled around on strings. Did you seriously believe I would forgive all manner of caprice simply because you are beautiful? Or did it perhaps cross that devious little mind of yours that I wouldn't be able to find another lovely, winsome wench anywhere in the Colony?"

Something in the way he lingered on the words *lovely* and *winsome* made Faith uncomfortable. She could not forget how bluntly he had warned her, the day she left for New York, that he would waste no time taking another mistress.

"Are you trying to tell me there's someone here you fancy?" she snapped tartly. "Who is the lucky lady? Samuel Hardin's plump little niece? Or one of Eleazar Carstairs' anemic daughters?"

The barb did not work. Brad's laughter was much too easy and confident.

"Haven't I told you? We have a charming new woman in the neighborhood. Lord Warren's sister. She came here to settle her son's affairs, and much to everyone's surprise, decided to stay on and run Oakwood herself. The Lady Elizabeth has two qualities I'm afraid you know little about. Courage and character."

Faith's cheeks reddened with indignation. The Lady Elizabeth indeed! No doubt she was every inch a proper lady, too!

"How—how . . . *prim* she sounds! Just your type. I suppose she is pretty, too."

"Oh, did I forget to mention it? Lady Elizabeth is the most beautiful woman I have ever seen in my life."

The words landed like a lump in the pit of Faith's stomach. She knew it was ridiculous to be jealous—she had no hope of a future with this man anyway—but the very idea of him with another woman was enough to make her physically ill.

"I hope—I hope you and Lady Elizabeth will be very happy!"

She hated herself for the childish way she whirled around and stomped away from him, but she could not help it. She had known all along that sooner or later Brad would find someone else, but that didn't make it any easier to bear.

Miserably, she wandered around the side of the house and into the narrow meadow that separated the street, where the blacks lived, from the rest of the plantation. She felt as if she had worked herself into a corner, and she could see no way to get out of it. Even if her worst fears proved groundless—even if she learned that Alexandre or someone else had killed Fleur—what would it matter if Brad had already begun a new life with someone else?

She sat down on the cold ground and tucked her skirt around her legs to keep the uncut grass from scratching her ankles. Now more than ever it was imperative to find out what had happened to Fleur, yet with each passing day the truth seemed farther and farther away. She had been so sure, when she came back, that the knowledge of what had brought Fleur to Havenhurst would solve all her questions. But far from solving anything, she realized now, that knowledge had only created new questions of its own. They were the same questions that must have faced her sister.

Faith rested her cheek on her knees and tried to imagine what Fleur would have done when she arrived at the plantation. Would she have accosted Brad, demanding to see the papers that supported Jeremy's claim to Havenhurst? But that was foolish, and Fleur had never been a fool. Even if Brad turned the papers over to her, how could she prove they were forgeries after all these years? And where would she find anyone willing to testify on her behalf?

No, Fleur would not have gone to Brad—not when that would only tip her hand. She would have looked for something else, some hard, tangible piece of evidence. But what could it have been? And what would she have done with it even if she found it?

Faith got up slowly, brushing broken ends of grass out of her skirt. That was the question of questions, wasn't it? What *would* Fleur have done with the evidence? How could she turn it to her advantage? It was all well and good to sit in New York and think lovely, melodramatic thoughts about being an heiress, but in reality, things did not work quite that way. Adam Eliot had owned only half of Havenhurst, the share he acquired through his marriage to Desirée. The other half had belonged to Olivier, and Jeremy, as Olivier's nearest male kin, had a good claim on that. Who would have won in a legal battle, Faith wondered: Jeremy's younger brother, a man who had already proven he could run the plantation efficiently—or Adam's daughter, an inexperienced woman without a husband to press her claim in court?

Faith pulled a stalk of grass out of the earth and ripped it apart in her fingers as she stared idly at the river. The more she thought about it, the more hopeless everything seemed. The sun was sinking behind pine forests on the hill, and the golden water had deepened until it was a melancholy thread of darkness winding through the fields.

She died there, did you know that? They died together.

The wind rose, cutting sharp ripples into the placid surface of the river. Adam and Katherine, her father and Estee's mother—lovers, for all that the thought made both their daughters uncomfortable. More than ever, now, Faith was certain the roots of today's tragedies lay buried somewhere beneath the tears of yesterday, if only she had a way to draw them out.

She wished desperately there were someone she could talk to about the past. Not Brad, of course—he was already antagonistic enough as it was. Nor Alexandre, that poor, sad shell of a man, his memories reshaped by his own self-absorption. Nor could she go to Estee. . . .

But there was one person left. One person whose remembrances of yesterday would be as clear as perceptions of today. One person who had always had the power to reveal the secrets of the past, if only she were willing.

Faith found Beneba sitting in the doorway of the cookhouse behind the main dwelling. Although it was dusk, she had not yet lit a candle, choosing instead to come out and take advantage of the last rays of the sun. A mound of string beans, dulled in the twilight to a soft gray-green, rested on the ground beside her. She swayed back and forth, humming to herself, as she took up handful after handful of beans and snapped them into a large iron kettle.

Faith stood in the shadow of an old live-oak and studied her in silence. It seemed strange to remember how strong and frightening Beneba had once looked to her. There was little of that primitive forcefulness left, except perhaps in the square set of her jaw or the superstitious talisman that still dangled from her neck. She had lost a great deal of weight in the past months, and the faded calico dress that hung on her once-impressive bosom only added to a sense of smallness and frailty.

Faith stepped toward her, then hesitated, waiting for her to look up. She remembered the touching, maternal softness she had sensed in those stern features the day they brought Estee home in bonds from Cypress Hill, and she prayed she had not misread it. Beneba's devotion to Katherine's daughter was the only key Faith had to unlock the dark secrets stored in her memory.

She went over to the woman and dropped to her knees beside her.

"I saw Estee today," she said quietly. "Standing on the hill-side, staring at the river."

Beneba did not look up, but kept her eyes focused on the pile of vegetables at her side. "Ain't no crime in that. The river's there for ever'one, even a slave."

"Yes, but she said something strange to me. She said, 'My mother died there. . . . In that . . . dark water.' "

The woman caught up another handful of beans. "Doan' see nothin' strange in that." Snap, the beans went in her fingers. Snap, snap, snap. "Katherine did die in the water. Yo' think they's sum'pin strange in a girl wantin' to call her mama to mind ever' now and then?"

"No. Not if that's all there is to it. But you see, I know what she was thinking. She was looking at the water, and she was saying to herself, How cool and pretty it looks. How inviting. And she was thinking, It would be so easy just to walk down that hillside and take a step into the water, and another—and then another."

She had not guessed wrong. Beneba started to take up another batch of beans, then gave up and let them drop back onto the pile.

"Why yo' doan' leave well enough alone, chile? Doan' yo' know no better than to drag an ol' corpse out in the sun? Yo' see a snake lyin' in the grass, what yo' gonna do? Wake it so's it can bite yo'? Better yo' let yo' ghosts lie, or they's gonna rise up an' hurt yo'."

"But that's just the point, Beneba. Our ghosts *are* rising up—and they are hurting us. You can't make a ghost lie still, just because you want it to."

"Cain't yo', girl? Well, mebbe not. But yo' cain't pull it up outa its grave neither, if it doan' wanna come. Estee's got all her ghosts buried inside her from way back when she was a girl. Jes' lak' yo' do. If they ain't come out yet, it's 'cause they ain't ready. Or 'cause she ain't ready to have 'em."

Faith drew back a little, trying to see the woman's face in the dark. For the first time, everything was becoming clear.

"So that was why you didn't want me here. Right from the very beginning. From the day I arrived, and you stood on top of the steps and glowered down at me."

Beneba did not try to meet her eyes. "What fo' I should want yo' here, girl?" she grumbled. "Some things, they is better left alone. Too bad you doan' got the sense to see that."

"Then it *was* you. That night I fell on the stairs. You weakened the board so it would break under my weight."

"Yo' wasnt' hurt none. Couldn't be, what with the landin' only a few steps down."

"No, but I could be frightened. And that's what you wanted, isn't it? To frighten me so much I would run away. Only it didn't work."

She paused to study the old woman. And that, of course, was why the other slaves had been so uncommunicative when she tried to question them. Such was the force of Beneba's personality that not a one of them would dare to cross her. "Oh, Beneba," she said softly, "don't you see how foolish you're being? Whom do you think you're protecting? Estee? But I saw Estee on the hillside this afternoon, and I wasn't lying. She *was* staring at the water—and she was thinking those things. What could be worse than that?"

"What could be worse? Where yo' put yo' brains, chile? I'll tell yo' what could be worse. She could stop standin' there thinkin' what it would be like to walk down that hill, and she could start walkin'."

"And you really think that would be worse? Worse than the terrible emptiness inside her? Oh, Beneba, don't you see? She doesn't feel pride anymore, she doesn't feel hatred—she doesn't even feel anger! There's absolutely nothing inside her. Nothing at all."

Beneba rose with an effort and hobbled over to the side of the yard, staring at a clearing halfway down the hill. Faith waited for a few minutes, then followed her. There was a quiet resignation in the woman's bearing that made her loath to intrude.

Beneba did not glance at her, even when she spoke.

"I tole yo' befo'. Estee's got it all inside her. I doan' know if I can git it out."

"But you will try?"

Beneba turned toward her at last. There was more than

sadness in her eyes. There was something that looked like pity.

"It ain't only Estee's gonna be hurt, yo' go on with this. Yo' gotta know that now."

The air was cold, but Faith did not notice it. The only chill she felt came from inside herself.

"You will try," she said again.

"Yes, I will try. Tonight."

Two

An eerie mist swirled through the darkness, enclosing the circular clearing in a world of its own. Faith squatted with the others at the edge of the ring of warmth cast by a blazing bonfire in the center. Fresh pine boughs crackled in the tall flames, catapulting red and yellow sparks into the air.

The low, subtle rhythm of drums seemed to rise out of the earth. A trio of elderly men, barely visible in the mist on the far side of the clearing, looked more ghostly than real as they beat out a solemn tattoo on the primitive instruments cradled between their knees. Directly in front of the flames, so motionless she almost seemed a statue, Beneba stood like a guardian of the night. There was in her bearing none of the frailty Faith had sensed that afternoon. Formidable and forbidding once again, she defied the darkness in a crimson apron, with a bright crimson kerchief knotted around her head.

Faith watched, intrigued, but confused. When Beneba had told her to come to the clearing after sunset, garbed in red like the slaves who would also be present, she had expected the smoldering excitement of heathen rituals as old as time. Yet here everything seemed remarkably still and restrained.

Tugging a scarlet shawl around her shoulders, she turned to the young man at her side.

"What's happening? Why isn't she moving?"

The lad grinned, showing brilliant white teeth in a large mouth. "Yo' is disappointed, missus."

"Not, not disappointed exactly. But I did think *something* would happen. You know, something—well, something . . . dramatic."

The boy chuckled under his breath. "Doan' you' worry,

missus. Yo' gonna git all the dramatic yo' want. An' mebbe more."

Faith settled back uncomfortably on her heels. The boy, like the three old men across the clearing, was a drummer, but because of the recent rebellion and the growing fear of blacks throughout the area, Brad had forbidden any music that might carry beyond the boundaries of his own plantation. Faith felt sorry for the lad as she watched him tap out a silent beat on the unresponsive earth, but she could not help being glad he was at her side. Without his explanations, she would never have been able to understand what was going on.

The sound of drumbeats increased so gradually, Faith barely noticed at first. They were still soft, but a new power touched their depths, a new urgency that seemed to draw Beneba out of her reverie. The old woman moved slowly, her body swaying only slightly as she raised her arms to shoulder height. In one hand she held an *asson*, a ceremonial gourd filled with beads and snake vertebrae. Responding more and more to the rhythm of the drums, she began to shake the *asson* back and forth in front of her.

"To drive away de *baka*," the boy whispered in Faith's ear. "De evil demons dat inhabit de night."

In spite of herself, Faith could not help being caught up in the strange ceremony. The superstitious ritual, so unlike the stylized rites of her own religion, was just alien enough not to seem blasphemous, and she found herself drinking it in with growing fascination. Tonight, the boy told her solemnly, she would share in an experience few white men or women had allowed themselves. Tonight, she would witness not merely the naive strivings of man to reach his gods, but a primitive celebration of the continuity of life. A communion of the living with those who died before and those who had not yet been born.

Faith did not, of course, believe in the *loa*, the gods the blacks had brought with them from Africa in the stinking holds of a thousand slave ships, but she listened avidly as the boy described them. It was to Legba, the guardian of the gates, the spirit who inhabited every crossroads, that Beneba appealed as she laid aside the *asson* and began to chant. It was a deep, chesty sound, starting low in her throat and rising until it filled the fiery circle of light. Come Legba, she called enticingly. Come, open your portals and let the spirits enter in.

They were an odd assortment, Faith decided, these dieties

of many tribes and African cultures who had come together for the first time in the New World, but they were strangely satisfying in their simplicity. There was Agwé, the *loa* of the sea, and Tonnere, the god of thunder; Simbi, the patron of springs and running water, and Ogun, *loa* of war and vengeance. Especially intriguing to Faith, who had herself been a twin, were the Marassa, the twins of the *loa* world. A child born a twin, the boy explained in hushed tones, was like a child born with teeth—he came into the world under an ominous sign.

Central to the ceremony, as he was central to every slave ritual, was Damballa, the snake god. Faith looked at Beneba, and at last she understood the twisted bone talisman that always dangled on a leather thong around her neck. It seemed to Faith a sinister symbol, though in reality, Damballa represented not only everything that was frightening in the world, but everything that was good as well. Damballa was the snake, but he was the rainbow, too, and the umbilical cord—the god of fertility and the determiner of all favorable and evil fortune.

Beneba ended her chant with an abruptness that made the silence in the clearing seem heavy and unnatural. She did not try to hurry, but worked her way slowly around a large earthenware jar, an object called a *canari*, that had been filled with water and bits of food. She moved carefully, making sure the torches at the edge of the circle blotted out her shadow with each step she took.

"Doan' neber let yo' shadow see itself," the boy warned Faith in a whisper. "Ef it does, it might git to thinkin' it were independent an' slink off to habe a life o' its own. Den yo' wouldn't habe a soul no mo'."

Beneba stopped before the fire. Faith could sense a kind of anticipation in the air. Even without turning, she knew that everyone was leaning forward to watch. Beneba bent down and, picking up a handful of gray ashes still warm from the fire, began to sprinkle them in a crude ring on the soil. In the center of this symbolic circle—a *vévé* the boy called it—she made the crude form of a snake, accenting the curving lines with white flour so they would stand out sharply against the dark earth. She worked with her right hand, holding her left hand behind her back, proof that she was no two-handed practitioner of black magic, serving the *loa* with one hand, evil with the other.

When she had finished, she picked up the *canari* and raised it with seeming ease over her head. She held it there for a brief moment, then released it suddenly, letting it drop with a bold crash to the earth. Food and pieces of broken crockery splattered across the ground.

The effect was electric. No sooner had the jar hit the earth than the drummers increased their tempo, beating out their rhythm with a sudden frenzy that defied Brad's commands and sent a tremor of excitement through the spectators. Beneba began to dance to the sound, shifting her weight from side to side with an uncanny grace that seemed uninhibited and controlled all at once. Faith watched, mesmerized by the unexpected sensuality of her movements. This was no longer the Beneba she knew, this woman before her eyes. This was the last alluring echo of a girl who had lived years ago. A lithe, limber creature, earthy and exciting—and filled with the vitality of passion and life.

One of the women in the circle of watchers got up, as if to join the dance, but Beneba ordered her back with a brusque wave of her hand. The woman pouted, but did as she was bid. Faith could feel the frustration that must have been hers as she slithered back into the shadows and rejoined the silent watchers. The beat of the drums was a relentless temptation, vibrating through the muscles of her own legs and hips, her shoulders and arms, until she, too, longed to leap out into the forbidden circle of light and submerge herself in the cathartic rhythm of the dance.

It was only minutes before a second figure rose from the shadows and moved into the scarlet glow of the fire. Faith was startled to catch sight of dark, feminine features, so serene and composed they were almost unrecognizable. Estee had remained so quietly in the background, Faith had not even realized she was there.

She was dressed, surprisingly, in a simple white sacque. Sheer linen, a striking contrast to the faded calico she usually wore, floated around her body like wisps of white fog in the darkness around the clearing. Long black hair fell loose down her back.

She moved forward slowly, taking one tentative, gliding step, then another. Her hands were stretched out in front of her like a sleepwalker's. Her eyes were open, but they were glassy, and she did not seem to be able to see.

Beneba stopped her dance and turned to watch the girl. Reaching out her hands, she beckoned her forward, like a puppetmaster working a marionette on long, invisible strings. The drummers hesitated, then picked up their beat again, beginning softly, as they had before.

"The *loa*," the boy whispered excitedly. "The *loa* got her now."

Estee did indeed look like a woman possessed. Faith crouched on the sidelines and watched with growing uneasiness. The *loa*, the spirits of the pagan underworld, took form on earth only by mounting a human, much as a man might mount a wild horse, and they would not let go until they had broken her.

Estee seemed to sense the possession almost at the same moment Faith recognized it. Fighting desperately, she twisted her body back and forth in wrenching, convulsive movements. The drums made a fitting accent, highlighting each moment of struggle and ultimate defeat with bursts of sound. Estee made it a battle of strong wills. Again and again, she challenged the power of the gods, but they only seemed to laugh as they caught her up in their frenzied dance and whirled her helplessly around the fire.

It was, Faith thought, fascinated and horrified both, a violent act, appalling to behold, yet strangely compelling. There was about it a savage beauty that could not be denied. A timeless wonder that belonged not to the present but to the dark unknown past from whence the *loa* had sprung.

Vibrant sensuality marked every movement. Sheer linen clung to Estee's body, teasing the full curves of her hips and bosom until she no longer seemed a frightened girl, fighting the demons that threatened to possess her, but a woman longing for the embrace of her lover. The firelight held her captive. Streaks of red saturated her gown with color, and her dark tresses blazed with flames of their own.

The drumbeats intensified, forcing Estee to move ever faster, until finally her features were no more than a dizzying blur. Her hair whipped out around her body, daring the flames to catch hold of it as she spun closer to the fire. Her hips writhed and twisted, no longer rebelling against the *loa*, but surrendering to the potency of their possession.

The rhythm rose to an excruciating peak, crashing at last in a crescendo of violence. Suddenly, all sound ceased, and the night was plunged into an abyss of silence. Estee stopped with the drums. Her body jerked upward, an abrupt, compulsive motion, as if those same invisible strings that propelled her before had been tugged sharply toward the sky. Then the illusion was shattered, and she collapsed in a heap on the ground.

With a cry of horror, Faith leaped to her feet. She did not know what Beneba was doing, but she wanted no part of it.

Not if it was going to hurt Estee like this. She took a step forward, turning with a frown when she felt a hand catch her arm.

"Stay where yo' is!" It was the boy's voice, hoarse and urgent. "Dat girl b'long to de loa now. Doan' yo' be gettin' in de way."

Reluctantly, Faith let him pull her back to the ground. She was sick with fear, but she knew the lad was right. Whatever was happening to her friend now, it was beyond her experience and understanding. If she tried to interfere, she would only make things worse.

Instead, it was Beneba who stepped forward. Stopping a few feet away, she squatted on the ground in front of the fallen girl. She did not touch her, but Estee seemed to sense her presence for she pulled herself up until she was in a kneeling position on the soil. Her eyes were cast downward.

Beneba took hold of Estee's hands, pulling them out until the girl's arms were stretched rigidly in front of her. When she released them, Estee did not move but stayed where she was, her limbs poised unnaturally in the air. As if in answer to a cue Faith had not seen, two women moved out of the shadows at the side of the clearing. One bore an earthen pot, the other a flaming torch.

Beneba turned toward the first woman. Extending her hands, she waited as the woman tilted the pot and poured a warm, oily substance over them. When they were completely coated, she clasped Estee's outstretched hands once again, rubbing first one, then the other, until they glistened in the light. Then, wiping her fingers on her apron, she took the torch from the second woman and signaled them both to retreat.

Holding the flame in front of her, she stared at it with a long, dispassionate gaze. Then, suddenly, she thrust it forward, bringing it up under Estee's palms.

A shudder ran through Faith's body at the sound of oil sizzling in the fire. But if Estee even felt it, she did not let it show on dark, impassive features. When at last Beneba pulled the torch away, Faith was stunned to see that the girl's hands were smooth and unblistered.

Beneba gave a low grunt of satisfaction. Raising the light, she let it play on Estee's features. The girl sensed the warmth, and she looked up. Her eyes were clear, but they held no more expression than they had that first moment when she stepped into the clearing.

Beneba leaned forward to peer into her face.

"Yo' knows who yo' is, chile? Yo' knows yo' name?"

The girl tilted her head to the side. She looked somehow different, softer and younger than she had before. Her skin was so dark in the firelight, she seemed as black as the other slaves.

"Of course I know who I am, old woman. Do you think I am a fool?"

Faith jumped at the sound. The words had come out of Estee's lips, but the voice was not Estee's voice at all. It was deeper and heavier, so husky it might almost have belonged to a man.

Beneba hardly seemed to notice. "No, yo' ain't no fool. Neber was, that's fo' sho'."

"Then why do you ask me if I know my name? You know perfectly well that I do."

"Tell it to me then?"

The corners of the girl's lips turned up in the vaguest hint of an impish smile.

"My name is Katherine."

Faith was too startled to hold back a soft gasp of surprise. Katherine? Of all the things she might have heard in the strange, unsettling voice that was not Estee's, this was the one she least expected. She glanced over at Beneba to see if the old woman was as disconcerted as she, but Beneba seemed to be taking it all in stride.

"No, not Katherine," she prompted gently. "That ain't neb-er been yo' name. Not yo' *real* name. Yo' knows that well as I do."

The girl glanced up sharply. For the first time, Faith caught a glimmer of rebellion in her eyes, and she thought she was going to resist. Then, as quickly as it had come, the look vanished, and she seemed to fall into a trance again.

"No," she admitted softly. "No, my name is not Kather-ine."

"What is it, then?"

"Kit—Kituga."

"Tha's better." Beneba's voice, soft and low, was filled with a tenderness Faith had never heard in its depths before. "Close yo' eyes, Kituga. Jes' close yo' eyes now—an' go back where yo' come from."

The words puzzled Faith, but they seemed to have a hyp-notic effect on the girl. She did as she was told, dropping heavy lids over her eyes, and turned her face upward to catch the heat of the fire. She looked incredibly young now, no more than fourteen or fifteen years old.

Beneba reached out, touching the girl's hand for a brief second, then drew away again.

"Tell me what yo' see, chile, with yo' eyes closed. What does yo' see, there in the darkness?"

"Nothing. I see nothing."

"Nothin? Doan lie to me, girl. It ain't no good fightin'. Yo is jes' fightin' yo'self."

"But I don't want to remember. Oh, please—I don't want to go back! Not—not . . . *there!*"

"Not where?"

"There . . . where it happened."

Faith crept forward, so engrossed in what she was hearing she did not even notice she had moved into the light. This was the past Beneba was coaxing to the surface now—the past she had been so anxious to discover—but if she had dared, she would have leaped up and begged her to stop.

Not that it would have done any good, she thought with a glance at Beneba's resolute expression. The old woman was not about to turn back now.

"Yo' *is* there, Kituga," she said in slow, even tones. "Where it happened. Doan' yo' know that?"

The girl who called herself Kituga opened her eyes. She leveled them on Beneba's face, but Faith had the feeling she did not see her.

"Yes . . . I am there."

"An' what does yo' see?"

"I see . . . I see funny-shaped green leaves with drops of rain sparkling on them. I see vines as big as my wrist, trailing in puddles on the ground and twining up the trees. It smells clean here. Clean like the earth and the rain and the sun. I have not smelled anything so clean since I left home."

"Where is this place, Kituga? How is it called by men?"

"I do not know. It is not home, but it seems like home. It has the smell and the feel of home. I remember once, when I was a little girl, I was still free and I could walk about as I chose in the forest. That is what it feels like here. Warm and clean . . . and free."

Beneba lowered herself painstakingly to her knees. Her eyes were even with Kituga's now.

"What is yo' doin' there, chile? All by yo'self?"

The girl shook her head slowly. "I—I do not know, but it does not matter. That other place is terrible, the place where they took everyone from the boat. It is worse than the pens in Africa. They are like animals now. No, less than animals, for men take better care of their livestock."

She paused. A flicker of pain crossed her features.

"I know I must go there, too. It is the lot of a slave, and I do not complain—but oh, sometimes it is hard. I think he pities me, the man with the yellow hair who was kind to me before. I think he wants to give me a day of happiness before he takes my life away again. At least it is pretty, this place he has put me. It is pretty and it smells of home."

Slowly, Faith began to understand. This was the Islands the girl was talking about. The Indies. The last stopping place for slaves on their way to the auction blocks of the New World.

Kituga seemed lost in her reveries now.

"The rain has stopped, but I can still smell it. The drops on the leaves are turning to steam in the heat, and the mud feels soft beneath the bare soles of my feet. I look up, and I see rainbow in the sky. And I know then that Damballa has followed me here from Africa, and I will be all right."

She folded her hands quietly in her lap and dropped her head. Beneba watched for a moment in silence, waiting for her to go on.

"The stream, Kituga," she pressed at last. "Doan' fo'get the stream."

"No. . . ." The girl looked up questioningly. "No, there is no stream."

"Sho' they is. Yo' done tole me 'bout the stream. 'Member?"

"Oh . . . the stream." Her voice was soft and insubstantial, like the mist on the wind. "Yes, there is water . . . I can see it now. It is clear and shining, and the white sand at the bottom sparkles like diamonds. It is so tempting I have to dip my fingers into it. I love the way it feels, cool on my hands, and I take off my clothes and step into it. I cup my hands and fill them with water, and laugh as it splashes over my naked breasts. There is a strange flower, a big burst of red like the rising sun, floating on the current. I turn to follow it with my eyes and then I see. . . ."

Her voice drifted off. Her lips continued to move, but no sound came out of them.

"Then yo' see . . . ?"

"Then I see . . . *him*. The white man. He is standing on the bank and he is staring at me. And I know what he is thinking. They are strange, these men with their light skin and their unnatural ways. They think only one thing when they see a woman with no clothes on her body. *He* is thinking that now. I can see it in his face."

"An' yo' recognize him."

"Yes, yes, I recognize him! He is the man who was kind to me. The man with the yellow hair. But there is no kindness in those pale eyes now. He is looking at me the way the others looked at me—the men on the boat with their gold earrings and their kerchiefs to tie around a black woman's waist—and he wants the same thing they wanted."

She half rose, her eyes dilated with terror. "I try to run to my clothes where they are lying on the bank. I try to put them on and cover my nakedness so he will not think those terrible things. But I am not as fast as he. His hands are hard on my arms. He hurts me, but I do not cry out. I am too afraid. His shirt is rough, and I feel the warmth of his sweat as he pulls me against his body. And his mouth——"

She stifled a cry of anguish as the sensation overwhelmed her.

"Oh, it disgusts me, that awful, gaping mouth, closing in on me. Like a jungle beast devouring its prey. I have seen white men force their vile lusts on women before, but I did not know how terrible a man's mouth would feel. Filthy and wet, full of tastes and smells. And then . . . then. . . ."

"Doan' stop now. Get it all out."

"No, I can't. I can't go on. Please . . . *please* don't make me!"

"Say it, chile. Jes' spit it out o' yo' mouth an' be done with it. Ain't nothin' so bad once it's been said."

"Oh, please——"

"Say it!"

"He—he . . . Oh, Damballa, help me, he is pulling me down on the ground. I tell him I am only fourteen, I tell him no man has ever touched me like that—and oh, I tell him I am afraid. But he does not understand my words, and it would not matter if he did. He forces me down to the mud, and I know that nothing—nothing!—will stop him."

The words died away in a low moan, like the sound of an animal in pain. The girl did not move, but sat absolutely motionless in the center of a circle of ashes and flour and stared at the white pattern on the earth. It was several minutes before she finally looked up. When she did, her eyes were dazed and confused, but they seemed to focus on the people around her for the first time that night.

Beneba took her hands and drew her to her feet. In that moment, Faith realized that it was Estee she was addressing and not the vague, disquieting spirit of her mother.

"Now yo' know. Ain't anythin' but what yo' always knew in yo' heart. But now yo' know in yo' head, too."

Faith could have wept for the girl. All her life, Estee had been terrified of one thing—that her father was a white man. Now her worst fears had come true.

Stepping over to the two women, she extended her hand tentatively. "Estee. . . ."

The girl did not respond. She glanced at Faith, but her eyes were veiled again, and her hands dangled limply at her sides. Helplessly, Faith turned toward Beneba. To her surprise, she saw that the woman was gazing with thoughtful eyes, not at Estee, as she would have expected, but at her. The look on her face was the one Faith had seen earlier when the old slave warned her that Estee was not the only one who would be hurt if they delved too deeply into the past.

Beneba did not let her eyes linger on Faith. Looking back at Estee, she opened her lips one last time.

"Yo' know that man, chile? The man with the yellow hair?"

"Yes, I know him."

"Who is he? What is his name?"

Estee did not face her, but stared into the fire. For a long time, nothing but the hiss and crackle of flames broke the silence.

"His name," she said at last, "was Adam Eliot."

Three

"You knew all the time, didn't you?"

Faith sat on the couch in Brad's study and stared at him with accusing eyes. He had been at his desk when she entered, working on the books that held the plantation accounts. Now he set them aside to meet her gaze.

"No. Adam told me a great deal about his life, but there were some things he kept to himself. Estee's parentage was one of them."

"But you must have guessed. You can't have known him that well and not have suspected something."

"Actually, I didn't. It never even occurred to me. I suppose, because I knew that Estee was five or six years old when she and her mother came here from the Islands. I realized that Adam was fond of the child, of course, but I assumed it was because she was Katherine's daughter."

Faith frowned distractedly as she looked down at her hands, folded in her lap. Brad closed the book in front of him and studied her uneasily. He had thought, in the months since she left him, that he had managed to erect a strong, protective wall around himself to keep her out. But now, with the first emotional crisis since her return to Havenhurst, she had come running to him—and damned if he could find it in himself to turn her away!

"What is it that bothers you so much about this? Are you worried about the pain Estee is suffering? Or do you feel as if you've been betrayed by your father again?"

"I really don't know. Both, I guess. But it's more than that. It was—oh, I know it sounds silly, but it was just so frightening."

"Frightening?" That was the last thing Brad had expected her to say. "In what way?"

"I wish I could explain. That pagan ritual of Beneba's . . . well, it was like some kind of magic. Not the magic children marvel at, but a deep-rooted, primitive force of evil. It was as if the dead were alive there. As if they walked the earth again. Only not in themselves—inside other people! I've never seen anything so—so *potent* in my life!"

A light quiver touched her lips at the memory. Brad pushed the ledger book firmly across the desk and wished he had not noticed. Damn! He could feel the whole wall tumbling in around him, stone by carefully laid stone, and there was nothing he could do about it.

"You don't seriously believe all that mumbo-jumbo, do you?" he said, a little too jovially to be convincing. "Beneba's a crafty manipulator, I'll give her that. And a damned good showman. She scares the hell out of half the slaves on the plantation. But you're too intelligent to be taken in by that."

Faith turned troubled eyes on his face. "You weren't there, Brad. You didn't see it. That was no show."

"Oh, I don't know. I may not have attended that particular performance, but I've seen enough of them to know what they're all about. African rituals are common in the Islands, I understand, although most of the slaveowners here don't allow them. Adam simply didn't have the heart to deny Beneba anything, and after his death the custom was so firmly entrenched Jeremy couldn't rout it out. It's become a religion for some of the slaves. They believe it implicitly."

"I don't blame them," Faith said with a shudder.

"Nor do I. But for different reasons. I've often thought of these ceremonies as a kind of hypnosis, practiced on a grand scale. You should have seen them in the old days, before the white man got it in his head that the slaves were using native drums to communicate with each other. The music was bold then and the beat provocative. Sometimes there would be as many as twenty or thirty slaves in the center of the ring at the same time, all dancing themselves into such a frenzy they collapsed to the earth unconscious. It was compelling—and, yes, I must admit, a little frightening—to watch. The pull was so strong, there were times I almost surrendered to it myself."

"I know what you mean." Faith could still recall the way the beat of the drums worked into her bones until she could barely force herself to sit on the sidelines and watch. "I felt the same thing. It *was* hypnotic in a way—the firelight and the music. But I don't think that explains what happened to Estee."

"Why not? That kind of spell can be very powerful."

"Maybe—but those weren't Estee's memories she was reliving. They were Katherine's. All that happened before Estee was born. She couldn't have known anything about it."

"Couldn't she? I'm not so sure about that. I suspect Katherine tried to tell her when she thought she was old enough to understand, and Estee was so upset, she didn't force it. Or perhaps she simply overheard her mother talking to Beneba. It's amazing the things a child picks up and understands."

"You could be right." Faith laid her head back against the couch and stared idly at a lacy cobweb in the corner above the window. "Beneba did say that Estee had everything locked away inside her. Only. . . ."

She let her voice trail off doubtfully. Brad did not look at her as he picked up the book he had been working on and put it on a sidetable, next to the pile of old ledgers that had belonged to Adam. Hell, he had used enough women in his time, and he'd never before held a grudge against one of them for getting the best of him. There could be only one reason he was angry with this woman now—because he was afraid to let her get too close to him.

"Only it still seems like magic to you?" he prompted, filling in the words she had left unsaid. Crossing the room, he leaned against the back of the couch and looked down at her. "Well, maybe you're not so wrong at that. Who says magic has to originate with some supernatural power we cannot see or touch? Maybe whatever magic there is in the world comes from somewhere inside ourselves."

The warmth in his voice touched a chord of longing in Faith. She had not realized until that moment how terribly alone she felt.

"Oh, Brad, she is my sister. My *sister!* And she wouldn't let me touch her."

He watched helplessly as tears of frustration welled up in her eyes. Confound the woman, she was going to cry! If she did, he would have to take her in his arms and comfort her—and he knew damn well what would happen then.

He sat gingerly on the edge of the couch facing her.

"What did you expect, Faith? It must have been a double shock to Estee, learning not only that her father was a white man, but that he was one she had always resented. To accept you as her sister, she would have to accept Adam as her father. I don't think she can do that. Not yet."

"But to reject me so completely. . . ."

"In a way, you know, that's exactly the same thing that you're doing."

"Me? But I'm not rejecting Estee. I would never do that."

"No, but you are rejecting Adam. Just as Estee is. Every time you find something that reminds you he was a human being, with human weaknesses, you use it as an excuse to push him farther and farther out of your heart."

"That's not true." Faith's eyes were wide and confused, like a little girl who could not understand what was going on around her. "I'm not the one who rejected my father. He rejected me. All those years my sister and I were growing up, he never sent so much as a halfpenny to help us. Or penned a single letter. I had plenty of room in my heart for him—he just didn't have any for me!"

Her pain was transparent, making her look soft and vulnerable to Brad. At last, he did the one thing he had wanted all along. He put his arm around her and drew her toward him, easing her head down on his shoulder.

"Your father loved you very much, my dear. If you don't believe anything else, at least believe that."

"How can I, when he didn't even take the time to send a letter?"

"Of course he did. He sent letters all the time—and money, too. Your mother returned everything with the seal intact."

Faith lifted her head from his shoulder and looked up at him. Brad could see the doubt in her eyes—and the hope.

"I'm not inventing this, you know. You were always your father's special joy, almost from the day you were born. Sometimes I think—though Adam never spoke of it—that you made up to him for all the things he looked for in your mother and never found. Haven't you ever been curious about your name?"

"My name? No. Should I have been?"

"Didn't it seem a strange combination to you—Faith and Fleur. Except that they both begin with the letter F they have little in common."

Faith shook her head, puzzled. "I never thought about it, one way or the other. But what does that have to do with my father?"

"Apparently he and your mother quarreled about it. Rather bitterly, Adam said. It took forever for them to choose names for you. Desirée wanted her baby girls to have elegant French names, but Adam was determined to hold out for something simple and meaningful. In the end, they compromised—Fleur for her, Faith for him.

"The next morning, when your father went into the nursery to check on his daughters, one of the babies opened her eyes and looked toward him. And she smiled, or so it looked to him at least. Right then and there, Adam said to himself, 'That's my little girl. That's Faith.' "

Brad paused for a moment, studying her in silence. She was still much too solemn—and much too sad.

"What do your suppose would have happened," he teased, "if the other baby had been awake that morning and she had opened her eyes? Would she be you then—and would you be Fleur?"

He could see that she was trying to smile, but her lips still quivered and he knew she did not trust herself. What a rotten life she must have had, he thought angrily. A mother who doted only on her sister—and a father who seemed to have deserted her. Not that he came from such a loving background himself, but things were different for a man. A man could say, To hell with it all, and go off and command a regiment or explore a continent. Or carve a great plantation out of the swamps at the edge of a half-tamed river. But a woman's world, like it or not, centered on home and family.

He rested his hands lightly on her cheeks. The warmth of tears spilled over his calloused fingers, and he knew he had lost the last battle with himself.

"Do you remember one day, a long time ago, when we stood on the steps of the piazza and I touched you, just like I am touching you now? I told you then to go home. You should have listened to me."

"I remember," Faith said softly. "You said that because you didn't want me here."

"I said that, my naive little girl, because I knew even then we were destined to destroy each other."

"But you didn't want me," she persisted.

There was more than a trace of irony in his smile. "Didn't I?"

"Do you want me now? Tonight?"

Brad drew her closer into his arms. He was keenly aware of the warmth of her body, soft and yielding against his, and for the first time he dared to admit what his heart had always known. He still could not speak the words aloud, but he could say them to himself. He loved this woman. Loved her as he had never loved before and never would again.

"You know I do."

Faith met his lips halfway, moving upward to greet the hard pressure of his kiss. There was, in that ravenous challenge, a power that took her breath away. She had not understood before how deep was the hunger within her body. The loneliness. The need to feel, not just any man, but this man, holding her, touching her . . . loving her. Theirs might be a passion conceived in hell and doomed forever to damnation, but it was a passion that fulfilled her as a woman and she could fight it no more.

She felt deliriously free as she abandoned herself to him. All her inhibitions, bred in innocence, nurtured by convention, were cast aside at last. Her hands seemed to have a will of their own as they raced over his flesh, luxuriating in the masculine hardness of a body too long untouched except in dreams. The sinewy muscles of his thighs felt hard against her fingers, his hips were tantalizingly slim, his back broad and virile. She slipped her hands under his shirt, feeling coarse hair and warm flesh. It no longer mattered how shameful she was. How wanton. She was with her man, and that was all that counted.

He had told her once that she belonged to him. He had not been wrong. Every breath she drew, ever sigh that lingered on her lips, was only for him.

Brad felt the pressure of her hands on his body, touching him in ways she never had before, and it heightened his desire until he could barely control his need for her. He had not been with a woman since she had left him—he had found no woman with the power to excite him the way she could—and his blood blazed with longing for her. He held her tight, feeling the sweetness of her body against his chest, then eased her slowly away.

"Not here, my darling," he whispered hoarsely. "Not here."

His arms were powerful as he picked her up and carried her into the dressing room. Laying her down on the narrow bed, he began to undress her. He was surprised to feel that his hands were trembling, but he did not let himself hurry, choosing instead to savor each perfect moment of beauty unveiled before his eyes. Her breasts—how ripe and seductive they were. How pink the nipples that tickled his tongue as he bent to kiss them. Her belly was smooth and gently rounded. Her hips, full and womanly, called out to him to come to her.

He did not refuse their plea. A shudder of surrender wracked his body as he buried himself in soft, welcoming flesh. Long separation had only enhanced their mutual excitement, and they gave themselves to each other with all the pent-up yearning that threatened to explode in their bodies. The rhythm of their passions worked in unison, rising and ebbing together, swelling swiftly to heights that both dazzled and overwhelmed them. When at last a soft moan of pleasure escaped Faith's lips, it was drowned in the flood of Brad's own cry of ecstasy.

Silence and darkness enveloped them like a warm quilt. The wind was no more than a sigh, rattling the windowpanes in the study. The only light was a ray of gold, seeping through the half-open doorway. The lovers lay in each other's arms, content for the moment to bask in the warmth of remembered lovemaking. When Faith finally drew away, sitting up on the bed beside him, Brad took her hand, but he did not try to draw her back.

"I warned you, you know," he said quietly.

"I know."

"You should have gone home."

"I know."

Faith leaned against the cold, whitewashed wall. Go home, he had told her, or we will destroy each other. She had not questioned his words before. Now she dared to ask herself what they meant. Was he merely reminding her that theirs would always be the clash of two stubborn wills, too inflexible to yield to each other—or did he know in his heart that there could never be any peace between a woman and the man who had murdered her sister?

"You told me once that you didn't love Fleur," she said. "But you must have felt something for her. What was it?"

He propped himself up on one elbow. Taking her chin in his hand, he tilted her face to catch the light and gave her a long, searching look, so intense it frightened her.

"Are you still jealous of your sister? Because I shared her bed, too? Does it hurt that much?"

"No," she said softly.

No, it did not hurt. Not anymore. Somewhere in the pain and struggle of the past months, she had found her own identity, and with that sense of self, she had finally lost her fear of Fleur. But she still had to know what her sister meant to Brad.

"Did she excite you?" she teased.

"Of course she excited me. How the hell do you think I made love to her?"

Once his crudeness would have driven her to tears. Now she only laughed at it.

"Was she more exciting than I am?"

"No, you little she-devil!" He threw his arms around her and thrust her down on the bed, pinning her beneath his weight. "No, she was *not* more exciting than you. No woman in the world is, damn you!"

Faith pursed her lips in a mock pout. "I don't believe you."

"Don't you? Well, good! Why the devil should I give you any more of a hold over me than you already have?"

He tightened his arms around her body, clenching her in a vise so rigid she could not move. His eyes flashed black in the faint light as he looked down at her.

"You are a beautiful, warm, responsive woman. Nothing is more exciting than that. Do you have any idea how masculine it makes a man feel to have a woman tremble in his arms the way you do in mine?"

Faith shook her head slowly. The sudden ardor in his voice confused her.

"But you're such a strong man, Brad. And so sure of yourself. You don't need anyone to help you prove your masculinity."

He eased his embrace, cradling her gently in his arms. "How can anyone who looks so earthy be so innocent?" He lowered his lips, playfully nuzzling her neck. "Don't ever make the mistake of thinking any man is so sure of his masculinity he doesn't need reassurance from his woman."

He ran his hands slowly down her body, tracing the soft, rounded curves of her hips and thighs. A new urgency vibrated in his touch, warning her that desire was quickening again, and the first tremulous waves of response began to rise within her. Lying back, she let her head sink into the pillow. His lips toyed with her, tantalizing first her neck, then her shoulders, then her breast.

The yearning pain that swelled her flesh in response to his kisses was both passion renewed and passion remembered. His tongue was bold, his teeth enticing, as he moved slowly down her body. Only when he finally lifted his lips from her thighs and began to draw her legs tenderly apart did she at last understand why his touch had seemed so familiar. This was what he had done for her before—the same sweet gift he had given her that first afternoon in the summerhouse—and she had reveled in it then. But it was not what she wanted now. Laughing lightly, she took his head in both her hands and drew him up again.

She waited until she could see his eyes before she spoke.

"Do you remember what you told me? That day you first touched me? You said that I would belong to you?"

"Was I wrong?"

She tucked her fingers under his chin, tilting his face upward as he had done so often with her.

"But you said that you would never belong to me."

His face darkened, but he did not reply. Faith was sure enough of herself now to smile. What strange creatures men could be. All pride and ego, and afraid to admit their need for love. She had gone through too much with Brad—she had given up too much of herself to lie with him tonight, to let him get away with that.

Hands tender and firm, she pushed him back on the bed. He made a brief effort to draw her down beside him, then gave in to her whims. Long golden hair trailed across his body as she bent over him, touching her lips to his neck. It gave her a heady feeling to be so in control of this man who had always dominated her.

She could feel his heart begin to race, beating wildly against his chest, as her fingers tangled in the hair that thinned to a narrow line across his belly. Her lips followed greedily, aching to play the same games with his body that he had played with hers. He stiffened suddenly when her mouth slid down to his groin, and she knew he had figured out what she had in mind.

She was more than ready for him. So he thought lovemaking made man the master and woman the slave, did he? Well, he had a few lessons left to learn.

"What, my love? I am supposed to tremble beneath you, poor frail woman that I am, to make you feel more masculine. Yet you would deny the same satisfaction to my feminine ego. I ask, you, is that fair?"

There was no answer to her challenge, and he knew it. Faith sensed the rebellion still raging in his body, and she thrilled to the tremors of resistance that greeted the renewed assault of her lips and fingers. For the first time in his life, this strong, stubborn man was finding in himself the same potential for subservience that characterized the weaker sex. She delighted in toying with his body, using him with her hands and mouth, molding him like a piece of raw clay to be formed into any shape she chose.

Her fingers became explorers, searching every hill and crevice of this warm terrain, already half familiar, yet still tantalizingly new to her. Her lips were a pair of bold adventurers, daring exploits that would have been beyond their dreams before. When at last she reached her goal, that hard, throbbing proof of his need for her, there was no modesty left in her. No hesitation. Willingly, eagerly, she gave to him the gift that he had planned for her.

No longer did he resist. He was her partner now, her fellow conspirator, twisting his fingers in her hair, guiding her, showing her how to give him ever more and more pleasure. Faith's own excitement mounted, drawing her into paths of passion she had not known existed. Never would she have believed that the mere act of giving could stimulate physical reactions so potent—and so satisfying. That final moment, when she felt his body quiver in ultimate surrender, was as sweet a victory as she had ever known.

She lingered lovingly, giving him one last shower of tender kisses before she finally pulled away. Gently, she drew her hand along his cheek. His face was pale and drained, his eyes misted with the residue of passion.

She smiled down at him.

"And now . . . you belong to me."

The sky was dark and clear when Faith finally stepped out onto the piazza. Behind her, alone in his narrow bed, Brad lay asleep, unaware that she had left him. A light wind rose from the river, but it was warm and benign, more reminiscent of gentle spring breezes than the howling gusts of autumn.

Faith leaned against the veranda railing and stared at the distant hills. The moon was nearly full, and blue-green pine forests stood out against the horizon. How strange it seemed now that she had ever thought she could escape her passion for the one man with the power to rule her heart. What was it he had called her before? A naive little girl? How right he had been.

She looked up at the stars, illusively cool and serene against a backdrop of deep blue velvet. What a tangled web she had caught herself in, she thought bitterly. She could not accept her love for Brad until she knew what part he had had in her sister's death—and she would never know that as long as her eyes were blinded by that very same love.

Logically, of course, it was simple. Faith turned her back on the hills and began to walk slowly along the piazza toward the front door. One of three things had happened to Fleur that last day at Havenhurst. First, she had gotten bored with the plantation and decided to leave, crossing dangerous swamplands in the dim light of dawn. Second, she had played one game too many with a man's heart and found out the hard way that Alexandre had already crossed the brink into madness. Or third. . . .

Faith hesitated, steadying herself with a hand against the railing. Third, Fleur had tried a little too hard to stake her claim on Havenhurst and Brad had caught her in his study at midnight.

The study at midnight. No matter how many times she turned everything over in her mind, it always came back to that. How much did she dare to trust her dream? Was it literally true? Had Fleur really put on a shimmering green silk dress and stepped through half-open French doors into a silent, moonlit study——

She broke off, realizing where her thoughts were leading her. For the first time, she let herself focus on the one thing that had always eluded her before. She had been so preoccupied with rooms that might have been stored in her memory and portraits that might have influenced her perception, she had forgotten that there was one detail of her dream that was concrete and indisputable.

And it was the easiest thing in the world to prove.

She waited until morning, when she knew she would find Fibby hunched over her work in the sewing room at the rear of the house. Pausing in the doorway, she waited for the girl to look up before she spoke.

"Fibby, did you make a green silk dress for Miss Fleur? A pretty gown, the color of an emerald?"

The child's eyes widened and she looked frightened. Faith took a moment to reassure her before going on to describe the dress. She took care to make the account vague, so Fibby could not agree just to please her.

She needn't have worried. The child shook her head emphatically when Faith had finished.

"Oh, no, Miz' Faith. I ain't neber made a dress lak 'that in mah life. Not fo' Miz' Fleur."

Faith's heart skipped a beat. If Fibby did not remember the dress, perhaps she had imagined it after all.

"You're sure," she pressed.

"Yes, Miz' Faith. I is sho' as I kin be. I ain't neber made nothin' lak' that. Miz' Fleur, she git all her fancy dresses done up proper in Charles Town."

Faith caught her breath as she stared at the girl. "Then she did have a dress like that."

"Oh, sho', Miz' Faith. An' she looked real purty in it, too."

"Do you think you could copy it for me, Fibby? Exactly the way it was?"

"Co'se I kin." Fibby fairly beamed with pride. "Ain't no dress I cain't copy, I sets it to mah mind. Ef I stay up all night, I kin have it fo' t'morrow."

And that, Faith thought wearily, as she stood in the hallway outside the sewing room, was that. She leaned against the wall for a moment, trying to make herself comprehend what she had just done.

By some time tomorrow, tomorrow evening at the latest, she would know if Fleur's emerald green dress was the gown she had seen in her dream. And if it was—if that one detail was accurate—then all the other details would be, too.

Including the face of her killer.

Four

The gown was ready by the time Faith returned to her room to dress for dinner the next evening, but she did not get a chance to look at it. She barely had time to catch sight of a vivid profusion of green silk stretched across her bed when a slave appeared suddenly at her elbow. Turning in the doorway, she was surprised to see one of the kitchen maids, a timid girl who had never ventured into that part of the house before.

"Please, missus . . . Ol' Beneba, she done sent me. She's terrible sick, missus. Ah ain't neber seen her lak' this befo'."

The anxiety in the girl's face was contagious. Faith cast one last glance at the dress on the bed, then put it out of her mind as she followed the girl through the long hallway and down the stairs. If Beneba was really ill—and she would not have sent for her if she weren't—then she could hardly refuse to go to her. Besides, she had already waited more than a year to learn the truth about her dream. She could wait an hour or two longer if she had to.

Unlike the other house servants, Beneba did not live in the main dwelling, but in a hut of her own at the end of the street, where the common slaves resided. It was, Faith thought as she stood on the threshold and stared in at a single small room, remarkably like every other hovel in the area. Except for smooth planks covering the earthen floor and a recent coat of whitewash on the walls, there was nothing to separate Beneba's status from that of the lowest fieldhand on the plantation.

A grease lamp hissed on a table in the center of the room, throwing a rancid odor into the air. There was no other light, for the window shutters had been closed and barred, and it took Faith's eyes a minute to adjust to the darkness. Only with difficulty was she able to make out the motionless form of a woman reclining on a crude wooden bed against the far wall. Beside her, on a three-legged stool, Estee sat straight-backed and silent.

Faith crossed the room slowly, stopping beside the bed. Beneba's body, frail and surprisingly thin, seemed to sink into the moss-filled mattress beneath her. Her features were so gaunt and strained, Faith was frightened. She had not seen anyone look like that since the last time they took her in to see her mother and she knew she was dying.

The illusion lasted only a moment. As soon as Beneba caught sight of her, standing beside the bed, her features took on a new animation. Amusement flickered in dark eyes as she looked from Faith to Estee, then back to Faith again.

"Lak' two little peas in a pod yo' is. Ornery as anythin'—an' so righteous yo' cain't see to the tip o' yo' nose. I look at the two o' yo', and I see Adam Eliot all over again."

"Adam?" Estee drew back indignantly. For the first time since she had come back to Havenhurst, pride and anger flashed in her eyes. "There is nothing of that man in me!"

"Ain't they tho'? Seems to me, girl, yo' is the stubbornest mule along the river. Yo' looks at sum'pin and yo' says to yo'self, 'That's the way it is, and ain't nobody gonna tell me otherwise!' If that ain't Adam, I doan' know what is."

She paused, shaking her head back and forth. "An' what it's all fo', I ain't neber gonna know. Yo' carries all that anger 'round inside o' yo'—and it ain't eben fo' sum'pin was done to yo'. Yo' think mebbe yo' mama sat up nights lak' this, frettin' 'bout the terrible wrong was done her?"

"You know very well what I think." Emotion vibrated in Estee's voice. "I think my mother's life was ruined by what that man did to her."

"Ruined? Well . . . mebbe. But not by Adam. An' not by what he done all them years ago. Yo' mama done forgive that long time ago."

"Forgive?" Estee's features contorted with disgust. "He used her. As vilely as a man can ever use a woman. He . . . he . . . *raped* her."

Beneba gave her a long, shrewd look. "An' cain't no woman neber forgive an insult lak' that. Is that it?"

Estee looked away quickly. She could not help remembering another afternoon, when a strong young man had waited for a pretty black slave at the edge of dense pine groves. Some might have called that rape, too—and it had been easy to forgive.

"That was different. You know it was."

"Mebbe fo' yo'. But not fo' Katherine, it warn't. Yo' ain't heard but half the story—the half yo' is willin' to listen to. It's time yo' set yo' ears to the rest."

Speaking slowly, with long pauses to marshal her strength, the old woman took up the tale where Estee had left off the day before. It was, Faith had to admit as she stood in the semidarkness and listened, not at all what she had expected to hear.

Katherine had been young that day Adam Eliot found her in a sultry rain forest, but she was not a child. Her heart was already a woman's heart, her instincts the instincts of a woman, and when the savage act that robbed her of her innocence had been completed, she looked up from her pain to see a man moved to tears by what he had done. He was kneeling on the ground a few feet away from her, his head bowed, his hands stretched out in front of him in a gesture of utter defeat.

Thoughts of her own suffering ebbed away as the girl crouched on the warm earth beside a gently rippling stream and stared at him in wonder. Even young as she was, she understood that this was a man who prided himself on his strength—a man who had never let himself weep. She dared to creep toward him, touching her fingers softly to the back of his hand in a mute attempt to tell him there was a capacity for forgiveness in her heart. But when he looked up, she saw in those strange, pale eyes an anguish beyond anything she had ever dreamed, and the first stirrings of a womanly compassion beyond her years awakened in her breast. Opening her arms, she drew him comfortingly toward her.

They clung to each other for a long time, absorbed in their own separate needs for solace, until at last the instinct for generosity in Katherine's heart gave way to an instinct for love, and she discovered that the touch of a man's mouth was not abhorrent at all, but sweet and satisfying. She did not question or even think about what she was doing, but gave herself freely and completely to a man she did not even know. Their union was for her not an act of passion, but an act of love. It was a love that was to endure throughout the years.

They touched each other tenderly afterward, speaking not with the words they could not understand, but with the gentle caresses that had served as the language of lovers since the beginning of time. It was the first moment of tenderness Adam had known for far longer than he cared to remember.

Had he realized it would be the last for years to come, he might well have wept again.

Beneba let her head sink wearily into the pillow as she finished her story. The only vitality left in her face showed in the dark eyes she leveled on Estee.

"Yo' mama, she always hoped yo' was born o' that second time. But we know different, doan' we girl? They is too much anger in yo', too much hate, to o' been born o' love."

Estee did not try to speak. Pushing her stool away, she went over to the large stone fireplace and stared absently at the dead coals of yesterday's flames. Pale, anguished eyes haunted her thoughts, and she tried not to imagine what Katherine had seen in those tormented depths. It reminded her too much of the pain she herself had seen in other, darker eyes.

Only with Rodrigo it was different! Angrily, she jabbed her foot at one of the blackened logs, sending a spray of ashes over the hearth. Rodrigo was a slave, one of her own people! He was a man driven by what he had seen and suffered . . . and feared. There were reasons why the anger and frustration inside him exploded into violence.

She spun around to face the woman on the bed.

"At least my lover was black!"

Beneba gave her an impatient look. "Black, white—yo' think that made any difference to yo' mama? She didn't look at Adam and see a white man. She looked at him and saw a man she loved."

"But he used her, Beneba. Don't you understand? He *used* her. Not just that day, but afterward, too. Adam's wife was still living with him when he brought my mother here from the Islands. What was she to him then? A—a *convenience?*"

She spat the word out with all the pain and anger in her heart. Beneba tried to pull herself up, but the effort was too much and she fell back on the bed.

"Adam didn't bring yo' mama here to use her, honey. Yo' gotta know that, 'ceptin' yo' is too stubborn to admit it. Yo' 'member what things was like in them days. Yo' didn't live in the big house then—yo' lived on the street with ever'one else. An' Adam didn't neber come near yo'."

"But he brought us here. We were on the Islands and he brought us here."

"What was he s'posed to do, girl? Leave yo' on the sugar plantation? Ain't no harder life 'n that. When he learned 'bout the chile and he knowed it was his, he took the 'sponsibility on his shoulders. That's why he brought yo' here—an' not for no other reason. Adam worshipped that little doll-wife o' his. He wouldn't neber o' laid eyes on another woman, not long as she was with him. Even that terrible day she left him, it warn't Adam what went to yo' mama."

Estee looked confused for a minute, then slowly the truth began to dawn on her.

"You mean *she* went to him. After what he had done to her."

Beneba nodded her head. "I 'member it jes' lak' it was yeste'day. Adam was standin' there on the veranda, kind o' lost an' broken lak'. With the sun all 'round him, lightin' the spring flowers, an' him not even seein' 'em. She jes' watched him for a while, an' then she brought the chile to me—that was yo', honey—an' she went up to him where he was standin'. Right there, in front o' ever'one, she put her arms 'round him an' drew him toward her. An' she didn't neber regret it, not one day in her life."

Faith stood a little to the side, listening in mounting horror to the things Beneba was saying. How could anyone have sympathy for a man who was nothing but a common rapist?

"Estee was right!" she burst out, appalled. "My father *was* using her. He didn't love her. Why, he didn't even have enough respect for her to call her by her own name. He called her Katherine, because it was easier for him to remember."

"Now where yo' git an idea lak' that?"

Beneba threw her a sharp, puzzled look. Then, catching a glimpse of Estee still glowering by the fireplace, she began to smile to herself.

"That one o' yo' notions, girl? Adam didn't choose that name fo' yo' mama. He called her Kit—fo' Kituga. An' he would o' gone on callin' her that, right to the end o' his days, ef he didn't once make the mistake o' tellin' her it was an English name. Short for Katherine, he said it was. Well, when she heard that, wouldn't nothin' do but she had to have the name fo' herself.

"Katherine always had a fascination fo' anythin' English. 'Cause o' Adam, I 'suspect. Mebbe she wanted to be a part o' his world, tho' warn't no world he was particular partial to hisself, 'specially in them last years. She called yo' Esther, after the name o' his ship, 'cause that were the only English name she knowed."

She stopped, chuckling under her breath at the memory.

"Ummmm, how Adam hated that! It was a constant 'minder o' his shame, he always said. But warn't no stoppin' Katherine once she got her mind all set up. She had named her little girl Esther, an' that was all they was to it.

"Sometimes when Adam was lookin' to tease her, he'd call her Kituga again. Didn't neber fail to git her goin' neither. Katherine, she was the sweetest thing yo' ever hope to lay eyes on, but when she got riled—oh, oh, couldn't she git the fires goin' then!"

Faith stood beside the bed and watched in silence as the old woman closed her eyes. She could not help wondering if she was telling the truth or if she had made the whole thing up. That Adam Eliot might have had a passion for his dark-skinned mistress was hardly surprising—or even that he loved her, if she was anywhere near as beautiful as her daughter—but affection? Lightness? Teasing laughter? Those were things Faith had not been prepared to find in her father.

She glanced toward the fireplace, curious to see if Estee was as confused as she, but to her surprise, she saw that her half sister was staring into the cold ashes with a strange, faraway look in her eyes. There seemed a new softness in her proud features as she turned and went back to the bed.

Sitting on the stool again, she reached out to touch the old woman's hand where it lay on the coverlet.

"She loved him then? My—" She hesitated, stumbling on the unfamiliar word. "My . . . father?"

"An' he loved her, doan' yo' neber let yo'self forget that. How many times yo' seen Adam Eliot sneak out after dark to find yo' mama in some dirty hut on the street 'cause he was 'shamed o' his woman? No, he kep' her in the big house lak' she had a right to be there. An' that warn't nothin' she asked o' him."

She paused, curling her fingers around Estee's in a warm, comforting grip. Although Faith stood only a few feet away, she knew that both of the women had forgotten her.

"He would o' married her, honey," Beneba said softly. "After Desirée died. Ef only the law had let him. Yo' know what he did? Right befo' the end? He petitioned the gov'nor to let him take a black wife. Oh, didn't that cause a stir tho', all up an' down the river. Would o' got his way, too, ef he had lived a little longer."

Faith took a step backward, feeling unwelcome and strangely out of place, a white woman caught in a black tableau that no longer included her. Caused a stir indeed! If she hadn't heard it with her own ears, she would never have believed Beneba capable of such gross understatement. No wonder Jeremy Alleyn had had such an easy time of it when he stole Havenhurst. Even if the other planters suspected what he was doing, who would lift a hand to help a man who not only insisted on keeping his black mistress right in the main house, but wanted to marry her as well? Why, a man like that was dangerous. The next thing you knew, he'd be talking about setting his slaves free. And giving them nice little houses right in the neighborhood.

No one noticed when Faith slipped out into a world that had darkened from twilight into night. The air was warm, and a full moon bathed the world in iridescent blue. The light was so bright, it almost looked like dawn. No deep shadows plunged the garden into a pit of black; no frightening secrets lurked behind each tree and shrub she passed.

No secrets. Faith smiled a little as she stepped off the path and onto the lawn. The grass felt cool and damp through the thin soles of her shoes. No secrets. It seemed an appropriate conceit, now that Havenhurst had finally begun to yield up the past.

The image of her father came to mind, a vivid picture, fleshed out in every detail, though he had been no more than a vague memory when she first returned to the plantation. She could still see him, as she had seen him once, through a child's eyes, a dynamic, exciting man, laughing as he bent down to pull a little girl into the saddle in front of him, and she knew he must have looked like that when he teased his mistress and waited for an answering flash of fire from her eyes. She was glad now that she had finally found the courage to face the secrets of the past. Nothing could ever be quite as painful—or as frightening—as dark half-truths nurtured in the imagination.

She was surprised to realize she had taken the long way around to the house. Instead of cutting directly across the lawn, she had made a wide arc past the stables, and she found herself approaching the darkened facade of the north side of the building. Once this entire wing had belonged to her Uncle Olivier, and every window was ablaze with dancing lights, even on the darkest night. Now only a single candle flickered feebly behind rippled panes of glass.

Faith stopped to look at it. How long had it been, she dared to ask herself, since she had taken even a moment to think of the man she married so impulsively a year ago? She tried to visualize him the way he had looked the day she met him—dashing, handsome, gay, charming. But the memory was elusive and she could not catch it up. It was almost, she thought sadly, as if none of it had ever really happened. As if Alexandre did not exist at all.

She had just started to move on when suddenly it occurred to her that the secrets at Havenhurst belonged not only to the long distant past, but to yesterday and today as well. And perhaps, she reminded herself guiltily, the greatest of these was the secret she had kept from Alexandre. In her own way, she had been as dishonest with him the day they were married as he had been with her—and they had both paid for it dearly. She hesitated a second, then began to climb the steps that led up to the piazza. If she was going to sweep all the dark secrets out of her life, the time to begin was now.

Her courage faltered briefly when she reached the door to Alexandre's room. She had not tried to see her husband since she came back from New York, and she had no idea what she would find inside that candlelit room. The temptation to turn and walk away again was strong, but she did not let herself give in to it. She was going to have to face her husband sooner or later. She might as well get it over with tonight. Taking hold of the handle, she slid the door slowly inward.

Alexandre was seated on a straight-backed chair beside the window. He did not seem to feel the warm breeze that drifted through the open doorway, nor had his ears picked up the slight sound of Faith's footsteps on the wooden planking outside. He was looking straight ahead, staring blankly at the reflection of candlelight on the darkened window pane.

Faith stepped slowly into the room.

"Hello, Alexandre."

He jumped at the sound of her voice. His face, as he turned toward her, was confused and disoriented.

"Faith? Is that you?"

Faith remained where she was, just inside the doorway. "You know who I am?"

"I know you are not Fleur, if that's what you mean." An ironic smile turned up the corners of his mouth. "I am not quite so mad as all that, my dear wife."

The last traces of a wit and charm that had once captivated Faith still lingered in his tone. The memory saddened her. If they had not been so involved in their own needs, she wondered—if they had been honest with each other right from the start—would things have been different between them?

She crossed the room and dropped to her knees beside his chair.

"I am afraid I have wronged you, my dear. I do not ask

your forgiveness, for I do not deserve it, but I want you to know how desperately sorry I am. I have kept a terrible secret from you, and I had no right to do that."

His smile turned pensive. He touched her hair with his hand, twisting a golden curl between his fingers, then drew it back again.

"We have wronged each other, *chérie*. Badly, I fear. But must we dwell on that now? We cannot go back and remake the past, neither you nor I."

"No, I cannot remake the past—I grant you that. But I can be honest with you now. I can tell you that. . . ."

She drew back a little, aware that she was watching his face for any sign of emotion.

". . . that Fleur is dead."

The reaction she looked for was not there. Alexandre sat absolutely still for a long time, not moving so much as a single muscle. When at last he spoke, his voice was so cool he might have been inquiring about the weather.

"What makes you think that?"

Faith rose slowly and turned toward the window. Candle-light coated the pane, making it into a dim golden mirror of the room inside.

"I was there, Alexandre. I saw it all—in a dream."

He did not question her as she related the details, nor had she expected him to. There was, within Alexandre, a deep mystical streak which enabled him to understand the special bond that existed between twins. He did not even ask whether Faith had recognized the man who raised a gun to her sister's breast and pulled the trigger. It was almost, she thought, puzzled, as if it were of no significance to him.

There was still no expression in his face as he raised his hand and ran his fingers lightly across the window pane. It took Faith a minute to realize that it was her reflection he was tracing on the cold glass.

"What do you see?" she asked softly. "When you look at me and think of her, what do you see?"

He did not take his eyes from the window. All the color had gone out of his face, and his skin looked white and translucent.

"Does all that matter . . . now?"

Yes, Faith longed to cry out. Yes, it matters desperately. Fleur had been killed by one of three men: a stranger she had encountered in the swamp, the lover she shared with her sister . . . or Alexandre. Faith had to know what he was thinking.

"I want you to remember everything that happened, Alexandre. The last day, those last few days—they are terribly, terribly important."

Her voice seemed to reach him, for he turned to face her, but his eyes were blank and uncomprehending.

"What?"

"Oh, Alexandre, please. Try to think back. It was April then. Don't you remember? A beautiful April, warm and sultry, just like it is tonight. With a bouquet of spring in the air."

He began to smile, a subtle, dreamy look. "It wasn't the way they thought, you know. All those other men. They thought she was theirs, but she wasn't."

Faith stared at him in dismay. This was what she had been afraid of, when she first came into the room. That he would retreat so far into his own private world she could not reach him.

"What other men?" she prodded gently. "Do you mean Fleur's . . . lovers?"

"She was mine all the time. Only mine. She never really belonged to any of those other men. She never cared about them. She was going to marry me. We hadn't told anyone about it, but it was going to happen. Soon."

"Oh, Alexandre. . . ." Faith hated to hurt him, but somehow she had to jolt him back to reality. "Fleur wasn't going to marry you. Don't you know that? She would never let any man have that kind of control over her life."

Alexandre's blue eyes were wide and soft as he looked up at her. "Oh, but she was. She told me so. Many times. We were going to be married, she said. Then we would run Havenhurst together."

"Havenhurst?" The first hint of foreboding touched Faith's heart. Havenhurst. She had thought often enough that Fleur could never acquire it without the aid of a husband. Why hadn't she realized that the same thing would have occurred to her sister? "She actually said that? That you were going to run it together?"

"Of course. We were going to get rid of Brad—then it would all be ours."

Faith shivered in the heavy silence that fell over the room. How diabolically cunning Fleur had been. And how cruel. She *was* going to marry Alexandre—but not until she had made absolutely sure of her own independence. That was the reason for all the sadistic games she forced on him. Not because she enjoyed flirting with danger, but because she wanted to drive him so far into his madness, she would always be able to control him.

"I think you're right," she said gently. "I think Fleur was planning to marry you."

A sudden coldness came into his eyes. "Yes. She was."

And did you know why? Faith wondered, trying to read something into those impassive features. Had Alexandre realized that Fleur was only using him? That she was fully prepared to destroy him merely to serve her own ends? What might a madman do with knowledge like that?

"Please, *please*—try to remember. What did Fleur look like the last time you saw her? What did she say to you? Did she do anything . . . unusual?"

She might as well have been pleading with one of the boulders set into the dirt on the hillside. The coldness left his face, but it was replaced by the same dreamy vagueness that had been there before.

"She used to talk about you, *chérie*. She called you *ma petite soeur*, as if you were much younger and she had to look out for you. She would never admit it, of course, but I think she was envious of you."

"Of me?" The idea was so startling, Faith forgot everything else. "But why on earth would Fleur envy me?"

"Because you were always your father's favorite. She said she used to compete frantically for his attention, but whatever she did, you got there first. You could run faster than she, and you weren't afraid of the dogs—and you could ride bareback on a horse while she could barely hold onto the saddle."

"I rode a horse? When I was a little girl?" So that was why she had taken so easily to riding when she came to Havenhurst. "No wonder Fleur always refused to get up on a horse. It wasn't because she thought it looked unfeminine—she just wasn't good at it! Fleur never liked anything if she couldn't be the best."

"And you were best at everything when you were little. I think that's why she loved to torment you so much. And you, *petit démon*, always repaid her in kind. She said once you put a frog under her pillow and she screamed half the night. But the next day, she got back at you. She hid your favorite sash in a place you could not find it for months."

"I . . . I think I remember that." It was strange, the way some memories were so vivid and others came back slowly. "She hid it in the clock in the library. The funny one, built into a case. By the time one of the maids found it, it had gotten caught in the works and was torn to shreds."

And oh, how furious Desirée had been when she learned the clock was broken. But Adam had only laughed and refused to have it repaired. Let the girls enjoy their fun, he had said indulgently. If they want to play with the clock, they can have it and welcome.

"After that, it became our own special place. We used to hide things inside, our treasures we called them, and we felt very grown-up and important because we thought no one knew they were there. It's funny the way Fleur remembered. . . ."

She left the words hanging in the air. It *was* funny the way Fleur had remembered the clock, and she had completely forgotten. Fleur must have remembered it all the time, right from the moment she first arrived at the house and saw it still standing in the library. And she must have remembered what they used it for.

Without so much as a word of explanation, Faith turned away from Alexandre and raced through a half-open door in the rear wall that led into the main part of the house. The clock! How could she have forgotten it? If Fleur *had* found something at Havenhurst—if she did have secrets to protect—where better to hide them than the place that had served her so well as a child?

The tall case clock stood alone on the far wall of the library. As Faith had hoped, there was no one in the room and the hallway outside was deserted. She did not waste time, but hurried over to it, looking for a way to get it open.

She must have known the secret once, but now it defied her. If there was a catch or handle anywhere, she could not find it. She ran her fingers up and down the crack that separated the front panel from the side of the case, but she could find nothing to give her leverage. She was about to go to find some kind of tool to pry it open, when she noticed that the lower lefthand corner moved slightly when she pushed it. Grasping the edge as tightly as she could, she began to tug at it. She was rewarded with a loud snapping sound as the fragile rosewood broke in her hand.

The opening she had made was small, but there was more than enough space to push her hand through. Almost instantly, her fingers came in contact with something hard and cold. A slow shiver ran down her spine as she realized what it was. Drawing it out of the clock, she held it in her hand and looked down at it.

It was a gun.

Faith studied it dispassionately. It was not the gun that had been used to kill her sister, not if her dream was accurate, but there was something oddly familiar about it, as if she had seen it before. She had the feeling, though she was not sure why, that it was one of a pair of dueling pistols. But when she reached back in the case, groping again with her hand, she could not find its mate. She was about to give up when her fingertips brushed the edge of a sheet of paper that had been wedged against the back wall. Working it loose with her fingernails, she pulled it out.

She recognized it instantly for what it was—a piece of ledger paper, ripped carelessly out of an account book. Horrified and fascinated both, she stared down at it. It was exactly the same size as the pile of dusty old ledgers she had seen on a side table in Brad's office.

Firm, forceful handwriting met her eyes. The same handwriting she had seen once before—in Adam Eliot's journal.

Even before she began to read, she sensed what she would find. Still, she forced herself to scan it carefully, checking and rechecking each sentence to make sure she had gotten it right. By the time she was finished, she knew she had the evidence her sister had been looking for.

And she knew what Fleur had done with it.

Five

Brad looked up from the papers spread across his desk to see Faith standing like an avenging Fury in the doorway of his study. The illusion, created by a play of light and shadow on her features, was as compelling as it was eerie. Wisps of soft blond curls, caught in moonbeams, floated around her head like a burst of golden fire. Her eyes were lost in shadow.

An avenging Fury? He allowed himself a wry half-smile at the thought. A trick of the light—or a trick of his own conscience? Sometimes it was hard to tell.

The smile died on his lips as she stepped into the room. Now that he could see her better, he realized that his first instinct had been appropriate. There was no warmth, no trace of greeting, in the hazel-green eyes that seemed to bore through his face.

She stopped just on the other side of the desk. Her gaze was steady as she held out a folded sheet of paper.

"I believe you have seen this before."

The certainty in her voice surprised and puzzled him. Taking it from her, he unfolded the paper slowly and looked down at it. No expression showed in his face as he began to read.

> Old friend Friday—
>
> I call you that because that is what you are. Not my slave, not even my faithful servant, but my friend. I am leaving this where no one but you will find it, in the record book in my study. If that swine Jeremy Alleyn succeeds in what he has planned for me this day, it will be safe here. If he does not—well, if he does not, then you and I will look at this together and enjoy a good laugh at his expense.

I am leaving this morning on what will be the most dangerous journey of my life. Alleyn has forged papers (and damned clever documents they are, too) showing that I have signed Havenhurst over to him to pay my so-called "debts." Naturally, he does not expect me to be alive when he produces them. I look for no help here, amongst my sanctimonious neighbors, but I dare to hope I can make it downriver to lay my case before the governor. Alleyn is a sly man, but a stupid one. If I move swiftly, I may catch him off guard.

Trust me in one thing, dear friend. Whatever happens—whatever you may hear in the days and weeks to come—I did not lose Havenhurst, or sell it out from under my heirs. If Alleyn succeeds, I charge you to find help. Do not let him get away with this. Do not let me die unavenged!

I am taking Katherine with me, not by choice but because she insists on being by my side. I accede to her whims only because I know there is no other way. Without my protection, I shudder to think of the price she would be forced to pay for sins that were only mine. We leave the child behind, the child whose secret you and Beneba alone know. I will trust you to tell her the truth when you deem the time is right.

Do not try to find either help or sympathy locally. You know as well as I that they will not be forthcoming. Send instead to England—to Bradford Alleyn. He is a young man, but strong beyond his years, and though he be Jeremy's brother, I trust him to demand justice in my name.

Brad lowered the paper and turned to stare vacantly at the darkened window. It was strangely painful to see his name written out in handwriting he had almost forgotten. *Trust.* I trust this man, Adam had said. Damn! Trust like that was a burden he didn't need.

He forced his attention back to the paper. The final paragraphs contained only a hastily drawn will. Brad was not surprised to note that Adam Eliot had left everything he possessed, including Havenhurst, to his two young daughters. But he was surprised to see his own name spelled out one last time—as guardian to the girls. Adam's terms were characteristically generous. In return for his services, Brad would be granted a half share in the plantation and all its proceeds.

All that remained was the final instruction Brad had always instinctively expected from the man who was both his teacher and his friend. Adam Eliot set his slaves free. Every legal choice was to be made available to them, the document stated, save only one. They could remain in the employ of the new owners of Havenhurst, receiving a fair wage for their work; they could move to any area or Colony that allowed free blacks; they could even demand passage back to Africa if that was their desire. The only thing they could not do—even if the alternatives intimidated or frightened them—was choose to remain in bondage.

Brad was keenly aware of Faith's eyes as he looked up at last. Refolding the paper, he laid it down on the desk.

"No, you are wrong. I have never seen this before in my life."

Faith raised a skeptical brow. "You don't expect me to believe that, do you? You see, I know my sister found it before she . . . well, before her last day at Havenhurst. She would never have been able to resist flaunting it in front of you. I know her too well for that."

Brad gave her a long, shrewd look. Faith had the uncomfortable feeling he was trying to decide whether she was bluffing or not. Then, with a shrug that seemed oddly careless and out of place, he bent down and unlocked one of the lower drawers of the desk. The envelope he pulled out looked plain and innocuous, as did the single sheet of notepaper it contained.

"This is all your sister ever gave me. Not quite what you had in mind, I suspect."

Faith took the paper tentatively from his hand and stared down at it. It took her only a second to recognize, amidst the frills and flourishes that had always embellished Fleur's penmanship, an exact copy of the first three paragraphs of the document she had just given Brad. It ended melodramatically with Adam Eliot's plea for vengeance.

Not what she had in mind? Dear heaven, it made her stomach turn just to look at it.

"Then you did know that Jeremy stole Havenhurst from my father."

"Hardly. I suspected it, of course. Long before Fleur ever came and waved that thing in my face. It didn't seem plausible that Adam had lost the plantation—or that Jeremy had somehow managed to accumulate enough resources to buy it. But that's just the point. I *suspected* it. I didn't *know* anything."

"But surely after Fleur showed you this . . . ?"

"You don't think I took that seriously? Oh, come, my dear. It was in Fleur's handwriting, you know. Not Adam's. Your sister was not exactly a mental incompetent. She was perfectly capable of forming the same suspicions I had—and quite crafty enough to invent a little ploy like this to see if she could worm anything out of me."

Faith wavered uncertainly. For the first time since she came into the room, she was not quite so sure of herself. The copy *was* in Fleur's hand. And that was just the sort of stunt her sister would have pulled.

"But I don't understand one thing," she said hesitantly. "If my father left that message where he said he did, in one of those old ledgers, why didn't the slave Friday find it and send it to you?"

"I don't suppose he had time. You forget, Friday died a few days after your father."

Faith's eyes widened in horror. "You mean Jeremy killed him, too?"

"Good God, I hope not. Jeremy had enough sins on his conscience when he went to meet his Maker without adding that. Besides, I doubt if my brother was bright enough to realize that the man might be a threat to him. It would never have occurred to Jeremy that a white man might consider a black slave his friend—or dare to trust him. No, I think it was only a sad coincidence."

A *sad* coincidence? Faith shook her head slowly, trying to sort things out in her mind. *Sad* was hardly the word she would have expected him to use.

"I would say it was a fortunate coincidence—for you. You wouldn't be sole owner of Havenhurst now if it weren't for that." Frowning, she glanced down one more time at the paper in her hand. "Are you sure this is all you've ever seen? Just these three paragraphs? Fleur didn't show you the rest? Or tell you what was in it?"

"No. She hinted that there *was* more. But it seemed to amuse her to keep it to herself."

Yes, Faith thought ruefully—that was exactly like Fleur. The whole thing would indeed have amused her. And no doubt, when Adam Eliot's last message finally came to light, that revealing section would have been neatly trimmed away. Fleur would not have taken kindly to the idea of sharing her inheritance with anyone.

"I don't suppose she told you where it was? The original, I mean. The one in my father's handwriting."

He gave her an incredulous look. "So I could tear it up and toss it in the fire? Does that sound like Fleur to you?"

"No. . . ." Faith had to admit. "No, it doesn't."

"Your sister was much too cunning for that. Fleur told me only one thing, that the document was in a safe place. A place where it was sure to be found—if anything happened to her."

The emphasis in his voice was chilling. Faith shivered as she stood opposite him and stared at this man who had shared so much with her, and yet in the end, kept so much that was essential to himself. His face did not give away even a trace of emotion, but she had the terrible feeling they were both thinking the same thing. Something *had* happened to Fleur. Only a short time after she uttered those fateful words.

"What were you planning to do?" she said at last. "If you found out my sister was telling the truth?"

His lips turned up in the vaguest hint of a smile.

"What do you think I was planning to do?"

In spite of herself, Faith could not help admiring him. He had to know everything was all over—the truth was bound to come out now—yet he looked as cool and collected as if absolutely nothing had happened.

"You were going to fight her, weren't you?"

"Was I?"

"Of course you were. You've always been a fighter. It's in your nature. Besides, I've seen you working this land. You love it too much to give it up, especially to a frivolous girl who wouldn't care a fig for anything beyond the cash she could squeeze out of it."

Brad did not try to reply. Perhaps, Faith told herself sadly, it was all for the best. What reply could he give that she would want to hear? Still silent, he laid the envelope he had been holding down on the desk beside the folded sheet of ledger paper and headed toward the outer doorway. Only when he had reached it did he turn to let his eyes touch hers.

It was like a plea, Faith thought as she met that penetrating gaze. A plea and a promise. Forget your sister, haunting blue eyes seemed to say to her. Forget Fleur and her tragic death, and I will give you everything your heart has ever longed for. In that silent communion, Faith recognized at last the bittersweet truth about her relationship with this proud, independent, unfathomable man. Brad was in love with her, as deeply in love as she was with him—and there was not a thing either one of them could do about it.

"Well, now you do know," she said softly. "Fleur *was* telling the truth. What do you plan to do about it now?"

His eyes burned with a blue fire that seemed to sear into her flesh.

"I wish to God I knew."

The silence that filled every corner of the room when he had gone was so complete it was frightening. Faith began to tremble, lightly at first, then so violently she had to hold onto the edge of the desk to steady herself. What on earth had she been thinking of? she asked herself, horrified, as she realized for the first time what she had done. She had thought she was so clever, coming in here to confront him boldly with what she had discovered. But all she managed to do was blurt out everything she knew—and he had given her precious little in return.

And she had brought the only piece of evidence she had with her!

She cast a nervous glance at the ledger sheet, barely noticeable in all the clutter on Brad's desk. She did not know why he had chosen to leave it behind when he could easily have wrested if from her and destroyed it, but she did not for an instant make the mistake of thinking that it meant she was safe. Fleur had been much more cautious than she. Much more cunning. And Fleur had lost in the end.

She ran her fingers along the paper, feeling the rough edges where it had been torn from the book. Seeing the envelope beside it, she picked it up idly, expecting to find nothing more than a blank, empty receptacle. To her surprise, she felt something inside it. Tilting it to one side, she slid the contents out on her palm.

A simple round object of gold glowed against her skin. In the center, Faith was stunned to catch sight of the brilliant green glitter of a tiny but perfect emerald.

It was all she could do to fight the wave of faintness that flooded over her as she stood in the silent room and stared down at the object in her hand. Fleur's locket. The mate to that same locket she herself had always worn around her neck. How long had it been since that day they snipped a lock of each other's hair and put it inside their lockets? How many years since they vowed never to take them off again?

Now Fleur's locket was lying on a broken chain in her hand.

Well, one question answered at least, she thought grimly. Fleur had not been killed by a stranger one misty morning when she decided impulsively to flee Havenhurst. Nothing in the world would have induced her sister to go off and leave the locket behind.

The golden token, warm and familiar, seemed to pulsate in her hand, as if it had a life of its own. The nearness of something so closely associated with her sister had an almost hypnotic effect on Faith, bringing back feelings and memories she thought she had forgotten. For the first time since that morning in London when she woke to the certain knowledge of Fleur's death, she could feel her sister with her again, as real and tangible as if she were still alive.

Moving slowly, more by instinct than will, Faith began to make her way toward the doorway that led into the interior of the house. Her mind did not know where she was going, but her feet seemed to have marked the path, for they did not falter as they carried her forward. It was almost, she thought musingly, as if Fleur were beside her now, guiding her every step of the way—leading her back one last time into a past she had never quite escaped. The illusion of her sister's closeness intensified as she passed through the empty dressing room and into a darkened hall beyond, until at last the sensation was so powerful, it almost seemed as if Fleur had merged into her body and they were one single, indivisible entity.

It was an eerie feeling, and a frightening one. More and more with each passing second, Faith was certain that it *was* the past she had sensed in the darkness around her. Only it was not her past—it was Fleur's. She pressed the locket against her breast, feeling her sister's strength flow into her body, and tried desperately not to be afraid. The thoughts she was thinking now were not her thoughts, the memories she was reliving not her memories, but Fleur's.

Perhaps, she told herself rationally, trying to cling to reality, this was the same thing that had happened to Estee at Beneba's ritual bonfire. Perhaps it was no more than a form of self-hypnosis—a trick her mind was playing on itself to tease her into remembering some story Fleur had told her long ago.

Or perhaps, she thought, shivering, Fleur *was* with her now.

Not that it really mattered. The pull of the past was so strong, she could no longer deny it. Slowly, she felt her own identity begin to slip away from her. Illusion or no, she was not herself anymore. And this was not today. She was six years old again—and she was Fleur.

The hallway was dark, but the child she had become was

not afraid. She had never been afraid inside the house. She hated it when it got all black outside, and slimy things like frogs and snakes lurked in shadows to jump out and bite you. But inside, the darkness was like a warm, cozy secret. There, you could be anything you wanted, a pirate or a princess—and even one of those funny African slaves—and no one could see you and prove that you weren't.

She ran a few steps, then slid along the polished floor. Her shoes made a delicious scraping sound on the boards. That was the best part of sliding down the hall—all the wonderful noises you could make if you did it right. She started to run again, then caught herself just in time. It was already well past the dinner hour, and good little girls were supposed to be sound asleep in their beds.

She tugged at her robe, pulling it tightly over her thin nightdress, and stood quietly in the center of the hall, listening to see if anyone had heard her. When at last she was sure it was safe, she shifted her weight forward on the balls of her feet and tiptoed down the hall.

She had made the same foray often. The most dangerous moment, she knew, would come when she reached the end of the long passageway and saw the bright lights of the entry hall just ahead of her. Her goal was the stairs, but the stairs were treacherously open, exposed to the view of anyone who wandered by, and she knew it would take all her cunning to get up them unnoticed. She waited until she was nearly there, then dropped to the ground and pulled herself along on her elbows, like a jungle cat slithering through tall grasses. The edges of the steps bumped her stomach and knees, but she ignored the pain as she crept stealthily to the top.

Once there, she sat down and looked around with disappointed eyes. It had been a great adventure, working her way boldly up the stairs, now the excitement was over. She pressed her face against the banister rails, letting the light shine daringly on the tip of her nose, but there was no one below to see her, and she soon tired of the game. Sprawling out, right in the middle of the hallway, she wriggled her toes against the banister and tried to figure out something else to do.

None of the tapers in high brackets on the wall had been lit, and the darkness was oppressive and boring. The only light was a lone candle flickering on a tall stand at the end of the hall, next to the door to *Maman*'s room. The child turned toward it, eyeing it speculatively, and a plan began to take shape in her mind.

Papa had gone off to see one of the neighbors. She knew that because she had heard him talking about it with *Maman* at lunch. He would not be back until late that night, he had said.

That meant *Maman* would be all alone in her room!

The child got up and began to tiptoe down the hallway, moving every bit as cautiously as she had downstairs. *Maman* would be furious, of course. *Maman* was always furious when one of her daughters disobeyed her, but she knew how to get around *Maman*. She would giggle and pout, and she would make all sorts of funny faces—and then when *Maman* was laughing so hard she couldn't speak, she would climb up in bed beside her and everything would be all right.

When she got to *Maman*'s door, she was disappointed to see that it was closed. She always hated it when *Maman*'s door was closed. That meant she had one of her headaches, and no one, not even Papa, was allowed to go inside. The child's lower lip jutted out rebelliously. She was nowhere near ready to go upstairs to the attic room she shared with her sister, but there didn't seem to be anything else to do.

Reaching up tentatively, she took hold of the door handle. She always tried the handle whenever *Maman*'s door was closed. It was always locked, but she tried it anyway, just in case. This time, to her surprise, she felt it turn in her hand.

The door made a dreadful creaking sound as she pushed it inward, and she stopped instantly, horrified at what she had done. She knew the game had gone too far, but she couldn't do anything about it. She stood absolutely still, just like a little statue, and waited the longest time to see if anything was going to happen. When it did not, she took a step forward and peered into the room. Then, because the door was open anyhow, she decided she might as well go inside. She wanted to shut it behind her so no one would see what she had done. But she was afraid it would make that same awful sound again, and she left it half open.

She had always loved *Maman*'s room, more than any other place in the house. Everything in it was soft and feminine, and it smelled like roses from the garden. The draperies over the windows were *Maman*'s favorite color, a deep, rich pink, just like the flowers in the patterned carpet. Curtains of a lighter shade hung over the wide double bed, veiling it in privacy. There was only one candle, on a table across the room, and tantalizing shadows danced on the walls and ceiling.

The child was startled to hear the sound of laughter, coming from somewhere near the bed, and she realized *Maman* was not alone. Perhaps she did not have a headache after all, she thought hopefully. Perhaps the door had just been closed by accident. She crept around to the other side of the bed so she could see through the parted curtains.

She frowned a little when she caught sight of her uncle Olivier sitting on the edge of the bed beside *Maman*. It was not that she did not like her mother's boyish younger brother. Quite the contrary. Olivier was never too busy to tease a little girl or stop and sing a special song, just for her. But whenever he was around, it seemed to her that *Maman* never had time to play with her daughters. The child crawled under one of the chairs, settling back in her favorite hiding place, and looked out at them.

Maman was laughing lightly. She liked it when *Maman* laughed. She looked so young and pretty then, as if she were a little girl herself. Olivier seemed wonderfully handsome as he bent his head over her shoulder, slipping a lacy pink wrapper aside to tease her skin with his lips.

"*Comme tu es belle, chérie*," he whispered hoarsely. "You know it drives me mad when you look at me like that."

The child curled her legs up under her and shivered with satisfaction. Sometimes Uncle Olivier could be so romantic, just like a chivalrous knight in one of her fairy tales. She absolutely loved it when he was romantic! She did not wonder that he called *Maman* beautiful—truly she was a beauty!—but she could not for the life of her figure out why something nice like that would drive anyone mad. Madness was a dark, terrible thing.

Desirée was still laughing, but she pulled away from her brother, giving him a playful slap on the wrist. Then, as if to make up for her halfhearted scolding, she caught his face in both her hands and leaned forward, touching her lips first to one cheek, then the other, the way she did with her two little daughters.

She tried to draw back then, but Olivier would not let her go. Taking her in his arms, he forced her body against his and kissed her full on the lips. From her hiding place, the child could see that *Maman* was trembling, and she did not know if she ought to be fascinated or frightened. Desirée clung to her brother for a long, lingering moment, then pushed him away.

"No, no . . . we mustn't."

"*Pourquoi non, chérie*? You know that you desire this as much as I."

"Oh, Olivier, we have promised ourselves we would not do this again. It is much too dangerous. You know it is."

"How can it be dangerous, *petit ange*?" He ran his hand across her shoulder, letting it come to rest on the front of her negligee. "He is gone for the entire evening. He said so himself. And besides, the door is closed."

Desirée's eyelids seemed to grow heavy. Long, dark lashes fluttered against her cheeks.

"Closed, *oui*. But is it locked? At least get up and make sure it is locked."

"Ah silly, silly little girl." Olivier slipped his hand inside her robe, caressing the contours of her breast. "It is closed, *chérie*, that is all that counts. He would never dare come into your room when the door is closed."

She did not resist again. Her lips parted one last time, not in protest, but only to accept the hard, unyielding pressure of his mouth, and her arms coiled around his neck. Pink bed linen echoed the soft flush of her cheeks as he eased her down onto the pillows and slipped the lacy wrapper from her body.

They were so absorbed in each other, they did not notice the sound of footsteps in the hall outside, but the child, still hiding under her chair, heard them all too clearly. A moment later, the angry crash of a door slamming against the wall shattered the silence. Crawling deeper into the shadows, the child peeked out. There, framed in the eerie golden light of the hall, stood a tall man, dressed in riding boots, with a pair of riding gloves clutched in one hand.

It was Papa.

"*Mon dieu!*" Desirée sat up suddenly, clutching the lacy wrapper over her slender breasts. "Adam!"

Adam took a step forward, controlling himself with visible effort. His eyes were cold with rage as he stood at the end of the bed and looked through parted pink curtains at the woman he had always adored to distraction—and never been able to please.

"None other, my dear. You should have closed the door if you didn't want company."

Desirée shivered at the savage anger in his tone.

"Oh, please. . . ." she pleaded, so frightened her voice was barely audible. "You—you don't understand."

"Don't I? I should have thought it was perfectly obvious."

"But it isn't something ugly, the way you're thinking. Or dirty. It's the only thing that's ever been good or pure in my life. You can't imagine what it was like—that terrible time in

France. I was just a child when they threw me into that dungeon. A little girl, completely innocent of . . . the ways of men."

Her voice dropped even lower, until it was hardly a whisper. Her face was so pale she barely looked alive.

"Oh, the things they did to me there. The unspeakable perversions they practiced on my body, I had not known before that anything could be so painful, or so terrifying. It was almost more than I could endure. When at last I escaped, it was only Olivier, only his tenderness—his *love*—that saved my sanity."

Adam gave her a long, searching look. She almost seemed like a rag doll, all curled up in a corner of the bed. She was too frightened even to cover her nakedness anymore.

"All right, Desirée. I pity you, if that's what you want. Only pity isn't enough now, is it?"

There was a quiet finality in his voice. Desirée wrapped her arms around her body, contracting protectively into herself. She looked very little now. And very lost.

"Adam, I—I don't know if I can live without him."

Her husband's expression did not change. His hands were steady as he drew them together, separating one of the riding gloves from its mate. Flicking it almost carelessly between his fingers, he looked down at her on the bed.

"You should have thought of that before."

Six

The past was still with Faith as she stood on the top step of the piazza and looked out at the moonlit world around her. The road was a band of gold, sweeping in a graceful arc down to the river. The air was warm and humid, the wind no more than a faint rustle of leaves in the trees. It frightened her a little to realize that she had caught a glimpse of the truth at last—and a glimpse was not enough. Something else had happened that night fifteen years ago, something still hidden in the deep recesses of her memory, and she had to find out what it was.

She looked down at her hands, surprised to see that they were empty. She must have lost Fleur's locket somewhere, perhaps in the musty darkness of the faded pink room that had once been her mother's. It did not matter now. She did not need a sense of her sister's closeness to guide her any more. The memories she had yet to relive were her own.

She had stood on the exact same step that night, too. She could see it all as clearly as if it were happening again. It was springtime then, a balmy April eve, with just a hint of sultry breezes blowing up from the river. The darkness had almost come to an end, and a soft gray light glowed on the edge of the horizon.

She had not been frightened at first, only a little puzzled. Tall, somber men were carrying lanterns back and forth across the yard, stopping every now and then to talk to each other in voices so hushed they did not reach her ears. She had been alone on the shadowy veranda. Fleur was upstairs, sound asleep in her bed. She had been crying half the night, refusing to tell even her twin what was wrong, but toward morning she had finally drifted off, and she did not hear the sound of approaching hoofbeats.

But Faith had heard them, and she had been consumed with curiosity. Horsemen had never come to Havenhurst in what seemed like the middle of the night before. Putting a robe over her nightdress, she slipped downstairs to see what was going on.

The men were already in the yard by the time she got there. It seemed to her there were half a dozen of them, though she could not be sure for they kept moving around and they all looked the same with their dark clothes in the darkness. She was careful not to let them see her, for she sensed they would be angry and send her back to her room. It was only minutes before they began to move, solely and in pairs, down the road to the river. She waited until the last of them had disappeared from sight, then padded down the steps in her bare feet and set off after them.

The memory was so compelling, Faith could not resist it. Moving slowly down the stairs, she began to retrace the path she had taken that fateful night, seeing it not as she saw it now, but as she had seen it then. Dawn came quicker than she had expected. The sky was already vivid with streaks of blood-red when she reached an open meadow that fronted the old swampland. Most of the men had scattered, fanning out to various sections of the field. Only two still stood together. They made a strange silhouette against the shimmering brightness of the sky: two men, unevenly matched in height, standing back to back, their right hands raised in front of them.

Faith squinted into the light, trying to figure out what they were holding in their hands. Then one of the men raised his arm slightly, and the first dazzling rays of morning sun glinted off the barrel of a pistol. Faith recognized the gun at once—it was one of a pair Papa always kept in his study—but she had never seen anyone use it before. A funny, tight feeling constricted her throat as she watched. She wished she understood what was going on. Things she did not understand always made her nervous.

She crept forward a little, trying to see the men better. She was surprised to realize that one of them was her Uncle Olivier. He looked so slight and fragile, he almost seemed a boy. His skin was deathly pale, his eyes dark and clear as he stared into the hills in the distance. The other man was Papa.

Faith was even more frightened now. She longed to run to Papa and beg him to tell her what was going on, but something in his face stopped her. She had never seen Papa look like that before. He was so stern he might as well have been a stranger. His back was rigid with tension, and his face had turned a deep, ruddy color. Even from a distance, she could see veins throbbing in his neck and temples.

The men began to move at last. Eyes straight ahead, they walked away from each other with slow, measured paces. The air was so quiet, Faith could hear the sound of their footsteps sinking into the soft earth. She was sure now that something terrible was going to happen, something she did not want to see, but she didn't know what to do about it. Perhaps if she called out to Papa, she thought unhappily—if she told him how afraid she was—then he would stop whatever he was doing and catch her up in his arms, and everything would be all right again.

But she was paralyzed with fear, and she could not move.

Then suddenly the men whirled around, and the early morning silence was torn apart by an explosion so violent it deafened her for an instant. She clapped her hands over her ears to blot out the sound, but she could not take her eyes off the men. They stood where they had stopped, absolutely motionless for the briefest fraction of a second. Then, slowly, even as Faith watched, Uncle Olivier began to sink to the earth. A red stain, bright as the streaks of crimson in the sky, spread across the pristine white of his shirtfront.

At last the memory was too painful to bear. Faith sank to her knees on the marshy earth and, throwing back her head, opened her lips in a terrible mute scream. It was a terrifying sensation. No matter how hard she pushed the air out of her lungs, all she could hear was that horrible shrill screech inside her own head. She knew the same thing had happened that day, too. The day her Uncle Olivier had died. She had screamed and screamed, and no one had heard. And she had been left alone in the swamp.

The emptiness that surrounded her now was not as frightening as it had been fifteen years ago, but it was no less dismal. Faith felt completely drained as she forced herself to her feet and began to walk back along the road toward the riverbank. Poor Uncle Olivier—he had never had a chance. He had always been the gay one. The charming one. More interested in song and laughter than learning how to hold a gun in his hand and shoot. Nothing in his life had ever fitted him for the role of a duelist.

And he must have known it. Faith paused at the edge of the road and pondered the irony of it all. He must have known that day as he stood in the first light of dawn and stared into the hills, that he was about to die. Just as Adam had known that the act he would soon commit was nothing less than murder. But the gentleman's code of honor demanded satisfaction, and they were both too proud to back down.

A full moon flooded the earth with light, giving Faith the uncanny illusion that she was trapped in that same despairing dawn again. A white mist rose from the swamp, softening the landscape until it seemed mystical and serene.

And she could have stopped it all.

Faith stood at the side of the road and watched trails of mist blow across her path. She *could* have stopped it—if only she had had the courage to trust her father's love. All she had to do was call out to him. She was Papa's favorite, his "little diamond." He would never have shot a man to death if he knew she was watching and crying in the shadows.

Even at the time, Faith suspected, she had sensed her own part in the tragedy. Even then, when she was so little and everything seemed so strange. It was a terrible burden for a child to carry.

The mist had thickened by the time she began to move forward again. She could barely see where she was going, but she did not falter. Her feet had known these same paths once when she was a child. They would carry her safely now.

The swamp was an unseen presence in the haze around her. She could smell it in the air; she could feel it in the soft, moist earth beneath her feet; but her eyes caught only occasional glimpses of tall, brooding cypresses and tangled undergrowth, and she paid them little heed. Only when she caught sight of a lone tree—a massive live-oak, illusively ethereal with its streamers of gray moss dangling in the mist—did she stop to stare at it in wonder. She had seen that same tree once before. On a foggy April morning in London.

She had not understood then what it meant. She understood now.

Even before she approached, she knew what she was going to find hidden in the cavernous shadows beneath those mossy branches. She was not wrong. There, on the earth in front of her, barely visible in the moonlight, was a long, low mound. The kind of mound left by a gravedigger's shovel.

Faith did not try to deceive herself. This was not Olivier Devereaux' grave she had stumbled on in the darkness, for Olivier's body had been carried up the hill by those same sober men she had seen before and laid in a graveyard beside the house. The ornate headstone that marked it today had been her mother's last act in the New World.

So that was what it meant, she thought dully. That terrible, suffocating vision that had frightened her so badly the morning after her dream. Not the moment of Fleur's death at all—but the moment of her burial. It had been dawn in London then, the beginning of a new day, but it would still have been the middle of the night in the Carolina Colonies. The perfect time to mask an act of secret shame.

The mist thinned perceptibly as Faith climbed back up the hill toward the house. Everything was beginning to come into perspective now. One night, one single night—a few brief hours in time—and her destiny and her sister's had been shaped for years to come. Fleur, with her promiscuity, mistaking sex for love; Faith, afraid to trust all men because of the violence she had seen in one man—what were they but prisoners of the past?

The air was clear by the time she reached the top of the hill. The house stood out boldly in the moonlight. Candles flickered in some of the front windows, but the entire north side was dark and inscrutable. It seemed a fitting image. A symbol of all the tragic secrets that would remain forever buried within those walls.

Faith had just started toward the front steps when she realized suddenly that something was strangely amiss in that solemn setting. Puzzled, she turned back and examined the north facade again. It took her only a second to realize what was wrong. There should have been at least one light showing in one window. The window of Alexandre's room.

Changing course, she began to hurry around the side of the house. The first tremors of apprehension crossed her mind, but she tried not to let herself dwell on them. Still, she had to admit, it did seem strange. Alexandre always left a candle burning in his room, day or night. She could not imagine why he would have blown it out now.

Her apprehension increased when she reached the side stairway and saw that one of the double French doors into his room was open. The wind, a steady force now, blew it back and forth with a monotonous *clop-clop, clop-clop, clop-clop* against the frame.

The sound was like an ominous warning. Faith shivered in the darkness as she listened to it. *Clop-clop, clop-clop, clop-clop.* Her hand was shaking as she reached out to catch the door and hold it back. Tensely, she tried to tell herself that everything was all right. But she knew it was not.

The instant she stepped across the threshold, she understood why her husband had sought the privacy of darkness.

She stood in the doorway and stared in at him, and at last she realized what she should have known earlier that evening when she blurted out the truth: a world without Fleur was a world in which Alexandre could not live. He seemed nebulous and unreal now, no more than a dark shadow in the moonlight, hanging by a rope from the ceiling at the far side of the room. His body moved only slightly in the warm wind that swept through the open doorway.

Faith backed slowly out onto the veranda and shut the door behind her. The night was so sultry, the scent of fall flowers so heavy in the air, she could almost believe it was all a dream. She tried to feel something for this man who had been her husband, she tried to pity the pain that had scarred his life, but there were no tears left in her. No sorrow. There was space in her heart only for one chilling thought.

Alexandre had been deeply shocked by the news of Fleur's death. He could not possibly have known about it before.

Now two questions had been answered. Two doubts resolved. The third was not truly a question anymore.

She picked up a candle from the table in the hall downstairs and carried it up to her room. She did not need its light to tell her what she would see when she looked down at the gown on her bed, but she raised it anyway, letting warm rays play over cool green silk.

It was just as she had thought. The dress Fibby had copied for her was the dress she had seen in her dream.

Seven

The room was a deep midnight blue, the air heavy and brooding in its own stillness. Only an echo of moonlight played across the rippled glass of tall French windows. Faith stood just inside the threshold, a lonely figure in the darkness. The sweet, familiar scent of flowers, cloying in the sultry night, lingered in her nostrils.

Everything seemed strangely unreal, yet familiar all at the same time. This was exactly the way it was before, she thought uneasily. The sights, the smells, the sensory impressions . . . it was all the same. Only this time it was not a dream.

Faith hesitated a moment, uncertain and puzzled, trying to orient herself in the darkness. Then, slowly, she began to slip forward. Thrusting out her left hand, she groped blindly with her fingers to feel her way. Her right hand felt strangely heavy at her side, as if it had been trapped in the green silk folds of her skirt.

No, not *exactly* the way it was before, she reminded herself grimly, tightening her fingers over the butt of the gun in her hand. She had one advantage Fleur had not had. She knew how ruthless Brad Alleyn could be.

A sudden burst of gold bathed the room with light. Faith lifted her head, tilting her face upward, but she knew even before she turned what she was going to see. Masculine features, potent and strong in the rays of a solitary grease lamp. An iron will, too proud to unbend. She caught her breath, feeling for an instant the same savage passions that had stirred her sister. The boldness, the excitement . . . the challenge of a duel she could not lose.

She was intensely aware of his closeness now. He towered above her, a tall man, powerful, exuding vitality with every breath. Blond hair, caught in the lamplight, burst into coppery flames; deep-set eyes blazed with blue fire; strong, hard lips opened, ready to scorn or to kiss.

What would he do, she wondered, as her sister had wondered before her, if she opened her arms and went to him? The temptation was frighteningly sweet. The same virile magnetism that had drawn Fleur toward this man, even to her doom, compelled Faith now, and she longed to forget everything else and surrender to his embrace.

It took all her strength to resist. She had not come to this room tonight for love, she told herself bitterly. She had come for the final, inevitable resolution of that vow she had taken more than a year ago in her sister's name. Slowly, she began to draw her hand out of the folds of her skirt.

She did not see him raise his own hand until it was too late. A tremor of shock raced through her body as she realized what she had done. The gun! Brad had had the gun in his hand that night, too. How could she have forgotten it?

She cast a quick glance down at her own pistol, dangling uselessly at her side. She did not try to raise it. She knew only too well she could never aim it at his chest before he had a chance to pull the trigger.

Drawing a deep breath, she forced her eyes slowly upward. She was surprised at how cool she felt, now that the moment of confrontation had come at last.

"You killed her, didn't you?" she said softly.

His eyes did not waver as he gazed back at her.

"Yes . . . I killed her."

"But why?" There was as much pain as anger in her cry. "Why did you have to do it? You could have fought for Havenhurst in a dozen different ways. You could have said the paper Fleur produced was a forgery. Who would remember my father's handwriting after all these years? Or pressed your claim through Jeremy's relationship to my mother and Uncle Olivier. You didn't have to kill Fleur to hold onto the plantation."

The hardness in his face eased subtly. "You think that's why I did it? To hold onto Havenhurst?"

"Of course. What other reason . . . ?"

She cut off the thought in mid-sentence. What reason did a man like Brad ever have for taking a human life? The weight of the gun felt strangely heavy in her hand. Just as it had felt when she entered the room.

Just as it felt in her dream.

"You *were* going to fight for Havenhurst, weren't you?"

He almost smiled. "You told me I was a fighter. Remember?"

Faith could see it all so clearly now. Fleur must have been tingling with excitement that day she faced Brad with the evidence she had found—and he had laughed in her face! How that must have galled her. Go ahead and press your claim, he had told her, and see what good it does you. The duel your father fought with a man who never shot a gun in his life was murder, and a murderer cannot inherit from his victim. Jeremy, as Olivier Devereaux' heir, was always the rightful owner of Havenhurst.

Fleur would have wondered if he was bluffing, of course—Fleur never understood the first thing about matters of law—but she would not have been willing to take a chance. Not when there was an easier way to get what she wanted.

"She came in here with a gun that night, didn't she? Hidden in the folds of her skirt."

Brad nodded. "The mate to that lethal little beauty you're holding in your own hand. One of the pistols used in the duel with Olivier. God knows why Adam kept the damned things around. I suspect he was afraid of easing his conscience by letting them out of sight. Adam was always a great one for remembering his own sins."

The irony of his words was not lost on Faith. It might be Adam who remembered his sins, but it was not Adam alone who would pay for them.

"Now you're going to kill me, too. The way you killed my sister."

He did not answer. Raising the gun slightly, he leveled it at her breast. Faith was aware of a cold fear seeping through her veins until her body seemed to turn to ice. She stared in silence down the barrel of that deadly pistol and tried not to think, as she knew Olivier Devereaux had tried not to think fifteen years ago, of the terrible thing that was about to happen.

Brad held the gun steady for what seemed to Faith an eternity. Then, unexpectedly, he eased his hold, letting the barrel dip a fraction of an inch.

"I've lived with that moment every day of my life since then. I'll be damned if I'm going to live with it any longer."

He dropped his hand limply to his side. Faith barely dared to breath as she stood and watched him. She did not see the gun slip from his grasp, but she was aware of the sound it made as it fell to the floor.

She was too stunned for a moment to react. All she could feel was a kind of dull, uncomprehending relief. Only slowly did her mind begin to grasp the implications of what had just happened. Brad had not ordered her to throw down her gun, he had not even tried to wrest it from her—he had simply dropped his own weapon to the floor where it would be of no use to him. It was not merely life that this man was offering her now. It was the vengeance she had sought from the day she left London.

And she owed it to Fleur's memory to take it.

Her hand seemed to move with a will of its own as she drew it slowly upward. Now it was her gun that was pointed at his chest, her fragile strength that held him captive. She hesitated only a second, then tightened her finger around the trigger. Closing her eyes, she tried with all her might to squeeze it.

Oh, God, why was it so hard? Why did she have to think of the way his hands felt when he ran them across her cheek? Or the sound of his laughter as he teased her? Why couldn't she forget the sweet yearning that filled her body every time she looked up and saw him across the room? This man had killed her twin. Fleur's pain had been her own pain that terrible night in London; a part of her had died with her sister then. Vengeance *should* be hers, and it should be sweet!

"Couldn't you have taken the gun away from her?" she cried, angry and hurt. She felt betrayed as she opened her eyes to look one last time at features that would linger forever in her memory. "You were so much stronger than she. Surely you could have done something! Why did you have to kill her?"

"Do you think I haven't asked myself that same question over and over again?" The anguish in his voice was too intense to be denied. "It seemed inevitable at the time. She was raising the gun. I had only a split second to react. But afterward . . . ! Oh, God, afterward I just stood there and looked down at her, and all I could think was—I killed Adam's daughter.

"Do you have any idea how many times I've run that scene over in my mind since then? Would it have done any good if I'd tried to rush her? Could I have gotten to her before she pulled the trigger? Or maybe she wasn't planning to pull it at all. Maybe she was just playing one of those silly, melodramatic games of hers."

"No." Faith shook her head slowly. "No, Fleur was not playing games. I was there that night. Inside her mind. I don't expect you to understand, but I was. And I know—Fleur *would* have pulled the trigger."

She let her arm drop heavily to her side. The gun slipped unnoticed out of her fingers. It was all over now. All the anger, all the misunderstanding—all the terrible hunger for revenge that had consumed her heart. She loved her sister deeply and she would always grieve for her, but Fleur had created her own fate. The grave she lay in now was a grave she had dug with her own hands. Faith could not kill the man she loved for that.

Brad was at her side even before the gun touched the floor. He started to put his arms around her, then pulled away uncertainly. There was something touchingly boyish about him as he looked down at her.

"Are you sure?"

Faith tried to meet his gaze, but to her surprise, the conflicting emotions that had been struggling inside her all seemed to spill out at once, and she began to laugh. It was a ridiculous reaction, she knew, but she could not help herself. Was she sure of what? That she didn't want to pick up the gun again and shoot him?

"Of course I'm sure, you idiot. I—I love you."

At last he dared to take her in his arms. His hands were gentle as he drew her toward him, his embrace sweet and succoring. But the eyes that teased her face sparkled with lights of laughter.

"I suppose you think I don't love you?"

"Well, if you do, you have a funny way of showing it."

The laughter tumbled out of his lips. "Do I? I wonder if you'll still be saying that in twenty years. Or will you have gotten used to me by then? Come, my dear—what did you expect? That I would fall to my knees the instant I saw you and beg you to take my heart into your keeping forever? That's too much to ask of any man. Especially a man like me."

He turned suddenly serious, closing his arms even tighter around her. There were so many things he wanted to say to this woman, so many promises he would have made long ago if only he had been able to be honest with her.

"Dammit, Faith, I do love you. I'm not very good at saying it—I don't suppose I ever will be—but for what it's worth, my heart *is* in your keeping. I am yours, if you want me. Now and forever."

VI

THE MISTS OF MORNING

The wind howled through the eaves, but inside, a fire blazed on the hearth, and the library was warm and cozy. It was late morning, and a white mist drifted past the windows.

Faith sat in front of the fireplace and gazed dreamily into the flames.

"Do you know what I would like to do? More than anything else in the world?"

Brad tossed another log on the fire, then turned to her with an indulgent smile. "What, my pet?"

"My pet?" Faith wrinkled her nose playfully. "You make me sound like a housecat. What I would like to do is tear this whole place down and build a new home. Up on the highest hill I can find. Too many awful things have happened in this house. There are too many sad memories here."

"Well, why not? You can do anything you want with the place. Havenhurst is yours now."

Faith reached out her hand, coaxing him to take hold of it. "Havenhurst is *ours*," she reminded him gently.

They had been married the day before. It was a quiet ceremony, for the idea of any kind of festivities so soon after Alexandre's death was distasteful to both of them, but Brad, with a characteristic stubborn streak, had refused to wait the decent interval convention demanded. Faith could not resist an impish smile as she turned back toward the fire. Tough, rugged Bradford Alleyn. The man who would never belong to any woman. The man who was not the marrying kind. And he was the one who had to drag the minister down from Charles Town without so much as an hour's notice!

She took a pine cone out of a basket by the hearth and tossed it into the fire. A burst of yellow sparks exploded into the air.

"Wouldn't it be nice," she said softly, "if sparks were like shooting stars? Then I could make a wish on every one of them—and it would be sure to come true."

Brad sat on the floor beside her. Putting an arm around her, he urged her head down on his shoulder. "And I know exactly what you'd wish, too. On every one of those 'shooting sparks.' You'd wish that Estee would come back to Havenhurst."

"She is my sister, Brad."

"I know, my—" He caught himself with a grin. "—my little housecat. But even sisters have the right to lives of their own. Estee made her choice. We have to respect that."

"Yes, I suppose so."

Sighing, Faith nestled closer into his arms. Brad had wasted no time in implementing Adam Eliot's last instructions. The very next day, he had called his slaves together, gathering them on an open hillside overlooking the river. They had come a little tentatively, Faith thought—except, of course, for Beneba. The old woman might be wobbly from her recent illness, but there was not a tentative bone in her body.

It had been an awesome experience. They sat side by side in the dying leaves, these black-skinned men and women who had come from Africa and the Islands, from households in the North and other plantations in the South, and listened to the words that gave them their freedom, some for the first time in their lives.

Most of the slaves, as Adam himself had no doubt expected, opted to remain at Havenhurst and work for fair wages. But a handful of the younger and more adventurous decided to set off for a community of free blacks in Virginia. Among them was Estee.

Even now, it hurt Faith to think of it. "I wish she hadn't gone, Brad. Life can be so hard for a black woman with no one to protect her."

"I think she knows that, darling. Even better than you. But it was important for her to be free."

"But she could have been free here."

"Not in her heart. Estee had been a slave in this house too long. If she stayed here, she would never feel free—no matter how many pieces of paper she had to prove it."

Faith did not try to argue. Much as she hated to admit it, she knew he was right. And at least Estee had stayed long enough to see her sister marry the man she loved. Somehow, it had made the moment of parting less painful.

"She did look beautiful this morning, didn't she, Brad? Standing in the mist on the shore, waiting for the boat to come and carry her away. How fiery and majestic she seemed. Just like the first time I saw her. I think my father would have been proud of his daughter, don't you?"

Brad touched her cheek lightly with his hand, turning her face toward him. His eyes were filled with love as he gazed at her.

"I think your father would have been proud of both his daughters today."

Faith leaned back in his arms and stared contentedly into the fire. The mist cleared slowly, and the first rays of morning sun glistened on the windowpanes. The light caught Faith's eye, and she turned toward it, fascinated by the way it seemed to dance across the glass. Easing herself out of her husband's embrace, she went over to the window and looked out.

It was hard to believe this land had ever seemed strange or alien to her eyes. Every bend in the river was so familiar now. Every tree on the hillside.

Brad came over to stand beside her. "Why so solemn, my sweet?" he teased. "Are you having second thoughts? About having married such a ruffian?"

Faith smiled a little to herself. "No . . . not yet."

"Not *yet?* What is this, woman? Don't tell me you're already dissatisfied?"

"Well. . . ." Faith stifled a roguish grin. She would love this man as long as she lived—but she would never quite forget the torment he had put her through. "There is *one* thing about you that doesn't truly please me."

His brow did not have quite the insouciance he intended as he arched it slowly upward.

"Only one?" he said lightly.

Faith took a long, deliberate pause. It would not do to let a new husband get too complacent.

"We have been in this room nearly an hour," she said at last. "With the door discreetly closed, mind you. And you have not tried to steal so much as a single kiss from me!"

There was a husky sound to the laughter that greeted her words. Gathering her up in strong arms, Brad carried her back to the fire. The floor felt hard beneath her body as he laid her down. The heat of the flames was a warm caress on her skin.

His eyes were only half teasing as he bent over her.

"That can be remedied."

About the Author

Susannah Leigh was born in Minneapolis and raised in St. Paul, Minnesota. After graduating from the University of Minnesota she moved on to New York City, where she worked at a variety of jobs and appeared in many off-Broadway productions. She stayed in New York for twelve years and then left for a year of traveling to such spots as Morocco, Nepal, and Afghanistan.

Ms. Leigh is currently living in the San Bernardino Mountains of Southern California, where she spends her nonwriting time indulging her interests in reading, travel, history, and lying in the sun.

She is the author of *Winter Fire*, *Glynda*, and *Wine of the Dreamers*, available in Signet editions.